The Sisters of the Crescent Empress

ALSO BY LEENA LIKITALO

The Five Daughters of the Moon

The
Sisters of the
Crescent Empress

LEENA LIKITALO

A TOM DOHERTY ASSOCIATES BOOK
NEW YORK

To Inka, the lady with two dogs,
one brown in color, the other silver gray

THE SISTERS OF THE CRESCENT EMPRESS

Edited by Claire Eddy

Cover art by Anna and Elena Balbusso
Cover design by Christine Foltzer

A Tor.com Book
Published by Tom Doherty Associates
175 Fifth Avenue
New York, NY 10010

www.tor.com

Tor® is a registered trademark of
Macmillan Publishing Group, LLC.

ISBN 978-0-7653-9544-3 (ebook)
ISBN 978-0-7653-9545-0 (trade paperback)

First Edition: November 2017

Acknowledgments

Writing *The Sisters of the Crescent Empress* was a journey much different from crafting *The Five Daughters of the Moon*. Working against a deadline—even one that you've chosen for yourself after careful planning and calculations—is a rather different experience from perfecting one's precious debut, and that's when the importance of the people near and dear to you kicks in in full force.

I had a clear vision for the story and an extremely detailed outline—big thanks go to the Hunts family who welcomed me to stay at their farm in Australia and drove me to the nearest town to send it onward in time. That was a wonderful beginning!

Very big thanks are due to my friends and family who took it rather well when I disappeared off the face of the earth to finish *The Sisters* last autumn. Sorry about that. And thanks!

I was moving houses the week I'd promised to deliver the first version of the manuscript. Hence thanks of a massive magnitude go to my parents, my husband's parents, and my very dear friend Inka, who pretty much cleaned the new place with my mother, unpacked the furniture, and put everything in the right places while I wrote and threw tantrums. As mentioned, these thanks are rather massive in nature, but still probably not quite enough.

Without spoiling too much of the plot, I can reveal this much: most of the events unfold in the same place, and thus getting the details right was of the utmost importance to me.

Colossal thanks go to my friend Satu for helping me figure out which way shadows fold in north and what materials to use in the house to achieve the desired sensory details. Also, I want to thank my mother-in-law, whose encyclopedic knowledge in gardening came in handy indeed.

While writing, I cried through most of the chapters, and I still do so even after having read the novel through about a gazillion times. For this, I want to thank my agent, Cameron McClure, who pushed me to go deeper, still deeper until the daughters took over, until the end became almost too much to bear. And then my superb editor, Claire Eddy, hinted ever so gently how to make the story even better, just a touch more tragic, and voilá! I'm so proud of what we've achieved together!

I'm extremely happy to work with the phenomenal people at Donald Maass Literary Agency, especially Donald Maass and Katie Boutillier.

And then there's the Tor.com Publishing team, a group of absolutely fantastic people I had the honor of meeting this past summer. Thank you Carl Engle-Laird, Kristin Temple, Katharine Duckett, and Mordicai Knode! I loved-loved-loved the cover of *The Five Daughters of the Moon,* but I'm head over heels in love with the cover of *The Sisters of The Crescent Empress,* art by the Balbusso sisters, design by Christine Foltzer—this cover is the very definition of stunning!

Finally, I want to thank my darling, dear husband, Matti. Whenever I slip into the worlds of my own making for too long, he cooks me the most fantastic dishes you can ever imagine and pokes me with that famous squeaking stuffed toy shark until I realize I should probably take a break. What more could a girl hope for?

Chapter 1

Alina

It's too dark outside. The world has been broken since the shadow of a swan brought the news of Mama's death. There's no Crescent Empress now, and it's the time of the month Papa looks aside. My sisters are Daughters of the Moon, just like I am, but I fear they will grow even more worried about me if I mention this aloud. Yet I must say something, anything, for the train is already slowing speed.

"Merile . . ." The train rattles as though it, too, were unhappy about approaching Angefort. I cling to the thick, white curtains with both hands and force myself to face the night. Maybe I'm just imagining the wrongness. That used to happen often enough. "Why is it so dark here?"

Merile balances on her knees next to me on the divan that yellows more with each day. She looks out through the frost-dimmed window, but it's as if she's not seeing the things that are so obvious to me. Rafa and Mufu stir from their shallow sleep, from where our hems form a nest for them. My sister smiles at her beautiful dogs, then at me, and her expression turns wicked. "Weeks. There won't be a day in weeks still."

Is she teasing me or serious? I can't tell. But I shiver when I think of how long the shadows will grow if the sun remains captive behind the horizon for much longer. To have no light . . . All the shadows I've met so far have been friendly, even the swan shadow. And yet, I don't want to live amongst those who have lost their bodies and souls. I really don't. My sisters would miss me terribly much! "Why?"

Merile glances at her lounging companions, snaps her fingers. Rafa bounces up first and rises on her hind legs, to stare out with us. Her big, brown ears are perched, alert. She yaps once, and soon Mufu is there, too, black tail stiff between her legs. The dogs must think something important is about to happen outside. That is, something more important than what's happening in the day carriage. "Because. It's because we're so high up in the north . . . Or was it south? In any case. It's because of that thing."

My sister sounds as if she's repeating a line she's read from a book or heard from Celestia or Elise. I don't think she's teasing me, but there's no way to be sure. Outside, the night droops against the hard snowfields. With Papa in hiding, there's no one left to protect the empire, and all sorts of creatures might lurk in the dark.

But evil things may come to pass even under our father's gaze. I don't want to even think of *his* name, but Celestia says that pretending that bad things didn't happen won't make them go away. Rather they will let the people who did the bad things get away with having done them, and so I force myself to think of the name of the man who ordered poor Mama shot.

Gagargi Prataslav is evil. He's built a monstrous machine that he claims can see into the future. His Great Thinking Machine consumes souls for fuel, and for reasons I don't understand he wants to feed it mine. Even though I'm no bird whose soul could light up a lamp or bring a mechanical creation to life, even though I'm six and a half years old and have spoken my name aloud so many times that it must be solidly anchored to my body already!

The gagargi also wants to rule the Crescent Empire and keep us, especially Celestia, as far away from him as possible. He has put many people under his spell, including Captain Janlav, who thinks he's tasked to protect me and my sisters. But when we get the chance, me and my sisters must flee so that Celestia can marry the Moon, become the Crescent Empress, and reclaim her empire. I hope she'll order the Great Thinking Machine torn apart and melted the first thing.

"Do you really not remember a word of what you've read?" Sibilia's sharp question yanks me back from my thoughts, and I've never been happier of her and Merile's squabbling. Even though not a day goes past without them arguing. "It's dark here because of the curvature of the world and because we're above the Arctic Circle. Honestly, if you paid a bit more attention to something else besides your rats, you wouldn't be making a fool out of yourself every single time someone asks you a trivial question!"

Merile sticks her tongue out at Sibilia. It's a dull, graying red, rather than the bright pink of Rafa's and Mufu's tongues. Though I often do as Merile does, this time I don't. Sibilia's words calm me. Maybe there's still hope that one day we'll run free.

"Alina, could you move just a bit?" Sibilia's tone is kinder than the one with which she spoke to Merile. Sometimes I think they're afraid of me breaking, as if I were sculpted from glass. "Merile, you too. We need to take down the curtains."

I shuffle aside. Lately, it's been easier to get lost in my thoughts. My breakfast and lunch no longer stink and taste of Nurse Nookes's potions. Maybe the two are related. Maybe not. I miss Nurse Nookes. I hope she's fine. I think she is—if something were to have happened to her, the shadow of the owl would no doubt have come to visit me. "Why?"

Sibilia wobbles up onto the divan even as Merile and her companions jump down. The sofa squeaks like a duck and shifts under me like a pony intent on tossing me off its back, not that that has ever happened. Sibilia seeks support from the wall, and manages to get up on her stockinged feet. Yet, I'm not at all sure she won't fall on top of me at any moment. Maybe that's why she sounds annoyed. "You know why."

But I'm not sure what she means. I'm dressed in the white travel dress, the winter coat, and the fur-lined boots that pinch my toes because I'm wearing two pairs of socks. I've already bundled up everything that has been given to me during this awful journey: the nightgown, the simple woolen dress, and the sabots. The pearl bracelet Celestia and Elise made for me. Even the sheets and blankets from my bed. Throughout the day, Celestia and Elise have been . . . I'm not sure what they're doing, but it almost looks as if they're taking things apart. Elise has shredded her sheets and now wraps the pieces around the chipped teacups and saucers. Celestia is . . . it almost looks as if she's wrestling with the samovar perched on top of the cupboard by the door that leads to our cabins.

"Or then you don't," Sibilia mutters under her breath. She can't quite reach the silver clips holding the curtains up. She steadies herself against the glass, leaving behind a wet handprint. "It's because it's better to be safe than sorry."

But I still don't understand what she means. The last time we were about to leave the train, we didn't pack anything with us. Celestia had arranged her seed, General Monzanov, to meet with us at a town so tiny I can't recall its name. But then something happened, and we had to board the train again, leaving him and his troika behind.

"Sorry. Sorry lot," Merile whispers to Rafa and Mufu. Her

companions snuggle against her, heads pressed against the backs of her knees. Does she, too, ponder if we're really going to depart the train this time around, if her seed will be there to meet us at Angefort? "That's what we've been lately, haven't we?"

Celestia says that at Angefort, we'll be staying in a house that stands on a hill overlooking a lake. She says it's a very nice house. But maybe there won't be servants there either. Maybe that's why we're now packing.

"I want to be safe." I force myself to meet the night with a steady gaze. With the glass between us, the darkness can't touch me. I feel a bit better. "Will we be safe at the house?"

"Safe. You'll be as safe as a porcelain cup wrapped in cotton sheets." Merile grabs a corner of the white curtain. Rafa and Mufu bounce against the divan, needlelike teeth bared, trying to do likewise. "Sibilia, what do you think, should we wrap up our precious little cup?"

There's a pause as there always is when Sibilia considers something for longer than it should take her to make up her mind. She glances at Elise and Celestia, her plump lips pursing. Our older sisters are too busy to pay attention to us. "Yes."

I yelp as Sibilia yanks the curtain loose. It falls over me, and . . .

It's night now. I smell wet ground, rotting leaves, and it's not the train that speeds across the empire. No, it's me, running as fast as my four legs can carry me. And I'm not alone. I sense, if I were to glance over my shoulder, I would see who is with me. But I can't. For I must run.

Run as fast as I can.

"Ha-haa. Ghost!" Merile laughs. "Alina, you look like a ghost!"

I fumble to lean on the windowsill. It's cold. And someone is tugging at the curtains, lifting the edge. There's a growl. It's Rafa. No, it's Mufu. The black dog jumps up onto the divan, into the low, soft cave. She licks my hands, her tongue wonderfully wet and warm and sticky. But even though I'm in the carriage with her and my sisters, I'm still at the same time running.

"Sibilia." Celestia doesn't sound angry, but more like she's disappointed. "Are you almost done with the curtains?"

If I were to close my eyes, I would be out of her reach, everyone's reach. For my feet are the fastest, like lightning and gale. But why would I want to run away from my sisters? I force my eyes to stay open, as I've done on so many nights.

The curtain lifts as Sibilia speedily gathers it in her arms. Her round cheeks glow. She stammers apologetically at me, "Sorry. Couldn't resist."

"We're not sorry," Merile mutters, picking Mufu up from the divan. She hugs her companion fiercely. "Yes, my darling, we're not sorry at all!"

I stare back at them, afraid to close my eyes for even half a second. The rattle of the train is the rhythm of my running feet. No, not feet, but paws, and I don't know what it means.

"Alina, are you all right?" Sibilia sits down next to me. She cups my face between her palms. Her hands are sweaty. "We didn't frighten you, did we?"

I can no longer keep my eyes open. I blink rapidly. "No . . ."

The dream, or maybe it's a nightmare, fades, and I decide I won't tell my sisters about it, just as I don't tell them about every shadow I see. Maybe I can simply dream when I'm awake. Maybe it's not a bad thing. Though the shadows come and go as they please, they've never hurt me, just as the Witch at the End of the Lane promised. I haven't seen her since we visited her cottage, but I do hope to meet her again. She's the one who summoned me back when I spent too long with the shadows and almost forgot where my home is—here with my sisters. "It was nothing."

"Right." Sibilia lets out a deep breath, and the front of her dress strains in its seams. She still doesn't seem convinced, but she takes it out on the curtain, vigorously bundling it. "Merile, will you help me fold this thing?"

Merile lowers Mufu on the divan and picks Rafa up in her arms. The copper brown dog nuzzles her chin. My sister tilts her head back, and her black hair is wild and wonderful. She laughs. "You're so silly! Oh, yes! You are!"

"I'll do it," I say before Sibilia can chastise my sister. Folding the curtains is no doubt important, but so is cuddling Rafa and Mufu. I think it might have been one of them in the waking dream. But why only one? Why not both?

The train suddenly slows speed. A lot. I grip the curtain, as does Sibilia. It stretches tight between us. I stay up on my feet only because of that.

"No," Celestia commands.

Sibilia and I turn just in time to see the samovar teetering on the edge of the cupboard, then arch past our sister.

"Don't you dare fall." And for a moment I'm sure that Celestia has it within her power to affect the way the world works, that she will only have to say the words to change events to follow her will. But then she gracefully reaches toward the silver pot, and her shadow . . . It flaps her arms as if they were wings, the sleeves of her white dress tattered feathers.

"Oh," I gasp, blinking. Am I imagining again?

A crash. Clatter of silver. When I next open my eyes, Celestia has caught the pot, but the rest of the samovar has come apart. The body and the base and the screws that held them together have scattered, landing every which way around the carriage.

Celestia folds gracefully on her knees on the carpet that's not so white anymore. Elise, Sibilia, Merile, and I rush to her, for there can't be much time left before we're at the Angefort station and must leave the train with our bundles. Elise picks up the dented body of the samovar. Sibilia retrieves the base. I spot one of the small silver screws.

"How. How are we ever going to manage to put it together?" Merile asks, but it's as if she's not worried about the samovar but about something else altogether.

"Hush," Celestia says, and in her blue eyes live the calm seas and the cloudless summer skies. "We will make do with what we have. And no matter what awaits us once we depart the train, as long as we remain composed and quiet, I promise to you, my sisters, that it is in my power to keep us safe. As long as we are together, everything will be all right."

I purse my fingers around the silver screw, smiling. We'll be safe, after all. Celestia is blessed by the Moon, the oldest of us, the empress-to-be, and she never lies.

I don't know why I thought that Angefort would be a town. It's not, and I'm not yet sure what it actually is.

As we step out of the train, we're greeted by a gust thick with prickly flakes, but not even a tiniest hint of light. I'm still shivering, squinting to see beyond my own boots, when the guards flanking us switch on the duck soul lanterns that sway as the wind wills. Their serious faces are familiar to me now, though I don't know their real names. My sisters have named them Beard, Boy, Belly, Boots, and Tabard.

Then we're on the move already, and of that I'm happy, because I'm sure that if we'd stayed still for a moment longer, we would have turned into ice. Captain Janlav leads the way through the storm, his steps long and strong, toward the hut that acts as the station and the hunched shapes of . . . houses? Me and my sisters have to hold tight to our blankets, which is tricky because we also have to carry our own belongings. Celestia goes first, cradling the dented samovar against her chest. Elise is next with the bundles of wrapped-up porcelain. Sibilia wades with her head bent low, the curtains clutched against her sides. Merile has our sheets and pillows piled on her arms. I'm the last, and my load is the lightest and sweetest, but as the wind yanks at my blanket, I dread I'll soon drop the wooden box that contains what's left of the sugar and tea.

The silent guards accompanying us carry only their rifles and the lanterns, their coats buttoned all the way up. I think they might get to return to the train later. I envy them for both. I did feel safer on the move. This place doesn't feel friendly in any way. I don't think any of our seeds will be here to meet us.

"Welcome to Angefort," Captain Janlav says when we reach the small hut, the wind pausing just long enough for the words to reach us. He sounds the same as always, steadfast and steady, but he looks very different. No, it's his coat that's different, missing the epaulets and the silver buttons, the signs of his rank in Mama's service.

My sisters stare past him, at our destination, and I do likewise. My bones rattle in the gale, or that's how it feels, but finally I can make out what awaits us. It's a square with low log buildings for three sides, the platform we stand on closing it. The windows are shuttered against the winter, the chimneys puff gray wisps. In the middle of the square is a flagpole, and there flaps angrily a scarlet flag that bears black shapes I don't recognize from this far away.

Then, three men in bulky coats, with the hoods drawn up, swarm out of the nearest house, armed with rifles, bearing dim lanterns. They must have heard the train arrive.

"Garrison. This is a garrison," Merile mutters even as Rafa and Mufu dive under the hem of her white cloak. Her companions must be scared. Or then, though coated, they're freezing. Or both. "Here, at the end of the railway! Curious that . . ."

Celestia shakes her head very, very lightly. Even as the wind scrapes our cheeks, as the snow turns us white-haired and piles up on our shoulders, Merile—we all—should be silent, simply watch, but not be seen. Akin to shadows, no matter what.

Captain Janlav waves at the soldiers. He doesn't seem cold or concerned at all as he marches through the snow to greet them. He calls over his shoulder, "Come."

We do as he commands, though this means that poor Rafa and Mufu can no longer shelter under Merile's hem.

When we're but ten steps away from the soldiers, a frightening thought occurs to me. The sky is gray with clouds. Papa can't see us now. Anything might come to pass without him learning about it until much later. Though I've decided to remain brave, I tremble as we meet the garrison men. The pinprick snowflakes sting my eyes, and tears soon follow. But I mustn't make a sound. I must be as my shadow should be.

Captain Janlav salutes the soldiers, bringing his fist against his chest. He's wearing red gloves, just as they are—they're all on the same side. "Captain Janlav," he introduces himself, his voice barely loud enough to carry over the howling wind. He glances at each of the men in turn, frosted brows furrowing. "Where's Captain Ansalov?"

The garrison men shrug back at him, bearded chins clenched against their furry collars, cheeks already burning red. In the light of the swinging lanterns, their shadows are scattered, uncertain of which way to fold. But I know for sure they don't want to be out either. I know this sort of thing because I'm friends with many a shadow.

"Well?" Captain Janlav tilts his rifle toward the heavy clouds.

A gust sharper than any before swipes against my back, against my sisters. Our hair comes loose from the braids, and light snow flees before us like a hundred translucent snakes. I hold on to my blanket, though my fingers are so numb that I don't feel them at all anymore. But I won't say a word. I'm my own shadow.

"Waiting inside." The shortest of the garrison men motions in the direction from which he and the others came. I realize it then, they don't know who we are. Is this Celestia's doing? Can Papa help us even when he can't see us?

"Well, how about you take us to him?" Even I can tell that Captain Janlav doesn't want to reveal more of his mission to these men, only their leader. Is he concerned about our safety? Or is he, too, simply weary of standing out here in the storm?

"Friend, we've been waiting for you for weeks." The man reaches up to brush snow off Captain Janlav's shoulder, a gesture too amiable. He reeks of smoke and sweat and something pungent. My teeth clatter, and so do Merile's, and I can do nothing to stop it.

"And now we are here." Captain Janlav doesn't sling his rifle over his shoulder, but glances at me and my sisters, speckled white from head to toe. Celestia looks back at him as if she were the one giving him the permission. Maybe it's that way. "Lead the way to your captain."

The garrison men guide us the rest of the way across the square, through the thickening snowfall. It hurts to move, more than it hurt to stand still. Every step feels too long, but I must keep up with my sisters. Though they wouldn't leave me behind. They'd come looking for me, even if they might never find me.

I'm so intent on wading onward, warding off my own thoughts, that I don't even notice it when we at last reach the buildings. But that we do.

Despite there being three houses, I don't see one that would match with what Celestia has told us about our destination. But when we climb up the clean-brushed stairs leading to a narrow porch, I hear the faintest notes of . . .

Music! It's definitely music, and I've heard this tune before! Rafa and Mufu yap as they, too, recognize the song. It's from an opera that Elise at one time couldn't stop humming. A love story with an unhappy ending, I think. And yet the tune warms me more than my blanket does—we haven't heard music since . . . Not since we boarded the train.

The short soldier halts by the closed door, in the light leaking out through the small windowpanes. He rubs his hands together. "Yesaul Ansalov is inside. Go ahead. Have a look."

Captain Janlav lifts his left fist—it's some sort of signal for Beard and Tabard, who guard the rear. Both men cock their rifles up, to rest against their shoulders. The garrison men chuckle, as if nothing had happened here in ages. Or if something did, they don't think it likely that that something would come to pass again anytime soon. Captain Janlav peeks in through the window and then, without further ceremony, pulls the door open and enters the room.

It must be so very warm inside, with the fire blazing under the brick arc, behind the simple iron grille. But I can't enter yet. Not before Celestia does, and she won't before she knows it's safe. I do shuffle closer to her, to stare inside through the narrow gap between her and the doorframe.

A thickset man with curly brown hair leans back on a chair, feet lifted on a desk covered with tidy but tall heaps of paper. He has his eyes closed, and his somehow short fingers tap the rhythm sleepily against his lap. There are shadows in the room, but none of them belong to living animals. Or people other than him.

But it's not the sight of Captain Ansalov as such or the shadows or the lack of them that has Captain Janlav unexpectedly chuckling. On the desk, behind the tallest pile of papers, there's a gramophone, one with a brass horn and a black disc spinning under the needle. The music has lulled Captain Ansalov to dreams so pleasant that he doesn't wake up when the warm air flees the room, not even when Celestia finally nods and one by one me and my sisters let the train guards claim our bundles, and then enter the room, stomping snow at the threshold.

The garrison man clears his throat with a ragged, wet cough, then shouts, "Yesaul Ansalov! Visitors."

Captain Ansalov jolts in his chair, a man shaken awake. "Compeer Vasal, what have I said about . . ."

For a moment, I'm sure he'll lose his balance, fall over, and bump his head. But with a surprising grace, he swings his boots down and reaches to flick the gramophone's needle up. He leans toward us, beady green eyes glinting with interest. "Visitors. So, it was true after all. Very well then, Compeer Vasal, close the door and depart, if you'd be so kind."

But there's nothing kind in Captain Ansalov's voice, even though it's mellow and round. I feel cold, colder than I was outside, despite the fireplace.

"I have been tasked by Gagargi Prataslav himself," Captain Janlav says after Vasal is gone and the door is closed with both the garrison soldiers and the train guards on the other side.

Following Celestia's lead, me and my sisters settle into a crescent behind Captain Janlav. He thinks it's his duty to keep us safe, and for once I'm happy about that.

"By the great gagargi himself? Of course you are." Captain Ansalov slowly gets up and crosses the floor, which creaks under his leather boots that have seen many years and miles. The shape of his shadow is uneven. And it's not only his shadow that's restless. There are animal heads hung on the wall, glass-eyed deer, elk, even wolves, and the parts of the shadows that remain shift as if the animals, too, wanted to leave the room, but cannot.

"One, two"—Captain Ansalov points at me and Merile with his thick stub of a finger as he nears Captain Janlav—"Three. Four."

His finger halts, pointing at Celestia. He must know who she is, who we are, even though no names have been mentioned, though the blankets, heavy with snow, hide our white dresses, though our braids have come undone. He was waiting for us, though he wasn't sure we'd ever come, and now he can't make himself believe we truly stand here before him. "Five Daughters of the Moon. Well, this I didn't expect at all."

From the corner of my eye, I spy Celestia and what she makes of this. My oldest sister might as well be sculpted from stone. I'm still so very cold, but I don't dare to sneak to warm before the fireplace. For it's as if my sister wants us to pretend that we don't exist. Are things still going according to her plan?

"There was a change of plan." Captain Janlav tugs off his red gloves and unbuttons his coat, scattering small piles of snow on the floor. He produces a folded, red-sealed letter from inside his breast pocket and hands it over to Captain Ansalov.

Captain Ansalov turns the letter in his hands, grunting as if he's not entirely pleased. He runs his too-short forefinger slowly against the seal as if to check that Captain Janlav is really telling the truth. I realize he's missing the tips of all his fingers but his thumbs. "What now, I wonder."

My fingers, still squeezing the blanket, throb as if to remind me that I didn't lose them anywhere, even if they went numb for a while.

"How about you read it?" Captain Janlav suggests. There are words he doesn't want to say before me and my sisters. But he doesn't want to leave us out of his sight either.

As I stare at Captain Ansalov's stumpy fingers, I can't stop thinking about mine. I should stay very still, but my hand aches worse with each heartbeat. I need to move my fingers because if I don't, the tips might fall off on their own. They really might, and then there would be no sticking them back!

"A fine suggestion." Captain Ansalov's tone is flat and joyless. As he reads, his chafed lips moving with the words, I slowly bring up my free hand, to hold the blanket closed. I make sure my shadow doesn't shift an inch. "Interesting."

I dare to uncurl my fingers only when he rereads the letter. And it hurts, it hurts so bad that I almost cry out! But I won't because that would draw his attention, and that would be a bad thing.

"Is the house ready?" Captain Janlav asks, accepting the letter back.

"Liberated and cleaned." That voice, so soft, but hard still . . . Captain Ansalov glances at me and my sisters and then again at me, and it's almost as if he knew how much my hand aches. He smiles in the smug sort of way. My older sisters remain completely still, unaffected by his smile, his words, by any pain they might feel. But I . . .

I shiver.

Captain Janlav strolls past the older captain to lightly tap the brass horn of the gramophone. He runs his fingers that are just as long as fingers should be along the lacquered sides of its body, the shapes of swans carved into the shiny wood. When he speaks, he sounds as if he's disappointed to find the musical instrument in this room. "Seems like you did a thorough job."

Captain Ansalov turns sharply on his heels, and the floor squeals like a wounded pig, not that I've ever heard an actual pig squealing, and marches to the desk. With his back turned to me, he can't see me shuffling closer to Merile. And now that I look at my sister, she's not as still as I thought she was. Her chin trembles, though Rafa and Mufu shift under her hem, to warm her. Maybe she's feeling nervous, too. Maybe all my sisters are, but we're the only ones showing it.

The two captains hold gazes for a long while, and it's a very good thing that the desk stands between them. Neither of them wants to back off before the other. I'm counting on Captain Janlav, because I know he'll protect us, even if he's under the gagargi's spell. And maybe it's that which in the end plays in his favor. And that's terrifying.

"Shall we sort out the details, then?" Captain Ansalov's question is more like a statement than any sort of suggestion. He sits down and lowers the gramophone's needle. The song continues where it last ended.

"Please do." Celestia says the first word she's said since we left the train. She doesn't wait for an answer. Instead, she glides to the fireplace, and motions me and my sisters to follow her. We brush the melting snow off the blankets, from our wind-whipped braids. Elise takes tiny dance steps as she holds her palms toward the flames. Sibilia looks as if she's tempted to do likewise. Merile cuddles Rafa and Mufu in turns. With the warmth and my sisters around me, I feel a little bit better.

Maybe we haven't come to a really, really bad place. But we're not yet where we should be either.

The two captains make arrangements, voices so low that I can't make them out, but I keep on trying. I shouldn't forget for even a moment that we're not free to come and go as we please. Celestia doesn't have to tell me that now we can but wait and see what will happen next. Any attempt to resist wouldn't end well. It's too cold and dark outside, and we have no friends here. Even those who have our best interests in mind only obey the gagargi.

Both familiar and unfamiliar men enter and leave the room as summoned by both the familiar and unfamiliar captain. Me and my sisters listen to the same song a dozen times or more. Celestia stares intently at the flames as though she could hear the words hiding behind the music. Maybe she can—she's the oldest and she sees into the world beyond this one. But even though I try, I still can't do either.

Eventually the song ends once more, and the door opens for what I guess might be for the last time. I think we've waited for hours already. That is, my fingers no longer hurt, though my hair is still a bit damp, not to mention my blanket. There are small puddles on the floor at our feet.

"The troikas are ready," the short soldier, Vasal, calls out from the doorway. He has a lit cigarette sticking out from the corner of his mouth. The wind herds the stink in.

Celestia stirs. She turns around to face Captain Ansalov and Captain Janlav. The men shake hands, a sign they've agreed on something, even if both still seem tense. I don't think they'll ever become friends.

"Come, then." Captain Janlav waves curtly toward the door. I can see Boy and Tabard waiting outside. They must be cold if they've stayed out the whole time. But I don't feel sorry for them. Why would I, when me and my sisters are the ones who have no say in where we're going?

"Wait." Celestia's voice is soft and shiny, the words almost visible. "Captain Ansalov . . ."

And curiously enough, Captain Ansalov strolls past his desk, toward Celestia, his expression blank. He bows his head. He reaches out for my sister's pale, slender hands. She lets him touch her fingers. His chapped lips part, but not a word comes out.

"You are still a good man." Celestia's eyes grow very blue. The pale hair braided around her head glistens silvery. Though she has a gray blanket around her shoulders, like all of us, for a moment it almost looks as if she were wearing white. "You only did your duty, what you thought was right."

"Come, then," Captain Janlav repeats. Or is this the first time he says the words?

Celestia casts Captain Ansalov one last look, and somehow, it's ripe with understanding. He gazes back at her, confused, even as my sister glides past him, toward the doorway, into the darkness.

The storm has died while we were inside, leaving behind snowbanks and a calm that I know won't last. One of the buildings must be a stable, for troikas and soldiers astride furry horses wait for us on the other side of the square. As we plod toward them, I can't stop thinking of Celestia and what she said to Captain Ansalov. When I'm tired, I sometimes I imagine things, like earlier today. I'm not sure which was the case now, and it feels important to me to know for sure. But pinching the underside of my arm doesn't help, and so I turn to Merile. "What was that about?"

"What. What was what?" Merile whispers back at me, not

wanting our older sisters to hear us. "Nothing. It was nothing."

Which means that something definitely happened.

"Nothing . . ." But before I can say more, Rafa and Mufu suddenly halt before us, one paw up, ears tight against their delicate heads. They growl in turns, and then they start bouncing in place.

"Go on, sillies." Merile holds her blanket against her chest with one hand, claps her thigh with the other, even as our older sisters wade farther away from us. "Go on."

But her companions pay no heed to her. I glance over my shoulder. Boy, who keeps up the rear, is but a few steps away from us. He would never kick Merile's companions, but who says what the garrison soldiers might do if they were to cause a delay.

And then I realize what Rafa and Mufu must have seen, smelled before we did.

"Hunting dogs," I whisper. The soldiers by the troikas hold leashed great, gray-black hounds that from this far away more resemble wolves than dogs. The hounds lean against their collars as if they were intent on springing upon us. Yet, the horses harnessed before the sleds seem calm.

"Rats," Boy laughs as he strides beside us. I stare at him in horror. What will he do to my sister's companions?

Nothing evil. He picks up Rafa under one arm, Mufu under the other. He does so with ease, though my sister's companions struggle and squirm. "Can't stay here the whole night."

Merile sniffs. She doesn't want the guards touching her dogs. But I don't see it as a bad thing that the guards we've traveled with for six weeks turn out to be . . . kind of nice. Or perhaps they seem nice only because now we can compare them to Captain Ansalov and his soldiers.

Boy escorts Merile and me the rest of the way to our sisters, and once more, we gather into a crescent, this time before the troikas. The hounds study us with hungry eyes, leashes taut. They're brutes with clipped ears and clipped tails, their leather collars studded with spikes.

"Here you go." Boy hands Mufu over to Merile and Rafa to me. I clutch the still-growling dog against my chest. Though her kin is much bigger, grimmer, she'd protect me against them with all her might.

"What?" Merile tilts her chin up. She pats Mufu repeatedly, but her companion won't calm down. "What are we waiting for?"

Boy trots aside, avoiding the question. Maybe he has a soft spot for animals only, not for us. And then I see why he didn't linger. Captain Ansalov is marching toward us, through the knee-deep snow, ice crackling under each step. He brings his ungloved hand to his lips and lets out a whistle so shrill I want to cover my ears, but can't as then I'd have to let go of Rafa.

"Here, boys," Captain Ansalov calls. The soldiers quickly unleash the hounds, and the horrid creatures dart to their master. I'm sure he doesn't keep them for company, but for . . .

I glance at Celestia, at Elise and Sibilia, but they stand as still as ever, even as Captain Ansalov approaches us with his ugly dogs. If Captain Janlav and the train guards weren't with us, I would run. That's how threatened I feel. Rafa must sense this, for she nudges me, as if to tell me that everything will be all right.

"Your hunting dogs?" Captain Janlav notes, more for our benefit than for him to have doubted this for even a moment.

"Excellent dogs. Bred them myself. You can't find a hound with a sharper nose anywhere in the whole empire." Captain Ansalov pats one of the dogs on the side. No, it's not a pat, but more like a slap. "There's a good boy! There's a good, smart boy."

He straightens his back and faces me and my sisters. He smiles at us, but it's a wicked sort of smile, then whistles a short note. The hounds scamper to form a neat line before him. He addresses us. "Attention. Stay still. Unless you want to lose a limb."

He sets the dogs free with another shrill whistle.

I tremble as the hounds circle me and my sisters, their black nostrils flaring, yellowing fangs bared. If it weren't for Rafa, her warm breath against my neck, her paws against my shoulder, I couldn't remain unmoving as the hounds sniff my boots and hem. One of them, a dog leaner than the rest, seems particularly intelligent. As if it could count what it must keep track of.

"All right. That's enough." Captain Ansalov chuckles. He whistles once more, and the hounds scatter and regroup behind the last troika.

"You may board the sleds," Captain Janlav says. He doesn't have to tell us that Captain Ansalov's hounds have our scent now. Even I realize that any attempt to run away would end up in their teeth.

I wake up to a wail so cruel that my stomach knots up. Rafa snaps awake on my lap, but Merile and Mufu continue snoring. Elise, who sits on my other side, stares blankly ahead, though maybe it's because her lashes and eyebrows glitter with frost. As Celestia and Sibilia travel on the sled before us, I can only see their backs.

"What was that?" I ask. Amongst the sounds of the snow crunching under the runners, the horses' heavy breathing, and the riders' occasional muttering, my voice sounds terribly tiny and frail.

Another wail comes from the dark forest lining what might or mightn't be a road. The guards gallop onward as though they'd heard nothing. I crane over my shoulder, only to glimpse Captain Ansalov's hounds sprinting from one rider to the other as though all this was just a game for them.

"Wolves," Elise says, wrapping an arm around me. My blanket makes a cracking sound. It's frozen into a hard shell around me, but I know it's not thick enough to ward off the hounds' teeth. "But don't worry about them, my dear Alina. They won't dare to approach this many people."

Even as she speaks, two of the hounds take off. They leap through the snowbanks with ease, clipped ears pulled back, and disappear amongst the white-cloaked firs. The next cruel howl comes from farther away. Even the wolves are afraid of Captain Ansalov's hounds.

I pet Rafa both to warm my hands and remain calm. There are stars in the sky at last, so it must be night. The forest is dense and full of shadows. Though I can't know for sure, I think most of them belong to living animals. Yet I don't dare to close my eyes again. I'm afraid of Captain Ansalov. I don't think he'll ever turn out to be a nice man, any more than his hounds could turn out to be anyone's companions. I'm sure he doesn't have any friends, only enemies and those he commands.

Elise adjusts the gold-embroidered blanket that covers our laps. "We will be at the house soon."

I don't know how she can tell that. I'm pretty sure she's never been this far up in the north or away from home either. To me, the firs with branches bent under snow and the rare white clearings that the winter wind has combed hard all look the same in the light that's not our father's.

The hounds return behind our troika, panting, yapping. Captain Ansalov barks praises at them. He sounds too cheerful.

I lean against Elise, because I don't want him to hear what I have to say. "I don't think he's here to keep us safe."

"That's why you have sisters," Elise replies. But then she suddenly leans forward and raises her arm to point straight ahead. The wind pushes its way under the blankets. Rafa shivers on my lap. "Now, look!"

The forest ends, and then I do see it, our destination still so far away. A house standing on a steep hill, with a walled garden facing what might be a frozen lake. It does look very pretty, but terribly lonely, all at the same time.

"The Angefort House," Elise whispers, awed, but there's a trace of something else in her voice, too. She's heard of this place. But hers are grown-up secrets, and if she hasn't chosen to share them with me before, I don't think she'll do so now either.

The guards and soldiers whip the horses to gallop faster on the last, long stretch, but when we reach the steep hill, they let them slow down to a walk. Merile stirs only when we curve onto the snowy yard flanked by two smaller houses, maybe a stable and servants' quarters? Mufu twists her head to lick what's visible of my sister's face from under the gray blanket, the angry red cheeks and redder nose. "Are we there yet?"

Elise laughs, and it's the most beautiful sound ever. She reaches past me to nudge Merile's shoulder. "Yes, we are there."

Even as she speaks, Captain Janlav and Captain Ansalov dismount their snorting horses. Frost immediately forms on the necks and flanks, where the animals sweated. The men stride with Beard and Tabard and two garrison soldiers through the untended yard to the wide stone steps leading to the white double doors. Captain Janlav and the guards have their rifles at hand. Captain Ansalov is more at ease as he reaches out for the ring-shaped knocker. The sound it makes is heavy and lonely. Then again, who would live in a place like this?

"What do we do next?" I ask Elise, hugging Rafa.

She tilts her head minutely and studies the door, the six men waiting before it, then the troikas and horses and soldiers and even the hounds. Celestia and Sibilia sit quiet in their sled. My sister says, "We wait."

And that's what we do.

At last, the door opens, but it does so hesitantly and slowly. Captain Janlav wagers a step back, just to give it space to fully open and not for any other reason. A pale, bony face that's framed by a frilly cap peeks out. And there stands a woman as old as Nurse Nookes, in a servant's simple black and white dress, her eyes wide and gaze darting from side to side, gripping an iron poker in her hand.

I immediately know this servant is afraid, not planning to harm us. Which is good.

In the other sled, Celestia whispers something to Sibilia. Merile fidgets with her blanket, as curious as I am. Elise notices this. She says in a low voice, "She wasn't expecting company."

Beard brushes in past the servant. The two captains exchange hushed words with her. Or that is, the men speak. The servant's lips don't move. She eyes the horses and hounds, doesn't lower the poker. No, she does so only when she notices me and my sisters. Her expression draws blank as she stares at us in disbelief, as if she were seeing a gathering of ghosts.

Beard returns from inside the house. He nods curtly at Captain Janlav, who then turns to face me and my sisters and shouts, "Escort them in."

"Now we get up." Elise pulls the embroidered blanket aside

from our laps. She eyes it longingly and then quickly bundles it up and pushes it atop our other belongings. "It's safe."

It hurts so much to get up! My teeth chatter. My body is numb and useless once more. Even though the buildings shelter us from the wind, the cold claws at me worse now than before we boarded the sled, though I don't know how that's possible. Yet Elise seems unaffected. She climbs out first, then helps both me and Merile down. By the time we're ready, Celestia and Sibilia have been so for a while.

Tabard points toward the open door. The guards don't like talking to us when they can avoid doing so. Celestia and Sibilia obey the wordless command and go first, which is wrong, because we should be seen in the order of our ages!

"Elise . . ." I whisper, confused.

"Hush." She holds my and Merile's hand as we follow our sisters' path. Rafa and Mufu trot beside us, lifting their paws high, but there's no escaping the winter. "Don't worry about that now."

But it feels exactly the sort of thing that we should worry about. For us, the Daughters of the Moon, the right order is very important. Nurse Nookes always said that the very future of the Crescent Empire depends on it, though I never quite understood why and how.

We enter the house, and Belly closes the door behind us. Inside, the old servant studies us in the faint light of a very old duck soul lantern. Though me and my sisters are wrapped in gray blankets and ruffled by our long journey, it's as if the servant knows already who we are, but not because someone has told her, but because she recognizes us as our father's daughters. I like her, though still she doesn't say a word. Is she mute? I try not to stare at her.

As we tramp snow from our sabots and boots and brush it off the blankets, I hear a snippet of conversation coming from a room next to the hall, from what might be a library. The door is ajar.

"Once your men have unpacked the sleds, we will not be requiring further assistance," Captain Janlav says. "Though do make sure nothing disappears in their pockets, will you?"

Captain Ansalov chuckles, and how I hate that sound! "We will try our very best."

Captain Janlav grunts something under his breath. He may or may not have mentioned the gagargi's name. Hrr! Thinking of him makes me shiver worse than the winter.

The two captains emerge from the room.

"Follow me," Captain Janlav says. He takes us through the hall, past what indeed is a library, toward a wide, wooden stairway. I catch a glimpse of narrower stairs leading down, to the cellar. The simple, dark door gives me chills. Rafa and Mufu must have sensed the same, for they yap, but only once.

"Sillies," Merile laughs, but the laugh is forced. "Up. Up we go!"

Though the stairs creak like a forest of hollow trees, I remind myself that I shouldn't be afraid. Beard checked the house. Captain Janlav is tasked to protect us. He wouldn't have brought us here, led us upstairs, if he weren't sure.

And yet, with each step, I'm more terrified.

We don't stop at the second floor, not in the big room that might be a dining room. We hurry along the long hallway. We continue onward to the third floor, there to at last enter a drawing room.

No curtains cover the tall, arching windows, and the night floods in unhindered. On the far side of the room, three doors hide what might be bedrooms. A grandfather clock strikes time, with a fireplace facing it from the opposite side. There's no embers there, no flames, but the two chandeliers gleam silvery. I blink, and then I see more. In the light of the stars and the chandeliers, two elderly, pale ladies sit behind the oval table, facing the door, their faces sharp, eyes hungry.

"Olesia, you were right," the older one says. "We have visitors, imagine that!"

I gasp and stumble back, straight into Elise's arms. She looks around in alarm, and though she seems to be taking in everything in the room, her gaze slides right past the women. "What is it, Alina?"

I can't reply to her. For it's then that I realize, the light goes through the women. This house is haunted.

Chapter 2

Merile

Lambs. The gray blanket smells of wet lambs as Elise pokes it with the long, sturdy needle. She hums a light tune that fails to fill the drawing room with cheer. She can't fool me this easily. The coat will be ugly.

"Peasants," I mutter. We've stayed at this house for a full week already, but the winter here will no doubt persist for months still. Enough time for Elise to finish sewing coats for all of us. "We'll look like peasants."

Elise pauses both humming and sewing. She glances past me at Celestia, who stares out of the tall, arching window, into the walled garden beyond. She's only half visible from behind the no-longer-so-white curtains we brought with us from the train. Her face is pale in the light of the day that still doesn't last long enough to be of any use. The crown of her hair is paler, almost the color of swan feathers. She's present, but away. No doubt she's looking into the world beyond this one.

"And would that be such a bad thing?" Elise asks me, tapping the point of the needle with her finger. Once. Twice.

How can she even ask? Does she not realize how wrong that would be? We're only ever supposed to wear white!

"Yes. Yes it would," I reply, glad that Alina is taking her afternoon nap in our room with my dear companions and that for once I don't have to shy away from an argument. We're here to stay, though my older sisters won't admit it aloud. But even if apart from the guards and the mute old servant, Millie, there's no one around for miles, that's no reason to forget who we are. "We're the Daughters of the Moon."

Sibilia has paused reading on the divan before the fireplace. Her shoulders are hunched from the hours spent over the book of scriptures. She's intently listening to my conversation with Elise. Is this again one of those times they try and gauge if I paid any attention during Nurse Nookes's monotonous lectures back at the Summer City, ready to tease me if I reveal that I didn't?

Well, I did pay attention! I'll set them right!

"Our power comes from the Moon himself. When the oldest of us marries him, she becomes the Crescent Empress. Papa will then send the men he's blessed to her, and those men will become the seeds of her daughters, and then they'll be appointed as generals and court officials and to other high positions." There. Oh, wait, that wasn't everything. "And then she'll also tell the lords and ladies what to do. And then they'll tell their landowners and mine owners and factory foremen what they need to produce and how much and when."

Elise sighs as she kneels before me to check the front piece. Knowing my sister, there was nothing accidental about the sigh. But looking at the front piece, she's holding it higher against my chest than the one she already finished attaching. As my sister reaches out for the mint green tin box perched on the edge of the oval table, I realize she's somehow still unsatisfied with my answer.

"Simple. It's really all quite simple," I add, because really, it is, and I don't want the coat to be any uglier than it has to be. Once it's ready, I bet Elise will force me to wear it every single time I go out to play with my sillies, and I'll have no choice but to obey her. I don't know who lived in this house before us, but the only clothes they left behind are tattered summer dresses, ridiculously wide-brimmed hats with thinning plumes, and worn ankle shoes too big for anyone other than Celestia. No muffs or furs or anything else useful.

Elise attaches the front piece in place with two stitches. She eyes it critically. "Things are rarely simple in life."

I, if anyone, know that. Our lives haven't been particularly easy lately, not with the gagargi turning against Mama, not with Celestia's previous escape plan failing, not with us ending up here in the middle of nowhere in a house so sparsely furnished that our bedrooms don't even have carpets. It's very difficult to be a Daughter of the Moon when you have to consider not only yourself but also how things happening to your family affect everyone else! "Peasant. When you're a peasant, your lord makes sure there's food on your table and clothes on your back and you really don't need to think about anything at all. Being a peasant is really quite an easy life."

The front piece slips from Elise's fingers as she flinches away from me. It tangles against my belly, held back by the loosening stitches. I've never seen her gray eyes this wide.

"What?" I ask even as Sibilia lowers the book of scriptures on the divan and strolls to us. This is no longer about her waiting and wanting to tease me about something, I'm sure of that. And yet Celestia remains by the window, staring out. No, she's not only staring out, but ever so slowly brushing her fingers over every inch of the sill. What is she doing?

"Don't ever say that sort of thing aloud when the guards can hear you!" Elise's chastisement gives me other, more urgent things to think about.

Because she's being very unfair! I only told her what I know and what I've been taught. But something in her tone makes me control mine. "Why?"

Sibilia holds out for Elise the mint green box that once must have contained hard sugar candies, but much to her disappointment proved to hide only sewing supplies. We don't talk with the guards in any case, not even with Captain Janlav, unless we absolutely must. But Elise does so out of her own will, and she might have learned something useful.

Elise gingerly picks up a pin from the box and glances at Celestia. Her eyes turn steel gray as if she decided to go on regardless of whether or not our oldest sister is listening to us. "For the guards, joining the imperial army, signing their very lives to be the subject of our late mother's whims, was the only way out to a better life. Imagine that, Merile, how wretched your life must be for you to willingly give it away in exchange for a few coins and a full belly. No, you can't even imagine what a hard life our people, even children younger than you, lead in the distant corners of this vast empire."

I don't know what to reply. She makes it sound as if being a soldier were a terrible fate. She also talks as if I were somehow very ignorant. Though that I'm not. I really am not.

"It's an honor to serve in the colors of the Moon," Sibilia replies before I can. It's a good thing she did so, because compared to her, I might have sounded just a little spiteful.

"Honor?" Elise shakes her head, the movement enviably graceful. "Dear Sibs, you clearly have no idea how rough life is outside the palace grounds, how the empire treats its veterans!"

"Tell us about the guards," Sibilia says, completely missing the anger and urgency in Elise's tone. It surprises me that Celestia has either chosen not to take part in this conversation or then she is too immersed in her own thoughts to really hear what we are talking about. We never really even broach these darker things when Alina and I are present.

Elise speaks very fast, very quietly, as if she were suddenly pressed for time but simply had to get the words out, off her chest. "Before Boots had a name, he worked in a mine up in the north, deep underground, pushing carts of ore until he fell down from exhaustion, being whipped to push more even after that."

I can't even think of her words, that's how fast she speaks. I commit them to my memory, to ponder about them later, during the nights I shiver next to Alina despite my companions snoring between us.

"Boy's mother cried for joy when he enlisted in the army, though none of the men in his village that went to war ever returned. But she was relieved to see him go because the previous winter two of his sisters starved to death when their lord did not leave them enough of the harvest to last through the long, dark months."

Sibilia clicks her tongue, tasting the flavor of the stories. I don't know what she makes of all this. Elise is saying such strange things.

"And Tabard . . ." Elise swallows as if holding back tears, though that can't be right. "Poor Tabard—"

"Elise." Celestia's voice is mellow and soft, and yet it cuts like a soldier's sword. "That is quite enough of such evocative tales. I agree we should not forget that the lower classes form the backbone of our empire. But neither should we dwell on the failures of a few personages."

Elise's right brow arches as it always does when she's about to disagree. But before she can say another word, the grandfather clock chimes three times. The swan on the pendulum paddles back and forth, neck straightened, beak tilted up for the silver song.

A mere moment later, the door of the bedroom I share with Alina flings open and Rafa and Mufu burst out, wagging their tails, and I'm so happy to see them, though we were apart for mere hours. Oh, my lovely companions are so very pretty! Their furs positively shine from the dedicated care Aline and I have bestowed on them. We brush them from tail to top after every breakfast, lunch, and dinner.

Alina darts to us. She leans over Elise's shoulder, panting. Rafa and Mufu poke at our older sister's hem with their glistening black noses. "Is it ready yet?"

Elise's expression draws blank as she reaches out for another pin. I realize the moment for darker truths is over, and we must pretend together that nothing else is going on than her trying to make my coat less hideous.

"Oh my dear darlings," I coo at Rafa and Mufu. Rafa stares at me with her big, chocolate brown eyes. Mufu sniffs my knees, her nose wonderfully wet. Both seem just a bit suspicious. "Of course I missed you! I missed you so much!"

Elise shakes her head, but whether at me or at the abrupt end of the conversation, I have no idea. She rises up to her full height, and she's tall. Not as tall as Celestia, but even so I reach only up to her chest. She takes a step back, and eyes me critically, head cocked to the right. Though sewing usually makes her happy, she doesn't look that way now.

"Well, will it take long?" Alina shifts her weight, wringing her hands as if she needed to use the pot-pot right at this instant. Though she's old enough not to need help when it comes to that. She doesn't look like she's distraught, either. I'm not sure what's going on. I need to find out what it is the soonest. My sister's mind is weak, and nightmares pester her almost every night.

The machine. She insists the gagargi intends to feed her soul to the Great Thinking Machine, no matter how I tell her again and again that there's nothing to fear. I'll keep her safe. Rafa and Mufu will keep her safe. Celestia would never allow anyone to harm her!

"A moment more still," Elise replies. She picks up from the table the slices of velvet that originated from the decorative pillows we brought with us from the train. She places them against my neck. She might be planning on creating a collar of sorts, but I can but bravely persist.

I click my tongue again, and Rafa and Mufu rush to Alina. They think whatever she has in mind concerns them. Which distracts her, and off she goes with them, to play before the fireplace. Sibilia follows them to the divan there and picks up the book of scriptures. But she keeps on glancing at them from over the book's edge. Worried. She's worried about Alina, too.

I want something else to think about than the gagargi and his horrid machine. But what could that be? There are days and nights when everything in this house that has fallen in disrepair reminds me of him!

"Coats," I whisper. Yes. That's a better topic. "Why don't we simply ask for coats? Or why don't we ask mute Millie to sew them?"

"Huh." Elise lowers the piece of velvet back on the table as if she'd changed her mind about the collar after all. "It's not polite to call people names."

I wasn't calling Millie names, just pointing out the obvious. Maybe Elise is simply having one of those days that she has to know everything better. Maybe that's what her earlier comments were all about. "'Mute' isn't a bad word."

"And she isn't mute!" Alina calls at us from before the fireplace, and then she's already scampering up. She bounces back to me like a day-old foal. My companions yap at her, wonderful, high-pitched barks. Alina falls on her knees on the undusted carpet, and they roll onto their backs, to be scratched more. "She's got her tongue still!"

Celestia lifts up her right hand, a sign that we should talk no more. But the routines we followed aboard the train are broken. We've reached our destination. We're where the gagargi wants us to be. The guards no longer rush to investigate every sound and shout. Which is a good thing.

"And how under the Moon do you know that?" Sibilia asks. Her lazily combed red hair shines dully compared to Elise's, even though she's the one sitting before the fire.

"I asked her to show it to me." Alina looks a bit sheepish, and I can tell she's lying and that my older sisters don't notice that. Liar. Alina has grown to be a very good liar.

Celestia and Elise merely look aghast, but Sibilia rolls her eyes at Alina. I fidget with my new coat's front. Worn. The wool feels thin and worn and smells like imprisonment.

"Now, is it ready?" Alina asks, her brown eyes lit with excitement.

I meet Elise's gaze. My older sister shrugs, if you can call the elegant movement that. She can't concentrate on her sewing anymore. "That it is not, but you can take it off now. Do go and play with Alina."

"Preferably in your room," Sibilia adds. "With the door shut."

The mirror. Sibilia's silver hand mirror lies facedown on the gold-embroidered blanket Elise snatched from the sled. There's something ominous in the way it glows in the light of the ceiling lamp, the one powered by an unreliable osprey soul.

"Come," Alina squeals as she jumps onto the bed we share. She roams on all fours across it, to sit with her back against the musty pillows. She pats the mattress, inviting both me and my dear companions to join her. "Up here!"

Rafa and Mufu glance at me, corner teeth peeking out. Odd. I smell something odd in the room. It's not the dank of a house kept cold for too long, only recently warmed, not the stink of cigarettes and frost that still clings to the embroidered blanket. No. It's neither of those, but something thicker and sharper. Ever since we arrived at this house, Alina has been acting strange. Sure, she's talked to herself—or to the shadows if you believe her claims—often enough in the past. But I've heard her talking as if someone were replying to her. That, along with this smell I can't name, gives me chills.

Mad. I'm not going mad, even though my sister is that already.

"Up here, silly dogs." Alina pats the blanket so hard it coughs dust. "Rafa, Mufu, there's no need to be afraid!"

Rafa and Mufu stay still, though I limp a step closer. The ankle I hurt months and months back still jolts. With the door closed, I can't hear what our older sisters say in the drawing room and I don't think they can hear what happens in this room either. I'm not sure if I prefer or detest that with Alina acting as she does. "What. Don't be afraid of what exactly?"

Alina gazes past me. That is, to my sides. But there's nothing there, only a vanity desk with a cracked oval mirror and an armchair so worn that if you sit down on it, you need someone to pull you up from amidst the cushions. The dank smell—is it that of a cellar? I've never been in one and hope to never visit one—intensifies. Maybe I should call for Celestia or Elise. Definitely not Sibilia, because she teases me already more than is fair! Elise might be upset for one reason or another. And Celestia is occupied by . . . I don't know what she's doing. Now that I think of it, she seems intent on running her fingers over every wall and panel of the drawing room.

"Alina, it's all right to tell me," I say, and still the mirror glints facedown on the blanket, Rafa and Mufu refuse to move. "Tell me what it is!"

Alina stares at the mirror as if tempted to flip it around.

"I can't. I can't. You're older than me." Her lower lip trembles, but at least she isn't crying. I bet that if she were to burst into tears once more, Elise and Sibilia would find a way to blame me for that, too. They've always been like that, pulling the same rope. "I can't tell you. They forbid it. But I can show you."

What should I do? What can I do? I sigh, and then I climb onto the bed, to her left side, with Sibilia's mirror remaining between us. It's after all just a mirror, not a rifle or a knife that Alina could hurt either me or herself with.

"Will you ask Rafa and Mufu to join us, too?"

I realize only then that my companions didn't trail after me. Mufu whimpers, black tail pulled between her hind legs. Rafa growls, floppy brown ears pulled back, teeth bared. I pat the blanket, and still they don't jump up.

"Oh, they're silly." I attempt a laugh, but I'm not exactly amused. Rafa and Mufu never disobey me. "Cold. Then, stay there on the cold floor. Yes. Cruelly on the cold floor."

They lie down and hide their heads under their crossed paws. What under the Moon is going on? I nudge Alina with my elbow. "Well?"

My little sister flicks the mirror over.

At first, I see nothing else but the reflection of the flaking ceiling plastering and the chipped dome of the osprey soul lamp. I can also see my face, and it's a pretty face. The winter hasn't paled me, and my black hair is as gorgeously wild as ever.

"Well?" I ask, relieved, but also annoyed. As usual, Alina was just imagining things. I should have known better than to let her lure me into believing her.

"You can show yourself now," Alina says.

A heartbeat later, two women lean toward us, their faces reflected in the mirror. They're not exactly old, but weary beyond any age, I guess. And there's something familiar in their bold faces and bolder gazes. The scent of the root cellar grows almost unbearable, and it has a vicious edge to it now. A bitter scent of . . . betrayal. Though I don't know where that thought came from.

"Merile," Alina says, and her voice doesn't tremble at all. "Meet Irina"—she nods at the woman on the left—"and Olesia."

I sit there frozen, with my back against the pillows. What is this that I'm seeing? It can't be real. Really, it can't.

I yank my gaze up, frantically glancing at my left and right. There's no one there. Rafa and Mufu spring up, leap to the door, nails scratching the floor. Their eyes bulge with fear. They whine heart-wrenching short whimpers. If I weren't almost twelve, I'd run to them and out of the room. But because

I am, I mustn't be afraid, not even if we're in the presence of ghosts.

"Well?" Alina whispers, anxious to hear what I think.

I peek again at the mirror, just to be sure. The women stare back at me, unblinking. Their gray-white hair is gathered atop their heads in onionlike buns. Their faces are graying, too. Their gray dresses have puffy sleeves and multilayered lace fronts. Gray. No, they're not gray all over but . . . "They're fading."

The two women smile at me, but it's a cruel and calculating look that chills me to the core. Does Alina not see that? No, she doesn't, because she's still so young and gullible.

"Out." I prod the mirror facedown with my forefinger, for I don't really want to touch ghost-things. I grab Alina's arm. "Let's go out. Now."

Despite Alina's weak protests, I haul her with me onto the floor. Rafa and Mufu rush to me, to flank us as if they were guards assigned to protect us. My dear, darling companions!

"Why?" Alina squirms, trying to break free from my hold. "You didn't even listen to what they have to say! You won't believe how long it took me to get them to agree to meet you!"

Of all things! I prod her toward the door. "Rafa and Mufu . . . Rafa and Mufu need to pee. That's why."

Dying. The day is already dying when Rafa and Mufu leap through the snowbanks, sending white clouds up in the crisp air. I run after them, though my fur-trimmed cloak flaps against my sides like floppy wings. Though we're allowed out only in the garden, after the weeks in the train my companions cherish every outing.

"Wait, Merile," Alina calls after me. "Wait!"

I don't. I'm not like her. I don't see shadows. I don't want to see ghosts. I need to get as far away as possible from both her and the house, from everything that's not how it should be.

Soon, I'm but steps away from the barren rosebushes framing the stone steps that lead down to the orchard and the lake beyond. Snow floods my sabots, chafes my ankles and toes, but I don't care. I have much bigger worries.

"Rafa, Mufu," Alina pleads with my companions. And being soft-hearted sillies, they stop. They keep trotting in place, though. Despite their coats, they're freezing.

"You want to wait for her?" I ask, annoyed that they've decided to side with Alina and not with me. No one ever sides with me these days!

My companions look anxiously at the house, at Alina. I realize they did sense the ghosts, and they're definitely not mad. Well then, I'm not mad either! "Fine then."

Alina scampers the rest of the way to us, her ugly gray coat open, her bootlaces undone. Frailer. Somehow, she's smaller and frailer each day, though she's the one who should be growing. It hurts to look at her, and so I look past her.

The house the color of a bruised peach looms behind my sister. Snow covers the black roof and makes the white sills even more so. Tabard smokes on the porch, his makeshift cloak barely shifting in the lazy wind. He's not alone for long. Elise and Captain Janlav join him. Neither our older sisters nor the guards ever let us out of their sight for long.

"Merile, the ghosts . . ." Icky yellow snot runs down Alina's thin lips. She sniffs, but it's too late. She brushes her nose on her sleeve.

"Later." I nod toward the porch. Our voices might still carry over. "And aren't you cold?"

Alina glances down at her open coat. She's wearing her woolen dress, but nothing else to keep her warm. Snow clots her hem up to her knees. "Yes. A little. Maybe."

"Let me," I say, swiftly buttoning her coat. My dear little sister, when she gets distraught, she forgets to take care of herself. I don't know what would happen to her if she didn't have us older sisters looking after her. "And if you don't tie the laces, you'll trip on those icy steps. Here, I'll do it for you, but just this once. All right?"

But once I'm done, it's darker already. The sky above the frozen lake is bleak blue and dull yellow. The garden walls cast shadows over the untended orchard. The iron gate has never looked as rigid, the stone steps leading down there as treacherous.

"Maybe we'll take another path?" Alina offers as if reading my thoughts.

"Yes," I whisper. We'll walk a bit along one of the other trails leading down. There's no reason to go all the way to the gate. We just need to find a place where we can talk.

We stroll in silence on the path that winds down the left side of the slope. The crisp snow cracks under our feet and my companions' paws. A bird of some sort croaks and cackles. The barren oaks and maples rustle, their shadows taller with each moment. I hold on to Alina's hand. I need to know what my sister knows, even if it means walking deeper into the darkness.

Soul and shadow. A person becomes a ghost when both their soul and shadow remain behind to sort out unfinished business. What caused these ghosts, Irina and Olesia, to decide to linger? Why are they being nice to Alina and attempting to be nice to me? What do they want from us? Why did Alina say it took her a long time to get them to agree to meet with me? As if we didn't have enough worries of our own already! Thinking of the things Elise said makes my head ache!

The path turns to the right, and we enter the orchard. My eyes have grown accustomed to the dimmer light, and though the garden wall is high and its shadow thick, I'm no longer that confused or nervous. Not even when I hear the croak. For it's but a magpie sitting on a branch of the hollow apple tree, right by the gate as black as true night.

"The white-sided one," I say, even as Rafa and Mufu pause. They lift their forepaws at the exact same moment. They want to give the bird a chase.

I smile despite myself. My companions are getting plump from lack of exercise. Soon they'll be as round as Sibilia once was. There would be more to cuddle then, but lifting them would become tricky. "Go!"

Alina and I admire them running, a brown and a gray arrow, a flurry of legs and tails. I have to remind myself we came down here for a reason. Alina must tell me everything she knows about the ghosts, for I don't trust for even a moment that they'd have our best interests in mind.

I'm just about to demand that Alina do so, when something even stranger happens. Rafa and Mufu skid to a halt by the tree, barking. The magpie takes to the air, the white-striped wings spreading wide, the mighty black tail straightening. It swoops toward my companions—no, back toward the apple tree—and between two eyeblinks, it simply disappears.

And then, a hunched shadow of a woman steps out of the hollow trunk.

"A ghost," I gasp.

Alina giggles. "No, she's not!"

Where my companions refused to approach the ghosts, they're not afraid of this woman in black who appeared seemingly out of nowhere. They bounce to her, heads bent low, ears pulled back in joy as if she were a trusted neighbor. And maybe she is something akin to that. "Can that be the Witch at the End of the Lane?"

"Yes!" Alina nods vigorously, and if I weren't holding on to her hand, she'd run to the witch at once.

"Unexpected." This is unexpected. Though I can't remember much of our visit to the witch's cottage, Celestia, Elise, and Sibilia all insist that the witch helped Alina when she was ill. I'm more prone to believe them than her. Or at least Celestia, because she never jokes.

"Let's go and greet her." Alina tugs toward the witch and my companions.

The witch must have heard her, because she turns to wave at us. Her black robes shift, not with the wind or because of her movement, but on their own. Rafa and Mufu poke at her hem, curious of the very same thing.

Should we? I glance over my shoulder, toward the house. Elise and Captain Janlav huddle at the top of the stone steps. They're not really looking at us, rather at what passes for the sunset here. They talk in low voices, immersed in some topic of their own. I don't think they have noticed the witch. It's quite dark already. "Fine."

But it's Alina who leads the way, pulling me behind her. And when we reach the witch, my sister speaks before I have the chance. "What are you doing here?"

The witch cackles. Though she's not much taller than me,

she seems much more so as she leans toward us, watching us—no, our feet—down her beaky nose. Her breathing, it doesn't form clouds like ours do, and her pupils are white as if she were blind. Which makes her next words even more peculiar. "Me come see you."

Rafa and Mufu fall completely still. They don't even shift weight, though the ground must still chill their paws. Stop. It's as if the witch could make time stop for them. I wonder if this is why I can't remember much of her cottage. That would be unfair, for her to have that much power.

"Why?" I ask because I really don't know that much about the witch and her motives. People don't visit these Moon-forgotten lands without a very good reason. And I don't think anyone would come here voluntarily. Even Captain Ansalov and his soldiers left as soon as they could, and of that I'm very glad indeed.

The witch shrugs. Her bundled gray hair and layered dress shift as if she were caught in between two gusts that don't know which way to blow. The dress is made of something gray-black and see-through, and yet she doesn't seem to be suffering from the cold like I do. Which is also unfair. "When me help, me take interest."

Allies. My sisters and I don't exactly have that many allies left, not with Celestia's previous plan going wrong and her seed being left behind at that desolate town to face the consequences. My seed. I don't know what has become of my seed, whom I miss so very much! Celestia says we have to do with what we have. Since the witch is here now, I might as well let her help us. For I can't tell my older sisters about what I saw earlier today or they'll think me as mad as Alina is. "There's ghosts in the house."

"Ghosts." The witch cranes her head toward the hill and the house. She sucks in the air, her pale blue lips pressing tight against her parted teeth. Smell. Can she smell the root cellar and old perfume? "Good? Bad?"

Alina gushes in, "Good, of course! They're very nice old ladies!"

I think of their hungry eyes, Alina keeping them secret from everyone for who knows how long. "I'm not at all sure about that."

"Wise," the witch replies. Her nostrils flare wide. "Trust no ghost. Trust me."

Which is a kind of foolish thing for her to say. I glance over my shoulder again. Elise and Captain Janlav seem to be arguing whether or not to descend the steps. Regardless of what they decide, there can't be much time to talk with the witch before they'll hear us.

"Why are you really here?" I ask.

"Moon, me, friends," the witch replies, meeting my eyes with her white gaze. Truth. I think she's telling the truth, but there's no way to be sure before Papa rises to the sky. "Come summer, you flee."

For a moment, my heart pounds so hard that I can't form a single word, let alone a sentence. I often dream of leaving the house for good, but since we have no horses and Captain Ansalov's hounds have our scent, even Celestia hasn't been able to come up with a plan. Or if she has, she hasn't shared it with us. Which would be so typical of her.

"How?" I ask, squeezing Alina's hand. Things that sound too good are usually not what they seem.

The witch smiles, blue lips drawing back. Her teeth are big, barely fitting in her mouth. "Me help."

Can I, should I trust the witch? It wouldn't hurt to know more. Up in the sky, the faintest round shape yellows in the horizon. Can Papa already see us? Would the witch dare to lie in his presence?

But before I can ask the witch for more details, Elise's voice carries through what may now be called night. "Alina, Merile!"

I dare not to move. Has my sister glimpsed the witch? Or did she hear us talking with her? Or even worse, did Captain Janlav notice her? That wouldn't be good. I force myself to merely glance at my sister's direction, rather than to spin around as if I were indeed doing something forbidden.

"Come inside, will you?" Elise waves at us, clinging to Captain Janlav for balance, halfway down the stone steps. I realize she doesn't want to descend the rest of the way any more than I want to return to the house when I still have so many questions left to ask both the witch and Alina.

"Soon," I call back at Elise, then turn back toward the witch. But there's no sign of her anywhere. If you don't count the lonely magpie perched on the gnarliest branch of the old apple tree.

Chapter 3

Sibilia

No, Scribs, I don't want to talk about it. Not yet, in any case, and not before I understand what happened today. As if I didn't have enough things to worry about already... What things, you might ask. Seriously, Scribs, you're a book of scriptures! There's absolutely no excuse for you to always act so dumb!

There's only four months exact left before my debut. We've huddled in this house for almost four weeks already, and it seems to me that we'll be here for many more not-so-splendid months to come. If we haven't left this house by the end of the last spring week, we won't make it back to the Summer Palace in time for the ceremony. Though I don't know if there's anything left of the city to return to, if the gagargi ordered the palaces torn down, if the people who once filled them fled or if they stayed and chose to serve him instead. Perhaps nothing changed or only very little did. Something as grand and glorious as our home can't simply cease to be, coup or no coup.

Spilled ink. Can't be bothered to even try and wipe it. I should get on with it, shouldn't I? Even though Celestia found me a new pen while rummaging through the rooms, there probably aren't that many more simply lying around.

Very well, then. Here goes.

This morning, as is our routine, after the breakfast we lingered in the drawing room. Celestia and Elise stylished our coats by the oval table, though I don't know if any amount of velvet ribbons (also known as former pillowcases) or decorative stitching (we'll have to do with stars, as Celestia forbade crescent motifs) will ever transform them into anything else than tortured blankets. I didn't offer my help because, to be entirely honest, I absolutely loathe everything that has to do with altering yarn or fabric with any sort of shape of wood or metal. Yes, this includes crocheting, knitting, and the apparently most-beloved pastime of all highborn ladies: embroidery. Though Celestia and Elise are bound to run out of things to stitch soon. I'm thinking, if reporting to you keeps me sane, what will my sisters do once they're ready with the coats? At times we're already at each other's throats! There are moments when I seriously think of strangling Merile, especially when she becomes obsessed with repeating everything she can recall of Nurse Nookes's lectures.

No, I would never really hurt any of my sisters. Not even Merile. Note: pinching her or tugging her hair doesn't count. Applied in right measures, it keeps her properly in tow.

Yes. I'm prattling. Putting off the inevitable. How observant of you, Scribs. But I have way too much time on my hands. If I were to write in a short and compact form of all that came to pass today, I would then have nothing else to do. Apart from reading the scriptures and dreaming of K. Though I don't want to write about K now. It might be that I won't see him ever again, and that would be the MOST HORRIBLE THING, worse than the gagargi betraying Mama and . . .

Let's not go down that path. Also, let's not think about K (but please feel free to refer to pages 1, 3–4, 7–9, 12–17, etc.

for a reference of what those thoughts might entail). Huh, a terrible thought just occurred to me. If anyone ever gets their hands on your pages, I will die of shame.

I don't want to think about that either. Onward to yet another topic.

Consider this when you get a chance, Scribs: we're stranded in a house in the middle of nowhere. It's decently enough furnished, though it seems that at some point someone snatched everything that could be taken with ease and hastily brought back what they thought we'd most urgently need. In any case, this is one of those places where people like us have been sent to exile for as long as there has been a Crescent Empire. Under the circumstances, it's wise to assume that no one is coming to take us home anytime soon. We must flee, and that's what Celestia no doubt has in mind. This far up in the north, the winter will last for a month or more still. Yet, I bet she's got a plan forming in her mind already. Celestia being Celestia, she won't share it with any of us. And who can blame her, given that even though she kept her previous plan a secret from everyone, including her own sisters, somehow the gagargi still found out about it and as a result, she lost her seed!

No, I'm not worried about mine any more than I'm hoping that he'd dash to my rescue either. General Kravakiv has been off fighting for the empire from even before the day I was born. Sure, Celestia says that he's been defeated, but that doesn't change a thing. Back when Mama (the Moon bless her poor soul) still lived, he would have never dared to switch sides. But I wouldn't put it beyond Gagargi Prataslav to manipulate my seed into thinking he's actually serving the empire better by siding with him. The gagargi is pure evil.

Argh. This is no good, Scribs. It seems like whenever I try

to avoid writing about a specific topic my mind drifts off to even more miserable ones. Brace yourself. And don't you dare to even hint that I might be going a little soft in my head, because what I'm about to write next is true, every single word of it.

Today, the strangest—well, considering what we've been through before, perhaps this categorizes only as strange—thing happened. I was sitting on the sofa by the arching windows so that I don't have to squint at the pages (freckles I don't mind, but I'm really too young for wrinkles). Alina and Merile were playing in their room with the rats. Lately, they've been acting, I don't know, or that is, I do know: suspiciously. As if they had imaginary friends. I've heard the names "Irina" and "Olesia" whispered, though the only servant around here is called Millie. I can believe Alina coming up with that sort of thing, but for Merile to encourage that when she knows how vulnerable our little sister's mind is to begin with! Note to self: talk with Merile. Even if she seems to detest me almost as much as I loathe her peeing, pooping rats, I should be able to sort this out. I don't want to bother Celestia and Elise. They need to be able to concentrate . . . Well, not in their sewing, but in forming a plan that will help us get away from this place for once and for good—and preferably in time for my debut!

Getting sidetracked. I swear, Scribs, this isn't intentional on my part.

As mentioned, I was once more reading through the scriptures (and yes, it's a bit challenging now, because I've written sideways over half of your pages already). I don't know if it was because of me lacking anything else to do or because it was blessedly silent in the house for once, but I got really immersed in the passages, and before I knew it, the letters floated off the pages, and just hung there, over the paper. And as I stared at them, they morphed into glyphs I'd never seen before. The hairs on the back of my neck jumped up, and I got goose bumps all over!

These glyphs were of a foreign language, and if I were to have tried to pronounce them, I think the sounds would have been guttural, something between a croak of a bird whose beak has been glued shut and a howl of a wolf that has lost its voice. Yet I knew what each meant instantly. They formed incantations, summoning our heavenly father's attention.

I barely dared to breathe, let alone move. I sat there, with the book open on my lap, with the slanting morning light wrapping around each glyph. I think the only movement was that of my mouth a-gaping.

Really, who am I to blame Alina and Merile for making up imaginary friends when I'm seeing things myself? Except that I'm not. The glyphs are real. They make sense to me.

"Sibs, are you dreaming of chocolate once more?" Elise's question made me blink, and the glyphs fled back onto the pages, there to completely fade away. My sister studied me from across the table, her embroidery on her lap, smiling mischievously.

"I . . ." I stammered, staring at what now was completely ordinary text. I fanned the page, hoping to somehow coax the glyphs forth again. But they wouldn't reappear. And what was it that Elise had asked? Scribs, you know it, there's one magic word that every older sister is always happy to hear when they're waiting for an answer. "Yes."

I'm pretty sure she mentioned chocolate, though. We haven't come across any since we left the Summer Palace. Though Millie seems to like us (at least much more so than the ever-changing servants that attended us during the train journey), the meals we eat are simple and there's rarely any desserts. And if there's dessert, it's lingonberry kissel or at rare occasions butter rolls with NO sugar sprinkled on top.

Luckily, the grandfather clock decided to strike eleven then. With the paddling swan that heralds every new hour with a different song, I find it very beautiful. Celestia says it's purely mechanical, which makes it even more marvelous to me. Speaking of Celestia, she swiftly rose up from her sofa chair, set the coat down on the table, and clapped her hands twice. "It is time."

And you know what eleven o'clock means in this house, Scribs! But today, I was so puzzled by the glyphs that I forgot all about the best part of the day, the dance practice! Can you imagine that?

I know I've said many things about Celestia in the past and not all of them have been exactly flattering. Back in our old lives, she was distant and cold toward us younger sisters. But now that I think on it, perhaps it wasn't entirely her fault—I suspect that back at the Summer City she may have been under Gagargi Prataslav's spell! In any case, now I've got my sister back, and she's a very good sister. We share the same room, and though we don't exactly talk the nights through, she's always there, ready to listen to my worries and comfort me, even if she doesn't exactly confide in me. Also, the dance practices were her idea.

"Gather around!" Celestia clapped her hands again, the movement smooth and graceful, even though I'm absolutely certain that, unlike Elise, she's never ever practiced anything before her mirrors, and I know for sure she hasn't done so since we arrived here. Yes, Scribs, perhaps I once swore that I would start practicing myself, but I haven't. Not even when I seem to have all the time under the Moon. "Elise, please help me move the furniture. Sibilia, would you be so kind as to fetch Merile and Alina?"

Herding in our little sisters is always better than hauling the furniture around (I'm pretty sure I would get bruised from even thinking of pushing a chair aside or moving the table against the wall). Yet, Elise never complains about the tasking. I wonder what's got into her. She claims she enjoys sewing, and she even partakes in setting up the table for the simple dinners we eat every night with the guards in the sparsely furnished second-floor hall. That, if anything, is peculiar.

"Sure I will," I replied. But first, I took you, Scribs, to the room I share with Celestia, there to hide you under my pillow. Only then I went to get Alina and Merile.

I don't know exactly why I did so, but for some reason I decided to press my ear against the door rather than knock. And true enough, I heard a curious exchange.

"So, this was your house?" Alina asked in a chiming child-voice that before this day I hadn't heard in months.

Merile sounded more skeptical than a twelve-year-old has any right to sound. "How did you come to live here?"

From this exchange, I concluded that my little sisters' imagination had taken over any sense either of them have left in their tiny heads. They can't fathom why these sorts of houses exist, scattered in the four corners of the empire. Scribs, I have a theory of my own about this house's former occupants, but it's something I want to talk about with Celestia in private. And even then, I suspect she mightn't answer entirely truthfully. Some subjects are too delicate even after decades.

"You can tell us," Alina prompted. "Really, you can."

"Secrets. I won't believe a thing you say if you keep secrets from us."

I knocked on the door then and proceeded to push it open without waiting for an answer, because being an older sister comes with certain privileges that I love.

Alina and Merile turned to look at me as one, gray and brown eyes wide, thin-lipped and wide mouths gaping. They sat on the bed with Merile's rats curled on their laps. They obviously wondered if I'd heard them talking. I pretended that I hadn't.

As expected, there was no one else in the room.

No, Scribs, I didn't get down on all fours to check if someone was hiding under the bed and neither did I pull open the wardrobe's doors. If someone had been in the room, they wouldn't have had time to hide. I'm sure of it.

I'm just a tad ashamed to admit that at times I'm happy that the train guards with their rifles share the house with us. This is an old, creaking, croaking house riddled with drafts that put out fires and lamps that turn off on their own. Sometimes I glimpse white shapes in the mirrors, though that's no doubt just dust catching rays of lights in odd angles. Even so, I don't know how Elise has the courage to sleep the nights alone. I would never agree to that!

"Alina, Merile . . ." I wiped my palms on my dress and clapped twice. It didn't sound or seem as refined as when Celestia did so, even to me. "It's time for the dance practice."

Alina and Merile glanced at each other. Alina studied me, as if to double-check if I'd seen something. She nodded to Merile, satisfied I hadn't (because there was NOTHING to see).

"Urgh." Merile stuck her tongue out at me, insufferably smug. I think it would serve her right if the magpie that frequents the walled garden were to try and snatch it on one fine afternoon. "Do we really have to?"

I waved toward the open door, at Celestia and Elise, who had by then almost finished hauling the furniture against the room's sides. Even here we must adhere to the routine. And when the dance practices are concerned, I'm happy to enforce Celestia's decrees. "Yes."

Merile sniffed, but Alina stared right before her, as if someone were sitting on the bed there. Then she blinked and snatched the silver hand mirror up. She pressed it against her chest as if to guard the reflection. "It's all right, Merile. They'll come with us."

I glared down my nose at the rats. Of course they'd come with us, to nip at our hems and bite at our ankles, and ruin our practice. Not that that has happened that many times to date, but I don't want to trip over a rat and sprain my ankle. Limping becomes absolutely no one. "I'd rather they stay behind."

"Hurts." Merile sniffed again as she ran her hand down the black rat's back. I felt just a tiny bit ashamed. After everything we've been through together, asking Merile to be apart from her beloved, adored rats verged toward being cruel. "My leg hurts."

But even if I was partially at fault, I couldn't exactly admit that or I'd lose my authority as a big sister. Besides, she injured her ankle months ago, enough time for it to heal three times already. I realized she was just trying to mess with me!

"No, it doesn't." I pressed my fists on my hips and shot her my best scolding look. "But soon it will, unless you get up right at this instant."

Alina and Merile glanced at each other. Then they jumped down onto the floor and dashed past me, into the drawing room with the rats at their heels. Celestia always says that violence isn't the answer, but threatening with it certainly gets things done.

We arrived just in time. Celestia and Elise were moving the last sofa chair against the wall. I checked my posture in the tall mirror that hangs on the door side of the room. Ugh, Scribs, whenever my concentration sways, I end up looking like a hunchback. And these long, too-loose sleeves, I want to rip them off. There's nothing I can do about the sleeves as such, because it's too cold in the house to consider altering them, but if I remember to roll my shoulders back and push my chest out every once in a while, I think that I do look rather good.

Celestia waited for us to form pairs. I always dance with Elise and Merile with Alina. We started the practice with a waltz—my favorite, as you know. I counted the one-two-threes in my head and let Elise lead me across the floor. My sister understands that I really need the practice and always lets me dance as a girl.

Though the dance practices are the best part of the day, they also fill me with melancholy. Scribs, I miss music. I wish we could have taken the gramophone with us from Angefort garrison, but I bet that even if we had asked (and a Daughter of the Moon is never supposed to ask for anything), that awful Captain Ansalov wouldn't have let us have it. The best we have here is Celestia tapping the rhythm against the paneling as she strolls the length of the drawing room, from the door of Elise's room, past the mirror, to the light blue door leading into the narrow hallway and stairs. When we first started the practices, Merile's rats trailed after Celestia, thinking she was hiding treats! The stupid rats still keep on trotting to her every now and then.

Today, Celestia did look very thoughtful as she tapped the rhythm, and I bet her mind wasn't busy with instructions on how to improve my pose or steps. Let alone those of Alina and Merile. Can you imagine this, Scribs, my little sisters danced both as girls! A waltz doesn't really work that way!

"Alina, Merile," I hissed at them from under my breath when the steps took us to the furniture clustered by the fireplace, as far away from Celestia as the room would allow. It was becoming increasingly difficult for me to keep track of the one-two-threes. Them messing around certainly didn't help. "Could you at least try and concentrate?"

I might as well have spoken to one of the rats. Merile sniffed, the tip of her wide nose pointed up. Alina lifted her hem high, revealing her knobby knees, and spun wild. They're hopeless, both of them! When they swirled toward Celestia, the rats in tow, they left so much space between Elise and me that another couple could have easily fit in there. And despite all the fooling around, they managed to maintain that space, even when I intentionally pushed Elise toward them.

"Sibs." Elise drew me closer as if she were indeed a cavalier of the opposite gender. Her hand pressed lightly against my lower back. She tightened her hold around my right hand. "On the dance floor, all that matters is you and your partner. Nothing else can really touch you."

My sister picked up a tune of a waltz and softly hummed it under her breath. I don't mind that she sometimes does so. It's very nice of her to help me. I don't want to make a fool of myself if WHEN I debut. Because we will return in time to the Summer City, and the palace will be there waiting for us in just the same glorious shape as we left it, and K will be there, and the lords and ladies will be there, and there will be servants with trays full of macarons and . . .

No, enough of that. For the time being, I won't fill another page with wistful thinking. I have, after all, only a limited supply of pages left. But let this be said, one day I will own the dance floors of the Summer Palace, just as my sister once did.

"Better." Elise guided me into a swirl, and I simply couldn't resist the temptation. I closed my eyes, tilted my head back, though I could feel my coiffure unraveling. I laughed, and at that moment I felt . . . free!

When I returned to Elise's arms, I opened my eyes and caught my breath. Only to accidentally lock my gaze with that of Captain Janlav and lose it again. He watched us from the door leading to the hallway, those gorgeous brown eyes of his gleaming with interest, lips drawn into a faint smile. He looked positively dashing compared to the scrawny Boy next to him. That poor creature is all limbs and pimples and wet, straw-colored hair, but then again, according to Elise, he does have a bit of a tragic past.

"Stop ogling him," Elise chided me, but there was a hint of amusement in her voice. Of course there would be. She's had her chance to sneak out and kiss with boys while I'm still waiting for mine!

I stepped on her toes. On purpose, I admit that, Scribs. I wasn't ogling Captain Janlav. I was admiring him. Bearded now, with his brown hair braided, he cuts a fine figure of a man. He's definitely not a boy. Now, given the completely hypothetical and unlikely scenario that we mightn't get out of this house in time for my debut, or in the worst case before we turn into old hags, if I had to ask someone to kiss me—because I do want to be kissed at some point of my life—at that moment, I did wonder what it would be like to kiss him. Would his beard scratch? Would he taste of smoke and cigarettes? Elise would know . . .

Elise sucked in her breath. "Do watch out for my toes, Sibs!"

The good thing about me blushing easily is that my sister thought me embarrassed of stepping on her toes, not because of . . . Scribs, guard my secrets well. No one must learn that I've fallen this low in my desperation. Because my first kiss is going to be with K, not with some turncoat guard, no matter how manly and handsome he may appear in my eyes after months of candy and eye-candy deprivation.

I gathered myself quite well, I think. My sisters and I danced for some time more and, as I checked myself from the tall mirror, I didn't look that terrible, not at all like a hunchback. Toward the end of the practice, Captain Janlav and Boy grew bored, though. They closed the door behind them, but didn't lock it. They're not concerned about us trying to flee. The nights are too cold and with the wolves hunting in the woods, we're not stupid enough to try! And then there's the garrison and Captain Ansalov and his hounds to think about, too. I'm sure Celestia has taken all this into consideration already. She'll share her plan with us any day now.

The grandfather clock's swan chimed twelve silvery notes.

"My dear sisters." Celestia knocked the paneled wall with her knuckles, and then she knocked again, just to get our full attention. "This suffices for today."

Elise and I paused, flush-faced, leaning on each other for breath—but we weren't so badly winded as we were when we first started these practices. My sister grinned at me, and somehow even that expression was dashing. "That was fun!"

I nodded, pushing the pins holding my hair up deeper to salvage what I could. But it occurred to me that Celestia mightn't be organizing these practices just for fun. She must have some ulterior motive of her own. I don't know what it is, but the sessions leave us sweaty and sometimes even exhausted. Which feels good! The Moon knows we do enough sitting around, sipping tea, and strolling in the freezing garden.

"I think we should let in some fresh air." Celestia glided past the oval table and the sofa, to the arching, tall window. I knew to expect this, but not her next words. "Why, hello there, bird black and white."

And true enough, there on the windowsill, on the other side of the glass, sat a magpie with a shining white belly and glistening black coat. Had it, too, been watching our practice? Hopefully so, as I really need to get accustomed to performing before an audience, and it's about time I don't mix up my steps just because someone is looking at me.

"A magpie!" Alina dashed past the furniture to the window. She placed her right palm against the pane. I really expected the magpie to take to the air, but instead it rapped the glass with its mighty beak as if greeting her. "Nurse Nookes once told me a story about magpies . . ."

"Now did she?" Celestia wrapped an arm around our sister's narrow shoulders.

"Yes, she did!" Alina leaned against our eldest sister. "But I can't remember it anymore. Do you know it? Will you tell me a story?"

Though this house has a library, it now serves as living quarters for the guards. Also, I've been told, the books are all gone, no doubt burned for heat or the pages used in other disrespectful ways. Sometimes my sisters and I reminiscence about the past, but we never tell stories as such. It really hadn't occurred to me earlier that back at the Summer Palace, Nurse

Nookes still told Alina bedtime stories.

"A story about a magpie?" Celestia mused. "I do recall one."

"Will you tell it?" Alina chimed. Merile and her rats drifted toward the window, too. I remained in the middle of the dance floor with Elise, though at that moment, I yearned for nothing as much as to hear a story, the sort where all ends well. "Pretty please!"

Celestia unwrapped her arm from around Alina and kneeled before her. She placed her palms on her shoulders. "I will."

And then she spoke in a melodious voice that filled every nook and corner of the drawing room, and somehow, even the hollows where longing had etched in my heart.

> *There once was a hungry magpie that the Moon took pity on.*
> *He bent his light into a ray and willed it to break into seeds.*
> *And when the magpie ate the seeds, its belly turned white as snow.*
> *Ever since that day, grateful, it has sung praises to the Moon.*

With the final word fading, the magpie took off. Celestia pressed a kiss on Alina's forehead and then rose up. She opened the window, sighed deep, and stared after the bird. I wonder, did she at that moment dream of flying away? Sometimes, she speaks in her sleep about white wings and fallen feathers as if she thought herself a swan.

"Can we go now?" Merile's question broke the wonderful, solemn moment. Scribs, my sister really has no clue on what's appropriate and when. "Alina, are you coming?"

Celestia tousled Alina's gray-brown hair. Though our little sister seems more cheerful these days, she hasn't grown an inch since we boarded the train. I wonder if there exists a potion for that somewhere.

"Go ahead, my dear," Celestia replied.

Thus liberated, Alina and Merile and her wretched rats disappeared back to their room, no doubt to continue talking with their imaginary friends, the Moon bless them.

I would have really wanted to cool by the window for a while, but Elise twined her long fingers around my forearm and guided me to the exact opposite direction. "Oh, Sibs, your hair is in quite a state!"

A part of me had realized that already. Often when I dance, my locks unravel regardless if they're braided around my head or secured with all the pins available in this house. I don't usually care that much about my hair (because once we're back in the hem of civilization, I'll have access to all the pins and combs I could ever possibly need). But then it dawned on me that my hair might have been in this state already when Captain Janlav watched us from the doorway. "Oh no . . ."

As Elise led me to one of the sofa chairs by the fireplace, I thought not only about that, but also about the things I might have been lately speaking about while asleep. That's the very reason I haven't dared to ask Celestia about her dreams. I might want to broach the topic that gives me tingles with Elise at some point in the near future, but I don't really want to talk about boys with Celestia. Though back at the Summer Palace Elise did suspect Celestia of having a lover, our oldest sister never made the official announcement. Elise, on the other hand, was romantically involved with Captain Janlav, even if neither of them seems to be particularly certain about how that affair eventually ended.

Elise patted my shoulder, and I think I caught a glimpse of

melancholy in her gray eyes. I sat down, pretending I hadn't noticed a thing, for I know how much it pains to be apart from your heart's chosen one. While I can imagine my happy reunion with K and some alternatives to that as well, Elise should know that Captain Janlav is forever out of her reach.

"Now then, shall we have a look at what we can still salvage?" Elise circled behind the chair and started unplucking the remaining pins. I nudged off my shoes (that is, the pair of heels Millie found for me), and pushed away sad thoughts. For my feet, they hurt, especially my toes! But it's the good sort of pain, the kind we pay to look pretty.

Soon Elise had her fingers around my locks, and thus when she asked the question, I was completely under her mercy. "Now tell me, dear Sibs, who's the lucky chap who has stolen your heart?"

And my heart stopped beating at that very moment, or that's how it felt. I fanned my face, to banish my blush. That had been the giveaway. It had to have been, unless she can read my thoughts. And if I'd earlier worried about Captain Janlav seeing me dancing with my hair in disarray, now I had to wonder, had I been radiating scarlet ever since I locked gazes with him?

"Do tell." Elise playfully straightened one of my locks till it was as taut as a ropewalker's wire. "It must be Boy. Please tell me it's not Tabard."

At that moment, I was overjoyed that she couldn't see my expression and that Celestia was busy with returning the furniture to its right places. Scribs, I really need to start practicing my expressions before a mirror. But how to do that in secret when I share my room with Celestia? Perhaps I can snatch back that silver hand mirror I brought with me, the one Merile has stolen from me for her own obscure purposes, whatever those might be.

Yes. Getting sidetracked. Sorry about that.

I did spend quite a while thinking of what to say. While Elise knows about K, it was obvious she wasn't talking about him, and thus revealing his full name would have gained me nothing. And I couldn't very well tell her that for one fleeting moment (that might have lasted for quite some time) I had pondered her former lover's merits.

"No one." I feebly tried. "There's no one. Really, it's just that I find myself terribly unaccustomed to exercise."

"Is that so?" Elise mused. She extracted a pin from my hair, twirled a lock even tighter around her finger, and then the tip of the pin was grazing against my scalp. I'm not saying she did this on purpose, but I think she might have done it subconsciously. Elise is used to having her way.

What could I reply? Could I ask her if the downright flirtatious thing she's kept up with Captain Janlav really is all for show, painstakingly maintained to soften and manipulate him to be more sympathetic to us so that he would help us flee when the time comes? Could I really ask her if she'd be fine with me dancing and perhaps even . . . Yes, Scribs, I know I'm daring and preposterous here, perhaps even kissing him!

No, Scribs, I'm not stupid enough to tell this to my sister, no matter how close we are. So, here's what I said: "My dear sister, I have no secrets from you."

"Oh, me neither." And with that said, she leaned over my shoulder and pinched my cheek. Not terribly hard, mind you, but firmly enough to leave a mark of endearment. "Never have had and never will have."

Sometimes I hate her, Scribs. That I really do.

Chapter 4

Elise

Five days ago, my sisters and I gathered in the icy garden at midday, there to perform the only rite that takes place under the sun's gentle gaze. As Celestia cited the holy scriptures of the spring equinox, I led Sibilia, Merile, and Alina six times around her in concentric, clockwise circles, then six more times around her in the other direction. Captain Janlav watched us from the porch, either as a silent observer or as someone afraid to stop us. I still don't know which, but he skied off right after, without a word said, without a message left behind.

As yet another dinner without him drags on, I can't stop wondering: did we anger him when we performed the sacred rites or has he somehow uncovered one of the secrets Celestia so carefully guards? Her secrets are more dangerous than mine, the deals she has crafted more intricate, the risk associated with them abominable. She bargained with the witch, swallowed the foul potion, and bled away the gagargi's seed—a deed, had it gone wrong, that could have harmed her permanently!

"Could you pass the salt?"

I stir from my darker thoughts to Sibilia's bony elbow. We sit at our usual places, in the second-floor dining room, by the large oval table with our backs against the windows that let in only night. The draft gnaws at our backs, for there are no curtains and the cream-colored tapestries must have been threadbare already years ago. In the light of the chandeliers that never shine as bright as those in the upstairs drawing room our meal looks more meager than it is: beetroot soup and rye bread.

"Please?" Sibilia grits her teeth as if the simple act of seasoning her soup could suddenly make a great difference in our lives.

It won't. What is done is done. These walls, these rooms have always guarded secrets. First those of the former occupants. Now ours, those of Millie, and those of the guards.

"There you go, dear." I hand over the white enamel salt cup. In this house, time stands still for long stretches at a time. But when it moves, it does so in great, uncontrollable leaps. The evidence of this is right before us. The salt cup doesn't match with the porcelain bowls or the plates that bear flowers that bloom stubbornly through the winter. Though we are only eleven—with Captain Janlav gone, with no idea if or when he might return—even the glasses form a mismatched assembly. There are only two or three from each setting, those that the former occupants didn't take with them when they moved on and that no one deemed pretty or useful enough to steal afterward. No, I'm allowing myself to foolishly fantasize that the former occupants had hope. Did I not hear with my own ears Captain Ansalov announcing this house cleaned and liberated?

"And pepper." Sibilia offers the salt back. Thank the Moon it's Celestia who has the pepper closest to her and not me. For lately when my thoughts have veered toward darkness, I have been struggling to keep up my carefully practiced charade of calm. And when I think of Captain Ansalov, my hands, they do shake.

That is how much I dread the day he returns to this house.

I know the sort of man Captain Ansalov really is behind his polite words and seemingly kind smile. I know this even though my sisters and I used to lead a sheltered life where all the evil under the Moon was hidden from us, kept out of our sight. Captain Ansalov is a man ready to follow instructions to the letter, who may not be able to pull the trigger himself, but never hesitates to order others to do so in his place. He takes, I believe, pleasure in seeing pain and misery, and this is what sets him apart from the man I thought I once loved. If there's a way to obey without hurting others, that's the path Captain Janlav chooses.

Or that is what I hope, but I can't be certain of it anymore. Why did he depart? Why hasn't he returned?

"And some more bread." Sibilia turns to me again, and from the corner of my eye I catch Merile rolling her eyes at our sister. Hers and Alina's is still the privilege of childish diversions and secrets that don't matter. "If you'd be so kind."

I understand all too well the underlying currents that no one ever mentions, and because of this my hands tremble so badly that I have to hide them under the table. Even if we are safe for the time being, my younger sisters haven't yet realized that we are treading in the footsteps of this house's former occupants. As history tends to repeat itself, we already sit on the same chairs and sleep in the same beds, and eventually we will come to see every twist and turn of their path.

"I say, the soup is good as it is." Beard lifts his bowl to his lips and gulps what remains of his portion down in one go.

Merile and Alina giggle, no longer frightened to share the

table with the guards, but rather amused by this willing display of bad manners. I'm happy about this distraction, something else to think about. I don't know whose idea it was in the first place that we start eating every evening together with the guards. Perhaps it was Celestia's—this might be a part of her grand plan, a piece that might not seem to fit in anywhere yet, but that will later prove to be crucial. Or then, perhaps, it was Captain Janlav's idea. His and the guards' duty is to protect my sisters and me. Be it as it may, this practice is very fitting for the new age of the empire, and it means less work for poor Millie, who never says a single word, not when she sets the table, not when she sits down to eat with us, not when she collects the dishes away. Not even when I offer to help her.

I might not have ever been able to connect the dots if it weren't for Millie and the drawing room's clock. Though the years haven't been kind to her, her eyes are still the same, gray as wisps of smoke, ever narrowed in suspicion. I remember them, even though I was so very young when I last saw her, no more than three. I was taught to forget her mistresses, pretend they never existed, and after so many years of denial, acceptance doesn't come easily. Celestia and I mustn't speak of their crimes to our younger sisters, for ignorance in this matter is bliss.

"Was really good." Beard burps, and his whole massive body expands, then shrinks. Boots and Belly and Tabard burst into laughter and drum their knees with their fists. They wipe their mouths on their tunics' blue sleeves. With Captain Janlav gone, it feels as if everything in this house were unraveling. It started with manners. These grown men have turned into boys, apart from Boy, who partakes only because not doing so would set him apart, but who at the same time feels ashamed to commit vulgarities.

I cherish this ray of normalcy, refuse to think of what my sisters and I might lose next. Boy has his eyes set on dear Sibs, who seems completely blind to this fact. My sister fancies someone else, but who that is, I don't yet know. She's too embarrassed to admit to admiring one of the guards to share his name even with me.

These silly avoidance games I play in my mind, they are of no use. It took me days to acknowledge that I'm not anxious only because Captain Janlav left, not knowing the reasons behind his decisions. I . . . I miss him. The unsteady jolting of my heart drives air from my lungs, knits my ribs together, and lets me breathe only in gasps. I can't stand the pain, the uncertainty any longer. I have to ask if the guards know more, though this single question might reveal to my younger sisters how little control we have over anything here. "When do you think that Captain Janlav will return?"

Though the guards have been with us for over three months now, they aren't as accustomed to us talking to them as we are to their perpetual presence. This isn't because of any sense of novelty or honor of being addressed by a Daughter of the Moon. According to the scriptures, under my father's gaze, we were meant to be equal in the first place. But perhaps during the train journey the guards grew used to us being silent and demure and would prefer things to stay that way, to forget that we exist, that we must stay here supposedly for our own safety, that any day, any moment someone might come to threaten us and these men might need to pay for the privilege of protecting us with their lives.

They might remain with us in this house, live in this flux, for mere days or then for decades.

"At some point." Beard grunts, lowering the bowl on the table in such a firm manner that it spins around on its own for two full laps. It's a miracle that any of the dishes have lasted for this long.

"But . . ." I do falter then, for I can sense Celestia studying me. She must be as worried about Captain Janlav's absence as I am; she must ponder if her secrets are no longer hers and mine. Though each of the guards has skied to the garrison on their turn, none of their visits has taken this long. I wonder then, and not for the first time, if he somehow found out about the deal Celestia brokered with the witch. If he did, did he see it as his duty to report directly to the gagargi? It's an understatement to speculate that the gagargi wouldn't react well to the news—his wrath would be beyond vile. But there is still a chance, a shivering, shrinking one, that Captain Janlav left simply because my sisters and I performed the sacred rites without asking his permission or acceptance for that matter. "He has been gone for five days."

The guards stare back at me blankly, and it occurs to me, they don't know why he has been delayed either and they must be anxious for their captain's whereabouts, too. For without him, who would lead? Beard himself? Or Belly or Tabard? Not Boy, for he can't be older than sixteen. And Boots likes following others, not going through anything unknown first, having spent too many months, years in the tunnels chipped under the mountains. Without Captain Janlav, one of them would have to talk with us when the need arises, escort us to our outings in the garden, ensure that the rumble of our dance practice is indeed merely our sabots and heels clacking against the floorboards, nothing more sinister.

Belly lowers his fist on the table. "Eat your soup before it gets cold."

———————

First, we hear the front door slam against the house's wall, as if someone had just yanked it open with much more force than required. Then there's the swaying steps up the stairs, muttered curses and expletives. These sounds should frighten me, but they do not. I can hear but one pair of boots, and that can only mean that . . .

"Who. Who can it be?" Merile demands, ever so impatient. Her dogs reply to her from upstairs with high-pitched whines.

"Hush," Sibilia replies, but to her or the dogs, I can't tell.

The guards get up sluggishly, gingerly picking up the rifles hanging at the backs of their chairs. Celestia, she nods in approval. If Captain Janlav were to have uncovered her secrets and reported them to the gagargi, he wouldn't be returning alone but with Captain Ansalov and his soldiers.

Yet my sisters and I remain seated as we are, for then both the table and the guards will stand between us and the doorway. Though, as the stumbling steps approach, I recognize their tone, the weight behind them, the cadence. This is no intruder. The cruel fingers clutching my heart ease their hold at last.

And this is the distraction Celestia must have been waiting for all along. For now that the guards and Millie have their backs turned toward us, she reaches out for the rye bread basket, picks up the loaves, and then they are gone, no doubt hidden in the pockets we recently have sewn into our day dresses. She notices me noticing.

Now she knows I know that she has a new plan. Should I ask her about that later or rely on her sharing with me what I need to know? The steps reach us before I can make up my mind.

"I'm back!" Captain Janlav bursts into the room, his cheeks and the tip of his nose glowing red, tiny icicles still clinging to his beard and moustache. He wears a wolf skin cap with the flaps tied under his square chin. His coat isn't the one he wore when I watched him leave through my room's narrow window, not the blue one with the wooden buttons and scars left where he tore away the epaulets. He has donned a trapper's fur coat, warm but soiled with death. "And look what I brought with me!"

Eleven pairs of eyes turn to stare at his raised hand, but I stare at his face, his expression. It's one of pure pride, not one filled with scorn. He doesn't know. Relief washes over me like summer waves against a lakeshore, but it is soon gone, replaced by ire. Oh, I can smell the stink of liquor from where I sit; the melting snow on his trouser legs and the rags tied around his boots is already pooling at his feet. How dare he show up like this when I have been fearing for the worst, wasting away in worry!

"A pheasant!" Captain Janlav cherishes the bird's carcass. He has tied the knurly gray feet together and the copper-speckled wings against the sides. As he shakes the bird, its beady yellow eyes bulge accusingly, though the white-collared neck has already been split, the blood drained. "Freshly shot. This calls for a feast!"

He's boyishly proud, and so very, very drunk, and this escapes no one. The guards clap hands and each other's backs. Tabard and Boots exchange bets on him vomiting or otherwise further embarrassing himself. Alina and Merile lean against each other, stifling giggles. Sibilia stares at him as if all her dreams had just been shattered. Celestia . . .

"Thank you, Captain Janlav," my oldest sister says, in a perfectly calm and collected voice as if she had never worried about him learning her secrets in the first place, "but we have recently finished enjoying our dinner. May I suggest that we spare this magnificent catch of yours for tomorrow so that Millie can prepare it with the dedication it deserves?"

Captain Janlav glances at the pheasant, then at Millie. Old Millie stays completely still on her chair, and yet I can tell she's hoping to sink so far back that she would disappear from our sight until everything is decided. If Captain Janlav has his will, she will be up all night. But she would never say a word in disagreement. Even in this new world, some things never change. She's still but a servant in the guards' eyes.

"I believe there is still some soup left. Celestia and I would be delighted to keep you company," I say in my girliest, silkiest voice. He's in a good mood now. Let him stay that way. "But please allow the younger sisters to retire upstairs, for the time for them to go to bed fast approaches."

Captain Janlav notices the empty plates and glasses only then, the bowls and stained beards and sleeves. When he speaks, his questions aren't aimed at me. "It's that late already? But not too late for a few more drinks, I hope!"

Beard and Tabard assure him that it's not too late. This is the cue for my sisters and me to return upstairs, first into the drawing room, then later into our rooms for the night. But he still holds the dead bird up in the air. I dare not to think what will be left of it come the morning if he starts drinking with the guards now.

"Why don't you take the bird to hang in the cellar first?" I suggest with the innocent tone that has never let me down.

He turns on his heels, and his eyes widen. Again, he looks at me as if he had never seen me before. The spell the gagargi worked on him has made him forget me so many times already that all I feel is mild annoyance. "Ah, yes! What a splendid idea!"

He sways back to the hallway, and I instantly regret my suggestion. Father Moon help me, he will fall on the stairs and break his neck. That wasn't my intention. His death would benefit no one. It would shatter me beyond repair.

"Should someone not go with him?" I ask.

But the other guards find his inebriated state only funny. Celestia and my sisters remain seated. Of course they do. Descending to a cellar for a man's sake isn't something any one of them would ever do.

"I shall come with you." And without waiting for an answer or protest, I rush to shelter the man who can't remember that once upon a time he swore me love under my father's light.

———

The arm of the man I once loved is around my shoulders at last. But this isn't what I imagined the return of his affections to be like. He smells of frost and smoke and brandy. His steps are heavy and unsteady, and if it weren't for me holding him upright, he would have fallen down the stairs multiple times already. The arm that isn't wrapped around me clutches the feet of the dead pheasant, and I'm sure he wouldn't drop it even after breaking every single bone in his body.

"And then I saw this pheasant, strutting with its head high and wings wide, and I thought—" Captain Janlav belches. He wipes his wet beard into the sleeve of his fur coat, then looks at the sleeve to see what he left behind. He seems boyishly happy to find nothing but an old, rusty stain. "A feast! I shall shoot it dead and bring it here, and we shall have a proper feast."

"And a feast we shall have, but for that Millie needs a bit more preparation time, don't you think?" I say as we pass the door that leads into the room that once was a library, but now serves as the guards' living quarters. I think of the third floor and the three chambers there. When we first came to the house, I insisted on having a room of my own. Celestia must have realized instantly what I had in mind, though not even once has she asked if I still intend to . . . "There are, after all, the feathers to pluck, the bones to break, the sauce to simmer, and meat to roast."

"Suppose so," he mutters when we come to the steep steps leading down to the cellar. Just as no soul lights the bird's eyes, none lit our way down. "But, mark my words, we shall have a feast to remember!"

With all the grandiose waving of his arms, I manage to keep us both upright only barely. Out of sheer annoyance, a part of me is tempted to let him fall, or even push him down the stairs. But my sisters and I, we might yet need him. Even though Celestia hasn't asked me to try and win over his trust, during the lonely nights, I have often asked myself: if it were to benefit us, would I share my bed with him?

I don't trust myself enough to provide an honest answer.

We reach the door of the cellar. It's plain and undecorated compared to the other doors of this house. And yet, a terrible sense of foreboding lands heavy on my shoulders. My gaze returns to the stain on his coat's sleeve. Is it blood? And if it is, is it from the dead bird or from someone else that the previous owner of the coat let out of their days?

"Mashed potatoes!" Captain Janlav pulls the door open triumphantly.

His voice doesn't echo in the corridor beyond. The walls are too porous to reflect back sound. But I sense . . . I don't know, a presence of sorts, something vicious waiting for us. No, it's just my imagination, a childish fear of the dark. If someone had been hiding in the house, the guards or Millie would have found them weeks ago already.

"We shall have mashed potatoes and roasted onions!"

This boisterous talk of his! I consider telling him to be silent, but I can't go around giving orders, for that might sow in his mind the idea that I'm not as meek and demure as he thinks I am. As my sisters and I must be in his eyes for the time being. Though I don't know what Celestia's plan is, I know it depends on this.

"I'll gut this bird myself and take the carcass apart!"

On the even, black floor he leans on me less. The smell of dark spring, of wet soil untouched by sun, and persistent mold and root vegetables floods my nostrils as we wander deeper down the corridor that is so very narrow, almost like a tunnel. He stumbles closer to me so that we can walk its length—a distance feeling longer than it possibly can be—side by side.

"And a sauce! What would a roast be without a decent sauce?"

I can't stand thinking of him as a fool, though he would very much deserve to be called such now. For to be so close to him, to reclaim what I once cherished . . . I still find this man too much to my liking regardless of whom he serves now.

"When did it get so dark, eh?" Captain Janlav laughs, a throaty sound accompanied by a friendly jab. "Can't see a thing!"

"Hold on to the wall, will you?" I'm more annoyed at him than anything else, and at myself for thinking of him and all that we once had. I really should have brought a lamp with me. But I didn't have time to think, and going back isn't an option. My sisters have no doubt retired for the night already. I don't want to face the guards alone. And given his drunken state, Captain Janlav might well end up piercing himself in the hooks if left unattended for even a minute. Some boys never grow up. Some never get the chance.

"The wall is gone," Captain Janlav announces, and he sounds both proud and smug, as if he were a particularly keen student of a particularly harsh master.

I can still feel the cold honeycomb of bricks against my trailing fingertips. But I sense the room widening off to our left, the tune of our soft footfalls changing. We turn, and there, right before us, faintly glows a narrow, rectangular window. A slanting ray of Moon's light paints a white beam on the floor, and in this light, I see that the walls here in this low-ceilinged room are made of bare, frosted granite.

"Ah, the hooks!" Captain Janlav sways toward the window, and I'm left behind.

Though I'm comforted by my father's presence, something in this space, in this sad room under the house, haunts me. It's not the wooden crates of beetroots and potatoes, onions and carrots, and other simple things that people who don't live in palaces rely on for sustenance during the long winter months. It's not the pile of empty bottles waiting to be reused come next harvest. It's something else.

Father Moon, will you show me what it is?

I step into the beam of the Moon's light. At this spot, on this stripe halving the room, I'm safe.

"Why, where is it?" Captain Janlav waves the pheasant in the air, near the wall where the Moon's light can't reach him. Feathers tall and small come off from the carcass. He will ruin the bird if I don't stop his fumbling. I don't like the thought of even one life lost in vain, not even an animal one.

I stride to him, into the void under the Moon's light. The darkness feels worse than it should. I want to return fast to where my father can see me. I crane at the ceiling while Captain Janlav mutters and meanders about. There, is that dull glint that of a hook? I reach up, rise on my toes. And it's then that something—of course it's but Captain Janlav—bumps into me, and my balance betrays me. I seek support from the wall to avoid taking him down with me.

The rough stones are cold, the spaces between them colder. But it isn't that which chills me. My fingers press against the round holes in cement, too many, too regular, to be anything else but . . .

"Aha!" Captain Janlav spots the hooks at last.

Breath flees my lungs. It can't be. I feel for the shape of the holes, the smooth edges carved by metal, hoping to find any other explanation. But it's always dark in this cellar and my father can't see those who stand under the window.

"Tangle-tang-tang-tangle there, birdy-bird-bird."

Holes carved by metal . . . I pull my hand away, cradle it against my chest. I know why this house was built here, in the middle of nowhere. I know the people who used to live here, the crimes they committed against the empire. Of course I have wondered before what became of them, had an inkling of the truth. But now the truth is here, before my eyes. The bullets lodged into the cement between the stones. The demise of my mother's sisters.

"See?" Captain Janlav grabs my shoulders and yanks me into the Moon's light. Dazed, I don't resist. Wouldn't, even if I could.

The pheasant's carcass, hanging from the string tied between its legs, swings on the hook, before the wall against which my mother's sisters were once ushered. There's no doubt in my mind that it was Captain Ansalov who oversaw the gagargi's order carried out.

"Did you know about this?" I grip Captain Janlav's right wrist with both hands. His skin is sticky, but warm. Life pulses strong in his veins. "Did you know he had them shot?"

Moon's light frames his silhouette as he stares at me, puzzled. He hasn't been the man I fell in love with in months. He has been but a soldier, fueled by his duty.

But now, in this room, under my father's gaze, his expression softens. The glaze over his eyes breaks, and they once more glow brown as young pines touched by the spring sun. "I didn't know of the order. Not before Captain Ansalov showed the letter to me."

I hate them both, but one more than the other, and even more so I detest the man who made them that way. Both captains are Gagargi Prataslav's pawns. He ordered my mother shot dead. He ordered her sisters executed so that no one could deny Celestia's right to rule. And this is a very frightening thought. Though neither me nor my younger sisters have ever even dreamed of becoming the Crescent Empress, in the light of this new knowledge, does this not mean that in the gagargi's eyes we are threats, to be disposed of when he comes to claim Celestia?

"I..." How long would it take for people to forget my younger sisters and me, to start believing that we never existed, that we are just a myth, a story told to entertain children? I don't want to find out the answer. As soon as the snows melt and we can think to survive the nights without cover, my sisters and I will have to flee, regardless of the risk. I need to make sure Celestia understands this.

He cups my face like he did once upon a time, callused palms against my cheeks. His gaze, it is kinder, caring, familiar. "Elise, what is it?"

And it's as if he had never fallen under the gagargi's spell.

"Do you remember?" My voice trembles, and it's not so by my choice. Would he help us if I so pleaded? Would he let us go without trying to stop us? Would he delay in reporting to Captain Ansalov, to give my sisters and me a head start so that we would be too long gone for the hounds to detect our scent? How can I know for certain without alerting him—he still thinks he's keeping us safe, not captive.

"I . . ." He stares at me, and the Moon's light is so bright. There's understanding and pain in his eyes. A personal struggle behind them.

That night when the train halted in the snow, I didn't want my father to intervene. But now I lay the safety of my sisters and I in his celestial hands. For surely it can't be considered wrong to help the man I once loved to break the spell that makes him forget where his loyalties should lie.

He jolts. His hands fling to cradle his head. He moans as if he had been punched and sways away from me, away from the Moon's light, to lean against the vegetable crates. I rush after him. He's hurt by my wish, by my father's interference.

"Janlav?" And now it's me brushing his shoulder, comforting him.

"The cause is just. The cause is right," he repeats under his breath, his chest heaving as if he had fled for miles, until his legs could carry him no more, but he still needed to keep on running. "The cause is just. The cause is right."

"Hush, my dear, hush." I wrap an arm around him, and there I am, so close to him, as if our ways had never parted. He remembers, even if it's only for a mere moment, and that feels like a victory to me.

"I'm only protecting you." His knees give way, and he sits heavily down on the rough edge of the crate. "You know that, don't you?"

I take a seat next to him. I lean my head against his shoulder, so wide and muscular and familiar. I don't care if he smells of cheap brandy. I don't care if his coat is shedding fur. "I know."

"I was in the war." He sounds confused, torn between what he thinks has come to pass and what actually happened. "I learnt life's lessons the hard way. The life of one person doesn't matter before the greater good."

I remember the night at the train depot, the gathering of the insurgents, the hopes and fears of the people who had had enough. The railway men and factory workers, the fathers and mothers and sisters and brothers of the soldiers that marched into the war and never came back, that once believed in making a difference in the ranks of my mother, only to be bitterly betrayed. I remember and shall never forget them.

"This new world . . . I don't know if it will be better than the one we so easily discarded. But trying to turn back now, after so many lives lost, would be just needless waste. For my people, things are better. Things will get better. They have to get better. We're almost done with the fighting. Only a rare few dare to stand against the gagargi's might anymore. It will soon be over. It will soon be over."

These tidings... they are the first news I hear from the world outside this house. They aren't good from my perspective. It seems like the report Celestia's seed gave her before his demise was indeed correct, not just the gagargi cruelly toying with us. "I know."

The revolution isn't only about my family but about our people and what benefits them the most.

We sit there on the crate, side by side, both staring into the distance, seeing nothing at all, but too much still. It's clear without either one of us saying it. If Celestia were to try and depose the gagargi, the wounds that have yet to heal would tear open again. The blood spilled would be that of the common people. Thinking in the grander scale of things, my life, that of my sisters, doesn't matter a thing. For what is a drop compared to a tidal wave of blood?

"Do you hate me now?" he asks.

"Hate you?" I press my head more firmly against his chest. No matter how I were to try and persuade the man who once loved me, he won't go against the cause. This stand comes from his heart, not from Gagargi Prataslav's spell. "No, how could I when you only have the best interest of our people in your mind."

And that is the truth. I don't hate him. Not yet, in any case.

But one day I might.

Chapter 5

Celestia

I watch my sisters play Catch the Goose in the garden through the window of the room I share with Sibilia. Even though the sun has reclaimed its brightness, the lake is still covered with translucent gray ice that the slowly warming days haven't yet managed to melt. Here, behind the Moon's back, winter lasts long, spring is feeble, and summer comes only when all hope is lost. This is the time of the year when my people starve, when my aviating kin freeze from their feet to shallow waters. And yet, as Elise, Merile, and Alina run down the slippery paths, they look happier than they have been in weeks, if not for months.

It is curious how soon people get accustomed to new circumstances. Even though my sisters and I have been through some hardship, it is nothing compared to that which my people must suffer in the inevitable aftermath of Gagargi Prataslav's coup. I am certain he has exerted his wrath upon those loyal to my family, regardless of rank and personage, age or gender. I know this is just the beginning. Once the initial resistance has been crushed, he will start enforcing his rules upon my people, state new laws and put them into action. The cost of that will not be light.

Outside, Elise the goose catches Alina, lifts her up, and

spins her around. Though glass and distance stand between us, I know that my little sister squeals with glee. A year ago this time, she wouldn't have been considered a full human yet. If the law the gagargi has in his mind had been in place then, he would no doubt have demanded that she be fed to the Great Thinking Machine, to fuel the mechanical creation that tirelessly crunches through numbers and instructions to distribute every resource available equally to all corners of the empire.

It is insanity, the equal redistribution of resources a logistical impossibility. The gagargi's promises may sound good in the ears of those who feel oppressed by the way the world works. But taking something one's family has possessed and cherished for centuries, dividing lands and property earned by hard work, sending one's fathers and mothers and sons and daughters to the other side of the empire because the machine so decides, will bring only mayhem in its wake, not the time of plenty.

I can't let this happen to my people.

Neither this idea of equal redistribution of resources nor the law he plans on setting in place to fuel his foul machine comes from my father, regardless of what the gagargi might insist. I know by heart every single line of the holy scriptures. Our souls anchor to our bodies at the age of six, when we announce our names for the first time. But that doesn't mean that it would be by any means right to extract souls from children younger than that. For I remember knowing my name already before my sixth name day. Elise knew hers before as well. She whispered it to me, boldly, accompanied with a smile. The thought of the gagargi going through with his plan, of enforcing the law to tax every other child, chills me more than what he did to me.

I lost a part of my soul. I may not ever be able to bear children. I will never fly again.

The hollow of my stomach aches as I lean against the windowsill, my palms flat against the cool, white stone. Even after three months, sometimes I still wake up to blood dripping through my nightgown, occurrences Sibilia has noticed, but hasn't dared to ask about—I must make sure she doesn't mention them to anyone, not even Elise. But even more frighteningly, I find myself thinking that I should have let the gagargi's seed grow into a baby. Residues of the spell he imposed on me still linger behind. Perhaps it is because I couldn't fully reclaim my soul, because in my body dwells now the soul of a swan he killed on the night of the coup.

Be it as it may, considering everything that unfolded after that night, what happened to my soul and my body doesn't matter. An empress must place her empire above her own needs, and at this point, my people are the ones who have suffered the most, and will continue to do so. I don't need Elise to tell me that too much blood has been shed already, that if the fields aren't plowed in time, if the mines don't remain open and the factories productive, our people will soon perish of starvation, exposure, and poverty. I have no right to feel sad for the demise of my mother or my seed, for blood spilled on the palace floor or trampled on dirty snow. That is a luxury that I am not entitled to. Not anymore.

A magpie, a bird blessed by my father, lands on the other side of the glass, and I think it might be the same one that has been watching our dance practices lately. Its charcoal gray beak parts, but the pane between us prevents me from hearing the croaks. I tap the glass with my forefinger, but the bird is bold. It cants its black head toward the garden where my sisters play under the half-watchful eyes of Captain Janlav and Boy. The wind tugs at the hair of my younger sisters, and yet they beam with smiles. Merile's lean dogs bounce from one girl to another, the silver-black dog slightly faster than the copper brown one. They could run for miles and miles without tiring. But my sisters and I, we can't, not even after months of building up our stamina with the daily dance practices.

"My sisters trust in me," I say aloud, for words spoken have always borne more weight than those said idly in one's mind.

There is no one around to hear me but the magpie. The door of the room I share with Sibilia is closed. Now that it is finally warm enough to spend time outside, the guards take full advantage of this. I can see Beard and Belly and Tabard and Boots smoking cigarettes on what will be untended lawn come summer. "I will not fail them again."

Ever since my seed's demise, I have been working on a new plan. Given the information and resources available to me, this new plan is not as refined as my previous one, and I consider it riskier by a wide margin. But it would be more dangerous to stay here, in this house that was built here for one and one purpose only, to isolate those deemed dangerous, but perhaps one day useful, from the rest of the empire, with no letters ever reaching them, no hawks knowing the way. When the gagargi summons me, and summon me he surely will, my sisters and I must be long gone, even if it is by foot, through the wilderness that bears no other name than that sung by swans when they compare the most favorable routes across the empire that one day still will be mine. It will be mine, and under my rule it shall be as great as it ever was under my mother's rule.

The magpie taps at the glass with its beak, three clicks too regular for them to be a coincidence. I meet the beady gaze of this curious bird. A thought comes to me, one that may or may not prove to be a significant realization. There is a grain of salt in some stories. "Are you sent by my father?"

My swan-self knows the way through the wilderness, to the Southern Colonies that the gagargi has ever despised. Even though I can't know it for certain, I believe that there my sisters would be safe. The southern rulers and princes yearn for things only I can promise: a child conceived together—though this might remain but a promise—tax alleviations for a negotiable period of time. I am even willing to consider granting them autonomy, provided they agree to protect my sisters and support my campaign to reclaim my throne. This magpie could be a herald of my father, a confirmation for this plan, one I would much cherish.

The magpie taps at the glass again, twice this time. Then it takes off, blue and white wings beating slowly, the long, black tail glistening. I don't know if this constitutes a yes or no or neither. I do know that I am desperate enough to leave this house, that my plan is so feeble still, that I am ready to welcome help in any shape or form that it might arrive.

Even so I am not foolish enough to rely on my father providing us sustenance on our daring journey to come. Regardless of what old stories may say, his light doesn't fill one's stomach. Otherwise my people would have never starved and turned against my family.

I glance once more at the closed door before I march to the massive wardrobe that takes up the whole corner to my right. My swan-self still remembers every flavor of the winds, the rain hiding behind the clouds, the frost that sometimes follows the warmer days. If it weren't for her, I would have ordered my sisters on the road already, doomed them to a grueling journey that might have led us no place better. But as soon as my swan-self announces the weather safe, my sisters and I will depart the house.

I slowly pull open the wardrobe's door, so that the verdigris-stained hinges don't make a sound, and move aside the meager collection of clothes hanging there, the dresses that my mother's sisters once wore, moth-eaten garments with frayed lace hems that used to be in fashion years and years ago. They made alterations in them, though. The deceitful creatures tried to imagine how life in the palaces went on without them. Perhaps they, too, entertained the idea of returning to the place that once was their home.

I do wonder at times how the Summer City has changed in my absence. Has the gagargi torn down the statues representing the past empresses? I am sure he never ordered one to commemorate mother. Has he relocated his horrid machine from his island to the palace's great hall as he once said he would do? Does he extract the souls of my supporters in public ceremonies, to make examples out of them?

I push the clothes aside, tap the corners of the back panel one after another, in clockwise direction. I wait for the soft click and then slide the panel aside. This is the third secret compartment I found while searching through the areas of the house that are accessible to us. Though I have tapped through every wall and patted every cushion, though I have run my hand over every decorative knob and inlay in search of hidden levers and switches, I didn't find what I was looking for. It is too well hidden.

In the secret compartment, my collection of supplies rests untouched. It took me weeks to secure the suitable tin boxes.

The blue and silver one is already full of biscuits—hard, dry things meant for the guards' provisions when they travel to the garrison and back. The men don't like the taste, aren't hungry enough to touch them, and often leave them carelessly lying around the house. I flip open the lid of the light green box that once held the sewing kit. There is still space for more rye bread. I shall have to grow bolder, though this will increase the risk of someone in addition to Elise noticing me stealing food.

The flint lies on top of the canteen, next to the tin boxes. Yesterday, when Beard chastised Boy for losing them, I was certain they would realize that neither of them was to blame. In the end, they didn't, but it was too close of a call for my comfort. I will not snatch more equipment from the guards. Praised be my father that, according to my swan soul, the rivers and rivulets are clean here and teeming with fish.

The footsteps are silent, the low screech of the door opening barely audible. But I hear them because I never allow myself to slip too deep in my thoughts.

I am on my knees, half inside the wardrobe. I don't have time to close the tin box, let alone slide the panel back. I collect myself, though, before I back out and turn and see who has entered the room. For if it is one of the guards . . .

It is not, the Moon be blessed. Sibilia stands in the doorway, and though she cradles the book of scriptures against her chest, as she so often does, there is something very frightening about her. Gone is the daydreaming, awkward girl. Before me stands a woman whose red-gold hair gleams even though the lamps in the room are unlit. Her face is pale, her freckles like scattered embers. But it is her gray gaze, wide and intense, and it is as if . . . No, not as if.

My sister sees through me.

"Celestia," Sibilia says, pushing the door closed behind her. "Tell me the truth."

For a moment, I am too shocked to speak, let alone get up from the floor. I have kept many secrets from her. I don't know what truths she has managed to uncover on her own—all of them or only one?

"What do you wish to know?" I ask, for I never expected my sisters forever refrain from asking questions.

Sibilia strides toward me, and there is nothing clumsy in the way she moves. There is but pure determination and unsated hunger as she halts three steps away from me. "Tell me, what happened to Mother's sisters."

That one, then. Even though I am not yet the empress, my control over my mind is fitting for one. I rise on my feet, to face my sister. Has Elise told Sibilia about mother's sisters, about their plans, their fate? If she has, what are her motives?

I meet Sibilia's sharp, gray gaze. No, even though Elise and Sibilia are close, Elise hasn't told her about the bullet holes in the cellar. She knows some things have been kept secret for a reason. Sibilia's thirst for knowledge stems from a different source, from a spell, I sense it now.

"What do you mean?" I need just a little more time to evaluate the best course of action. Where does this spell originate from? Who is behind it? How is it powered? Surely not by a gagargi!

"You know what I mean." Sibilia advances toward me until nothing separates us but a paper-thin slice of air. Her gaze is almost level with mine. She has grown tall, as if she had stretched during the winter months, and I wonder, what else has come to pass before my eyes without me noticing. And then I know it and chastise myself for not realizing it sooner.

This spell is not of any gagargi's handiwork. The days my sister has spent with the scriptures, they have yielded fruit. She has learned to read the words unwritten, the spells that the gagargis so jealously guard. A feat I never accomplished, though not for the lack of trying.

"Who are Irina and Olesia?"

I am proud of my sister, but my posture stays unchanged, expression unwavering. For those names . . . I haven't seen or heard them said since the day my mother summoned her younger sisters into the sacred observatory, there to hear their feeble pleas only out of kindness before she ordered them exiled and their names obliterated from all official and unofficial records. Now my sister stands before me, demanding to know what I might have done in my mother's place. But there are benefits in ignorance, pain in knowledge. "Irina and Olesia?"

Sibilia snorts. Her nostrils flare. She senses that I am not telling her everything. This spell of hers, could it really be . . . Yes, it must be, a truth spell. She will sense if I lie.

I say what is true from every measurable angle. "It is a long time since I last heard those names."

Sibilia stomps the ground, dissatisfied with the answer. But before I speak more, I must know for certain that there is no one else around. My senses have grown precise indeed in this house. I have trained myself to recognize every creak of the stairs and floor planks, the wail of every hinge. I hearken my senses, but I hear no sounds that would betray someone moving around the drawing room, suppressed sighs that come from holding one's breath for too long. I don't like breaking eye contact with Sibilia, but that is what I must do to confirm my conclusion. The guards are still outside, in the sun, as are Elise, Merile, and Alina. Sibilia and I have a moment or two to speak of things that then must not be ever voiced again.

"Shall we take a seat?" I motion toward the bed that we share at nights, when we are close but far apart still. Let my sister agree to sit down with me, for I doubt she knows what she is fueling her spell with. Sooner or later it will abandon her and leave her weak and confused, momentarily drained of a part of her own soul. "No doubt, you have many more questions to ask."

Sibilia blinks, and a veil of confusion clouds her eyes. Then it is gone, and back is the burning thirst. "A trick, perhaps? No, you wouldn't trick your own sister. Or would you? I really think not. Yes. Let's sit down."

And so I gain myself a few precious seconds to think of what to tell. The truth, yes, but truth has many flavors, some more bitter than others. My sister deserves some version of the events. Back at the Summer Palace, during the train journey, she was still a child, and I under an obligation to protect her from the information that would only hurt her. Now she is but two months, three weeks, and four days away from her debut, from the rite of passage that marks her an adult. Perhaps the time has already come to treat her as one.

I speak in a low voice only when we both perch on the bed's edge, the book of scriptures between us a neutral ground that neither can occupy without breaching peace. "They were our mother's younger sisters."

Sibilia clings to every word, holding her breath, and it is as if the house, too, were listening to us. It occurs to me that I might have made a grave mistake in immersing myself in my plans, by considering only the guards and the gagargi as a threat. I have failed to take into account the other parties that may yet become involved.

"And what happened to them?" Sibilia asks, and at that moment I am certain that she has never really heard of them. But that can't be it. How would she have then known their names, something even Elise is too young to remember!

"They plotted to assassinate our mother," I reply, even as I wonder from which source my sister's knowledge stems. There is but one way to find out. I must tell her more and read from her reactions how much she really knows. "They acquired a swan soul and sweet-talked a talented young gagargi into their service. It was only at the last moment that our mother learned of their plan and put an end to it."

A family secret that soon became a state secret. I was taught to forget mother's sisters, and it was by no means a difficult feat to accomplish with their names forbidden in conversations that steered around their absence, their faces skillfully altered in portraits to resemble no one at all, their friends and allies silenced with unsaid threats and punishments so terrible that any grain of loyalty still lingering in their bones withered willingly away. Only now, I realize that their fate could have been mine, even though I did not and I will not betray my sisters.

But in conspiring with the gagargi and plotting a coup together with him, even if I was under his spell, I did betray my mother. That night, there was so little time, and the guards escorted my sisters to the observatory before I had a chance to explain that I had merely intended to seek the gagargi's counsel, nothing more. Though she forgave me, sealed this with one last kiss pressed on my forehead, I am sure she went to her grave thinking I was behind the coup. I can only wish that our father has revealed her the truth.

"Would-be murderers then?" Sibilia nods to herself, seemingly satisfied for a moment at least. But I have to ask myself: is she still on my side? How much can I trust her, or any of my sisters for that matter? These are ghastly questions, but ones every empress must consider, regardless of how fond they are of their sisters. Questions that my mother no doubt asked herself.

"What do you do when your sisters plot your downfall?" I ask her as much as myself. If the world had turned out differently, if it weren't for the gagargi and his machine, my sisters might have eventually conspired against me in lust for more power. Now I know they won't. If I have to be grateful for one thing, the gagargi's actions have resulted in that. "She could have ordered them shot. Empresses of the past have done so more than once. But they were her sisters. She loved them, despite their betrayal."

Sibilia stares blankly ahead. No, not blankly, but at the oval mirror above the vanity desk. She isn't interested in her reflection. It is as if she is hoping to see more, but what? Surely not into the world beyond this one.

And then I know the answer. Ghosts can gaze into this world through reflecting surfaces.

I say, as much to those who might be watching us as to my sister, "Instead, our mother sent them here, into a house built so far away that any plot conceived could be stopped in time."

Even without Millie's confession, there was so much evidence, my mother told me after the guards had escorted Irina and Olesia away. The young gagargi cracked under the truth spell that mother's advisors enforced on him. Come next full moon, her sisters would have poisoned mother with arsenic. Irina, as the older one of them, would have married the Moon. But even though the guards searched the palace from attic to cellar three times, the swan soul bead the sisters had acquired was never found. And that might yet turn out to be a blessing. Knowing the cunning of mother's sisters, I am certain they smuggled it with them here, even if I haven't been able to locate it yet.

Sibilia nods at her reflection, satisfied with what I have told her so far, if not by what she saw. "When you were still under the gagargi's spell, you wanted to send me, Elise, Merile, and Alina here."

She has grown indeed, for this I haven't told her either. It was originally the gagargi's plan. But it was I who decided that we should all come here—that night in the sacred observatory, it was the best course of action. Though, back then, I didn't know what he had in mind for my mother's sisters. Had I known, I don't know how I would have chosen.

"It's not as safe here as you thought it would be," Sibilia continues in a voice too deep, too old.

I think of the bullet holes in the cellar, the ones Elise so vividly described that even though I haven't seen them myself, I can feel them under my fingers as I brush the worn velvet coverlet. I don't know if one of mother's gagargis cast a spell on me, to make me forget Irina and Olesia even faster. I was only nine when they were exiled. But now I suddenly recall things I haven't thought of in years. My nostrils fill with their perfume, white midsummer roses in bloom covering the bitter scent of cigarettes. I taste the hard, colorful candies they always carried around in their purses. My ears lock and pop. My heart pounds too loud.

Sibilia pokes my shoulder as if nothing had changed. "So, what's the plan?"

I must be present, with her. I can't think of what the past

meant to me or what the coming days may bring in their wake. My sisters rely on me to find a way to leave this house, and leave this house I must, for my empire is torn asunder and my people suffer in the throes of a civil war. But only a secret untold is safe.

"Tell me," Sibilia commands, playfulness gone from her tone.

I know it then: if I don't tell her, I will put us even more at risk, even if a careless slip of tongue could ruin the plan beyond recovery. For it is clear now that though their bodies have bled dry, the souls and shadows of my mother's sisters still remain behind and haunt this house. They distrust me as I am . . . will be the empress. If given half the reason, half the chance, they will sow seeds of distrust amongst my sisters, and this will then endanger so much more than the escape plan.

I face the mirror and speak as much to the ghosts of Irina and Olesia—if they indeed are present—as to my sister who sits beside me in the flesh. I shall tell them what awaits us. "We will flee on foot to the south. If we leave at midnight, that will give us from six to eight hours of head start before the guards notice us gone. If we walk through the night and the following day, down the streams and rivulets, by the time the guards reach Captain Ansalov, his hounds may not be able to determine our path."

Sibilia nods to herself. "They will think we've headed toward the Summer Palace, that you are intent on reclaiming the empire as your first action."

My sister is no longer a silly girl, but a woman of reason. Though, relying on the guards to draw the right conclusion without carefully scattered hints would be to count on luck too much. Toward this end, I have composed a letter that I will leave for Millie to find. She will give in under pressure, before the guards have to resort to more than threats. She has done so once in her life already.

This, I can't share with Sibilia. Irina and Olesia were fond of Millie. They wouldn't approve of me using her. But I consider this as Millie's chance to redeem herself in our father's eyes.

"You mentioned 'we.'" Sibilia squints her eyes, rubs her forehead. The spell is fading, and she senses it. She can have but a question or two left to ask before she has spent all that her soul can spare. "What's the definition of 'we'?"

Mother once said that each difficult decision will carve a hollow under my heart. I feel it now, the emptiness that tugs at my lowest ribs. Does my sister know? How could she? I never shared that part of my previous plan with anyone, and I don't like being reminded of what I might have been willing to do. "All of us."

Sibilia shakes her head. "No, I wasn't sure earlier, but now I am. You're holding back information. Tell me what it is."

I can see from her widening pupils that she isn't quite in control of the spell anymore. As she reaches toward me, to grab my shoulders, the compulsion hooks into the cogs and wheels of my mind. It is a feeling that . . .

After being subject to a harmful spell before, I should be repulsed. Afraid. But instead, I am proud of my sister and what she has achieved on her own. Proud enough that if it had been my choice, I might have told her the truth without the spell's interference. But now, it isn't my choice. "The previous plan."

"I'm sorry, I'm sorry . . ." Sibilia kisses my forehead, tears streaming down her cheeks. My mind was tampered with not so long ago, to coerce me into actions I wouldn't otherwise have agreed to. In my sister's eyes, she has hurt me in the worst possible way. "I didn't mean to really use it. I . . . I can't take it back."

And I wish I could take back the words that I hear myself saying. "That day my seed came to our aid, I chose you to remain behind with me."

Sibilia draws away from me. She stares at me, unable to comprehend what I am talking about. No, that isn't it. Unwilling to comprehend.

"There was but one troika . . ." Out of control now, the spell seeks firmer hold of my mind. Images of the day my seed met his end flash past my eyes. The sun clinging to the zenith. The waiting horses tied to the wooden rail. It seemed like such an easy choice then. When I saw that my seed had brought but one troika with him, with the future of the empire at stake, I realized I could send only three of my sisters away to safety. At that instant, I had to decide who would stay behind and face the grim consequences with me. That role fell on Sibilia.

But now that I have slept next to Sibilia, now that I have heard of her hopes and dreams, I do regret ever making that choice that in the end didn't matter. "I would have ordered him to leave with Elise, Merile, and Alina."

"You were . . ." The hurt in my sister's voice is primal. Though an empress should never be guided by her heart, my sister's pain makes me regret what I thought back then—what I knew—as the best course of action. "You were going to leave me behind."

I focus my mind on one word and one word only. It took my father's help to break through Gagargi Prataslav's compulsion. But my sister's spell isn't as intricate. What I need is a breach, one word through the spell. One simple word. "No."

"You were going to leave me behind," Sibilia repeats, blinking slowly as if she weren't seeing properly anymore. She shakes her head, and her faith in me leaks out with the tears. I, her honored eldest sister . . . in her eyes, I am that no more, but a calculating empress-to-be. "You were . . ."

"Listen to me, Sibilia, it was the only possible choice." And even with her spell cast aside, I hide nothing more from her. I don't want my sister thinking I wanted the events to veer to that direction. "This empire needs a future, and weak and bleeding, I chose Elise before myself. And our little sisters, dear Alina and Merile, they rely on our protection. Tell me, how would you have chosen?"

But Sibilia doesn't hear me anymore. She gropes for the book of scriptures, holds it against her chest, slumps against the pillows. "Abandon me . . ."

I rush to help her onto her back, though her accusing gaze stabs me like hunter's knives. I have seen spells invoked many times before. When not powered by a soul bead, the gagargis draw from their own souls. My sister has come upon this knowledge on her own. This might be the very first spell she has ever invoked.

"It never came to pass," I whisper as I tug the coverlet over her, to keep her warm. She shifts waveringly, yearns for me to leave her alone. But I sit down on the bed's edge, next to her. "My sister, it is all right now."

"Is it?" she mumbles, wounded by more than the secrets uncovered. Her spell has faded and left her weak. I hope it hasn't harmed her soul permanently. "Celestia . . ."

I gently brush my sister's wet cheeks, dab the tears away with my sleeve. Even though her body is that of an adult, deep inside she is still but a girl, prone to be afraid and confused. For a reason, though.

I lean to speak softly in her ear, though I know the hurt I have caused her may not ever mend. "We will go to the south together. All together or not at all."

She grows too weary to say more. Her eyes keep open only barely, but the piercing gray sadness is unmistakable. As her breathing deepens, I hold her hand in mine. It is no longer plump, but delicate. She has changed. I haven't, for I am already as I must be.

I sit by her side, until I am certain she will not stir to the sounds I might make. I glance at the mirror. I am not yet the Crescent Empress. I don't see into the world beyond this one. My expression is unreadable as I get up and glide to the vanity desk.

Swiftly, I cover the mirror with my shawl. What the ghosts can't see, they can't tattle onward. I return to Sibilia, and I carefully pry the book of scriptures from her sleepy fingers.

I turn the pages and read the first unsteady line. It gives me no pleasure to break the trust that my sister has placed in me. But in this house, I can't afford to let her keep secrets from me. If we want to survive, I must know everything.

I must know who has been talking with Irina and Olesia.

Chapter 6

Alina

Celestia knocks the paneled wall with her knuckles as she always does at the end of the dance practice. Rafa and Mufu trot to her, convinced this must mean treats for them, though I don't think she's ever given them any. She shakes her head at them, says to us, "My sisters, this suffices for today."

"Good." Olesia wipes her ghostly forehead. Her kind doesn't sweat, but it's as if she hasn't realized this, and I don't really want to remind her that she's actually dead. "She failed to stay in rhythm once more."

What a mean comment to make! I didn't notice anything off with the rhythm, but I must admit, I wasn't following the steps either. Maybe I missed a thing or two as I swirled round and round with Merile and her pretty companions.

"What did you expect?" Irina links arms with her sister and leads her toward the window. They can't leave the house, but I'm quite sure they dream of doing so just like we do. "You can't trust the eldest sister."

Merile and I exchange looks. I keep many things secret from my sisters, but two I share with her. At some point, we might tell our sisters about both the ghosts and the witch. But not yet, I think.

"Shall we let in fresh air?" Celestia asks. Sibilia glares at her as if the question had somehow hurt her. When Celestia says nothing in reply, our sister stomps to the fireplace, unraveled red-gold locks swaying with her steps.

Merile nods at me. Something is definitely going on, but she doesn't know what it is either, and neither do the ghosts. It started a bit over a week ago with Sibilia being very upset with Celestia. They won't talk about it, not even when we're *not* in the room. The ghosts say that keeping secrets like that is very typical of older sisters.

Celestia strolls to the window, her steps so fine that she might as well be still dancing. She unlatches it, closes her eyes, and breathes deep. Usually she remains silent, but this time around, she says very softly under her breath, "At last."

Irina's thin gray brows arch. "She has a plan."

"Younger sisters, beware." Olesia drifts to stand right behind our oldest sister, who doesn't notice her at all. I don't like the ghost speaking of Celestia like that even if she does keep quite a few secrets from us. Maybe Merile is right. Maybe the ghosts have their own ghostly agendas. Maybe we should reconsider telling Sibilia, Elise, and Celestia about them.

Then again, Irina and Olesia say that only people who want to see ghosts will see them, and hence if we were to tell our older sisters about the ghosts, they simply wouldn't believe us. I really don't want to tell our sisters anything that might make them even more concerned about me—my meals might start to taste funny again!

When Celestia leaves to help Elise with the furniture, Merile and I and Rafa and Mufu rush to the window. I look out for the magpie, and Merile does likewise. We lean against the sill, squinting at the sun. Our shadows fall against the house, unable to reach the porch's tin roof below. They shift back and forth as the cool breeze tousles our hair.

"Spring," Merile mutters, no doubt upset because the magpie didn't come and watch us dancing. "It still doesn't feel like spring."

Irina leans out from between us. "The day is not as it should be."

I wonder if the magpie felt it, too. Though it's five weeks since the equinox, the garden remains murky, the paths muddy, and the grass wet and brown. Only a few shy coltsfoots bloom amidst the muck. The days are now twice the length of the nights, but last night was the first that Merile and I didn't shiver and quiver under the blankets with Rafa and Mufu. I have to ask, "But summer will come before too long, won't it?"

Irina and Olesia share a somehow very sad look. They don't know that come summer all will be well at last, and once more I'm dying to tell them about the witch. She promised to help me and Merile flee, and though we haven't seen her since, we've glimpsed the magpie almost every day. Once we do see her again, once she shares her plan with us, we can finally tell our older sisters and maybe even the ghosts about her without fear of being ridiculed! Hopefully that's going to happen soon!

"The days will grow longer until midsummer," Olesia says, brushing her plump fingers against the window's frame.

I glance over my shoulder at our older sisters. Celestia and Elise are pushing the chairs and tables back to their usual places. Sibilia broods by the fireplace, the book of scriptures on her lap. They're not paying attention to us. It's safe for me to speak with the ghosts. "That would mean less time for darkness, wouldn't it?"

Though we've lived in this house for months now, I keep on seeing the same nightmare. I'm hoping that once the nights turn light, my dreams will do likewise. I really don't want to be reminded of the gagargi and his machine every time I close my eyes. If it weren't for Rafa curled at my feet and Merile snoring beside me, I wouldn't dare to sleep at all.

"Yes," Irina replies. "Midsummer marks the end of night. During the nightless days, our father . . ."

"Wait." Merile suddenly leans farther against the sill, so far out that her feet no longer touch the floor. She kicks for balance, loses a sabot. Rafa and Mufu jump after her, nip her hem, and hang on to it.

"Merile," I shriek. She can't fall! She can't! She's my favorite sister, and I wouldn't know what to do without her! "Help!"

One moment the ghosts are there, puzzled, even shocked. The next they're gone as if they'd never been present in the drawing room at all. But Merile still teeters on the window's edge, half in, half out.

"Oh dear, Merile . . ." Celestia glides to us. There's no haste in her steps, and yet I'm sure that if Merile were to slip any farther, Celestia could still catch her in time. "I do advise for a certain degree of caution when high places are concerned."

She grabs the back of Merile's dress and swiftly pulls her back in. I bite my lips together. It's a pity the ghosts disappeared like that, that they didn't see Celestia coming to Merile's aid. Our older sisters really aren't as unreliable as they think. They don't know our sisters like Merile and I do!

"Magpie." Merile tosses her gorgeous black hair over her left shoulder as if she hadn't just been in danger and then been properly chastised. "I thought I glimpsed the magpie, but it was just some other bird."

"Now did you?" Celestia gazes into the garden as if she already knew why we're so interested in the bird. But she can't know. Really, she can't.

"Shall we close the window?" Celestia asks, already reaching out for the handle. "It is still a bit on the chilly side outside."

"Fine." Merile tilts her chin and scoops Mufu up, into her arms. She shuffles to reclaim her sabot. "But since you're older and know everything, why didn't the magpie come and watch our practice today?"

Celestia secures the window with a latch. She stares out for a moment, looking very thoughtful. "A bird has all the sky as its playground. As long as a soul rests behind its eyes, it is free to come and go as it pleases."

"Poetic." Merile gives Mufu a wet kiss right in the middle of her black forehead. "How very poetic."

"Oh, Merile." Celestia laughs and pats our sister's hair. I happen to look at their shadows. Celestia's is very tall and her arms feathery. Merile's shadow retreats from her, faster than she could possibly shy away from our sister. What I see in the shadows is something I don't tell even to Merile. "How about we play a game, then?"

"A game," I squeal in excitement, and forget all about the shadows. Though Elise and Sibilia sometimes play with us, Celestia never joins us. Though the ghosts keep me and Merile company, they say they're too old for idle amusements. "What sort of game?"

"It is called the Silent Path." Celestia places one palm on my shoulder, the other on Merile's. She leads us past Elise, who, ready with the furniture, has moved to braid Sibilia's hair. Somehow it always comes loose when we dance. Maybe that's what's been making her so gloomy lately.

"I've never heard of it before! Is it as much fun as Catch

the Goose? Is it played outside? Say it's not! It's still so muddy there!"

"Gah," Merile mutters, less interested. She presses Mufu tighter against her chest. Her beautiful companion treads the air, tongue sticking out of her mouth. "We're tired. Yes! So very tired!"

My feet are a little sore from dancing, too. I'd rather dance barefooted than wear my sabots, but my sisters won't hear of that. And I won't hear more protests from Merile—if we ponder our answer for too long, Celestia might change her mind and we might miss this treat for good!

"Come now, Merile!" I pat my knees to summon Rafa. For if she joins the game, then Mufu will want to play too, and then Merile can't say no.

"Yes, go," Elise says, the words clipped. I don't know if she meant for us to hear her or if she forgot that she's no longer whispering with Sibilia. Either way, she looks very interested in the rules of this game we've never played before. I'm not sure if Sibilia's hair would be better off without her.

"Fine." Merile follows us slowly and sluggishly, as if she'd turned into a snail. Wouldn't she look funny then! Though I really hope that Papa doesn't turn her into one. Nurse Nookes once said that a girl who doesn't behave herself might one morning wake up changed to another creature. "But it had better be fun."

Celestia stares at Merile, her gaze as blue as the summer seas, calm now, but reminding us both that a wise girl doesn't try the temper of the empress-to-be. "That, we shall find out together, shall we not?"

And that's exactly what we do. The game starts from the room I share with Merile. Celestia presses the door closed behind us. She leans down to whisper to us, "Now, my dear little sisters, open the door as silently as you can."

I reach out for the handle, but Merile is faster than me. We've opened this door a hundred times at least—no, I need a bigger number than that—but now I want to do it more than anything else in this world. For who knows what awaits us outside?

It turns out, nothing out of the ordinary. That is, if you don't count Elise and Sibilia staring at us. They're whispering once more. I don't know what possible gossip they can have left, but it might be about Celestia. Lately, Sibilia and Celestia have barely greeted each other. The ghosts say that Celestia has been sleeping curled in the armchair, though why she would do that when their bed is wide enough for two, I really can't even begin to guess.

"Now, memorize this path," Celestia says, and then she drifts across the room; not the straightest path, but one that takes her first to the oval table, then right toward the mirror on the paneled wall and along that way to the side table with the dented samovar, then a step left and straight until she reaches the door that leads to the hallway and stairs beyond. She halts there and turns to look back at us. "Do you remember it?"

"Boring." Merile pouts her lips and squats down to pet both Rafa and Mufu. Her companions offer their paws to her. She grasps their delicate feet in turns. "This is a boring game. Isn't it, my dear darling companions?"

I like boring. So many strange things have happened in this house that I think I've just about had enough of it. When I keep my eyes open, I see both shadows and ghosts. And though Irina and Olesia are very nice old ladies, I'd like to see them only in reflections like Merile does, because seeing them whenever they're near us feels wrong in a way I don't know how to explain.

"This is just the beginning." Celestia smiles, a sight so rare I have to pinch my arm. I'm wide awake. I pinch a little harder, just to be sure. "Now, close your eyes."

Merile hugs Mufu. Of course I need to do likewise to Rafa. Merile nods approvingly at me. There's nothing better than cuddles! "What if I don't?"

"Then you lose," Celestia replies.

Merile closes her eyes right at that moment. I follow her example, though whenever I close my eyes, I risk losing myself in a dream. In this house, my dreams are sharper than on the train. I often run, and it's always away from this house. Sometimes I descend narrow stairs, into an unlit cave that smells of mold and old onions. I wander down a low corridor, until I come to a wall of stone. When I run my fingers across its length, I find scattered holes, and for some reason, this makes me very sad.

Though both of these dreams are better than the nightmares I keep on having about the gagargi.

"Follow me," Celestia says.

I hear Merile's hem swish and sabots clack as she hurries toward Celestia's voice. I tiptoe after her. All the planks in this house make a different sound, but now I mustn't make any. I'm lucky that I'm light and know how to move quietly. Merile . . .

My sister steps on a plank that shrieks like a goat stuck between two fence posts. Not that I've ever seen or heard a goat do such.

"You lost," Celestia says.

I open my eyes, just in time to see Merile sniff and stick her tongue out at Celestia. She got only as far as the mirror. I think

I could have made it the whole way.

We start again maybe a thousand times. That is, I'm not sure. I don't know how much that really is. But it's not easy to remember the way Celestia goes, even after she shows it to us many, many times, for we must step on the exact same spots as she did or the planks will betray us. Sibilia and Elise watch us from their sofa chair before the fireplace. They're done with their gossip and braiding and first cup of tea.

"May we join as well?" Sibilia's tone is pointed as Merile's sometimes is when she wants to prove that she's right. Though most often she's not. My sister's face is pale, the thick, blue circles around her eyes like bruises, and when she continues, her voice wavers. "Or is the Silent Path only for the youngest daughters?"

"Please do." Celestia reaches her hands out for them, a gesture to join her on the dance floor. "Sibilia, dear, please start from our room. Elise, you from yours."

Sibilia gets up from amidst the cushions almost hesitantly, as if she wanted nothing more than to play with us, but was sure the invitation would be called off at any moment. As if that had happened to her again and again in the past, though of course nothing like that can have possibly come to pass!

At first it's fun, playing with all my sisters. We compare the sounds the different planks make. Some purr like happy cats, some grunt like old men. There are planks that are angry for no longer being trees, some so old that they've forgotten where they came from. Though this I don't tell to my sisters. Neither do I tell them that their shadows act out of order. Elise's sways as if the lamps were lit and swinging, though they're neither. Sibilia's is pierced by tiny holes.

"Fun," Merile says as she finally reaches the pale blue door without making a sound. I managed to do so way before her, as did Elise. "This was not as fun as you promised."

Celestia stares past her at Elise and Sibilia. There's something in that look, a word of advice left unsaid. Elise nods back at her. Sibilia looks somehow hurt. Did she accidentally walk into the furniture at some point? "I don't recall promising fun."

Merile sulks off back to the sofa by the window. Rafa and Mufu remain with me. I don't know if I should follow Merile with her companions or stay with Celestia. It doesn't matter, for it's then that Irina and Olesia reappear. They slip into the room through the mirror on the wall.

"The door is ajar," Olesia whispers.

"But it is the front door," Irina adds. "Someone is coming. He doesn't wear red gloves."

_____

Rafa and Mufu race down the flight of stairs so fast that Merile and I can barely keep up with them. A whole forest of creaks follows us, sounds high and low and all the hushed tones in between, too. If it weren't for my excitement, I would run back up and then down, just to hear them again. But now we're already at the hall. And . . .

"The front door is open," I gasp as much to Merile as to the ghosts. It's only then that we realize to check for the guards. The door of the library is closed, thanks Papa! The guards must not know that we're about to be rescued at last!

Though I hear our older sisters descending the stairs behind us, I rush to the front door. Rafa and Mufu beat me to it. Merile is just a step behind, the hand mirror lifted before her. We push the door fully open together, only to stagger to a halt on the wide stone steps beyond.

The spring day is so bright that I must blink again and again to see what awaits us. We're not alone. Rafa and Mufu bark and bounce next to Boy, who stands at the front yard, a hand raised to shield his eyes. He cranes into the distance, down the hillside of brown grass dotted with tiny yellow flowers, toward the forest where the birches are still too shy to show their new leaves.

"Well?" Merile turns around slowly, to catch the ghosts' reply. They can't leave the house, but they aren't often wrong.

"There," Irina replies, backing away from the daylight as if it hurt her.

"I can't . . ." Olesia trails off, and with that, both ghosts fade away.

I'd call them back, I would, but just then, the most beautiful black horse I've ever seen bursts out from between the trees. Its long mane flutters in the wind, and the oiled hooves glint in the sunlight. The rider stands on the golden stirrups, dressed in the reddest of red coats. His white grin is wide, and his skin is akin to Merile's. No, darker. The rider is . . .

"The Poet," Merile chimes, and runs to the yard, past Boy, who's spotted the rider too, and is struggling with his rifle's strap to unloop it from around his shoulder. "Don't shoot! It's my seed!"

I hurry after my sister as the Poet gallops the long, even stretch of the road, past the fields like starry skies. I bless his name! At last, Papa has sent someone to our rescue! I can't wait to see my sisters' expressions!

But then another rider emerges from between the bare trees, one on a leaner, meaner pony. His leather coat flaps hurting-sharply against his sides. Great, gray-black dogs leap barking behind him. This second rider . . .

"Get back inside!"

I swirl around just in time to see Captain Janlav and Belly and Beard striding down the stone steps. They look startled and . . . even furious to find me and Merile in the yard. Our older sisters, they didn't follow us out! I know it then, I'm definitely somewhere where I shouldn't be, but also that I can't leave even if I should.

"Will you get them inside now," Captain Janlav snaps at Boy as he leads Belly and Beard past us, to the closed gate. He's angry, but also excited, as if something he'd awaited for a long time were finally about to come true.

Boy flounders to me and Merile, but we repeatedly ignore him pointing toward the house. Then Belly and Beard are already leaning their elbows against the gate, rifles unslung, aimed toward the riders. As the Poet reaches the slope, he glances over his shoulder, at the rider behind him, and he's so close now that I recognize him.

"It's Captain Ansalov," I whisper.

Boy stops waving. His mouth gapes, but no words come out. This is no rescue. This is something else, and it feels as if the very ground were giving in under my sabots.

"Drat," Merile curses as the Poet digs his spurs against his horse's sides. His grin widens as he leans forward. He buries his head against the fluttering black mane. The horse speeds up, hooves scattering gravel. "They're racing."

"Lower the rifles!" Captain Janlav orders. He must have realized the same thing. "And move aside, unless you want to get trampled."

He has just enough time to swing the gate open and dodge aside before the Poet canters to the yard, past the dazzled Boy and Merile's companions. He draws his horse to a halt so sharp that it ends up sitting on its hind legs. He pats the horse on its foaming neck and then swings down from the saddle. "My sweet, little Merile!"

Merile dashes to her seed, even as Captain Ansalov enters the yard at a trot, his hunting dogs leaping behind him. I don't dare to look at him, and so I run after Merile. Rafa and Mufu follow me, barking over their shoulders. I'm happy that they have my back.

The Poet's oiled hair is twisted into a dozen braids with silver crescents tangling at the ends. He wears a fine red coat with golden epaulets that toss and turn as he lifts Merile up in the air. His black, soft trousers are tucked into shiny boots. He doesn't wear any gloves. The ghosts were right about that, at least. But there's still more questions than there are answers.

"I do apologize for taking so long to find you." The Poet swings Merile around. My sister laughs, her head bent back, her black curls bobbing. Rafa and Mufu yap around them, running small circles. I stand there, hands tucked into my dress's pockets. I don't know what to do. I'm confused and excited and a bit afraid, if it's possible to be all of that at the same time. "No doubt my visit is long overdue!"

"Captain Janlav." Captain Ansalov's call is more like a jeer. His hounds sniff the air and growl, maybe at me. I shuffle closer to the Poet's magnificent horse. Its tack is splattered with mud and the leopard skin under the saddle is soaked through. "It seems like these days your prisoners run around rather freely."

It's the first time someone calls us that, but it might just be the truth. For Captain Janlav grits his teeth, glances at me and Merile, as if thinking what he can say when we're within earshot. But before he can make up his mind, Merile's seed lowers her. He hooks his thumbs on his wide belt and speaks in a loud, booming voice. "And are we not all prisoners of our body, minds knotted inside skin and bone shell? Do we not deserve to run when we can, before the empress rings the last bell? Those young of age, those unconcerned, let them remain that way. For rather sooner than later, I'm sure of it, darker will be the day."

Everyone, including the two captains, turns to stare at the Poet. Merile beams at her seed's words, though I bet that she didn't understand either what they were about. Captain Ansalov's frown turns smug. I realize he likes this sort of thing, operas and poetry.

"Captain Ansalov! We meet again." Captain Janlav strides to Captain Ansalov, Belly and Beard in tow. Their rifles are strapped against their backs once more, though their elbows bear wet stains from aiming the guns earlier. "What brings you here on a fine day like this!"

"Come, Bopol!" The Poet reaches out for the reins and pats his horse on its sweaty neck. He grimaces and wipes his hand clean on his trousers. "Daughters, let us walk. For soon, I think, adults must talk."

Adults . . . Celestia must be disappointed and upset with me and Merile slipping out on our own. Maybe we should return inside.

But Merile couldn't seem less concerned about that. She slips her arm around the Poet's, and though she reaches only up to his chest, her smile is like the rising sun. It dimples her cheeks, and her teeth flash white. Seeing her so happy is almost enough to make me forget the awful Captain Ansalov and his hounds and everything else that's broken or wrong in this world. Almost. For the captain's shadow is very dark, and it almost seems as if . . . as if it were reaching out toward us.

I hurry to keep up with my older sister and her seed. I'll tell Celestia this outing was Merile's idea.

Poet's horse—Bopol, and that's a fine name for a fine horse—follows us like a tame giant, neck arched and ears bent forward. I bet he's as gentle as a lapdog. Though unlike some lapdogs, like Rafa and Mufu, he doesn't bounce after his master but walks majestically. I wait for either the Poet or Merile to speak, but neither does, not until we reach the wooden rail before the stables.

As Bopol extends his teeth to gnaw at the rail, the Poet reaches out for the saddlebags and unclips the closest one. He rummages through the content. Merile's big brown eyes sparkle. "Did you bring me something? Did you?"

I'm getting curious, too. Or I want to get curious. I only glance at the two captains, who talk in voices so low they don't carry this far. But there, beyond the gates, I see more soldiers arriving, some of them riding ponies, others sitting on a horse-drawn cart. There's one, two, three . . . five of them, I think.

"Indeed I brought you a fitting present." The Poet pulls out from the bag a red silk scarf. He flourishes it before Merile so that the sun shines through it and I can see the shape of his face, now colored red, behind it. "The very thing is Moon-sent!"

"White." Merile's forehead wrinkles. She taps her sabot against the gravel. "But it's not white!"

"Ah yes, it's not the color of snow, that is something we should know. But wear it about your person at all times, and there might come a day that you'll be all smiles."

Merile gingerly accepts the scarf. She must be as puzzled as

I am. Why would her seed give a Daughter of the Moon something we're not supposed to wear! Though, since we left the Summer Palace, we've worn the gray blankets that Elise turned into coats quite a few times. Celestia says Papa doesn't mind that, as otherwise we would have frozen or at least gotten sick during the winter.

"I also brought chocolates with me, but I confess that I couldn't resist the temptation. While I was crossing the nation, I did sample a few. But worry not, my sweet Merile, I know the selection varies. With great care I picked only the bitter ones, leaving you the ones filled with berries."

Merile accepts also the chocolate box that, having traveled through the empire, is rather dented. "Alina, hold this, will you?"

And so I become the guardian of the treat that Sibilia has been longing for for months. Maybe she'll finally cheer up.

"Poet . . ." Merile pulls him with her toward the flowerbed flanking the stone steps. I quickly peek inside, through the open doorway. Boots and Tabard guard the main stairs. Celestia argues with them, Elise and Sibilia behind her on the higher steps. I turn my gaze aside before they notice me noticing them. They'll be so mad at us! "I want to show you something Elise taught me."

"But of course," the Poet says, and then he calls over his shoulder at Bopol. "You may rest now, my steed. You kept up a decent speed."

Merile snaps the longest coltsfoots from the flowerbed that no one has tended in a while. I'd help her, but I can't, not without lowering the box of chocolates. Rafa and Mufu settle behind us. They'll watch over the two captains and the hounds and let us know if anything of importance happens in the yard.

"Crown. I learned how to braid a crown! And as you're a prince, I want to make you one!" Merile beams at the Poet as she struggles to weave the stems together. "Short. These are a bit short. Elise says it'll be easier to braid from dandelions . . ."

"Ah, dandelions," the Poet sighs. And now that I look at him closer, he looks very tired. When Merile concentrates on the weaving, his smile tightens. His clothes, though sewn of velvet and silk, are stained and wrinkled. He also stinks quite a bit. "Yours is not the glory of the first summer days. Yours is the whiteness that disperses in the wind. There is nothing a single man can change, no matter how he prays. Sometimes, in the end, ignorance is more kind."

The way he speaks . . . So sadly, as if he'd lost something he much liked. Though it might be that I'm just imagining this, for as Merile braids the crown, his smile broadens.

Rafa growls. Mufu barks. I turn around to see the soldiers on their ponies and the cart enter the yard. The day fills with their harsh laughter and . . . clucking. Yes, there, on the cart, is a cage that holds speckled brown chickens and a redheaded rooster. And behind the cart, with a rope around its neck, oinks a real pink and black pig!

"Look!" I point at the chickens and then at the pig and then again at the chickens. Now I know what sort of sounds they really make!

The Poet bends down on one knee before Merile. "Do not look. Do not look back. Do not think of what you may now lack. Keep those you love hidden, deep in your chest. Cherish that which you love the best."

She embraces him, the unfinished coltsfoot crown swaying in one hand. I want to embrace this dejected man, too. He can no longer hide it. But he's my sister's seed, not mine. My seed is far, far away. I don't know exactly where.

"Poet Granizol." Captain Ansalov's voice cuts through the day like a dull knife. When we turn toward him, he smiles at us. If I'd never met Gagargi Prataslav, I would call it the most terrible smile I've ever seen. Captain Ansalov's cheer, with the wind tugging at his curly hair, flapping his dirty coattails, ranks only second compared to that. "Join us inside."

"It seems that I must go." The Poet squeezes Merile's shoulders. He presses a kiss on her forehead. "Please let me depart with the deepest bow."

He gets up and does just so, flourishing his left arm, the sleeve so very red. As he turns to leave, Merile reaches out for his hand. "Talk. We will talk again, won't we?"

Maybe he didn't hear her. Or maybe he did but doesn't dare to answer. He gently shakes himself free, and as he strides to the two waiting captains, I can only guess.

"I'd be very curious to know what they're talking about," Sibilia says once we're back in the drawing room, her tone more bitter than any potion Nurse Nookes ever tricked me into swallowing. My sister paces to the arching window closest to her room and glances out. Though, no matter how many times she'll do so, she will see only the garden and the lake. None of the windows on this floor open to the front yard.

"Yes, what could they possibly discuss in the absence of their younger sisters," Olesia agrees, though Sibilia can't hear her.

Rafa scratches the door leading to the hallway beyond. I press my ear more firmly against the panel, but I can't hear a thing. In the drawing room, the ghosts sit on the white sofa nearest to the windows, a spot from which they can easily watch everyone in the room. But as Merile can see the ghosts only through a reflection, she stands before the tall mirror and stares fixedly beyond the gleaming surface. Mufu leans against her legs, ears pressed back. She's still shy about the ghosts.

"Adult things," I reply to both my sisters and the ghosts as I straighten up. I'm pretty sure that no one stands guard on the other side, but I'll stay by the door and check again in a few moments.

Celestia and Elise want to protect us from the gagargi. Though me and my sisters have gone through quite a lot since we left the Summer City, the revolution Elise has mentioned quite a few times must have affected other people, too. Merile says she saw burning houses on our way here. I don't dare to think what else might have happened. Yet I sense that many shadows have been lost, their bearers fallen limp in snow or mud.

"That man, Captain Ansalov, I do not like seeing him here." Irina clenches the top of her closed fist against her mouth.

"He is very dangerous." Olesia drifts from the sofa to Merile, to stand behind her—no, to lean over her shoulder. Mufu backs away from my sister. "Listen, little one, listen closely. Do not ever follow Captain Ansalov into the cellar, no matter what he tells you."

"The cellar?" Merile wonders aloud even as Mufu shrinks down on her hind legs and growls. "Why would I ever want to go to the cellar? Elise says it's dark there, and her clothes smelled of moldy onions for days afterwards."

I don't know how Merile doesn't see it. Hear it. Olesia's words are a warning. Not that she should have needed to tell us not to trust Captain Ansalov. Though he smiles when he addresses us, his shadow is spiteful and hungry. I would never trust anyone with a shadow like that!

"Merile . . ." It's Sibilia who speaks as she strolls to our sister, and at that moment I'm glad that I'm still watching the door, at the other side of the room. I don't remember her being as tall as she now is, but with her shoulders pulled back and her back very straight, she resembles Celestia more than I've noticed before. "What are you talking about? And to whom?"

Merile spins around, and Mufu spins with her. Her brown cheeks redden. She's spoken out of turn! Can she possibly come up with a story that doesn't reveal to our sister that we see ghosts! For if she can't, I don't know what to do! With the Poet arriving, but then with Captain Ansalov and his soldiers arriving, too, too much has happened already today without Sibilia getting mad at us!

"No one. I'm talking to no one. No, I'm thinking aloud. That's it. I'm thinking aloud."

Sibilia pats Merile on top of her head, sending her curly black hair bouncing. But she stares past her into the mirror. No, somehow *beyond,* as if . . . My sister is powerful in a way very familiar, but which I don't really understand. And yet, her shadow is fraying around the tiny pinprick holes scattered across its length.

"Irina, Olesia, reveal yourself to me. I know you are here." Sibilia pauses. Her lips press together as if she were thinking hard. "Or there, if that's what you prefer."

I bite my fist then, though it hurts quite a lot. Guilt isn't a nice thing to feel. And neither is it nice to be caught redhanded in . . . not lying, but holding back things from my sisters. How did Sibilia find out about the ghosts?

Irina merely sighs. "Well, this was bound to happen eventually. What do you think, Olesia, should we? She is not the oldest, after all."

My heart pounds heavy as I wait for Olesia to make up her mind. I understand that the order of birth is very important for Daughters of the Moon, but Irina and Olesia keep on bringing it up even when it doesn't matter. It's over a month since the last sacred ceremony and almost two until the next one.

"I shall have to consider this carefully," Olesia replies. Oh, it would be so much easier if she just agreed. But if she doesn't . . .

It will all be so very embarrassing. Sibilia will want to know why Merile and I didn't tell her of the ghosts earlier. And what will we do if she then speaks with Celestia and Elise? They'd be so very disappointed in me and Merile. I know it for sure!

"We might as well," Olesia says, and the ghosts waft together to hover behind Sibilia.

They reveal themselves exactly at the same moment. I imagine how they must look to my sister. Two elderly ladies in white, with proud, pale faces and paler hair gathered atop their heads. Faded, but strong at the same time.

"Thank you," Sibilia says, not in the least bit spooked!

Irina and Olesia glance at each other, brows arched. No doubt they expected my sister to gasp upon finding them craning behind her, seeing this in the reflection, but not with her own eyes. But our older sister looks smug instead.

She says, "Now, you can move through the walls, can you not?"

"Of course we can." Irina cants her chin up. Olesia nods curtly as if the very question were silly to begin with.

"Well, I, for one, would like to know exactly what's happening in the dining room."

"Yes! Me, too!" Merile echoes Sibilia, though the two of them never agree on anything.

I'm not sure if I really want to know. Adult things are adult things for a reason. Celestia and Elise will share everything we should know with us as soon as they return. I rub my fist, the white toothmarks there. Come to think of it, maybe Merile and the ghosts are somewhat right. Maybe our older sisters don't exactly keep secrets from us, but maybe they don't tell us everything either.

We're kind of guilty of the same thing.

Irina and Olesia glance at each other. Irina flickers, and her expression is one of fear. Olesia's shape, on the other hand, hardens. "And what would you be willing to give in exchange?"

When Sibilia speaks, her braided red hair glows. She's more than herself today. Does that sort of thing come with age? "My word as a Daughter of the Moon that I won't mention your presence to Celestia and Elise."

Which is a very curious thing to promise. Merile and I kept the ghosts' presence secret because we decided to do so. But Sibilia's suggestion makes it seem as if the ghosts don't want Celestia and Elise to know about them. I'll need to think about this later when all is not so confusing.

"Deal." Olesia reaches a ghostly hand toward Sibilia. My sister grabs it without hesitation. If she feels anything at all, she doesn't say a word. "Irina will speak in my place."

An eyeblink later Olesia is gone. Irina drifts to the mirror, to speak in her sister's place. Sibilia waves curtly at me and, thus summoned, I hurry to join my sisters with Rafa. Mufu welcomes us with nervous tail-wagging. Merile nudges her companion with her shin. "Hush, silly."

"In the skirmish of Skatanor, fought under the Crescent-lit snowfields that come summer will grow a plentiful harvest of rye, the Equal People, armed with scythes and pitchforks, triumphed against the dispirited, ill-prepared Enemy, killing eleven hundred foes and bringing their callous commander, Captain Orinov, to justice. He will be judged in a fair trial, and when found guilty of breaking the laws degreed by the Moon himself, he shall face the choice between the shameful death of a traitor or donating his soul to remedy the harm he has caused when he decided to side against our good, devoted people."

"Who's saying this?" Sibilia squints at the mirror, one thick eyebrow higher than the other. I'm confused, too. What sort of news is this? Why was Papa's name mentioned when there's no Crescent Empress to speak his will?

Irina lifts both hands up as if she were holding a scroll. Her knuckles are bony and white. "The man in the fancy red coat."

"The Poet?" Sibilia muses at the same time as Merile chimes, "My seed."

"It doesn't sound like him," Sibilia comments.

Merile licks her lips as if she's not sure whether she could and should agree with Sibilia again. Mufu stares expectantly up at her, though she must know this is no time for treats. "It really doesn't. Not his. The words aren't his, even if they come out of his mouth."

But it's not even that which bothers me the most. It's the thing the Poet said about choosing between . . . I kneel down to pet Rafa. I really don't want to think about it, but I don't think that's an option.

Irina clears her throat and glances at us from over the scroll that doesn't really exist. "Do you want to hear more? The list is very long. Olesia says he has been reading it ever since they retreated into the dining room."

I glance at Merile, then at Sibilia. Merile bends to pick Mufu up. She's confused by the way her seed speaks. I'm terrified by what I have heard.

"Yes," Sibilia says. "Do go on, and leave out nothing."

Irina closes her eyes and speaks of what her sister sees. "The resourceful people of the fine town of Opitap ambushed the convoy of the greedy Count Sukisov, who foolishly attempted to smuggle gunpowder and ammunition to the Enemy to support their ridiculous pretense of a resistance."

I don't remember hearing Count Sukisov's name before, but . . . I realize it then, the Enemy must be the people supporting Celestia. How can those fighting for the empress-to-be be called that?

"After inflicting heavy casualties on the opposing side, the Equal People escorted the justly dispirited traitor to the Winter City, where he received a fair trial. He was sentenced to pay his soul for the crimes committed against the Crescent Empire."

Merile shakes her head slowly. She cradles Mufu against her chest, chin pressed against her companion's silvery forehead. "No . . ."

I don't know what she means, and I can't think of it now. For a memory comes to me, and it's a dark, frightening one. Last summer, Merile and I saw the gagargi's engineer feed an amber bead to the Great Thinking Machine. Since then, I've been certain the gagargi wants my soul. My sisters say I'm just imagining it, but having heard the Poet's words . . .

"So, regardless of what you do," Sibilia says, tapping her fingers against her thigh, "you'll be fed to the Great Thinking Machine?"

My mouth goes so dry that when I whimper I don't make

a sound. Rafa rises on her hind legs to lean against me. It was true all along then. I wasn't imagining. I really wasn't imagining it.

"Alina?" And then Sibilia is there, squeezing my shoulder. Rafa whispers warm air in my ear, but I can't make out what she might want to tell me. "I didn't mean to . . . It's all right, my little Alina. It's all right."

I hug Rafa. How can it be all right? If anything we've heard today is true, people are dying in our name, not one or two, but many, and the gagargi is stealing their souls. And yet, the way the Poet speaks, how Irina conveys this to Olesia makes it sound as if Merile's seed believes he's delivering good news. It simply doesn't make sense.

"Is he really the only one speaking?" Merile asks.

Irina pushes the scroll aside. "Yes." Then her face—or is it only her expression and pose?—changes. Any distraction, even an unsettling one, is a welcome relief from the ghastly news.

She listens with her head held high, expression unflinching. I recognize Celestia straightaway.

She looks sickened, confused, and yet so very beautiful. That can only be Elise.

She drifts to hover very close to where Elise was, as if to protect her. This must be Captain Janlav.

And then she smiles as if indeed the news were good, and the most terrible thing is that this smile reaches her eyes. The sight of Captain Ansalov, her as him, scares me. If Sibilia and Merile and Rafa and Mufu weren't there, right next to me, I'd flee into my room, under the blankets, never to get up again.

"Perhaps we go on with the rest of the tidings?" Sibilia suggests, patting my shoulder once more, almost apologetically.

"Perhaps we do." Irina resumes her own face, and I'm happy she does so. I hadn't realized the ghosts could appear as other people. Maybe I don't really know everything about them. "It was by no means a pleasant experience for me either."

I brace myself for more bad things to come. But with Sibilia and Merile by my side, with Rafa nuzzling my palms, I will be safe. I'm safe, and as a Daughter of the Moon, I must honor the ones who lost their lives fighting for us. That's what Celestia would do.

"In the battle of Fornavav, where the enemy blood turned the snow to scarlet, the vigorous soldiers of the Equal People's army defeated the ruthless General Monzanov, who has been known to butcher innocent women and children in his mindless pursuit to support the losing side. The gallant, untiring efforts of our men yielded expected results. He was captured alive, to bring him to justice and to bring justice to those who have fallen under his cruel sword. But after a dastardly escape attempt, for the Equal People's absolute victory frightened his cowardly soul, a well-aimed bullet to his heart put an end to his deceitful life."

"Huh." Sibilia breathes deep. She pulls her arm from around me and, again, starts pacing the length of the room. With her head bent down, she bumps into the divan. She looks around, startled to find herself already by the fireplace. "None of that can possibly be right. Celestia's seed was the finest, most righteous man this empire has seen! We know what happened to him!"

Do we? Yes, I guess we do. Celestia met with her seed that day when the train halted and we got to walk around the station. She'd planned that we'd go with him. But something went wrong, and we had to board the train again, with him remaining behind.

Irina motions Sibilia to return before the mirror. My sister does so. I hug Rafa, trying not to look at my sister's shadow. I must be imagining the holes. Though I'm not. This day is full of foul things.

"We know," Irina says. "None of it is right or true. Dear daughters, this is propaganda."

"Propaganda?" Merile's voice is muffled because she speaks with her lips brushing against Mufu's gray forehead. I've never heard this word before either, but I don't like the sound of it.

"People believe what they're told to believe." Sibilia grimaces as if the words left a bad taste in her mouth. "All this talk about redeeming crimes by . . . The gagargi is feeding our supporters to the Great Thinking Machine. And now his supporters repeat his twisted words again and again, making people accept that it's perfectly fine to steal a man's soul."

Papa can't approve of that, but maybe the gagargi has never respected our father's wishes. Maybe Sibilia didn't get it right. Though I'm sure she did. I've seen the machine. I've felt its hunger. And now I know that I'm not safe in this house. The gagargi wants my soul and will come to claim it any day now.

But there must be something me and my sisters can do. Anything. I ask, "If none of it is true, why doesn't Celestia or Elise say something?"

"What could they say to make a difference?" Irina asks in return. Sibilia shakes her head, face reddening as if she had something else stinging her tongue, but knows better than to say it aloud. Merile seeks comfort from Mufu. "This is not the first house where Poet Granizol has read this scroll. He is the voice of the gagargi. And I think you have heard enough for now."

I think I've heard too much already. Rafa must sense that

I'm feeling unease. She nibbles my fingers, gently so that her teeth don't hurt me.

"Why." Merile's eyes brim with tears. "Why would my seed side with the gagargi? My seed is good. The gagargi is evil!"

Olesia appears alongside Irina. She looks . . . maybe slightly shaken. It's difficult to tell when they're so pale and see-through to begin with. "We all do what we must to survive."

"But still!" Merile insists, swallows hard. "Still!"

Irina reaches out to wipe a tear from my sister's cheek. Her finger passes through the teardrop, but Merile doesn't notice this. "You should try and forget him."

"You will not see him again," Olesia adds.

Chapter 7

Merile

Twelve. Right after the swan clock in the drawing room has sung twelve times, there's a knock on the window, a sharp and hard scratch against the glass.

"Merile..." Alina whispers, the blanket drawn so high up that only her little pallid face shows. Rafa and Mufu stir, too. They crawl the low alley between us. Mufu lies down next to me. Rafa curls against Alina's side.

"I heard it, too," I reply, hoping for the sound to simply disappear. My seed. Neither me nor Alina has slept well since my seed left, but for different reasons. I still can't make myself believe the things the ghosts said that day, my seed becoming the voice of the gagargi and supposedly being completely fine with the task. Alina is convinced the gagargi is coming for us and dreads every sound, smell, and shadow. There's nothing I can say to make her stop believing that he intends to feed her to the Great Thinking Machine.

Knock. Knock. The sound is too regular.

"What is that?" Alina's voice trembles, though Rafa licks the tears from her cheeks as soon as they appear.

I don't want to get up from the bed. I really don't, because who knows what I might find from behind the curtains. But I must or my little sister won't sleep at all and then I won't either. "Look. I'll go and have a look. Rafa, Mufu, you stay with Alina."

Alina nods. She wraps her arms around Rafa. She believes she'll be safe with my companions. Of course she'll be safe with them.

Though it's late spring already, the floorboards are cool under my bare feet. They creak, too, and with every step the smell of the old house, that of moist dust that rises from between the planks, grows stronger. When I reach the window, I hesitate to even touch the curtain. I have to firmly remind myself that I'm twelve already. I can't be afraid when Alina can see me.

I pull the curtain aside. And then, I chuckle.

"What is it?" Alina peeks out from under the blanket, and my companions peek out with her.

"A magpie!" I whisper back at them. How silly of me, to be spooked by a bird we know so well! But with my seed's betrayal, I don't know what to think of anything anymore. Though I've demanded multiple times that Celestia and Elise tell us what really happened in the dining room that day, neither has replied anything useful. Why did my seed have to go without saying as much as good-bye, but then that horrid Captain Ansalov and his soldiers could stay and overtake the old servants' quarters at the front yard? It makes no sense!

The magpie studies me with its beady eyes. It tilts its head to the right, and behind it, mist rolls in from the lake, the white, light blanket creeping up the hill, toward the house. Soldiers. In the Moon's soft light, I can see no soldiers patrolling the paths.

"What are you up to?" I ask the magpie. A few pale rays reach out to me, all the way up to the third floor. Yet, Papa's embrace is lacking, dulled by distance.

The bird hops off the sill. The white-striped wings split the night as it swoops down into the garden. Then it pecks the lush new grass, as if waiting for me. Moon's light strengthens, and . . .

I know it then, and I know it for certain. Papa is summoning me. This is the night my sisters and I will finally leave the house. With the magpie waking us up, there's no doubt about it.

I dash back to Alina, excited. "It's the witch."

"Oh, that's wonderful!" Alina squirms up to sit cross-legged before me, with poor Rafa struggling to stay on her lap. "Did you see her?"

"No." I frown. That I didn't. But if I've ever been sure of anything, it's this. With the curtain still partially drawn, I can feel Papa's call clearer with each heartbeat. "But I'm sure she sent the magpie, and she must have Papa's blessing."

"I don't know . . ." Alina stares past me at the window. A beam of Moon lights the way there. Rafa and Mufu climb up to her sides, every single muscle tense. They sense this night is different, too. "Should we wake up our sisters?"

Hesitant! Why is she so hesitant when we're about to finally leave the house! Though we haven't seen the witch since she first showed up here, she promised to help us. The magpie, however, has checked on us almost every day. It's her companion, just as Rafa and Mufu are mine. But, as we haven't told our older sisters about the witch and her promise . . .

"No." I firmly walk to the sofa chair, pull my day dress up from the pile of clothing heaped there, and slip it on. Wrong. In the unlikely case that I might be wrong, I don't want our older sisters to know anything about the witch and the magpie. "Not yet. I'll go and see if it's really her. And when it is, I'll send Rafa back for you."

"You promise?" Alina's voice is so frail, her eyes so wide. "You wouldn't leave me here alone."

I return to her and my companions and kiss their foreheads in turns. I would never ever abandon any one of them. "I promise."

A glint of silver draws my eye. The hand mirror shines softly in the Moon's light, on Alina's nightstand. I grab it with me, just in case I run into the ghost. Not that I trust them even if I agree with them on certain matters, but they do have some very useful skills.

I lead Rafa and Mufu through the silent path across the drawing room. The path never stays the same for long, and Alina and I must search it anew every day. Game. Celestia would have us think it a game, but that it's not. She had an escape plan, but I think it fell apart when Captain Ansalov decided to stay in the house. If she's got another one, she hasn't shared it with us. I understand she wants to protect Alina from everything, including disappointment, but me! She should tell me the truth, especially when I ask her directly. Maybe the ghosts are right when they say that you can never really trust your older sisters. Though there's something bitter in their comments, something that makes me weigh their words carefully.

I've almost reached the door leading to the hallway when a soft, wet sound carries to my ears. Rafa tucks her thin tail between her hind legs. Mufu turns to look over her shoulder, toward Elise's room. I tilt my head, not daring to voice the question.

Then I recognize the sound, and I wish I hadn't. My sister is crying, though she smiles the days through. She pretends that the arrival of Captain Ansalov and his soldiers changed nothing, though it definitely did. Awake. And also, since my sister is awake, I could go and tell her about the witch, the magpie, and Papa. But . . .

Rafa raps the door leading to the hallway. Mufu nods. My dear companions agree with me. It would take too long to explain to her what's going on. Alina can do it, once I send Rafa back for her. Even if they don't believe her, they will at least follow my companion out to look for me.

I turn the door handle. It's stiff and, for a moment, I fear it won't budge. But my sisters and I have been stranded in this house for three and a half months already. The guards may worry about someone galloping to our rescue—not that that's likely anymore with the gagargi feeding all our supporters to his machine—than us simply walking out one night.

The handle shifts and the door opens, creaking, but not screeching. I tiptoe through the length of the hallway. My sabots don't make a sound, but my companions' nails click against the planks. I hope it's not the sort of sound the guards are drawn to come and investigate.

This thought in my mind, I stop at the top of the stairway. I gaze into the awaiting darkness. Though only two flights of stairs and one more hallway separate me from the night and the Moon's light, the way out feels much longer. Going out on my own . . . Millie is asleep for sure, but what about the others? In addition to Captain Janlav and the five guards that came with us on the train, Captain Ansalov brought with him five more soldiers, and I don't like the look of them in the least. Hounds. He's got his hounds with him, and though he keeps them locked in the stable, he sometimes lets them out in the garden. They're vicious beasts, and they remember our scent. But if we flee tonight, Papa will guide them off our tracks.

I boldly stride down the stairs and enter the hallway that always reeks of cabbage, beetroot, and pork. And then, I find myself under the dark gaze of the gagargi.

Posters. I chastise myself as I slip past the posters that Captain Ansalov has glued all over the house and across the garden wall, too. I hadn't known that Alina could read before she started asking what the messages written in bold red letters meant. I know the words, but what's written and shown in the posters isn't right at all.

In the poster announcing Age of Equality, muscular men and women work side by side in golden fields, in clean white clothes that for some reason reveal their arms and legs and bellies. They smile as though they couldn't be happier about the gigantic shape of the gagargi looming behind them, arms spread as if he were about to cradle them. Elise says the peasants are happy to be free of their lords and ladies, but I wonder if they understand that their new master is much harsher.

In the Gagargi of the People, the gagargi writes a letter under the full Moon. His black hair is braided against his head, and his robes are blacker than the night. He holds a white quill pen—it must be made of a swan feather—in the air, as if waiting for Papa to speak to him, though I'm sure Papa never has and never will!

And then there's the Age of Progress poster, the one that Alina always runs past, and to be honest, I don't like to look at it either. Scarf. I fidget with the red scarf my seed gave me that I always carry in my pocket, but never dare to wear. Tonight is different, though. I slip the scarf around my wrist and boldly face the poster. Rafa and Mufu do likewise.

The Great Thinking Machine gleams under the Moon's light. The gagargi stands before it, his smile knowing, waving at the children gathered before the machine, urging them to come closer. Action. Celestia says this one is a call for action. I'm not sure what she means. But the poster reeks of ominousness, if that's a word.

I walk past the posters quickly. Yet the images burn in my mind. They're all lies, and surely everyone sees it. The words that my seed said aren't true. The gagargi doesn't have Papa's blessing, no matter what he claims.

Stairs. I'm relieved to reach the second and last flight of stairs, to leave behind the posters, and soon this house altogether. I run down the stairs with my companions. I slow my pace only when I enter the hall.

"Shh!" Irina hisses at me.

I turn around, holding the mirror at an arm's length. Ghosts. Where are the ghosts and what are they doing up this time of the night? There, Irina hovers before the library with Olesia, behind the mute Millie, who has her ear pressed against the door. She keeps her finger raised to her lips. What. What can possibly be happening inside the room?

"What does it mean?" Beard's rough voice is low, dimmed by the door and the wall no doubt, but I'd recognize it anywhere. "Read it again. Will you?"

"The great Gagargi Prataslav." Someone chants, and many voices join the chorus. It's almost as if both the train guards and Captain Ansalov's soldiers were gathered in the library. But usually the guards and soldiers avoid each other! What can be going on? "The Gagargi of the People."

Then I recall, there was a rider earlier today, one of Captain Ansalov's men. We've grown used to seeing riders come and go to the garrison, but it seems this one bore a message in addition to the new set of posters. A thought occurs to me. Maybe this is why the magpie woke me up, to hear whatever is happening in the library. Or maybe I'm supposed to both hear this and then go out? That must be it.

I pad to stand next to Millie. The ghosts make way for me, but the servant doesn't notice a thing. Maybe she's turning blind in addition to being mute already.

"Did it say when it'll take effect?" Boots asks when the cheering ends. I know it's him because the words are followed by the heavy stomp of his feet. Though I'd want to, I can't make myself forget what Elise told me about him. To grow up in a mine, so deep underground, no wonder he's hesitant to ever enter a room first. "And was it mentioned if it affects children who are already on their sixth year? My Marisa . . ."

"My compeers, you heard the same words as I did." Scythe. The mellow voice that hides a scythe interrupts him, and I'd recognize it anywhere. Captain Ansalov. Does this mean that all the guards and soldiers are indeed in the library? That would be so very convenient. "The machine knows everything. The machine cares for us all. This is the end of injustice."

Injustice? The word burns me, and if I weren't out on my own, in the middle of the night, I'd march in the room and confront him. The gagargi's men are the ones who shot Mama dead and broke the rules that had been set in place for everyone's benefit. It's them that dragged the lords and ladies out of their houses and herded them before the gagargi to be judged for crimes that don't even exist so that he could apparently justly feed their souls to his machine!

"For every soul we selflessly share, two more are guaranteed a good life." It's the utter agreement in Captain Ansalov's voice that frightens me the most, the willingness to serve the gagargi regardless of the orders. But then again, Elise says that he's the kind of man that likes breaking things, people, too. "No price is too great for such freedom. No price is too great for a better world."

The ghosts shake their heads. They're not believing a word said either. How could a coup like this, Mama's murder, possibly lead to peace? How could anyone ever forget all the death and those dead? Even if Celestia will at some point claim her throne from the gagargi, how can the people continue on from where they left, as if no hand had ever grabbed a weapon, no soul was ever pulled from an unwilling body!

"I shall read the manifest once more and address your questions, one at a time."

Mufu nudges the back of my knee. I should go. Outside, the magpie—or the witch—and Papa must be already waiting for me. But I need to hear with my own ears the gagargi's plan. How can I otherwise protect my sisters from him?

"On this first day of the fourth month, with the greater good of the Crescent Empire and the Equal People in mind, I—Gagargi Prataslav, the Gagargi of the People, thus appointed by the Moon himself—degree a law to be equally shared with every subject of the Crescent Empire, effective immediately."

Shiver. I do shiver, despite Rafa and Mufu huddling against me. Now I understand why the guards are so confused. Evil. Evil lurks beneath the tide of words.

"Together we have glimpsed the new Age of Equality and Progress, and the Great Thinking Machine shall forge us the brightest future. But as all machines need fuel to continue functioning, so are we also privileged to together provide for ours. My brothers and sisters, my fathers and mothers, I humbly appeal to you to let every other child become a part of the empire."

Surely he can't mean! From the corner of my eye I catch Irina and Olesia shaking their heads. They don't want to believe it either. Because it's a whole different thing to yank a grown man's soul from his body than . . .

"A parent may choose which of their children with an unanchored soul to honor with this privilege. It is to be noted that families with one child only may choose whether they wish to grant their child the ultimate opportunity of fueling the greater good."

Captain Ansalov sounds happy to deliver this horrid news of a tax that demands every other child to be fed to the machine! My heart jolts as I think of Alina . . . No, my little sister is over six already. She's exempt.

"As we are all equal before the Moon, no title or rank shall be a reason for exception."

The words. Then I think of the words and the man who wrote them and the man who read them aloud. That day in the pavilion, when he first presented his machine to Mama, he fed it a grown man's soul. Since then, he's been stealing souls from the people loyal to my family. His evil knows no limit. There's nothing preventing him from falsifying Alina's age and saying that we lie about the naming ceremony ever having taken place, though he himself performed it.

"The machine belongs to us all and benefits every one of us."

Leave. Alina and I must leave the house now that it's still possible. The gagargi, he will be back, and he shall demand her soul. Papa must know of this. Yes. That must be why the magpie knocked on our window this night of all nights.

As Captain Ansalov continues reading the gagargi's manifest, I tiptoe to the back door with Rafa and Mufu right behind me. Both Millie and the ghosts are so concentrated in eavesdropping that they don't notice me leaving.

I slowly push the door open. The spring night, alight with a half Moon, greets me with moist, warm air that tastes like upturned soil and new grass. There's not a hint of cigarette smoke, none of liquor or horse sweat either. As all the guards are really in the library, the hounds must be locked in the stables.

I slip out, leaving the door ajar.

Magpie. On the porch's railing perches a magpie as black as the night, as white as winter Moon's light. It stares at me, beady eyes glinting with a shrewd savviness that is very familiar.

"Witch at the End of the Lane?" I dare to barely voice the question, for the air smells of freedom, so sweet I must lick my lips.

The magpie nods.

Mufu rises to her hind legs, leans against my knees, and pokes me with her nose. Rafa turns to stare at me expectantly. They want me to hurry. I ask the witch, "What do I do next?"

A thick beam of the Moon's light sets the path leading away from the house ablaze. Didn't Celestia once say that the Moon and the magpie—the witch—are old allies? Yes, she did say that. And the witch helped us once before already, when Alina got sick during the train journey.

I'm sure of it then. Together, the Moon and the witch are helping me and my sisters flee.

"Go. Go fetch Alina," I whisper to Rafa. "Go and get my sisters."

My companion stares in turn at the misty garden and me.

Then she slips through the narrow crack of the door. I want to wish her good luck, but I won't. Better not to make too much noise.

The magpie hops twice along the railing, then takes off. It glides over the wet lawn, wings beating slowly. I hurry after the bird with Mufu. Rafa will lead my sisters to me.

I stride the stone steps two at a time, toward the iron gate that bars the way to the lake. The garden wall casts thick shadows, but my path keeps me out of their reach. As I leave behind the house the color of a bruised peach, no one calls after me. The guards and soldiers are still in the library, too confused to care about me and my sisters. Freedom. For the first time in months, I feel something akin to proper freedom. Mufu trots beside me, fur silver under Papa's light, and everything is at last as it should be!

Gate. And then I'm but a mere three steps away from the gate. The magpie lands on the handle. The simple iron rod budges under its weight.

The gate has always been locked before. But tonight, the world is different, and I dare to hope. Dream. As if I were in a dream, I drift toward the sound of the gentle waves washing against the lakeshore. I reach out for the handle. Red. My seed's scarf is red around my wrist.

My fingertips touch the cool metal. A stink of rye liquor and sweat floods my nostrils. A mountain of a man waddles forth from the wall's shadows, a rifle cocked against his shoulder.

"You halt right there. You halt right there, girl, or I'll shoot you dead."

Chapter 8

Sibilia

Hi Scribs,

I know without you reminding me that I haven't written a single word in the last six days. Trust me, it's for a very good reason. Everything has been horrible and getting even more so since the INCIDENT. I don't actually want to talk or write about it. But I'm willing to detail the resulting consequences. Though be warned, Scribs, I might have to pause at a moment's notice. The guards keep on checking on us at odd hours.

It's tough to write in the dark, so please ignore any poorly stroked line or the more than likely smudges. Even though both of the chandeliers are lit the long days through, the corners of the drawing room remain so shadowy that I don't want to even glance that way. My sisters and I are constantly on edge, and so are the guards and soldiers. Even that dreadful Captain Ansalov is terrified, but for a different reason.

This is of no use, Scribs. I must tell you more: why it's dark and why my sisters and I are confined to the drawing room. Otherwise you won't understand why I've come to hate this house so much more than I ever loathed the train journey. At least then we were moving and not stuck!

It's all because of the INCIDENT. The first day after, the guards painted the windows black with tar. Once this was completed, poor Millie had to sew shut the curtains in the drawing room and in our chambers, too. Yesterday, when my sisters and I were escorted out for our daily walk in the walled garden, I saw the soldiers building ladders and piling planks next to the house. All this because Papa saw what came to pass, and no matter what Captain Ansalov said that night, he's afraid of our celestial father. He's properly and thoroughly frightened, though we're less than a month away from midsummer and soon all that remains is one long summer day when his power will be at its weakest (which is not a very cheery thought either).

Scribs, you might have figured this out already, but just to be clear, it's not only the light we lost, but also our freedom, and the confinement here feels worse than it ever did on the train. I couldn't sleep on the first three nights after the INCIDENT, and it wasn't because Celestia returned to sleep next to me (even if I do hate-hate-hate her, under these trying circumstances, her being closer to me does make me feel better), but because the guards kept on peeking in through the door crack. This must have tired them too, for now they sleep in turns in the drawing room, way too close for comfort.

Gone are the lazy mornings when we could crawl out of bed when we so wished. These days, after we've dressed, we have to wait for Captain Janlav and the guards to unlock the doors and let us into the drawing room. We never meet Millie alone anymore—the breakfast of the blandest sort awaits us on the oval table. We shift the gluey porridge around in the bowls till eleven. Then we dance, because routines are all that remain of the time that (now in hindsight) seemed so easy and carefree. Scribs, remember how I used to love the practices? They're ruined for me now, and at times I stumble on the steps simply because I'm so focused on holding back tears!

Did I already mention that our lunches are beyond awful? Cold beetroot soup, sometimes hard rye bread with pickled white fish (not sure what sort of fish and not sure I want to even find out). But when it comes down to choosing between the porridge and the soup . . . Ugh. Both options are bad, but so is wasting away, and so I eat, but only enough to chase away the worst hunger pangs. There's no desserts—Scribs, I'm so desperate for something sugary that I'd kill even for one spoonful of kissel. At times, I dream about chancing upon just a piece or two more of the Poet's chocolates. Though they were filled with berries, they did taste delicious.

Quarter past two Captain Janlav returns to escort us to the garden. These excursions are the only time we breathe fresh air, but even then it's under the watchful eye of the guards and Captain Ansalov's soldiers. The latter stare at us from the porch, rifles ready, and if we as much as glance in their direction, they aim the guns toward us in the creepiest sort of greeting.

At three, Captain Janlav herds us (or that's how it feels) back to the drawing room and locks the door behind him. My sisters and I idle away, till the guards bring in our dinner at six and take the rats out. An hour later, they fetch away the leftovers (none of us has felt like eating lately), and then we're locked back into our chambers. At nights, I hear Captain Ansalov's hounds howling. I think he lets them out to patrol in the garden.

To summarize, my sisters and I are now truly and really prisoners, and it's Merile's fault. Oh, Scribs, I hate my sister so much that I can't bear to even look at her! How dare she lounge on the carpet, on her back with the rats snuggling against her, as if nothing at all had happened! As if she weren't to blame for everything!

Though I can't bear to look at Alina either. She stands once more in the darkest corner of the room, her back turned to the fireplace, facing the empty walls. Ever since the INCIDENT, she's been staring intently at shadows, including ours, when she thinks no one is looking at her. I don't want to ask (I really don't even want to know) what she sees. Even if I should.

Remember what I wrote on your pages after we'd visited the Witch at the End of the Lane? About her seeing into the world beyond this one, even though she's the youngest... I mentioned this in passing to Elise, and she said it's the illness affecting our little sister's mind, nothing more. I don't know which would be better, Elise being right or the impossible being possible. At this point, I'm really not sure about anything anymore.

Because even Celestia and Elise are rattled by our desolation. They sit with their backs straight on the sofa, sipping weak tea from the chipped cups we brought with us from the train. They may be able to fool Merile and Alina with their pretended calm, but not me! Elise no longer smiles. And Celestia... as you know, Scribs, we haven't exactly talked with each other since the truth-spell episode. I don't think I can ever forgive her, I really can't. I keep on imagining what might have come to pass that day she chose to abandon me.

Standing in the knee-deep snow, my heart turning into ice.

Watching the troika get smaller and smaller. Waving Elise, Merile, and Alina good-bye, knowing I'll never see them again.

Hearing the gagargi's soldiers loading their rifles, the snow creaking under their approaching steps. Knowing it could have been me in the troika if only my oldest sister hadn't decided that I'm the one that can be sacrificed for the so-called greater good.

Yet Celestia continues to insist she had no other choice. Scribs, that's why it's not worth saying another word to her ever again unless I absolutely must.

Bang. Bang. Ah, here we go at last. Bang. Bang. Bang. The soldiers have started nailing planks over the windows. Ugh, I really hate that sound. So raw and throbbing. Almost like a tooth pain.

Merile's folly ruined everything. I keep on thinking about the plan Celestia told me about while under my spell. It sounded plausible and well thought-out, but it's no longer of any use to us. The ghosts have as much as told Alina that our sister doesn't have another one. Not even one that would include abandoning us.

But I'd better brace myself for worse. The rats will soon start barking. Even as I write this, they bounce before the windows. Any moment now . . .

Oh, yes, here goes. Yap. Yap. Yap. Oh, the Moon, help me!

Now the rats are leaping against the sewn-shut curtains, and Merile simply watches them from afar, lying limply on her side. Bang. Yap. Bang. Yap. Insufferable cacophony. All this noise will surely give me a headache. Can she just not shut them up?

In fact . . .

———————

Scribs, you won't believe this! It's all so incredibly unfair.

Elise dared to chastise ME, and for no other reason than telling the rats to shut up! Well, perhaps I threatened to skin them and make muffs out of them, one for myself and one for Merile (the latter only out of pure kindness). I might have raised my voice a tad (but definitely not in a way that anyone could consider unladylike) because Merile simply doesn't get things when explained nicely and sometimes not even then, as we both so well know.

Merile, of course, started bawling her eyes out, but at least her rats then stopped barking and rushed into her waiting arms, as if she'd indeed suffered a major shock or trauma. Perhaps I should have tried crying myself, because Elise swiftly rose up from the sofa and glided to comfort our insufferable little sister. She shot a cold look over her shoulder at me and said, "Sibilia, dear, do try to behave."

I heard her loud and clear, because at that moment the hammering paused. My joy for that was short-lived, though. For Merile glared at me victoriously from behind Elise.

I bit my tongue, because apparently being twelve gives you certain freedoms that disappear as you near your debut (and in case you've missed it, Scribs, as we're still trapped in this house, there's no way we'll make it back to civilization in time for mine). Being an adult, or almost so, I maturely turned to Celestia, because her being the oldest of us, her word is final, and she does owe me for intending to leave me behind.

Scribs, what sort of person is so very eager to sacrifice her own sister? Why didn't she insist we at least try and steal horses? I'm a decent enough rider, and so is she, and I'd rather be shot in the back while attempting to flee than happily stand before a wall, waiting for the soldiers to pull the trigger!

But Celestia simply lifted her tea to her lips, though the cup had to be empty already! I stared at her in utter disbelief. Does she not understand how badly she's hurt me, that she really should have sided with me? To me, not taking sides is just as bad as choosing the wrong one!

Wait. I know that sound. Approaching steps. The key turning in the lock.

Back again, and let me tell you, that was an awkward encounter!

I admit, making Merile cry wasn't perhaps my smartest move. Because of course upon hearing the racket, Captain Janlav had to come and check on us. Papa bless us that it was only him and Boy, not Captain Ansalov or one of his mongrel soldiers. Though, no doubt that day will still come.

Naturally, when Captain Janlav pulled open the door, my sisters and I faked that nothing at all had come to pass, and though we're very good at pretending that something didn't happen (actually just really good at pretending in general), of course we wound up looking guilty, because that's what you do when you try and appear extremely innocent.

Celestia nodded him an imperial greeting from the sofa, her chin still somehow tilted up, her teacup held high. (I don't know how she does it, but I sure don't have enough time to learn that pose before my impeding debut, wherever it may take place. Also, why doesn't she need to pee all the time?) Elise buried her fingers in Merile's hair as if she were about to braid it. Our little sister managed to hold back her sobs, but her cheeks were vivid red still. And Alina . . . still lingering in the darkest corner, she stared back at Captain Janlav and Boy, her deep-set eyes so haunted that it scares me to think what she might have seen. I think the ghosts might have been talking with her, but I can't know for sure, because I have to see their reflection to hear them and that hasn't happened in a while. They avoid me, though I gave them my word that I won't reveal their existence to Celestia and Elise, and unlike some, I keep my word, no matter what.

"Carry on," Captain Janlav said after he became reassured that nothing more than a minor family dispute had come to pass. And then he just stood there, the heels of his once-fine boots firmly pressed together, as if we were soldiers under his command, as if he expected us to proceed with whatever meager daily activity he'd interrupted. As if all it took for us to resume being happy and content was his permission.

The silence stretched on, and I dreaded that he'd never leave. His gorgeous pine-brown eyes narrowed as they always do when he really starts thinking. I fidgeted with your spine, Scribs, for at that moment I dreaded him suspecting that my sisters and I were up to something (though we aren't and can't possibly be). And of course, because my hands turned instantly clammy, and him looking at me makes me clumsy, I wound up dropping you on the floor.

Boy shifted first, like a foal that doesn't yet have control of its limbs. I do sympathize about that, though not about anything else. Well, perhaps a bit about the pimples and scars they've left on his high, sharp cheeks. But definitely not for the voice that seems to have gone missing in action.

Captain Janlav simply watched Boy lurch toward you, Scribs. Perhaps he thought Boy would just pick you up and hand you over to me. But I knew that in his ungainliness, he'd most likely accidentally open you and then . . . he might see my writing!

I reached out for you, Scribs, as fast as I could. But Boy

was already bending down to retrieve you. He lifted his gaze (he has gray, rather large eyes) to meet mine, and our fingers met against your leather cover, in a brush of skin, so warm and sweaty.

I flinched back and, if I hadn't been sitting already, I would have surely collapsed on the floor. He did likewise, but with a guttural, breaking yelp (no wonder he never speaks). As I cradled you against my chest, Scribs, many thoughts I shouldn't, couldn't think crossed my mind. With everyone, and I do mean everyone, my sisters and Captain Janlav, staring at us, I felt like dying of humiliation right then and there.

It was so embarrassing! Boy retreating back to the door, his long limbs swaying every which way as if he had no bones. Captain Janlav eyeing me from under his furrowing brows. At that moment, I was certain he thought of confiscating you! And I couldn't let that come to pass. The Moon bless me if anyone ever reads your pages. You know way too much for your own good!

I did the only thing I could think of. I opened the pages at random. And though my scrawled lines cover the scriptures now, the holy words glowed under my gaze, and I knew I could summon forth the glyphs if I so wanted. Of course, I didn't dare to do so, but as I had to do something, I read the words beneath in a voice that was so steady that I don't think it actually belonged to me.

> *Come to me, join me under my Light.*
> *Let me make you strong.*
> *Let my Daughters strengthen you.*
> *Let us be stronger together.*

156 • *Leena Likitalo*

As a side note, I really like this part, and I can't wait to pronounce these glyphs, even though I have no idea what they might do and though they will most likely leave me exhausted for days. But they seem VERY important.

In any case, after the last word, I pressed you shut as if I'd just finished the section I'd been reading all along. Celestia and Elise looked genuinely comforted, though if you ask me, the former really doesn't deserve to feel good about anything. Merile dabbed her cheeks (she couldn't possibly still be crying because I threatened her rats). Alina nodded, though whether to agree with the ghosts or for some other reason altogether, I couldn't tell. But it was the guards' reactions that sent shivers down my spine. Boy stared at me in wonder, pimpled cheeks blushing, and Captain Janlav . . . he shook his head slowly, as if the reality of our existence, the roles we each have to play, had just dawned on him.

It's only starting to become clear to me now as well. But there's too many thoughts swirling in my head for me to go down that path. I must finish telling what happened first before I can think of the accidental brush of skin against skin and that waltz I once shared in secret with K, and how under our changed circumstances I might never get a chance to kiss a boy, let alone experiment with anything else that's still forbidden from me.

Enough! I shall finish this account first. Deal, Scribs?

Captain Janlav and Boy left without saying a word, locking the door behind them. My sisters and I listened to their fading steps. The hammering resumed before the steps could have possibly reached the stairway.

I counted to one hundred before I dared to speak. "Are they gone?"

Alina tiptoed to Merile and sat down cross-legged next to her. The brown rat crawled onto her lap. She wrapped her arms around it. "They're walking past the library. Going out."

I sighed in relief only then. The danger was over. And Scribs, I knew I was right. My sister is definitely talking with the ghosts, or at least the ghosts are still talking to her. Perhaps Alina can ask the questions I have in mind without alerting Celestia and Elise about the ghosts' existence. Though I don't trust them, they might know something useful.

I don't trust Celestia either, but I bet she knows less than she pretends to know.

———

Back again. The dinner was horrid, as usual, but at least the hammering has paused. And the rats are still out with the guards. I really hope that one of Captain Ansalov's hounds snatches them for a snack. Or perhaps not, because then Merile would bawl till she'd waste away, and though I still hate her, I . . .

I don't want to lose her, any of my sisters, to be honest. Not even Celestia, though I may have written things contradicting with this statement in the past.

Scribs, I know I've mentioned the INCIDENT multiple times without sharing the details with you. Now that I can think straight (or relatively straight) again, I'm going to tell you what came to pass that night, before I forget anything or add something that really didn't happen.

What's behind my newfound courage?

You recall when I dropped you today, Boy reaching out for you, our fingers accidentally brushing? It made me think . . . I miss the life we once had. I miss K (may he have fled in time to avoid being fed to the Great Thinking Machine) and living in a palace and being pampered. But all the things I've been looking forward to for the past year—my debut, the balls to come, waltzing the nights away—there's a real chance that none of it will come to pass. It's very much possible that my sisters and I will never leave this house. A morbid thought, isn't it?

I don't want to write about the bad things and speculate of what might follow them, in case my words become a prediction of sorts. But today I started thinking, if my sisters and I were to meet our end in this house, I want someone (that someone being you, Scribs) to know what led to our fall. I don't want to be simply wiped out from history as happened to Irina and Olesia.

Drat, my handwriting is shaky. Can you make out the words still? I hope you can't and yet, at the same time, I hope you can. So, do tell me if at any point my handwriting veers toward unreadable.

Here we go then.

Six days ago, at midnight, Elise heard a timid knock on her door. I know it happened for sure because I've talked with Elise about it on multiple occasions, and though she mightn't always tell me everything, she doesn't make up things like our younger sisters do, and neither does she omit important bits like Celestia does.

I mustn't get sidetracked. I must not!

Elise, who was awake at the time for reasons she wouldn't share with me (what is it with all my sisters keeping secrets from me these days), glided to the door. Behind it, she found Alina, and our little sister was even more agitated and incoherent than usual. She prattled about a magpie and the witch and shadows of all sorts, and Merile being gone.

Elise, the Moon bless her for being the sensible one for once, managed to coach the relevant details out of Alina. Mainly that Merile had wandered out into the garden with her rats. Upon learning this, Elise promptly proceeded to wake up Celestia and me.

I was still rubbing sleep from my eyes when we heard the commotion from downstairs. Boots pounding. Doors slammed. Shouts smothered by the walls. Without a word said, Celestia soared out of our room. Elise, Alina, and I rushed after her, into the drawing room. But we caught only a glimpse of her white negligee's hem as she disappeared into the hallway beyond.

I've never been as out of breath nor has my heart struggled to keep up as much as when I stumbled down the two stairways, then past the wide-open door of the library. I halted to catch my bearings when we reached the back door that stood ajar. Elise boldly pushed the door fully open. I followed her to the porch with Alina.

The night wrapped around us like a suffocating, wet blanket, but the sky was alight with our father's half-revealed face.

"Father, bless your daughters," Elise whispered, and then she skimmed down the porch's steps, toward the barked orders muffled by distance. Our father lighting our way, Alina and I hurried after her, across the damp lawn, down the stone steps, to the orchard where the black shapes of the trees and bushes bowed under the soft spring rain.

Oh, Scribs, I shall never forget the scene we witnessed that night.

The Moon, though only growing, shone with his full might as Merile stood before the locked iron gate, Captain Ansalov and his mongrel soldiers circling her, Captain Janlav and his men doing likewise. She held her arms out to her sides, with her head tilted back, a glittering cap of raindrops on her black curls, and it was as if she were completely unafraid of the weapons aimed at her.

Scribs, if you reveal what I'm about to write next to anyone, anyone at all, even under the greatest distress, I'll scorch your pages and shred you with the dullest knife. Understand this? Good.

As Merile shifted to defiantly stare at Captain Ansalov, she looked so very brave and beautiful that I did envy her! Yes, Scribs! I envied my otherwise so despicable sister, because out of all of us she'd acted, or at least tried to act, whereas the rest of us have remained docile and tame. For a good reason, too. But still!

Onward. I must go onward, though this is where things get darker.

"Stay back," Captain Janlav shouted at Elise, Alina, and me, or that's what I thought then. He and the guards must have arrived to the scene mere moments before us, for though they had their rifles drawn, their aim was still amiss. Within the next few heartbeats, they took places right behind Captain Ansalov's men with a grimness that revealed that they'd been to battle before many times in their lives.

"Stay back," he repeated, though Elise, Alina, and I had obeyed him the first time around. But then I saw Celestia stepping forth from the shadows of the gnarly apple tree by the gate. She strode before Merile, to protect our foolish little sister with her own body. In the searing white light of the Moon, she looked akin to a swan poised to strike.

The world held its breath, or that's how it felt. I could hear everything, the sounds faint and loud. The squeak of triggers under sweaty fingers. The howl of Captain Ansalov's hounds, barred in the stables. I smelled and tasted the night, too. Hot and humid with traces of iron and salt. Wet grass and ground and branches snapped under hasty heels.

"You shall not take my sister's life," Celestia announced, and her gaze promised a storm to come for anyone who dared to argue against her. I could tell the mongrel soldiers were afraid of her, for some of them lowered their aim.

"Compeers, don't listen to her," Captain Ansalov replied, and of all things, he sounded amused. "Though she may be the oldest Daughter of the Moon, she has forsaken her people. She cares not for you, only those she calls her own."

What an insult, and yet my sister didn't deny his words. I glanced quickly at Captain Janlav. He motioned his soldiers to keep their aim, his own rifle pointed at Captain Ansalov's chest, right between the two rows of brass buttons. "Will someone explain what's going on here?"

It was at that moment that I realized that if Alina hadn't woken up Elise, if Elise hadn't woken up Celestia, if Celestia had arrived at the scene just a moment later, Captain Ansalov would have had Merile shot already. And . . . it wasn't only my little sister in danger, but all of us!

I felt faint, and time seemed to slow. It was as if every image, smell, sound, and detail were being permanently, forever, imprinted in my mind whether I wanted them or not. And I wanted the moment to rather last than abruptly end in bullets. Scribs, this might sound silly, but I've found the simple act of living sweet and to my liking, which is cruel, because now I know for sure that my sisters and I may not have that many days left to live.

"Certainly," Captain Ansalov said, as if doing so pleased him immensely. Out of all the men in the orchard, he was the only one without a weapon. "We are under the great gagargi's personal order to shoot any who may attempt to leave the premises they have been ordered to be contained in."

Encouraged by the words, the mongrel soldiers pointed their rifles again at our sisters, fidgeted with the triggers. But Celestia remained unfazed. Though her negligee has frayed thin, though the moist air pressed it so against her frame that she could as well have been undressed altogether, it seemed to me as if she were wearing armor. And at that moment I realized that she would give her life away gladly to shield my sister, and I felt great regret, too, because for weeks now I've loathed her for the very same reason.

"Who is the one who holds the highest power, the Moon who watches us from the sky or the man who wields a piece of paper that anyone may have written?" Celestia asked, and in her voice sang the swans who don't tire even when they cross the skies from north to south.

As Elise, Alina, and I were standing higher, on the root of the stone steps, behind the soldiers and the two captains, I could see only a glimpse of Captain Janlav's familiar profile, the square jaw covered by beard, the posture of a man who cared not if it was night or day, only about fulfilling his duty. But I had no trouble hearing his voice.

Captain Janlav said, "We all serve the Moon. There is no doubt about it. He wants what is best for our people. Who are we to debate his wisdom, for we can't even begin to comprehend it. It's for us to follow the orders placed by those who can hear his voice and see what he sees."

Much to my horror, he lowered his gun and marched to

Captain Ansalov. A piece of paper was exchanged, as were some muttered words. I don't know what they agreed on, but I dreaded what might follow.

It may have been the longest moment of my life.

"I see," Captain Janlav said in a dry voice when he finally handed back the paper. He turned to signal his men, a frown marring his forehead. But before he could speak, Merile did so.

"I wasn't trying to flee." My sister shuffled next to Celestia, the black rat flanking her as though it could really protect her. "Walk. I was merely taking Mufu for a walk."

It was as if Captain Janlav hadn't heard her. He retreated back to his men. Much to my and Elise's shock, he motioned them to lower their rifles. Captain Ansalov's soldiers did no such thing. I felt Alina pressing against my side, but I couldn't comfort her then. Not when I needed someone to tell me that all would end well.

"Reasons behind actions don't matter." Captain Ansalov spoke louder again. "There are orders that must be followed. It's not for one man to think whether he is right or wrong or whether it pleases him to do so. For hesitance only leads to the ruin of common good."

Celestia wrapped an arm around Merile, drew our sister before her. Merile crossed her arms under her chest, and as she did so her sleeves rose up. It was then that both Celestia and I noticed the scarf around her wrist. It was red as blood.

Celestia twitched ever so slightly upon seeing the gift the Poet had given Merile. She'd called it inappropriate and insulting before. But now, a calmness I knew to mask high-stake calculations fell upon her. I pinned my hope on her.

"Wait." My sister's one word contained so much power that I was sure it was our father who spoke. "That is not the only order."

Time stood still again, but not as long as it did before.

"You may be the empress-to-be," Captain Ansalov sneered as he replied to my sister. He had his hand raised already. One motion, and shots would be fired, I was sure of that. Even Captain Janlav could do nothing to stop him. "But your words have no power here. Not in the house, not even in the light of the Moon. We have our signed and sealed orders. We obey the great gagargi."

"So I have been told," Celestia said, grabbing Merile's wrist. She held it up so that no one could miss the red scarf, despite my sister trying to tug her hand free. "My sister is under the great gagargi's personal protection. Do you not see what is before your own eyes?"

The mongrel guards gasped. Their holds on the rifles slackened. They craned at Captain Ansalov, but it was clear now. They saw the scarf as something much more than an ill-picked fashion accessory. Bloodred like their gloves.

"I wonder . . ." Captain Ansalov muttered. His expression stayed the same, pleasant and moderate, but no doubt his men's disobedience infuriated him. "Tell me, how did you come by that thing?"

Merile pulled her hand free. She pouted at Celestia as she rubbed her wrist, as if it simply hadn't dawned on her that she'd ever so narrowly escaped being shot. "Seed. It's a gift from my seed. Whatever for you that information need."

"A gift from the gagargi's voice himself?" Captain Janlav wondered aloud, and it took me a while to get it, why he'd said such an obvious thing. He'd said it for the benefit of everyone present, in case they'd somehow missed the connection. "A favor not to be lightly dismissed."

The Moon's light slanted and brushed against Captain

Janlav, as if welcoming a long-lost son home. I think it was Papa's way of saying that though under the gagargi's orders, Captain Janlav would keep us safe for as long as he could.

"Shall we not return indoors now that this unfortunate misunderstanding has been sorted out?" Celestia suggested, and without waiting for an answer, she guided Merile past Captain Ansalov and his men, toward the path leading back to the house.

"Considering the circumstances, I couldn't possibly allow you to walk back unescorted," Captain Janlav said to her, then to his men, "Please accompany the daughters to their rooms."

Celestia and Merile had just about reached Elise and me then. Beard and Belly and Tabard and Boots fell beside us before I could as much as even blink. The next thing I knew, my sisters and I were escorted up the hill. Prisoners, yes, but alive.

"Compeers, at ease. I commend you on your vigilance," I heard Captain Ansalov say behind us. "Captain Janlav, a word with you."

Though I yearned to return to the house the fastest, to pretend I was safe for a moment at least, I wanted to, needed to hear the conversation between the two captains, too. As I stumbled up the slippery stone steps, I strained my ears. But I couldn't hear a thing.

Scribs, I really need to ask Alina to talk with the ghosts. We need to learn what sort of understanding the two captains reached, and the sooner the better.

———

I can't sleep yet, Scribs. I have a bad conscience. Lately, I've had a lot of time to think, and having written what happened on that almost fateful night, I've come to realize that I may have acted just a little bit immaturely myself.

For weeks and weeks, I loathed Celestia, and a part of me still does so. My sister chose Alina, Merile, and Elise over me. Had things turned out differently, I might have been shot on that blue winter day alongside General Monzanov. But that's not how things came to be, and it's no use being mad about something that didn't happen. Or that's what I tell myself. And you.

Of course even the thought of being discarded like that hurt me immensely. But I've finally understood the rational reasoning behind my oldest sister's decision, and now I'm ashamed.

Remember when I speculated about Celestia having been under the gagargi's spell? What if that wasn't the end of his evil, what if he further exploited her while she was unable to comprehend which ideas were her own and which came from him? Yes, I mean what you think I mean, but I don't want to write those horrid words on paper. If Celestia wants to keep it a secret, then I must respect her wish.

But, you should ask me: what makes me think that the gagargi is guilty of more?

I'll tell you. You recall the visit at the witch's cottage, the bargain my sister made with her, the bloody aftermath. What if the gagargi's seed had taken root in my sister's womb? What if the witch helped her to get rid of it? What if my sister hasn't been since then suffering from the most irregular wretched days, but instead a condition much more severe?

As soon as I realized this, saw the pieces I somehow missed earlier, everything clicked together. The future of our empire rests on the shoulders of Celestia's daughters. Which she mightn't be able to bear anymore. And that's the biggest, most dangerous secret in this house, something that no one else must learn, Scribs. That's why I'll be smudging this over right now.

Celestia had to choose Elise. There was no other choice. Really, there wasn't.

Poor little Alina is so frail, with her mind rotting, clouded by things we others can't see. She won't ever be able to take care of herself. She will always need us to protect her.

And Merile . . . even if she's both stubborn and reckless, she's still our little sister, someone we must look after, though I don't always much cherish that thought.

Trust me, Scribs, protecting her was the very last thing in my mind when I confronted her the day after the incident. I had to, because she'd acted beyond selfish! I had to make sure she understood that she'd placed all of us in grave danger!

I let her hear a proper lecture, with my voice raised, and slamming my fists against the oval table to punctuate the important bits. Merile replied with a tall tale about the witch and the magpie. Though Celestia and Elise remained customarily restrained, I don't think they believed a word she said either. I told her as much.

There has been no sign of the witch since we visited her cottage. And she doesn't do favors.

Merile cried and protested rather heart-wrenchingly, and Celestia and Elise opted to rather soothe her than further chastise her. But I refused to do so, because I knew I was right. We can't possibly have anything more valuable to offer than the empress-to-be's firstborn.

Scribs, it just occurred to me that Celestia has put herself at risk already twice, first when she bargained with the witch to bring Alina back from the realm of shadows and the second time when she saved Merile. Of course I can't know it for sure, but I think that if she could, she would do so also . . .

No, I know that if Celestia had a choice, she would save me, regardless of the cost.

I'm much comforted by this thought. For lately, I've harbored such resentment toward her that I've wished ill things to befall her. Good thing she hasn't spoken to me and I haven't spoken with her that much either. She'll never need to learn how much I hated her for a while.

But I don't hate her anymore. No, I respect her.

Scribs, I'll go to bed soon, and I promise I'll speak with her then. I'll tell her I've forgiven her, and that if there's anything in my power to help her defeat the gagargi, then she will only need to ask. After all, we're the Daughters of the Moon, both of us, and if we don't have each other's backs, then no one has.

Chapter 9

Elise

I suck in the tainted air, and though my throat shrinks and my lungs blister, I don't cry out like a newborn child who instinctively fears the first breath and the ones thereafter. I don't cherish it like an exhausted athlete who has reached the finish line at last, who has given his all, and to whom, at that moment, it doesn't matter if he lost or won. I don't gasp for more like a soldier whose wounds are beyond healing, whose bravery or cowardliness no longer matters. I hold it in because I deserve the discomfort and pain that the world has in store for me.

In the end, I must breathe out, for I'm not yet dead, and all living things must breathe. The cloud of smoke veils my sisters, the ethereal creatures in white that gather midsummer roses from the bushes that mark the border between the untended lawn and the steep, mossy slope. Though only the porch's rail and the wet, overgrown grass separate us, it feels as if they were drifting out of my reach inevitably, irrevocably.

"That good?" Beard studies me from under his bushy brows as Tabard pockets the matches with one flick of his thin wrist. Now that the windows are nailed shut, the guards sleep in turns behind the drawing room's door. It's easier for them, to be farther away from us during the nights. But during the days, they're more and more drawn to us, as if my sisters and I were animals exotic and dangerous. This is because of Sibilia.

"Thank you." I favor Beard with a girlish smile that has never betrayed me and offer the cigarette to him. This isn't my first smoke but among the first dozen still. I can't pry my chamber's lock open with a hairpin, but I can work with locks of the other kind. It was I who insisted Sibilia continue reading the scriptures after every dinner.

Beard accepts the lit cigarette back, but he chuckles as he does so, my smile the key required. I watch him suck in the smoke, unfazed by the fact that his lips are now touching that which a Daughter of the Moon enjoyed mere moments ago. The world has truly changed.

The rain has paused at last, but the swallows still seek shelter from behind the planks covering the windows, the insistent knocking of their beaks providing an accelerating rhythm for the tune of the day. From the corner of my eye, I glimpse Celestia indiscreetly waving at me. The tilt of her head signals growing impatience. Our younger sisters seem happily enough preoccupied with the roses under the watchful eye of Captain Janlav and that of Boy that might miss a thing or two.

"I must join my sisters," I say to Beard. I descend the porch's steps, leaving him and Tabard behind. But only for a moment, for their duty is to keep us safe, if not from the gagargi, then at least from Captain Ansalov and his soldiers. The two captains have reached an agreement. The soldiers are not to enter the house. The guards are to keep us inside, the only exception being our daily outings. But as the rough jeers of the soldiers carry over from the stable yard, I wonder how long that exception will last.

The grand maples and lindens of the garden hum, scattering drops that land on my shoulders. My younger sisters, including Sibilia, are barefooted, their hems knotted up just below their knees. With white roses bundled on their arms, with smiles and giggles exchanged, they look carefree and free. But I can't bear the thought of joining them, for that we are not and shall never again be.

I head toward the path that follows the shadow of the wall. Celestia notices my intention. She speaks softly with Sibilia, whose whole posture changes, gaze sharpens. Celestia must have tasked her with looking after our younger sisters. It's a curious development, to see them again on speaking terms. For Sibilia swore to me on multiple occasions that she'd never forgive Celestia for intending to abandon her.

It was this revelation that propelled me toward the crucial realization. As we drift down the same paths day after day, we might as well be ghosts already. There's nothing we can do anymore to change our fates. But we may be able to affect that of the very empire.

As Celestia and I slowly stroll past the thickets of fireweeds and thistles, I indiscreetly study my sister, her straight posture and steady steps. But before I can make up my mind about whether she has reached the same grim conclusion or not, a breeze of the colder sort carries with it a hint of smoke, revealing Tabard and Beard trailing after us. Celestia shakes her head.

"What?" I ask. Did she somehow sense what I was thinking earlier? Is she the braver one of us, the one to bring up the topic?

"Must you really?" Celestia glances pointedly at Sibilia, Merile, and Alina, barely visible through the leaves and branches of the blooming rosebushes. But I can hear their giggling still, the playful growls of Merile's dogs. What bliss ignorance is! "That is such a vile habit."

My sister is worried about me sharing a cigarette with the guards, of me negatively influencing our younger sisters! I laugh despite myself and to despise myself. It doesn't matter what I do and with whom anymore, if I socialize with those we were taught to ignore if we needed nothing from them. "Yes. I do think I absolutely must."

Celestia sighs, but doesn't say a word. She knows that none of us apart from her will have time to regret any possible ill choices.

On the even ground, plants reach out toward us from both sides of the path, but it's not because they wish us to honor them with our touch. The rigid stalks of widow's lace stick out in steep angles. The hundreds of violet fireweed flowers gape open like maws to display their thin, white tongues. Stems of lupines, blue flowers sodden with rain, arch down as if they can't take, can't bear their glory for much longer. I pause to tilt water out of one of the stems. There's so much water. It's almost as if the whole world were drowning.

"Then I shall respect your choice," Celestia says after too long of a time has passed for her reply to be genuine. She approves of the guards listening to Sibilia reading, for she thinks it's our father's voice that draws them toward us, nothing more. But me smoking with them . . . it is too much for her, even though the scriptures clearly state that before our father rose to the skies, he intended everyone to be equal under his light.

At nights when I can't sleep, I often wonder what my sister would be like as a ruler. She says she would be fair and just, but how could she be that when she hasn't really comprehended the scriptures, our father's sacred will? She says she would put an end to all wars and launch social reforms to ensure that her subjects would no longer starve and die of disease and exposure. But she hasn't mentioned how she plans to accomplish this. I don't think she has given much thought to what she would do after reclaiming her throne. Yet she vehemently opposes the equal redistribution of resources, the one solution that might just bring a better life to everyone!

A thunder of shots fired. A chorus of shattering glass. Vicious jeers. Then, a moment later, the bitter tang of gunpowder.

My sister's steps remain equally spaced and graceful, though mine falter. A quick glance over my shoulder confirms I should have nothing to fear, for both Beard and Tabard are at ease. It's just Captain Ansalov's soldiers practicing shooting once more. Knowing that man, it isn't a coincidence that they always do so during our daily outing. He's preparing his men for the inevitable.

It's cold, suddenly colder in the wall's shadow, but this is the way the path winds. Here plants must grow in the dark, here they never bloom as vivid, with as much ardor, as their kin that get to grow in the sun. But that is the way of the world. There will always, eventually, be darkness.

I know for certain that one day soon Captain Ansalov will lead us down to the cellar. He will order everyone but Celestia to stand before the wall of granite. The soldiers will take aim. They will fold their fingers around the triggers, perhaps closing their eyes as they do so. How sounds must echo in the cellar when there's no way out!

"Elise?" Celestia reaches out toward me, to touch my shoulder.

I evade her, brush a stem of thorny thistles aside, change my mind, and snap it off. It's a law of nature that all beauty must eventually die. Our ruin is unavoidable. "Do you know when the gagargi will come for you?"

Where gunshots couldn't break through my sister's composure, my question wounds her, just as I knew it would. My sister pulls her chin high, higher still until the tendons of her neck are taut. Her pale hair glistens in the afternoon sun, a reminder of the crown she still yearns to wear one day. Though she's the empress-to-be, she lacks the courage to acknowledge the truth. "That I don't know. But he will come for me as certainly as the sun rises each morning, as certainly as our father will travel the skies during the nights."

It's almost a month since Merile's folly, and with the summer solstice but five days away, anything might come to pass here without our father being able to help us, for he's just a dim, white disc in the sky. That's why this house was built here in the first place, to keep the Daughters of the Moon that have fallen from favor out of sight, out of mind. Guarded by the winters too fierce to defy. Isolated by the nightless summers.

"Will you go with him?" For I can but speculate what happens to her and us if she does. But a more frightening thought is what may come to pass if she doesn't.

If she goes, my younger sisters and I will be shot, and of this I'm more than certain. The gagargi can't risk keeping us around for fear we might one day plot to claim the throne.

But if she doesn't... Celestia seems to think herself almighty, though I haven't seen any evidence that would suggest she possessed any power to alter our fates. Is she just perversely cantankerous? Or is she playing a game, one she thinks she might yet win? As much as I wish that she would emerge victorious, we must be realistic. If she doesn't go voluntarily, the gagargi will claim her by force and us younger sisters will meet an end much crueler in the maws of his machine.

Celestia and I are as far away from our younger sisters as the walls allow. I can glimpse but strands of Sibilia's red hair from over the lush rosebushes, can't see Merile and Alina. Yet the breeze carries over their muffled chatter. The gunshots didn't frighten them. They have grown used to ... to the confinement, the presence of the guards, and even the constant threat, it seems, though I find our strangling circumstances almost too much to stand.

"I will not go with him, unless I can bring all of you with me," Celestia says, and I do wonder what can possibly be fueling her confidence. Does she believe that our father will still somehow save us? Or does she have a new plan brewing in her mind, one she hasn't mentioned to anyone? Has my sister not realized that the time for futile planning is over?

Any escape attempt would be too risky, doomed to fail. Given even half a reason, Captain Ansalov's soldiers will shoot us dead. If it weren't for the Poet's scarf, we would have lost Merile the night she thought the Moon was calling for her. Oh, my poor, silly sister!

We have come to the stretch of the wall that blocks the view to the lake. Here, the gagargi is more present than elsewhere in the garden. I suspect Captain Ansalov ordered the propaganda posters glued across the wall's length to intimidate our younger sisters. And if this was his intention, he succeeded, for these days they prefer to play on the lawn. Even to me, it's more terrifying to see the gagargi portrayed as kind and generous. For that he's not, at least when my family is concerned.

"I was thinking..." Kindness should weigh little when the lives of our people are at stake. My sisters and I have been isolated for months, isolated but safe, and the guilt I bear for this grows greater every day. It torments me during the nights. I haven't slept an eyeful in ages. Back at the Summer City, before I knew that Gagargi Prataslav was the driving force behind the insurgence, I funded the cause most generously. Since then, I have done nothing toward those who suffer the most. Now, I have decided to stop wallowing in self-pity and take action.

"Yes?" Celestia prompts me, and I do wonder: what would she do if she knew that I, too, plotted against our mother? There was a time when I considered telling her everything, during our first few days on the train when she was weak and vulnerable, when she confided in me in whispers and revealed what the gagargi had done to her. I couldn't bring myself to tell her my secrets then, didn't want to hurt the one who was in so much pain already. I can't tell her now either, because then she would refuse to hear a word more from me, and mine are words that can no longer remain unsaid.

"What if you were to go with him regardless?"

Celestia halts, as if my words were iron chains snapped around her ankles. The rain has swelled the puddles before the wall vast. She teeters on the edge of the widest of them, glances at me from over her shoulder, and I have never seen such anger in her blue eyes, fear, too. "Do you not see, my dear sister, that that would gain us nothing?"

"I didn't suggest that lightly," I say, and mean it. It's a horrible thing for me to propose that she return to the gagargi, who would put her under his spell to make her his puppet ruler and impregnate her once more. Yet she would at least survive, live, whereas those of us left behind . . . None of that matters. It really doesn't. "Since we left the Summer Palace, people have bled in our name and died in the hundreds, if not thousands. Our people are divided, and every day sees this gap torn wider.

Brothers have drawn arms against their own brothers. Fathers have wielded their sword against their own sons."

Celestia listens to me, and oh, how she looks like a good ruler should, just like our mother always did when she had already made up her mind. But she looks different, too, attentive, contemplative, somehow stronger than I recall her being. Is it because of the way she holds her arms against her sides, like wings ready to lift her in the air, above us all? Or is it only the sounds of the swans nesting on the shores of the lake beyond that make me think this? Though, if our father could turn us into swans and let us fly away, he would have done so already.

"My people are right to stay loyal to us," Celestia replies only after she is sure that I have pleaded my full case. "Our right to rule comes from the Moon himself."

And with this said, she walks into the water, the puddle that could be an ocean for her, for that is how much space she wishes there were between us, I think.

I approach her slowly, so very slowly, but I will myself not to stop. I wade deeper, the surface rippling in my wake. The water creeps up my hem. Puddles form inside my sabots. But neither discomfort me as much as the words I have no choice but to say. I owe them to our people. "And that is exactly what the gagargi tells them, too."

Nothing but silence, not the stunned sort, but of the more dangerous kind. My sister knows I'm right, but that's not enough. She needs to understand, acknowledge, and act, not simply listen. With my drenched hem, I'm no longer a creature white, but gray as the clouds above, stained as the waters below. "Do you think our people even know what they are really risking their lives for? You see the posters before us. They have seen them, too. What does the return of the rightful ruler mean to them? They see the good old days of our mother as a time when children starved to death and soldiers were sent to meet their end at faraway continents for nothing more than profit."

"This has not escaped me." Celestia steps away from me, toward the wall. She places a hand against the poster that portrays golden fields of wheat, chubby children at play. She brushes the stalks as if she could really feel them, but she doesn't touch the children. She doesn't see the brighter future that lies there right before our eyes. "Rest assured that my rule will be different."

"Will it?" I ask, so cold inside, so miserable, because I don't believe a word she says. "Will it really?"

"Yes. It will be much better than the other option." Celestia glides to the next poster. In this one, a mother is handing her newborn baby over to a country gagargi. Happy children tug at their hems, smiling. Behind them, the Great Thinking Machine puffs soft, white clouds. "He feeds children to his machine."

Of course I know this. I have read the manifest and discussed its content with her many, many times. But sometimes a ruler must make difficult choices. During our mother's reign, more than every other child died of disease and starvation. Is it not better for a mother to voluntarily give away her child before she forms a deeper bond with it? If our people are willing to pay the price, so should we be. "Sometimes the price of peace is high."

Celestia shakes her head, the movement delayed but unhesitant. "Do you think that I have not thought of that? Do you think that I allow myself to feel pity for myself, that I cry at nights because of what he has already done to me?"

What could I possibly answer? Nothing. Nothing at all. My sister is placing our family's safety above that of our people.

"Do you think he would stop killing those who displease him if I were to stand by his side?" Celestia continues in a lecturing tone. She thinks me foolish, a girl throwing a tantrum in a puddle. But it is she who isn't listening!

For even a slight chance is better than none. "Once you marry the Moon . . ."

"It will be too late." Celestia strides to the next poster, the one after, and all the way to the gate that failed to lead Merile to freedom, and I have no choice but to follow her. "By the time he allows a gagargi to perform the ceremony, or perhaps he will choose to marry me to the Moon himself, there will be no one left to stop him. Even though our father may see all that comes to pass under his gaze, his capability to interfere is not as almighty as you might believe."

I halt a step behind her, my hem dripping dirty water. Where I didn't expect this conversation to be easy, it annoys me she considers me ignorant. The Moon would have saved our mother if it had been possible. He would have sent someone to our rescue. He would have unlocked the gate for Merile. "You are only thinking of the worst possible outcome."

"Am I?" Celestia stares through the gate's grille at the lake beyond. Swans paddle along the rocky shores, necks arched, wings pressed against their sides. Their cygnets are still gray, covered by down. When my sister speaks, she does so in harsh whispers. "My dear Elise, someone has to. Unlike you, I can't afford the luxury of idealistic dreams. If I am to ever depose the gagargi, I can't leave this house with him and leave you here alone."

This is the first time since we arrived at the house that I

have seen her composure crack, glimpsed raw emotion, the human being beyond the hard shell she so dutifully maintains. I realize it then, the only way she will listen to my words is if I pry this crack wider, anger her, make her feel even more vulnerable.

"My dearest Celestia," I reply in a steady, merciless voice. "Could you stop thinking of us as children for even one moment? Some of us might have an opinion of our own in this matter. Have you ever considered asking any one of us if we would actually prefer you leaving with him?"

Celestia's fingers tighten into fists, she clenches her arms against her sides. She's . . . disappointed in me. Good. Any emotion will do. "I didn't say that because I think you a child. I said it because I want to keep you safe."

She's acknowledging my opinion at last. She will hear, really hear, what I have to say. I must take advantage of that. "And what is more important to you, your sisters or your empire? There is nothing to be gained by resisting the gagargi. Just as much as he needs you by his side, you need him to put an end to the war you started together."

She spins around so fast that I don't even see the slap coming. Her palm connects with my cheek with such force that I stagger back. My sabots slip on the mud.

"Never speak of me needing anyone apart from the Moon on my side. Never even hint again that the harm he caused was somehow my fault. Never, ever dare to suggest that I forgive the man who killed our mother and tore my empire apart."

White dots pierce my field of vision, but I see her expression clear enough, her bared straight teeth, her flaring nostrils. I have accomplished everything that I desired. I will not take my words back.

Celestia straightens to her full height, pulls her shoulders back. "I expected more of you, Elise. I expected you to be able to stand against his manipulation and propaganda. But you are even weaker than I was. You do not deserve to be called a Daughter of the Moon."

With that said, my sister turns around on her heels. She climbs up the gravel path, past Tabard and Beard, toward the house that may be the last place we ever call home. Her words, the pain she inflicted on me, cling to me.

I am a Daughter of the Moon, just like her. And at the same time, nothing at all like her.

―――――――

Celestia leans on the wall by the arching window, staring what would be out if the curtains weren't sewn shut, the panes painted black and covered with planks. I let her fume there alone and take a seat on the sofa. Either she will come to her senses or then she won't. There's nothing more I can do. The pain on my cheek is an ample reminder of that.

Sibilia tosses a log in the fireplace, there to keep company with the others. The fire exhales smoke that smells of birch pitch, an odor sweet and somehow intoxicating even. "That should do it."

"My feet will never be this big," Alina announces. My sabots clack as she stomps from the grandfather clock to the fireplace. I'm afraid that she might be right, but I remain silent. Though I have acknowledged the bitter truth, it's better they stay blissfully unaware of it for as long as possible.

"Sure they will be," Sibilia says at last. She's lying, though. Celestia's selfishness will yet prove to be the downfall of us all.

"Now, place them to dry against the fender, will you?"

"I will," Alina promises, but she wonders at her tiny feet and the size of my sabots before she takes them off and places them next to my patched stockings. Her bare feet must be cold, no doubt as cold as those of Merile, who has curled up with her dogs on the divan. The three of them seem oblivious to the drama between Celestia and me. For that, I'm grateful.

My whole head throbs, and I wonder if Celestia really slapped me so hard as to cause me a mild concussion. I settle on my side on the lumpy sofa, for there's not much else I can do about the pain than sleep it off. I don't feel that comfortable, though. My toes are blistered and corpse-white. My dress is sodden all the way up to my shins, but I can't take it off. The guards may check on us any moment they so wish, and they still do so many times a day. Though nothing really matters anymore, I don't want to be caught undressed. That much is in my power.

That and nothing else.

The truth to be admitted, I'm more than tired. Exhausted. My cheek aches. My lids droop heavy. My body feels limp. I want nothing more than Celestia to be right, there to be a way to save my sisters. But even now, I know deep in my heart, the gagargi's soldiers are fighting against those who still support us. This fighting will not cease before she returns to him.

"Elise . . ." Alina tugs at my hem. I don't know how long has passed. Perhaps minutes. Perhaps hours. Perhaps I passed out. "Are you sleeping?"

I part my lids to find my sister peeking at me from the narrow space between the sofa and the oval table. Her deep-set brown eyes shine with sincere curiosity. And perhaps with excitement, too.

"Not anymore," I reply, though speaking hurts my jaw.

"Good." Alina nods to herself. "Sibilia and Merile and I want to show you something."

I sigh despite myself. If I were to close my eyes again, I would surely fall asleep. I could leave this room, this house behind for a blessed few moments of nothing more than fabrications of my tired mind. And anything, even nightmares would be better than our existence here, better than this prolonged pretense, this agonizingly slow wilting. "Can it wait?"

"No!" Merile calls out from the floor where she's cuddling her dogs in turns. Perhaps I really did pass out. I brush my cheek discreetly. It feels warm and swollen. "Oh yes, my dear sillies! It's important, so very important."

I force my eyes to stay open, though in the grander scale of things, whatever they are up to can't matter anymore. "How about I look at it from here?"

"Maybe." Alina gnaws her thin, colorless lower lip. She glances over her shoulder at Merile. Sibilia has joined our sister there. For weeks after our sister's folly, she simply refused to speak to her. Before that she wouldn't talk with Celestia. Soon, it shall no doubt be my turn, though once we were the best of friends. "Sibilia?"

Sibilia shrugs. "It's her call."

"It's your call," Alina repeats, though I heard my sister perfectly well. Before I can reply anything at all, Alina disappears farther under the table. The next I see her, she's petting Merile's dogs. The brown dog lies on its back, begging for attention.

My younger sisters, they are a sorry, endearing lot. A part of me does understand Celestia wanting to protect them regardless of the cost. But unfortunately, that isn't an option anymore. There's no such path of action that would result in all of us leaving the house.

"Celestia, Elise . . ." Sibilia clears her throat, and her tone turns solemn, though she's not reading the scriptures. "We have something to show you."

"Oh, you do?" Celestia stirs by the once-white curtains. A few pale strands have escaped her braided crown. Other than that, there's no sign of the inner turmoil that must so torture her. She manages to even sound enthusiastic. "Well then, by all means, do show us!"

Alina and Merile giggle as they dash to her, the dogs bouncing behind them. Sibilia follows, showing a bit more restraint, but not that much. Though I try, I can't muster up enough strength to push myself up from the sofa. I can barely crane my neck enough to watch them from afar.

"What might it be?" Celestia tousles Alina's gray-brown hair. She favors Merile with a smile that doesn't quite reach her eyes. For Sibilia she has nothing but the lightest of nods. Me, she ignores as if I were no longer a part of the family.

"We found it today," Alina replies. "It's a—"

"Alina! Surprise," Merile cuts in, crossing her arms across her chest. She pouts her lips. "It's a very good surprise."

Sibilia grins. "And you'll sure like it!"

Though I have come to loathe surprises, I'm growing curious. Perhaps this is because lately every single one of them has been bad. Another thought occurs to me. I should be there by the window with my sisters, for we may not have that many good moments left together. But after what I have been thinking lately, after sharing my realization with Celestia, I don't feel like I deserve any.

If Sibilia was mad earlier with Celestia intending to leave her behind, then how would she react if she learnt that I suggested Celestia leaving and abandoning all of us in Captain Ansalov's hands?

"Can I?" Alina glances at Merile, then at Sibilia. But before either of our sisters can reply, she produces a jingling key ring from the front pocket of her dress, the very same one I worked on when it was still winter here. "Ta-daa!"

No, I'm not mistaken. It's really a key ring, dark with age. I bless the name of our celestial father even as Celestia's pale brows furrow. She can't believe what she sees either. "Is this . . ."

"It is!" Alina squeals, beaming. She waves at me to join them before the curtains. My heart jolts, but my limbs, they are slack and won't obey me. I can't go to her, even though at that moment I want nothing more. "It has a key to our room and your room and Elise's room and this room, too!"

With an effort, I manage to sit up at last. But the world spins before my eyes. I clutch the table's edge, to anchor myself to this world, a trick Lily taught me the first time I tasted wine and drank too much. For almost a month now, we have been locked in and out upon the will of others. Regaining even a sliver of freedom is more than I have dared to hope of late.

Celestia accepts the keys, but she studies our younger sisters in turns, with no joy, not even a hint of a smile on her face. "How did you come by the key ring?"

As my dizziness evades, I realize Celestia is concerned rather than pleased. I see it then, too. If my sisters have snatched the key ring from one of the guards or, even worse, one of the soldiers, they will no doubt search the house from cellar to ceiling, and then there will be guns aimed and triggers drawn. Holes in the stone walls. Blood as red as wine.

"A magpie brought them," Alina chimes, just as Merile

replies, "Rafa and Mufu found them."

Which means neither of them is telling the truth. Leaning on the table for support, I maneuver myself up on my feet. I shall join my sisters soon, once the world steadies, when the glimmer of hope we glimpsed has already dampened.

"Will you tell me where you found them?" Celestia turns to Sibilia, the one who should be sensible, and I dread her answer. For dear Sibs is still but a child.

Our sister meets Celestia with a level gaze, one that mirrors hers. She's no longer a girl easily intimidated, perhaps not a child after all. "In the garden, while we were gathering roses. No guard or soldier lost it. It had been there for years."

While Sibs might be telling the truth, it's not the full truth, but at the moment I know it's all she's going to say. Gone are the days when my sister shared everything with me. I shouldn't be exactly surprised about that. She has learned her tricks by observing the best.

"Try. Can we try them now?" Merile tugs at Celestia's hem. The fabric has worn so thin that her fingertips slip through the wool. Yet, in her excitement, she doesn't notice that.

Before Celestia can answer, a scrape of metal against metal interrupts us. A muffled conversation comes from behind the door leading to the hallway.

"Later," Celestia replies. "Go on and play on the floor with your dogs. Alina, you too. Elise, sit down, will you?"

Captain Janlav pushes the door open with his shoulder, and for a moment I'm not sure if what I see is real or if I'm suffering from a hallucination. The light of the two chandeliers wraps around the brass horn of the gramophone he cradles in his arms. Though his is the wildest smile, the guards trickle in after him, each more hesitant than the other. Tabard and Beard enter side by side, one fidgeting with an unlit cigarette, the other a box of matches. Belly comes in next, his blue tunic looser now, Boots behind him, his namesake footwear worn almost undone. Boy enters the drawing room last, and he closes the door behind him. The guards are unarmed, and this makes them seem bare, as though a strap of leather and piece of metal were something grander, something behind which to hide all fears and hesitation. They huddle together, stare expectantly at their captain.

I blink twice, but neither Captain Janlav nor the guards disappear. I realize it then, they are here because of me, because of the cigarettes shared, the shy smiles exchanged. Whatever Celestia thinks of me, my plans are the ones that have proven to work time after time, not hers.

"I've brought you music," Captain Janlav announces with a grin, and he looks boyish once more, someone who has been up to mischief and knows he will eventually be caught.

Yet I don't really know what he expects to happen next. Or I can guess what some of them think. Beard and Tabard must have told Captain Janlav about the argument between Celestia and me, for nothing in this house stays hidden for long. He feels pity for us and what we have been through lately. He thinks music might ease the tense atmosphere. Boy no doubt imagines that we will start dancing upon hearing the first sweet notes, that we will forget our constraints and our captivity, that he can then swirl Sibilia round and round until she gets dizzy and upon looking into his eyes falls in love with him.

Though that won't happen. She has her eyes set on some-one else. Eventually, I will find out whom she's dreaming of. If I can lead them together, then I shall do exactly that. My sister deserves to experience the fluttering of her heart, the rush of blood in her veins. She deserves to experience that before . . .

"Shall I put a disc playing?" Captain Janlav asks.

The truth to be told, with my hem wet and stockings drying, I'm in no mood for dancing. Looking at my sisters, neither are they. We have navigated through the steps for months with-out a song to guide us, and this has turned the dance practices into a compulsory chore. Now that we could dance for fun, it doesn't feel like the appropriate thing to do. But how do you turn down kindness without insulting those who meant well? I turn my head slightly, to better see Celestia, who once more stands before the curtained window. She has her chin tilted up, and I can already hear in my mind the wrong words she's about to speak.

"Yes! What a wonderful idea!" I reply in my sister's place, for having failed to reason with her once already today, I'm past caring about the breach of etiquette. If we were to send the guards away now, they would never return, but resume the distance I have fought so hard to bridge. "Please, do place it down on the table and take seats if you will."

And with these words, the tiniest flicker of hope stirs in the depths of my heart. If you care for people, they will care for you. This is something Celestia has yet to comprehend. She is so set in her ways that I'm not sure if she will ever be able to see that.

"Thank you." Captain Janlav chuckles. He strides toward the table with the gramophone. Alina and Merile flee out of his way, to hide behind the sofa chairs, but not because they are afraid of him. Rather, as if he were their older brother, someone who might lift them up and spin them around or playfully hang them in the air from their ankles.

"Alina, Merile, you can sit here on the sofa with me." I pat the padded seat once, twice, to reinforce the invitation. Celestia won't dare to disagree with me before the guards, her mastery of self-restraint becoming a weakness for me to exploit. "If we move a little, there will be space even for Rafa and Mufu."

My little sisters do exactly as suggested, but Celestia and Sibilia are slower to realize how important this day may yet turn out to be. Sibilia shuffles to occupy the end of the table only after receiving a nod from Celestia. Our oldest sister broods opposite to her, her long fingers curling around the back of the sofa chair. After our heated argument, she doesn't exactly trust me.

"This is an old model." While Captain Janlav hustles with the gramophone, turning the metal crank a dozen or so times, the guards remain by the door. The instrument is ancient indeed. These days all machinery is powered by souls. "Boyek, you brought the discs, right?"

The guards exchange grins, relieved and proud as if this had by no means been an easy feat. But Boy's pimpled face flushes as if he were caught red-handed. And that he was. Because even as he meanders his way to his captain, balancing a pile of paper sleeves against his widening chest, he's still staring moon-eyed at Sibilia.

"May I see which songs we have to choose from?" Celestia speaks for the first time since the guards entered the room. I hope it's only me who recognizes the tone. She's more than slightly annoyed. This situation isn't in her control. But it is in mine. "Ah, do lower them gently! The older discs may be brittle."

Boy's shoulders draw up to his chin, so high that his neck disappears altogether. I feel for him, for my sister's chastisement. This isn't how one treats one's guests!

"Sibilia, dear," I chirp in, "would you pick the first one?"

Let my sister's presence bring back Boy's cheer! For he sees her as she is, a girl grown into a woman, tall and lush, though wearing a gown too short on the sleeves and hem, sagging around the frame she hasn't yet realized she possesses.

"Sure." Sibilia shrugs, waving Boy to bring the discs over to her rather than Celestia. She browses through them, unaware of the hope she has stirred in this young man's heart. She sees Boy only as he is, not as what he will become. He may be lanky, but soon he will grow to fill in his tunic and trousers, his narrowness will turn to pure muscle, his awkward steps to determined stride. "How about a waltz?"

Celestia studies us, lips pressed together as if she were a bird observing her subjects from between clouds, unwilling to sing, to let them even catch sight of her. I wonder if she will ever be willing to learn from me, acknowledge how well I handle this sort of situation. I doubt it. She doesn't understand how everyday kindness is akin to a pebble rolling down a hill to join an avalanche.

"If you will allow me," Captain Janlav offers, and soon the brittle black disc is spinning under the needle, and the grandiose strokes of the violins interlace with the bold brass notes. While my younger sisters lean their elbows against the oval table, the guards listen to the music from where each of them ended up. Captain Janlav is bent over the gramophone, cranking it when need be. Boy shifts his weight behind Sibilia's chair. The other guards are still clustered by the closed door.

I don't think they have heard music in ages either. For Beard has his eyes closed, lips parted under the brown whiskers. Boots taps the floor hesitantly. Tabard and Belly nod along as if they yearned to spin us—any girl, for that matter—around, but know that this isn't the right time or place for such.

When the song ends, the guards look disappointed, but hopeful, too. No one dares to speak, for we are dazed by the simple beauty of the waltz, by the memories of better times that it has stirred in our souls. Finally, Beard clears his throat. He brandishes a small rectangular cardboard box. "I've got cards. Anyone fancy playing?"

My younger sisters turn to Celestia, to see how they should react. But again, before she can say that it wouldn't be proper for us to play together, I hasten to reply, "Yes! That would be most delightful."

"Come join us," Celestia agrees, finally taking a seat herself, but the look she casts me speaks volumes. If I had hoped earlier that she would descend from the skies to join us, as a sister amongst sisters, that she hasn't. She sees only that even in captivity, there are certain protocols to follow. She's the oldest. The decisions should be hers. But she doesn't understand either that the world has changed, that we must change with it or cease to be.

Captain Janlav and Boy and Beard and Tabard take the free chairs on the other side of the table, opposite to me. It's an unexpected reflection of the dinners we shared during the winter months. Or not quite. Belly and Boots choose to stay by the door, leaning against the wall, with one knee raised. At ease, at least.

"A polka?" Sibilia suggests, holding another disc up for Captain Janlav. His hands tremble, barely visibly, and I don't think anyone else notices this. What is he nervous about?

Surely not being so close to us.

Then I realize it, and I should have realized it much sooner. The gramophone is the one from the garrison. Did he bargain for it or steal it? How much is he risking simply to cheer me up?

But as the buoyant polka starts, I push these thoughts aside. I shall not worry about the gramophone's origins, even if Captain Janlav's choices may have consequences later on. I shall enjoy that which is within my grasp now. Something I failed to do when enjoyments were available aplenty.

My sisters and I, we play family—no, Families, the card game—with the guards, and with a silent agreement, we let Alina win at least every other game. Perhaps not all change is for the worse. As I watch the guards laugh with my younger sisters, the grain of hope in my heart swells. To them, we are no longer only Daughters of the Moon, but also human beings, young girls, young women kept captive against our will. I hope Celestia sees this, too. We may not have the power to alter our fates, but it is within our power to make the last days of our sisters better.

I cast a warm look at Captain Janlav. He smiles back at me, arches his brow at the redness of my cheek. I shrug as if I had hurt it by accident. From his concern for my well-being, I know at last that I wasn't naïve in placing my trust in him. He and his men will keep us safe as long as we obey the rules of the gagargi's wicked game. That is more than I have asked for, hoped for.

And yet, no matter that I'm resigned to my fate, that of my sisters, I want more.

The polka ends, and it's then that the door flings open.

Captain Ansalov's beady green eyes gleam with ire as he

takes in the scene: us sitting around the table, fans of cards in our hands. The black dog on Merile's lap bounces up and growls at him. It senses the threat in the air, the promise of violence the captain carries with him everywhere he goes. "Ah, here it is."

The gramophone's needle scratches empty circles before it starts replaying the polka. I don't dare to say a word. Neither does Celestia. No one does apart from Captain Ansalov.

"But what is it that you, Captain Janlav, are doing here with your men?"

I pat Merile's hand, praying the Moon that she will echo the soothing gesture on Alina. For Tabard and Boots no longer lean on the wall. They are ready to spring into action if so much as half ordered. But Captain Janlav merely shuffles his cards. I wish Celestia would say something wise and calming, but she remains perfectly still. Her placid blue gaze reveals that she won't interfere unless things get much, much worse. She is punishing me for acting out of place, for speaking out of turn, for disagreeing with her. And seeing my younger sisters afraid is worse than any pain I can imagine.

"We are listening to music. And playing Families," Captain Janlav says at last, glancing at the other captain from over his hand, smiling all the while. "Would you like to join us, perhaps?"

The agreement between the two captains, the orders each follow to the letter. Bless the Moon, my sisters and I are exactly where we should be. But Captain Janlav and his guards . . . There must be no constraints placed on them visiting us, otherwise he would have never allowed them to enter the room.

Captain Ansalov chews his cheek. He must be trying to find a breach in the rules, and given time, he will surely be able to twist the gagargi's words in a way that benefits him and only him. The cheerful notes of the polka have never sounded so sinister. I hold my breath as I wait for his answer. Merile leans against me, Alina against her. If I'm scared of this man, my little sisters must be terrified! Celestia still refusing to interfere only shows how callous and spiteful she truly is!

"No," Captain Ansalov replies at last, but his gaze is drawn to the gramophone, as if he were a magpie mesmerized by all that glitters, greedy beyond its own understanding. I remember the evening when we first met him back at the garrison. He may be a harsh man, ready to follow any order given to him, but at the same time he likes music, and... "I didn't realize earlier you and your men are enthusiastic about music. Why don't we continue listening through my misplaced collection in the confinement of my office?"

This polite talk is just a veil, and both of the captains know it. Captain Janlav has stolen that for which Captain Ansalov cares the most. But it's a dangerous game he plays. For Captain Ansalov knows Captain Janlav has grown fond of us, that by hurting us he will also hurt the captain who has turned into his adversary.

"No, I don't think so," Captain Janlav says with a boyish bravado against a man twice his age, though we would have been better off with him taking up the offer. "We are quite comfortable here as it is."

I stare at him, perplexed. There is no shame in sometimes taking the easy way out. He can't possibly be doing this to impress me! We both know what awaits my sisters and me. There's no point in dwelling on what could have been between us. And then the game he's playing becomes so clear to me. He has always known it, but only recently understood that he, too, is at liberty to interpret his orders as he wishes. It's his duty to keep my sisters and me safe, not to treat us like prisoners.

"Is that so?" Captain Ansalov's soft question is more terrifying than a shout bellowed from the top of his lungs.

Captain Janlav drops his cards on the table face-side up and slowly rises. Belly, Beard, and Boy perch on their seats. Sibilia, the Moon bless her, pulls a card from Alina, a distraction meant to keep our younger sisters unaware of the rising tension. "I believe in the equal redistribution of resources. My men and I would much like to lend this player for a while longer."

Captain Ansalov chuckles. This horrid sound mixes with the gramophone's needle scratching the disc, at the outer edge, round after round. "So it seems my time is over and yours has just begun, eh?"

But what he's saying between the lines is that Captain Janlav's time might come to an end sooner than he can even begin to guess. And I wonder, does Captain Ansalov hold in his pockets more of the gagargi's orders, some that he hasn't yet shared with us? If he does, is Celestia aware of their content?

"No!"

We all, the guards and my sisters alike, turn toward the sound. For it's neither of the captains speaking, but the little, wide-eyed Alina who has sprung up from the sofa. The dogs bounce beside her, agitated.

I don't want to ask my sister what she means, but Celestia still holds her silence. As the guards turn to look at me, one after another, I have no choice but to ask, "What is it, my dear?"

Even though I know the answer. This is the way Alina acts when she thinks she has seen something in the shadows.

Indeed, Alina stares intently at the darkest corner of the room. The brown dog dabs my sister's tiny hand with its nose, and it's this that brings her back to us. Her lips part as she turns toward Captain Ansalov. Her face pales.

Captain Ansalov runs his stubby fingers along his upper lip, smug. He likes us terrified, the more so, the better. "Yes?"

"I . . ." Alina whispers, but before she can say more, a sharp crack interrupts her.

Jagged black shards scatter every which way. One of them hits me in the forehead. I blink, confused, but the guards act upon reflex. The next I see clear again, Tabard and Boots have drawn knives I didn't even know they carried about their persons. Captain Janlav has vacated his chair. He has his arms spread wide, as if to protect us with his body. Boy and Belly flank him. Beard hovers by Celestia. Only Captain Ansalov has held his ground. He has done so though a trickle of blood coils down his round cheek.

Why wouldn't he have when it was only the gramophone's disc that shattered?

"He's coming." Alina stares at the first drop of blood on the floor. Tears glint in the corners of her eyes. Her voice shivers. "The gagargi is coming for us."

First there's nothing but stunned silence. Then laughter, vile and deep, erupts from Captain Ansalov's throat. His whole body shakes with his amusement, even as blood drips down his chin. "By all means, Captain Janlav, keep the gramophone."

His words, those of my little sister, chill me to the core. He has no further need for music. Soon we will all be dancing to his tune.

Chapter 10

Celestia

As I lean against the window's frame, I feel the night, the darkening hour, the calm that falls over the garden and the lake, though I can't see it yet. The curtains were nailed against the white wood and sewn shut six weeks and four days ago. Until recently, we simply let them be that way.

"Is it the time?" Sibilia teeters on our bed's edge, opening and closing the book of scriptures in turns. Though this is the seventh time she is about to strengthen me, her nervousness hasn't eased. It haunts her through the days. "Ah, drat, I must use the chamber pot again. Sorry."

"Don't worry, dear Sibilia," I whisper at her, and seeing her smile back at me is more than I deserve. I chose to abandon her. Yet she has forgiven me, unlike Elise, who still refuses to see beyond the veil of the gagargi's propaganda. "We will see the Moon tonight."

I set to unraveling the thick black thread holding the curtains together, one stitch at a time. We can't let the thread snatch. Any knot could be easily detected by Millie when she tidies our rooms during our daily outings. She might choose to continue her silence, or then she might not. Fear does unpredictable things to people.

Elise has changed. I fear she has started to believe the

gagargi's lies. It bothers me that I don't know how this came to be. She is young. She is naïve. Perhaps that alone sufficed. The gagargi is very charismatic. I, if anyone, know that.

It isn't only this that contributes to my increasing disquiet. I don't know if Alina really saw a shadow the day that we heard music. She claims that an ape came to warn her about the gagargi's arrival, but that it was so faded by the distance traveled that it couldn't tell her more before vanishing altogether. Two weeks and six days have passed since then with no further news. But it would be pure madness not to prepare for the imminent encounter by whatever means available to us.

The thread tightens. A frayed part has caught on the edge of a blooming midsummer rose. I will my fingers nimbler, the movements more precise. Each day, the unraveling becomes a task trickier, the secrets weigh heavier on my heart. Even so, my sisters must not learn what Sibilia and I are contriving. Elise has become unreliable. She thinks me selfish, that I should abandon our younger sisters and just return to the gagargi, that this simple act would end the bloodshed. Merile and Alina are too young to benefit from the hope that may yet turn false. For even with Sibilia's help . . .

I am done with the unraveling. The curtains part slightly, and a thin sliver of night winds its way in. I inhale exaggeratedly slowly. My swan-self says the air tastes different, too moist and cold. I am tempted to believe her. The maples have turned bloodred, too early considering that it is still summer here. Perhaps it is because lately it has rained almost constantly. The house's pale orange paint flakes, revealing the gray plaster beneath. The posters glued on the garden walls disintegrate in the moisture. The gagargi's face is bubbling as if he were covered with warts.

He is not diseased, but a disease of which I must cleanse my empire.

"Please let it not rain." Porcelain scratches against the floor as Sibilia pushes the chamber pot under our bed. She is concerned that we might not be met with our father's gaze tonight, that instead she might need to guide me through the spell once more.

Though I have already smelled the air and know what awaits us, I press my ear against the curtains that wait to be parted. Some secrets are mine to keep, more dangerous than others. I think of the flooding lake, the ever-swelling puddles before the garden wall, the path that is fully submerged, the swans that nest by the lake, that can now swim all the way to the iron gate. They observe my sisters and me through the elaborate bars. As they sing throaty tunes, my swan-self yearns to sing back at them. But this I can't tell to my sisters any more than I dare to reveal that I might not be able to bear children.

I say, "It doesn't rain now."

"Great." Sibilia tiptoes to me as I slowly pull the curtains apart. I don't know how many more times we can do so without fraying them too much. Perhaps once. Perhaps two times. No more than that, I think. "You won't believe how glad I am that we're not practicing the spell. I'm so worried about you accidentally saying it aloud and wasting all of our father's power! Remember that once you do start pronouncing it, you can't say another word before you unleash it. And every word you say after that will drain more and more of your strength."

She has told me all that a dozen times before, but I smile at her as I reply, "I will remember that."

The black pane is cracked, and beyond it lies the gap between the planks. I broke the glass the first time we parted the curtains, to perform the sacred rites of the midsummer night. The crack has remained the same since, but the gap grows wider every day. Soon, no doubt, the soldiers will grow suspicious of the magpie that seems so intent on nesting behind the planks. I am not wary of the bird, but curious. While I am tempted to believe that the witch and the magpie might be connected—perhaps the bird is her companion like the two dogs are Merile's—that perhaps the Moon has chastised her for asking such a heavy fee from me, I have no proof one way or another. I haven't met the witch since we visited her cottage. She hasn't shown herself to me, and how could she with the guards shadowing my every step?

I can but rely on things I know are real. "I am ready."

"Me too," Sibilia replies.

Beyond the crack and the gap, the night is pale, just an imitation of the true darkness, but we know our father is still present. I nod at Sibilia, and she opens the book of scriptures. She hasn't marked the page, but as she knows each section by heart, it doesn't take her long to locate the right passage. She breathes rapidly as she prepares to read the holy words. She parts her lips, but no words come out. Instead, she pronounces a silent shape, powerful and arcane.

A ray of light slants in through the gap between the planks, the cracked black glass, and the parted curtains. It pierces the dimness of the room, paints a perfect circle on the floor, before my bare feet. I am pristine and white once more, even if only for a moment.

"Father," I sing softly under my breath as Sibilia has instructed. "Make me stronger."

The Moon's light grows denser, thicker. And then I feel my father's embrace, his thousand hands on my shoulders, caressing my cheeks, my hair. This is more than I deserve, and there are those who would be more deserving of his love. But it is I who must put an end to the gagargi's twisted rule. I who has to face him. I who must be able to persuade him to let me bring my sisters with me.

For I will not leave them here, no matter what Elise may think the best course of action. As much as it is my duty to protect my people, I must also keep my sisters safe. And now that my father has blessed me with his presence, I know that I am right.

I close my eyes. I let my father see into my mind, into my heart. He is gentle and caring. He knows I am earnest, that my reasoning isn't affected by selfish ambitions or lust for power. I hold only the best interest of my people and my sisters close to my heart. He will make me stronger. He will . . .

His presence feels different. Hurried and imperfect. Pale things, like sheets drying in wind, flicker before my eyes. They are like . . . Can they be? Yes, they are images, glimpsed from too far away, for too short a while.

"Father . . ." A ragged breath escapes my composure. I am not married to the Moon. What he yearns to show me, I can't yet fully see.

My father withdraws, the images disappearing, but his touch doesn't leave me vulnerable and lacking. Not like the one that hurt me so much.

"Celestia." Sibilia's voice brings me back.

I blink, but the images are gone. How long was I under my sister's spell? For a minute or for an hour? I always lose track of time when connected to my father.

"How do you feel?" Sibilia asks, curious of her own powers and our father's, too.

The circle at my feet has broken. The light trickling in is duller. The short night is over.

That day I first read my sister's diary, I resolved to never lie to her again. But speaking half-truths isn't the same thing. I reply, "Stronger."

But as I once more sew the curtains together, I don't know if I will ever be able to defy the gagargi. For it seems that even my father's powers have a limit.

At first, I mistake the approaching, rumbling sounds for thunder. It has rained for weeks, after all. But then the clamor travels through the house, from the library to the hallway and up the two stairways. From that I know that the moment I have dreaded for so long has finally arrived.

Elise stirs on the sofa where she dozes these days when she isn't playing her feeble games with the guards. She doesn't seem to realize that regardless of how fond the guards grow of us, in the end they will have no choice but to obey their orders.

Sibilia lowers the book of scriptures on her lap. She squints past the smoke at the flickering flames. She tosses one more log in, though she knows it won't make any difference.

Merile and Alina pause playing with the hand mirror on the carpet. The two dogs bounce onto their feet, alert. The brown one lets out a low growl.

I say in a voice in which I pray the Moon shall bear no trace of my terror, "Gagargi Prataslav is here."

Though I have had seven months and two weeks since we left the Summer Palace to prepare for this encounter, my statement frightens every single one of them. Elise, who so casually suggested I go with the gagargi and leave my sisters to face death or worse. Sibilia, who turned to the scriptures for comfort, who found something more, but still frets about missing her debut. Merile and Alina, who understand that the gagargi is evil, but blessedly nothing more.

"He's greeting the captains downstairs," Alina says, and Merile nods, avoiding looking at the mirror's reflection. From this I know that Irina and Olesia are present, a complication I would have hoped to avoid. Yet I can't reveal that I know of this—in this house knowledge is power.

"Gather around, my sisters," I say. I can't allow myself to be distracted by the past, mistakes made by my mother for which I may yet need to bear the blame. "We may not have much time."

My sisters do as I ask, even Elise, who no longer cares about traditions and rules. She has her arms crossed over her chest, her gaze downcast. Does she hope or dread that I will heed her advice? Sibilia meets my eyes boldly. The two of us share a secret. She thinks I have a chance against the gagargi. Merile and Alina know nothing at all. They are our little sisters. I believe every single one of us, even Elise, would do whatever is in our power to protect them.

"The gagargi will want to see only me," I say. Of that, I am quite sure. It is only I who is of value and importance to him. He wants me to stand by his side before the crowds and bear a child of his seed. It is only that way that my people will ever accept him as a ruler assigned by the Moon. "You are to wait here. Even if I may stay away for a long while, don't be afraid. Captain Janlav and the guards will not let any harm come to you."

For as long as it is possible, at least. Since the day we listened to the music, they have been more and more drawn to us. They visit us during the long afternoons, bringing the gramophone and the frail discs with them. We play cards until six, for then they must join Captain Ansalov and his soldiers in the dining room. But after both my sisters and the guards are sustained, they return to hear Sibilia reading the scriptures. Though Elise has been wrong about many things, I must approve of her cunning in ever so casually setting up these new routines, making our last weeks together that little fraction better.

"But you will come back?" Merile asks, glancing sideways at Alina, who is already in tears. It is as if they are both convinced that they will never see me again. The ghosts in the mirror must be whispering disconcerting things to them.

"I will come back," I promise, but there is a note of falseness in my voice. The gagargi is a magnificent opponent. Though the Moon has strengthened me, it may be that I can't resist the gagargi's spells. It is well possible that I may not be able to make him believe my words as his own. Yet I can but try, even if this may hurt me beyond healing. "But I might return changed."

"As a swan," Alina whispers, and breaks down in sobs that tremble her whole, frail body.

"Hush." Sibilia kneels to embrace our little sister. As she holds her, her sleeves reach barely over her elbows. She hasn't yet met the limits of her body. Or mind. "Celestia is strong. You needn't be afraid."

I wish only that I could believe in myself as much as Sibilia does. When the gagargi last put his spell on me, I was unprepared and weak. He did things to me that can't be undone. Yet I can't let the past affect me now.

"I must prepare myself," I say. The spell Sibilia taught me is similar to the one she first learnt. In principle, it should allow me to make the gagargi believe that he should take all of us with him. While this wouldn't guarantee us freedom, it would broaden our options. For in this house, hope is extinct.

Elise brushes my shoulder, her touch soft as a falling feather. "Will you accept an embrace for good luck?"

This I didn't expect. It is not an apology. I doubt she will ever ask for my forgiveness, but it is something, a concession perhaps. And though I should get ready for the encounter with the gagargi, at that moment it becomes more important to me to simply be close to my sisters, to soothe my aching heart, and that is what I do.

As I hold my sisters and they hold me, I think, there was a time when I could easily brush my feelings aside. How inconvenient it is to be overcome by emotions! How inconvenient indeed, and yet it feels like a blessing still!

———

There is a knock, followed by a nervous rattle of the key. I gently pry my hem free of Alina's grip. Her fingers are so tiny, thin and narrow. I don't want to let go of them, but that is what I must do. "This is where we must part, but it will be only for a moment."

Alina stares at my feet—no, at my shadow—and wipes her tears away with the back of her hand. "You will come back."

The door opens before I can ask for more or decide not to do so. It is Beard and Tabard. This time around, they have their rifles strapped against their backs. They also wear long knives at their belts, visible rather than hidden. These two things tell me everything I need to know.

"Gagargi Prataslav has come for me."

"Aya." Beard stares at his thick knuckles, the hands clasped into fists. "The great gagargi has indeed arrived."

I glide toward the guards without them having to order me. I know the role I have to play. I will not fight against it. "I am ready."

Tabard clears his throat, and yet he is hesitant to deliver the message. "He told us to bring all of you."

It is only because I am already moving that my steps don't falter. What can the gagargi possibly want with my sisters? Will he threaten them to make me do his bidding? Or does he have more sinister plans in store for us? I can but mentally prepare for that.

"Come along then, my sisters," I say lightly, as if I had known to anticipate this as well. "Gather in a line behind me."

I don't glance over my shoulder as I exit the room. My sisters know their places. And there is no place else for them to go, but to follow me.

It rains outside, something that we have grown used to, but that feels more ominous now that the gagargi shelters under the same roof. The stairs thud hollow under our steps. The hallway leading to the dining room feels longer. This doesn't disturb me—I shall use the time in my hands to prepare myself for the encounter.

It is the gagargi who told me to decide whether I will be a victim or a victor, and so I seek strength from the harm he inflicted on me in the past rather than let seeing him surface it all again and weaken me at the crucial moment.

He made me fail my people. His is the blame for the civil war, even if it was I who first sought his guidance.

He made me fail my mother. His is the blame for her demise. He put me under his spell and made me think the coup my idea.

He made me fail myself. His is the blame for my pain. It was him who stole my soul and sowed his seed in my womb. He did this when I was powerless to resist him.

As we reach the dining room's closed door, Boots and Belly standing guard before it, I make myself a solemn promise. I may have been a victim before, but tonight, I shall be the victor.

Boots nods at me before rapping the door with his knuckles. There is no reply, but he opens it nevertheless, announces, "The daughters are here."

"Please, ask them to join us." Gagargi Prataslav calls at us in a pleasantly low voice, as if we were about to share a cup of zavarka tea together and not discuss our fates.

Boots stomps aside, and I must remind myself that the gagargi is but a man—a wicked man, but just a man still. I am the oldest Daughter of the Moon. It is not I who will be facing him, but her. Holding on to this thought, I lead my sisters into the room that we might not leave with our souls intact.

"Celestia. The Daughters of the Moon." Gagargi Prataslav's black braids are glued against his skull. His face is still wet with the rain, and tiny drops cling to his voluminous beard. His drenched black robes hang against his wiry frame, and yet, he looks like a man who is delighted to have faced the storm.

I remind myself again that he is only a man. But it isn't only him who awaits us in the room.

Behind him stand at attention Captain Janlav and Captain Ansalov, the shoulders of their gray coats striped with rain, their boots covered in mud. When I still watched the events unfold from my mother's shadow, I met many generals, dozens of captains, and hundreds of soldiers of lesser rank. I know how to read their faces and postures. These two men have been reporting to the gagargi. Captain Janlav is a soldier delivering bad news, dreading his ruler's reaction, but who has braced himself for the inevitable punishment. Captain Ansalov smiles smugly. He is a soldier delivering good news, sure of rewards to follow, of praises and reputation gained.

Seeing this, my swan-self wants to scamper out of the room, regardless of the consequences. I push her opinions aside. For a true empress, there is no distinction between good and bad news. Both are information upon which to lay plans and make decisions. Rather than surrendering to my swan-self's terror, I ask myself two questions.

Why are the two captains present?

Why did the gagargi want to see my sisters?

"Gagargi Prataslav," I say as my sisters and I form a crescent in the order of our ages. Perhaps the gagargi thinks that the mere presence of the two captains will suffice to distract me. Perhaps, but guessing is never sufficient replacement for knowledge. "So thoughtful of you to travel all the way here to greet us."

"Yes. I am a very thoughtful man." The gagargi's smile reveals his slightly crooked white teeth, but there is no indication yet of a spell spun or cast. What is he waiting for? Or is he simply toying with me? I am tempted to form my spell, but I sense now is not yet the right moment.

Rain lashes against the planks covering the windows. From the corner of my eye, I catch Alina and Merile huddling closer to each other, unaccustomed to the absence of their dogs. The gagargi knows my mind and soul. Just as I have had time to think about this encounter, so has he. He must have realized that I am in full control of myself, that no mere isolation, loss of freedom, could ever break my spirit. But my younger sisters aren't as resilient. He summoned them, the two captains, into this room so that my sisters would react, so that their distress would disturb my composure, so that he could then catch me off guard and put me under his spell with ease. Just like me, he is merely waiting for the moment to strike.

Boldly, I take a step forward, to shield my sisters from the evil of this man. I will protect them with all the power bestowed on me by the Moon. This is no secret.

"Close the door," the gagargi suggests to Boots. Captain Janlav shifts his weight, but there are no orders for him. None for Captain Ansalov either.

"Now then, let me have a look at you, dearest Celestia." The gagargi approaches me, and though he is soaked, he still smells of incense, sharp and pungent. My swan-self screeches. She recognizes a predator when she sees one. "You have been gone for so long. I have missed your company on many a lonely night. But of course it isn't only about me. Your people miss you, too."

He speaks as much to me as to the two captains and my sisters. He knows me, knows I have considered every option and eventuality, and as a result reached the one conclusion that is almost too painful to admit aloud. But for me to be able to ambush him with the spell Sibilia taught me, he must feel in control. Though it pains me to have my sisters hear what I am about to say, I have no other option but to part with the words he wants to hear. "I have run as far as I can."

"Yes. That you have." He reaches to fondly cup my chin, his skin clammy against mine. And still, there is no sign of a spell, nothing to fight against. I meet his deep, dark gaze. What is this game he plays? "The time has come for you to return."

As he touches me, images of the night I followed him into his bed flash past my eyes, memories earlier suppressed. My head pressed against his chest. His skin rough against mine. I knew joy with him, but not out of my own will. He wanted me to think I wanted it, liked it, though that I never did.

I push the past aside. I refuse to be a victim a moment longer.

"Yes. That it has." I mirror his words on purpose, focusing on what matters now. I know from the propaganda reports, the manifest, and his very presence here that even though the gagargi is winning the battles, he hasn't won over the heart of my people. No matter how many souls he has stolen, he hasn't been able to make the bloodshed end.

"Join me now, and let us put all this unpleasantness behind us." His gaze intensifies, and I twitch my head sideways as if it were becoming unbearable. He must believe me weak, once wounded beyond recovery. "We shall stand before the gathered crowds at the autumn equinox. We shall greet the Moon together and receive his blessing to our rule and that of our future daughters."

Our daughters . . . he doesn't have a clue about how close he came to accomplishing his goal, what ridding myself of his seed has potentially cost me. Which is good.

But from the corner of my eye, I catch Elise beaming approvingly. This is what she has wanted me to do all along, though the invitation to leave this house is meant only for me. But it is an unexpected opening, one I can't leave unexplored. "My people would be relieved to see their empress and her sisters unharmed."

"Your sisters?" Gagargi Prataslav muses, removing his hand from my chin to stroke his wet beard. "Unharmed . . ."

I realize my mistake then. All this conversation, mere intimidation, the lack of attack on his behalf, it was just a maneuver for him to push me into revealing my plan. The Moon help us! No, our father can't help us now. It is up to me to reclaim what can still be salvaged.

"Yes." He strolls past me, to Elise, and when he does, his attention shifts to her. "The younger Daughters of the Moon."

I don't know if this is the optimal time to act or if I will only make the situation worse. But having revealed what I yearned to accomplish, I can but strive to turn the course of events toward a more favorable path. Pressing my lips tight together, I begin to pronounce the one hundred and seventeen consonants and three vowels that form the glyph.

"I remember you, sweet Elise," the gagargi says, a terribly pleasant tone to his voice. Drawn by this, I turn around, though I am but one-fifth through the letters. Captain Ansalov smirks at me. He thinks me distraught. "You contributed to the cause most generously. We funded many a strike against the Enemy, thanks to your donations."

Elise flinches, and just like her, I will the gagargi's words to be a lie. But of course that they are not. Everything that he says makes perfect sense. My sister's darker moods. Her fraternizing with the guards. The argument that led to our unbridged disagreement. This realization almost leads me to lose track of the glyph's letters. Almost, but not quite.

"Celestia . . ." Elise pleads with me, though she should remain silent. Can she not see from my expression that I need to focus? Does she not understand that apologies are of no benefit to us, that emotions may only lead us all to ruin? "Please, Celestia!"

I pronounce the last silent consonant, and the glyph surges to life in my mouth. Even if I wanted to speak words of consolation, I couldn't voice them, not without releasing the spell first. Even if . . . But I have nothing to say to my sister, not until I have considered through the full implications of her selfish actions. And that is something I can't afford to focus on now. It will have to wait.

"War is such a messy business. To see a sister turn against sister . . ." The gagargi shakes his head, and drops scatter from his braids and his beard onto the plank floor. The spell swirls in my mouth. "Ah, it breaks my heart."

Upset by what she must consider cold-hearted silence from me, Elise blinks back tears. The gagargi glances at me, to see if this revelation had any effect. I don't need to pretend shock, but it pains me to let him see it. Yet, he needs to believe that my plans have come undone, that I have lost my trust in my sister.

"I don't recall your name, younger Daughter of the Moon," the gagargi says as he moves onward, to harass Sibilia. He leers at the too-taut front of her dress, the too-short sleeves, and the dirty hem. "You are the one who doesn't matter, but you must have realized that by now."

Sibilia gazes past the gagargi, pretending braveness, pretending so much more. Out of my sisters, only she understands why I don't, can't say a word. She knows and believes in me, even though I was once ready to abandon her.

"Yes. That you have," the gagargi replies to his own speculations. To him, my sister is still expendable. He has no idea of her powers, and if it is up to me, he will never learn of them. "You are of no interest to me either. How does that make you feel?"

Sibilia blushes, but otherwise manages to hold on to her composure, and I am so proud of her that the spell almost manages to sneak out from between my lips. I tilt my chin up, clench my teeth together. To my sisters, the two captains, it must look as if my façade of calm were crumbling.

The gagargi chuckles, and the rain outside grows heavier. Wind knocks against the barred windows, loud and insistent. My swan-self warns me of approaching thunder. She tells me to fly away. But even if I could, now isn't the right time.

"You, on the other hand, little Merile," the gagargi says, turning on his heels, "have become of interest to me of late."

Merile glances at her feet, but her dogs aren't with us. There is no one to comfort her. I can but stand before her, teeth already aching from the eagerness of the spell, full of power I can use only once. I need to wait for the moment when the gagargi is, if not weak, then at least distracted.

Pray to Moon that there will be such a moment soon.

The gagargi slips his arms into the voluminous sleeves of his black robes. His fingers climb up his arms, shapes like colossal spiders under the wet fabric. Then he pulls his arms free, flourishing a scarlet scarf I instantly recognize.

"Mine," Merile shrieks, reaching up to claim the scarf her seed once gave her, though the gagargi holds it too high for her to reach. "That's mine, the scarf so fine!"

Captain Ansalov laughs. The gagargi doesn't so much as glance at the soldier, and yet his displeasure is obvious. The two captains may have been allowed to remain in the room to witness my humiliation, to allow them to see how powerless I am despite my heritage. But they aren't allowed to partake in it.

Captain Ansalov's expression grows somber and sour as he realizes this.

"No, no, little Daughter of the Moon." The gagargi closes his fist and the scarf disappears into the hollow formed by his bony fingers. "It is mine. A favor granted by me to the one who speaks in my name. I am by no means surprised to see him passing it onward to the daughter of his seed. But back, you shall not get it."

The gagargi cranes over his shoulder at me, and the spell barges against my teeth so hard I fear they will shatter. There is no time to think, only to act. I press my hand against my mouth to prevent the spell from claiming uncontrolled freedom. Oh, the Moons be blessed, let the gagargi think that the night of Merile's folly has returned to haunt me, that I am afraid of him harming my little sister and nothing more.

"He has been such a great asset to me. The people listen to his voice," the gagargi says, twisting a knife in the wound he knows I bear in my heart. Even our seeds, the ones that are still alive, have deserted us. He is responsible for the death of mine. "But enough is enough, I think. Having spared you, I have now favored him twice."

My dread is fuel for the spell that is growing ever so impatient. It forces my clenched teeth, my tight-pressed lips apart. I must clasp both hands over my mouth, bend my upper body down, to make it seem as if I were about to gag. The left corner of the gagargi's lips twitches. He is satisfied, rather than suspicious.

"Great Gagargi Prataslav," Elise chimes, and at that moment I don't know if the reverence is a mere practiced tone or genuine. I don't know my sister anymore. "You are the Gagargi of the People. Your kindness knows no limit."

"Kindness," the gagargi repeats slowly. Even if Elise's intervention was an attempt to sway the gagargi to granting us, Merile, mercy, he isn't a man capable of that. "Yes, I am kind. But I cannot be seen to favor any family over the others. Not even the one of celestial descent."

And with this said, his full, intense attention falls on little Alina.

My stomach cramps as if my intestines were boiling, and I am no longer faking my nausea. A guttural hum rises inside me. I retch parts of the spell into my palms, swallow back what I can. It isn't the time yet. Not yet!

"The youngest Daughter of the Moon." Gagargi Prataslav pats Alina's head, his long, skeletal fingers weaving into the gray-brown hair. "Still on her sixth year, is she not?"

Alina tenses and seems to shrink before my very eyes. I have never wanted anything as much as to rush to her, to hold her, but that I can't do. Elise, Sibilia, and Merile turn to me, hesitant, concerned, and afraid, seeking guidance on what to do. I can't provide them any, not when I am about to vomit out the spell that may not be enough to save us.

"Every family gives their every other child to fuel the greater benefit of the empire," the gagargi says, the terrible words preceding a suggestion unfathomable. "Imagine how it looks to the people, when the imperial family refuses to follow this rule."

It is clear to me now. He wants Alina's soul, though it is deeply anchored to her body. That he shall not have, even if this will cost us older sisters dearly. I force my back straight, lower my arms to my sides. And curiously enough, now that I am about to set the spell free, it no longer fights against me.

"It lives in his shadow," Alina whispers, filling the calm moment about to shatter. "It's growing."

The gagargi takes a step back and stares at his shadow, and with his gaze, with Alina's words, everyone's eyes are drawn to the black shape veiling the planks. This is the best I can hope for. I part my lips and release the spell.

"What do you see?" the gagargi asks, unaware of the threads of silver that coil through the air toward him. This spell will not be difficult to maintain once connected to a person, I know this from personal experience. But each word I want the gagargi to believe will drain more of my strength than the previous, both that which was bestowed on me by the Moon and that of my very soul.

"It's growing bigger." Alina hugs herself, her face paling as if she had not a drop of blood left in her veins. "There's two of them . . ."

My spell reaches the gagargi at the exact same moment as my little sister falls limp on the floor. The gagargi swats his palm at the back of his head. Does he feel my spell?

"What is this?" the gagargi asks his two captains, as if they were to blame for this deviation from his plan, merely annoyed rather than suspicious.

"Alina!" Merile shrieks, kneeling by our sister. "Celestia, help!"

I dare not to move a step now that I am connected to the gagargi, and so I can but watch from aside. The good man, Captain Janlav, rushes to shelter little Alina from anyone who might think to hurt her more. He gathers her into his arms, holds her against his chest. "It's all right. She's alive. She's breathing."

"Alina!" Merile cries as Sibilia pulls her up from the floor. Elise stands as if frozen, so far apart from our younger sisters. I pray the Moon our youngest sister has merely fainted from fright, nothing more.

The gagargi sighs, shaking his head at the scene, and I feel the thread connecting us pulsing. I sense that he got what he needed. My sisters are terrified. He thinks that they have lost faith in me. The two captains have seen us weak and wailing. "Captain Janlav, take them away, will you? They are of no more use to me."

The gagargi lies, for this isn't the case. But I am relieved as Captain Janlav carries little Alina out, as my sisters follow behind him, leaving me alone with the two most frightening men I know. If it weren't for the spell, the nights soaking in my father's light, this one and only chance I have to save my sisters, I would follow my swan-self's suggestion and flee the room regardless of the consequences.

Boots is already drawing the door closed when the gagargi adds, "Captain Ansalov, you can return to your duties."

This I didn't expect, and the lack of knowing the gagargi's reasoning behind this sudden decision unnerves me. The line of Captain Ansalov's jaw tightens, but he is a soldier too experienced to disagree. He simply salutes and strides out. I am glad to see him go, but also terrified of remaining alone with the man who stole my soul once already.

When only the gagargi and I are left in the dining room, his demeanor changes. He spreads his arms wide, as if welcoming me into his arms. There is still no sign of a spell, and yet his words are ominous beyond comparison. "It would be futile of you to try and resist."

Even with my spell latched to him, doubt nags my resolve. The gagargi masters his dark art. He has decades of practice and studies behind him. What chance do I stand against him? There is only one way to find out: to do the exact opposite of what he told me, to resist him for as long as I can.

"We might as well start." The gagargi chuckles, and when he finally pronounces the glyph of his own, I am appeased, but only for a moment. For I know that though his violence will not leave behind bruises, he will take pleasure in breaking me. He wants to, needs to take over my mind. He needs to leave this room believing he has achieved this. That is the only way I can save my sisters. "You do know, the less you resist, the easier it will be for you. Think about it, Celestia. Would it really be so terrible for you to simply enjoy my company? Once upon a time you did cherish my touch."

I gasp as the spell lashes against my face, half of it for show, the other half from genuine shock at how difficult it is to keep him out of my mind, even when prepared for the attack. The gagargi strolls to me in a leisurely pace, dripping water. I stand still as he reaches out to fondle the back of my neck, his breath so close I can smell his hunger, not a morsel devoured, not a drop drunk to quench his thirst. "You will stand by my side."

I dare not to move, not to breathe. Regardless of what I told myself before, I am not whole. I will never be whole. But my spell is still attached to him. If Sibilia is right, the gagargi will think my words his own. Yet I must be mindful of them. I will not have strength to make him believe many.

"Stand by my side." The gagargi lifts his hand to draw a circle on my forehead as he has done before. His spell intensifies. I feel it pushing through my skin. I wonder, does the same principle apply to him? Does he have only a limited supply of ideas he can press on me? Is that why he ordered the two captains to leave? "Before our people."

"The ceremony," I whisper. Him being closer . . . Him being closer makes it easier for me, too, to wield my spell. My confidence grows. My words hold my father's power and his do not. I press my will on him through the threads connecting us. "You will send for me."

For even if I want nothing as much as to leave this house right at this moment, this encounter will leave me drained. I am not yet married to the Moon. My sisters and I, we need more time, not only to plan but to start trusting each other again. I don't know if a month will be enough, but that is the best I can do.

"Send for you?" The gagargi blinks, shakes his head, but I am almost sure he doesn't realize the form my resistance has taken. Indeed, his next words, the cruel smile, confirm this. "I will send for you."

He thinks it his idea. The spell is truly working. But my expression must not betray how I rejoice over this small victory. Not when the battle itself remains yet unfought.

"In the ceremony, the imperial family will show example," he continues, and I know what he means without him saying it aloud. It is an idea too horrifying for me to voice.

"Show example," I repeat, and I think it is out of my own initiative, not his. The gagargi wants Alina, though she is almost seven already. He wants to extract her soul before the gathered crowd and feed it to the machine. He will not give up on her before his will comes to pass. I speak four more valuable words. "Hand over her soul."

"Hand over her soul?" The gagargi considers this for a moment. He knows my little sister is weak of mind, has seen it with his own eyes now. Potions don't work on her, and the guards will confirm this. She isn't fit for a public appearance, and extracting a crying child's soul before the crowd wouldn't be the best of propaganda.

"Hand over her soul," I repeat, and will him to draw the right conclusion. Let him want me to present a soul bead and feed it myself to the machine. When that day comes, the bead will not contain Alina's soul, but that of some other unfortunate person.

The gagargi's gaze sharpens. "Celestia . . ."

His spell only builds up while I feel mine already waning. Sibilia did warn me that the power charged on me would drain out all of a sudden. I don't dare to spend more on reinforcing my idea when there is still more I need to accomplish.

"You are very important to me," he says, and his words sink in. I am important. I have always known that I am important while my sisters are not. No, that is of his doing, something he wants me to believe toward his own myriad ends.

"You will send for me," I repeat, focusing my fast-fading spell on the one last idea that I must imprint onto the gagargi's mind. "You will send for my sis—"

The spell that ties the gagargi to me snaps mid-word, and I recoil from . . . not pain, but absence of power, that of my father is all gone. Desperate, I attempt to pronounce the glyph again, the litany of consonants, even if the resulting spell will be powered by my own soul.

The glyph refuses to take shape. It's a mindless, arcane thing. It doesn't care about my desperation, doesn't care that crucial words remain yet to be said.

"I will send for . . ." the gagargi muses, rubbing the back of his head as if he had a headache.

"For my sisters," I whisper, praying the Moon my mere voice will be enough. The only way I can ensure their safety is for us to stay together. But my words lack power now. "My sisters."

"It is agreed then, dearest Celestia." The gagargi nods, oddly satisfied, as if he had what he came for at last. "I shall send for you in time for the ceremony. You may bring one of your sisters with you."

Chapter 11

Alina

The roses bloom red and pretty, but even so there's something very wrong about them. I pick up Sibilia's dance card from the sofa pushed against the wall and squint at the flowers Elise had to paint during the night so that our sister wouldn't learn about the surprise. Every petal is as it should be, every leaf, too. But . . .

"Table. On the table. Next to the pastels." Merile raises her voice at Beard. She holds the silver mirror in one hand, a piece of paper in the other. Being five years older than me, my sister gets to oversee the preparations while Celestia and Elise ready Sibilia for her big night. Though I don't think she'd know what to do if Irina and Olesia weren't there to advise her.

"Are you certain you've ogled at yourself from all the possible angles yet?" Beard asks my sister as he lowers the tray of meringues on the oval table that has been moved before the windows. Irina nods both in approval and disapproval, two thin fingers lifted to her lips.

"No." Merile sniffs, tilting the mirror so that she can better see the ghosts. Rafa and Mufu spin with her. I've brushed their coats to shine copper brown and silver gray. "Punch. What's taking so long with the punch? They'll be ready any moment now, and we're not—there's still so much to do!"

But I think the drawing room looks like a different place already, as it's meant to look. We—or the guards actually—have already moved the furniture against the walls and looped the maple leaf chains to hang from the ceiling. There's not much left to do for me, apart from the very important task, but the time for that comes only later. I dangle my feet over the sofa's edge. I'm bored.

As if sensing this, like Nurse Nookes always did, Olesia turns around and drifts across the carpet that's been set very straight. She sits down next to me and brushes the roses with the tips of her pale fingers. "Beautiful, aren't they?"

"Pretty . . ." I whisper back at her, though with Merile overseeing—that's what she calls it—the guards entering and leaving the room, no one is paying any attention to me, not even Rafa and Mufu, because they're too busy hoping that one of the guards would trip and scatter treats. I glance at the roses once more. Though Papa looks at them fondly from the sky, he's not yet up in this world and won't be for some time still, as it's not yet even five here. The time for shadows . . .

I realize what's wrong with the roses. "They have no shadows."

Olesia leans closer to me, to flick the dance card open. Though of course it won't open. She doesn't have a shadow. Or she does, but not in the way living things have.

I turn the dance card open for her, careful not to wrinkle the paper. "Maybe they're ghost flowers."

"Perhaps you are right." Olesia tousles my hair that Elise refused to braid this morning and repeatedly told me not to braid myself either. Everyone has been tousling my hair lately, since . . . I'm not going to think about the gagargi or what I saw in his shadow. I don't need to think about that. Not for three weeks or so at least. Not until he sends for us.

"Do you think we'll start soon?" I ask the ghost.

Olesia glances at the locked door of the room Celestia and Sibilia share. Well, it's not really locked, but I like to think it's that way, because we have the key and if we wanted to, we could lock and open it at will! But we don't want to do that, and we don't need to do that, because Elise arranged with Captain Janlav that she and Sibilia and Celestia can use the room to get ready for the Ball, that's how she calls Sibilia's surprise. And that's not the only thing she arranged—the decorations and the treats and the dance cards are all of her doing. She talked and talked and smiled and smiled until Captain Janlav and the guards agreed that they'd never wanted to do anything as much as to celebrate my sister's debut.

"No, not yet," Olesia replies after thinking about my question for quite a while, though neither she nor her sister actually bothered to go and check up on my sisters. Lately, they haven't been very good ghosts. They haven't done much of the floating around or walking through the walls and they don't appear that often anymore either and when they do, they don't stay for long. It's as if they've grown lazy.

Though I could have, I haven't grown lazy, and Nurse Nookes would be proud of me. And Mama, too! I can read and count all by myself now. But there's not too many people around to tell about it. Nor that many things to read. Not that many things to count either, apart from hours and days.

"One. Two. Five." I poke each dance listed. There's five of them and then five again, with blank spaces left for the names of the cavaliers. Waltz, polka, the one with the tricky name that I call goose song, mazurka, and then there's the chicken dance. "Ten."

"I am looking forward to dancing," Olesia muses, gazing at the guards from under fluttering lashes. They look different today, too, with their clothes freshly laundered, with their hair braided with red ribbons and thick red belts tied around their waists. "We have never had a ball in this house."

"Surely you had at least one!" I say, because lately the ghosts have also started to forget things. They've always been pale, but now they're definitely beyond any color. I realized this upon coming back from visiting the shadows. I could have stayed with them in the dark. They were very friendly, and the ape and the swan were there, too. They promised to take good care of me. But I told them I couldn't stay for long because my sisters would grow worried about me. And when I woke up, my sisters were so relieved that I knew I'd been right to return.

"Perhaps we had." Olesia glances at Irina as if hoping her sister would agree with her. But Irina is too busy guiding Merile to notice either of us. As she drifts closer to the table, farther away from us, she dims so much that I can barely make out her shape. Maybe the ghosts are fading because they've let me and Merile and Sibilia see them too many times. "Yes, we definitely had."

I'm happy to see her happier, though I think she believes now what she wants to believe. But I don't mind. There's no harm in that.

"Tonight, I shall dance every single song. I shall start with . . ." Olesia purses her lips as she studies the guards. Then a man enters the room, and Olesia smiles as a cat with a full plate of cream just placed before her might. "That one."

The man with no beard or moustache, with his hair braided up and boots polished to shine, doesn't look familiar at all. As he crosses the room to join the other guards, his heels clack an excited tune. Who can he be? He laughs at something Captain Janlav said and tugs his shirt's edge down with both hands as if it were too short. It's only then I recognize him. "That's Tabard."

"Tabard? Yes, he is a fine-looking fellow, though those ribbons and belts should be white."

That's what Elise said, too, but red was all that Captain Janlav could find, so red is what we have to make do with. But I don't want to think of that now. I've sat nice and still long enough already.

"I want to dance the chicken dance," I announce, and jump down from the sofa. It's not fair that everyone else gets to have fun tonight but Merile and me! The guards pay no attention to me as I sneak toward the gramophone, past Merile's turned back. Done with the preparations, they're patting each other's shoulders and chatting, pleased with themselves.

"Which one is that?" Olesia asks, trailing behind me.

"It's the tricky one." I like how the steps form knots and watching my sisters stumble around, though usually it's only Sibilia who gets confused.

Olesia frowns at me when we reach the gramophone. "I am afraid I am not entirely sure which one you mean."

"Cot-cot." The discs are in a neat pile. I shift the sleeves to spell out the names. The one I want starts with the sounds chickens make. "Cot-cot-cot."

"Alina!"

I draw my hands away from the discs and spin around. Though I wasn't really doing anything forbidden. And I was careful!

"Away." Merile storms to me, Rafa and Mufu trotting next to her. Irina remains behind, a raised hand covering her mouth as if she, too, were upset with me. "Step away from the gramophone."

"Cot-cot-cot." I press my fists against my chest and wag my elbows, though Merile is taller than me. And older. She will always be older than me. But she can't really be telling me no all the time! "Please, just one dance . . ."

"No." Merile curls her fingers around my arm and pulls me away from the gramophone, past the table laden with so many treats that I can't even count that far, to the curtained-shut window closest to our rooms. The ghosts follow us, but they don't even try and make her stop. The guards barely glance at us. They're used to Merile's tantrums. "No. No and no."

"You're hurting me," I squeal, though really she's not. But she could if she wanted to.

"Too bad. Too bad for you." Merile squats down to whisper harshly in my ear. "The point. The whole point of a debut is that you need to be sixteen or older to participate. And today Sibilia turns sixteen, and Papa be my witness, I forbid you to ruin the only ball she might ever get to participate in."

I blink back tears, though I don't know why I'm crying. I did want to dance. But I also want . . . Sibilia has always been nice to me. She plays with us in the garden. She reads the scriptures every evening. She smiles and laughs, though the gagargi said that she doesn't matter to anyone, not even to Celestia. But then again, he said many horrid things.

He hinted that he'd feed me to his machine, as I'd known he'd do all along. He claimed that Elise had in some way I don't really understand sided with him and plotted against Mama. During those agonizingly long minutes that we waited for Celestia to return, Sibilia said that the gagargi is full of lies. That must have really been it, at least as far as Elise is concerned, because neither Celestia nor Elise ever brought the topic up afterwards.

"You can let go," I say in a tiny voice, placing my hand atop of Merile's. My sister stares at me suspiciously, black brows drawn together. I bet the gagargi was just trying to turn us against each other. Or maybe not. Irina and Olesia have warned Merile and me about the inherent deceitfulness of older sisters many, many times, whatever that really means.

"Eye." Merile taps her cheek with a forefinger. "I will keep an eye out for you."

I remain completely still by the curtains as Merile strides back to the table with Irina, to count the glasses or something else Elise told her to do. Though I have my one task, I'd like to help more. But asking Merile now would only end in her raising her voice to me again, and I don't want that. I don't like people being angry at me.

"That leaf might fall." Irina points at one of the maple leaves that the guards slipped through the thread holding the curtains together. The leaf does look lopsided, even before she prods it with her finger.

"I'll fix it." This is Sibilia's debut, and I don't like the way her shadow has acted lately. Maybe Merile is right. Maybe this will be Sibilia's only ball.

But as I shuffle closer to the curtains, something crunches under my right sabot. I squat down to pick it up. This something is black and sharp. No, not really only black, but kind of see-through. "What is this?"

Olesia cranes down at the black grain. Then she glances at the door leading to Celestia's and Sibilia's room. "You should ask your older sisters."

I close my fingers around the black grain so tight it bites my skin. I really don't like the way the ghosts speak of my older sisters. "Maybe I will."

But right at that moment, the door leading to Celestia's and Sibilia's room opens.

"Is everything ready?"

It's Elise, and yet as she lingeringly pulls the door closed behind her, she's not my sister. Or that is, she's more so than she's been on any day during this summer. With her gray eyes sparkling with mischief, the gleaming red-gold hair curled atop her head, and dressed in a thin white gown, she's the very Elise, the silly, wonderful Elise with whom everyone wanted to dance back at the Summer Palace.

"I think we are." Captain Janlav snaps his fingers once, and I wish his uniform were still decorated with silver ornaments, not with red ones. Beard and Tabard and Belly and Boots and Boy settle into a line next to him, at the edge of the carpet. There's some tugging of shirts and lifting of belts and slipping of flasks into the back pockets. "Right, lads?"

"Yes, we are!" The guards' reply is booming, cheerful—false, too—as if they really weren't guards, but . . . Elise beholds them with a warm curiosity, as if they were our guests. Are they? She calls them her friends, but I'm not sure they'll ever be mine.

"Merile?" Elise turns to our sister, still beaming at the guards. But her laughter doesn't chime like it used to. It's weary and worn, like the dress she wears, the one from which she and Celestia removed the sequins during the train journey. "How about you?"

"Ready." Merile hides the hand mirror behind her back, and though Rafa and Mufu rub against her shins, she doesn't bend down to pet them, which isn't right either. No one is as they should be. "I'm ready. Alina?"

My sisters and the guards all look at me, and I shuffle a step back, bump into the curtains and the window behind. It's as if we were playing a new game, but no one told me the rules. But though the guards play cards with us, they never play with us in the garden.

"Alina . . ." Elise tilts her head toward the sofa. I squeak as I notice the dance cards there. Maybe they did tell me the rules after all, but I just forgot them.

"Yes!" I dash to the sofa. The moment of the very important task assigned to me has come. "Yes! I've got them."

"Perfect." Elise claps her hands twice. Merile glowers at me from the gramophone, but Rafa and Mufu lay down on her hem, preventing her from moving. Irina wafts to her sister, who stayed by the curtains. The guards perch on the carpet's edge. "I shall bring her in then."

Elise disappears back into the room, only to appear a moment later with . . .

I clutch the dance cards with both hands as Elise and Celestia guide the blindfolded woman into the drawing room. She's Sibilia, though she doesn't look like her! A crown of maple leaves sits on her golden curls. The white dress that's whiter than anything we've worn in months makes her seem tall and slender and round all at the same time. I recognize the crescent-embroidered hem, the high neckline. It's the dress that Celestia wore the night we boarded the train!

"May I present you Sibilia, a Daughter of the Moon, of General Kravakiv's seed?" Elise asks Celestia as they halt before us. My oldest sister looks more like herself than Elise and Sibilia, though the dress she wears is funny. It has puffy lace sleeves that have been split at the bottom so that her arms are both covered and bare, even though she wears gloves. The hem is lacy too, but only because . . . she has cut it that way, maybe?

"You may," Celestia replies, the line that should have belonged to Mama. Her voice doesn't waver, though mine would have. My throat tightens on its own. I miss Mama so much! May Papa look after her soul in the sky!

Having received Celestia's permission, Elise glides behind Sibilia. Our sister stands very, very still while she unties the white blindfold. As Elise lets the blindfold drop on the floor, Celestia says, "Sibilia, meet the court."

But Sibilia keeps her eyes squeezed shut, as if she were dreaming and didn't want to wake up. My heart goes out to her. I know how it feels to see things, both the sort you never want to see again and those you don't want to let go of!

"Court—" Celestia gently pats our sister's arm—"meet Sibilia."

It's only then that Sibilia opens her eyes. Her gaze is gray and deep like mountain valleys and stormy seas, and it reminds me of . . . Mama. Our sister has grown so pretty and also very wise. I don't know why this thought makes me teary, but it does. I rub my eyes quickly, before anyone can grow worried about me. This is Sibilia's night.

"Father Moon." Celestia holds a white feather on her upturned palms. I think it's a swan feather, because though her hands are parted, the feather rests at ease. And though I've never been part of this ceremony before, I'm sure this isn't how it's supposed to go. She shouldn't be the one introducing our sister to Papa. She shouldn't be holding a feather. In her place should stand a gagargi with a swan soul bead. "Welcome your daughter to shine by your side, as in life also in death."

There's a heavy, swollen pause as we wait for the fall that must follow. My oldest sister's hands tremble under the feather's weight, just a little, but too much still. Though a week has passed since she sent the gagargi away empty-handed, she still tires easily.

"Honored swan, bear my message to the Moon." Celestia further parts her hands, and it's as if the two chandeliers decided to dim at that moment. I look around and realize, it's only me again. Or no one else has noticed this.

The feather falls. No, it doesn't fall, but floats, slowly, back and forth before Celestia. When it meets the floor, it should shatter and release the swan soul, though of course it can't, not when it's but a feather. And that's wrong because Papa will never learn that Sibilia has turned sixteen, that if she were to die she should become a star by his side!

The feather sways, lands on the planks, against Celestia's white hem. The guards start clapping, smile broadly at Sibilia. The ghosts clap, though their hands make no sound. Merile claps, and Rafa and Mufu wag their tails. I blink again and again because I've decided that I won't cry, no matter what, and when I next look at the feather it has turned black.

No, not black. A thinnest veil of gray has stretched out from Celestia's hem. It shifts through the feather, taking shape. I stare at the feather, glance at my sisters and the guards. They're still clapping. This is again one of those things only I can see.

The gray shape twirls into the faintest shadow of a tiny swan. It perches on its webbed feet, extends its long neck, lifts its delicate head up. I don't know where this shadow came from, or I know because I saw it. But I don't dare to even glance at Celestia. I need to, want to see what happens next.

The tiny swan tries its wings. Finding them light and steady, it rises with ease into the air, beak parted for a song even I can't hear. Three more flaps of the wings, and it soars past the chains of maple leaves, through the ceiling, and then it's gone, on its way to tell Papa about Sibilia's debut.

Though it's all so strange, I feel better now that I know our father will know.

"You may congratulate Sibilia," Celestia announces. I try and meet her gaze, but she is talking to the guards. I'm curious to find out if she noticed what just came to pass. Where did the swan come from? Was it of her doing? It wasn't the same one that brought the news of Mama's death, I'm sure of that.

"Thank you." Sibilia giggles, a hand lifted to cover her plump mouth. Celestia smiles as she places a palm on our sister's shoulder. She knows how the sacred ceremonies should go. She'll follow them as well as we can here. Yes, she must have been the one who brought the tiny swan to life, though I can't even begin to guess how she did it.

Sibilia straightens her back and extends her right hand toward the guards. Captain Janlav is the first to approach her. The ghosts watch in silence as he presses his lips on my sister's gloved fingers and meets her eyes. She jiggles on the spot, giggling. Captain Janlav laughs. I'm pretty sure this isn't part of the ceremony, but there's no swans left to witness anything.

Beard, Tabard, Belly, Boots, and Boy follow their captain's lead. They don't laugh, though. Apart from Boy, but his snickering sounds nervous, and he blushes awfully lot, even worse than Sibilia!

"Now."

Who spoke to me? I have to glance around me twice before I spot Olesia waving at me. Why is she doing so? Ah, yes, the dance cards! My very important task!

I tiptoe to Sibilia and curtsy as Elise taught me. "May I present you this evening's dance card?"

"Why, Alina . . ." My sister's cheeks glow in the same shade as the dance card's roses. "That you certainly may!"

I give her the first dance card. Celestia accepts hers with a smile, as does Elise. I like seeing my sisters cheerful. But there's something off in their smiles, something I can't quite name. They're happy, though we're locked into this room, though nothing is quite as it should be. But they're really happy, and maybe that's all that matters.

———

After the official ceremony is over, which is pretty soon, Elise announces that it's time to enjoy the refreshments, as she calls them. Merile cranks the gramophone, and the notes of the opera flap across the room like swallows with soaking-wet wings. Though I like music, my stomach knots. It's the same sad song that the awful Captain Ansalov was listening to the day we first met him. My sisters and the guards chat by the table moved before the windows. They don't seem to care about the music. They trust in the agreement between the two captains. It has the gagargi's blessing, after all. Captain Ansalov won't dare to break it.

I remain by the curtains closest to our rooms. I should join my sisters, but I don't want to, not even if Rafa and Mufu are both there, as are the ghosts. I don't feel like it, and I can't make myself feel like it either, even though I try really hard.

"Punch?" Elise hands over glasses filled to the brim, though no two are matching and some should be called cups or mugs. There's pastel cookies and treats of many sorts, but I don't want any. Sweet things always make me dizzy, and I'm already confused and lonely.

Boots stomps to claim a cup. "Yes, please!"

I fidget with the black grain I found earlier. Everyone is in a great mood, even Celestia, though she has had to sit down on a sofa chair to rest. The guards jest with my older sisters and the bravest of them even ask to be favored with a dance or two. They think that everything that has happened so far will soon be over, though it won't be. It won't ever be over for me and my sisters.

Someone pokes at my knee. It's Rafa, her big brown eyes wide and pleading. She's mistaken the grain for a treat. I've got nothing for her. "Sorry, Rafa."

And it's because I talk with Rafa that I miss whatever happened by the table.

"Oh, well . . ." Elise laughs, flicking her hand, spraying red drops around her. Boy stands before her, blushing terribly, a half-empty glass in his hands. As the red drops land every which way, on Elise's hem and the guards' tunics, he mutters apologies. My sister will have none of that. "It's only a glove!"

But it's not only a glove. The white satin is no longer so, but very, very red, and for some reason this fills me with dread. I shrink back, toward the curtains, though it's not night yet, and even if it were, Papa couldn't see me.

"Really, it's quite all right," Elise repeats.

Rafa presses herself against my knees, back arched. I pick her up and hold her against my chest. Nothing is all right. My sister is lying.

The grandfather clock strikes six then, and everyone falls silent. Though I know what's to come, I'm afraid. But I'm also sure that I'm the only one who realizes the foulness of this night.

"Why," Elise exclaims, "I believe it's time to dance!"

My sisters, the guards, and the ghosts gather onto the dance floor. Merile remains by the gramophone with Mufu. That's her part tonight. She's the orchestra.

"What's my part?" I whisper to Rafa.

She tilts her head to lick my chin, floppy ears drawn back. Her brown fur glows under the light of the chandeliers. Dressed in white, next to the curtains, I'm invisible.

"Am I a ghost?" I ask her, glancing at Irina and Olesia. But even they're more present than I am. Olesia has her arm hooked around Tabard's, who has no idea about this. Irina fans her face with her palm, eyeing Belly rather coyly.

Rafa shifts in my arms, to stare at them. No, not them, but their shadows. She's so much smarter than I am. I whisper in her ear, in agreement. "Tonight, I'm a shadow."

And I won't be in anyone's way. No one will see me apart from those who know where to look for me. I tiptoe further into the hem of the curtain.

Merile changes the song. The needle scratches the disc for a while before violins announce the waltz. Captain Janlav strides from Elise to Sibilia and bows deep. "May I?" he asks my sister, though his is the name my sister scrawled down first on the dance card.

"You may." Sibilia waits still as a statue, but not as still as I am, for him to step closer to her. She places her hand on his shoulder only after he's positioned his behind her back. Though he smiles, she doesn't move an inch. But when the waltz really starts, she melts in his arms.

He's a fine dancer. His steps are sure and firm and never stray from the rhythm. When my sister stumbles he's always there to save her, swirl her around or bend her back to make it all seem right. Sibilia's smile widens with each note of the violins. Her crown is red and her hair is gold, but it's her hem that's very white, swirling up and down and up and down. My sister is a striking sight, but when she next turns, I catch a glimpse of her eyes, and for the shortest of moments, her gray gaze is keyhole-hollow.

"Shall we join them?" Tabard bows at Elise as the first part of the waltz is almost over. Beard strides to Celestia, to ask the same question.

My sisters curtsy at the guards, and it's . . .

"We've never curtsied to them before," I mutter to Rafa.

She nods in agreement. I don't know if it's a good or bad thing that everything is unraveling tonight.

Led by Tabard and Beard, my sisters join Sibilia on the dance floor. Under the light of the two chandeliers, they're wonderfully graceful, swans soaring across skies. I want them to stay that way forever, and that's why I won't look at their shadows. I don't even glance at them as the polka starts and the dance partners change, not even when the polka ends and the couples shift to dance our version of the goose song.

Halfway through the goose song that reminds me of a three-legged table, Rafa shifts in my arms. She wants to stretch her legs. I lower her down. "There you go."

And as soon as her paws meet the planks, she runs to Merile, without as much as glancing over her shoulder at me. My throat shrinks, though she's her companion, not mine. Now I'm as alone as a shadow should be. As I know my shadow will soon be.

"Here you are!" Olesia glides to me, past Boots and Boy, who stomp in the merry rhythm of the mazurka. She looks different, too, a lady invited to a feast, though none of the other guests here can see her, dance with her. "Oh, why are you crying?"

Am I? I wipe my cheeks with the back of my hand. They come away wet. I don't know why I'm crying, or I do, but I can't say it aloud, because then everyone will grow worried about me.

"My dear, what is wrong?" Olesia bends down to cup my cheeks.

I swallow back tears, though my shrunken throat hurts. This is Sibilia's night, not mine. Real shadows never draw attention to themselves. "My sisters look so happy . . ."

Olesia shifts so that she can look at my sisters. They swirl in the arms of the guards, not only happy, but somehow wild, too. As if we were someplace else, maybe back in the Summer Palace and not locked into the drawing room of a house so far up in the north that during summers there are no nights.

"I know, it is sad . . ." Olesia trails off, her gaze fixing on Sibilia, my sister crowned by the too-early autumn, "that she won't ever leave this house."

That sounds wrong. I grip Olesia's ghost hand, but my fingers go through hers. "What do you mean?"

Irina and Olesia weren't present when Celestia confronted the gagargi. They remained away when she returned victorious, when she spoke slowly the news that filled us with joy, when she drifted to sleep that lasted for three days. But I did tell them everything, word for word. When the gagargi sends for us, either we all go or we all stay. And if we all go, Celestia won't let the gagargi feed me to his machine, she promised me that.

So why did Olesia then single out Sibilia?

"Nothing." Olesia pulls her hands away and straightens her back. "Nothing at all."

But I don't believe her. Merile has always said that I shouldn't trust the ghosts so blindly. I've always defended them, but now . . .

"Oh, this is the cotillion!" Olesia tousles my hair. "You will be all right." And without waiting for my answer to the question that may not have even been one, she hurries to the dance floor, waving at her sister. "Irina, come and dance this with me!"

The cot-cot song, my favorite, has never made me as sad. I wish Rafa would return to me, but she's busy with begging treats from the guards, and I don't want to call out to her, because shadows are supposed to stay silent. When I'm silent, people sometimes forget I'm present and say things they didn't mean me to hear. But for the ghosts, I'm the only one who can always see and hear them. I think everything they say is always of great importance, though I don't always understand what they mean.

Waltz and polka and another goose song. No one misses me during the dancing, as the evening behind the sewn-shut curtains and tar-black glass and barred-shut windows arrives, but doesn't darken. Yet, the room darkens so that all that remains is the brighter glow of the chandeliers, the whiter shapes of my sisters, and the redder belts and ribbons of the guards. Though the music is the same, each song is somehow faster than the previous, the steps of the dancers fierier than before, followed by soft pops. The guards spin and fling my sisters. They soar from one man to another, their feet moving in patterns so quick and complicated that I fear they might hurt themselves.

But faster they go, even faster, and soon their heels no longer touch the floor, and it's as if both they and the guards are dancing in the air, rising higher and higher, toward a ceiling that's no longer there, but replaced by a black sky as vast and wide as the one outside these walls.

And it's all so impossible, so very impossible, that I need to know that it's not true, that they're not about to leave me in this house alone, and that is why I decide to look at their shadows.

The guards' shadows are heavy, black and right, but those of my sisters . . .

When Celestia spreads her arms wide, in the deepest curtsy, she extends the wings that she doesn't have, but still has, that I know aren't strong enough to carry her.

When Elise spirals at the center of the dance floor, arms raised and twined together, head tossed back in a pealing gale of laughter, her shadow sways in a way that doesn't make sense, as if it were hanging from such a great height that her feet can't reach the ground anymore.

When Sibilia . . . I can't look at her shadow. I can't. My sister's hair has come loose and she's lost the crown of maple leaves. Yet her steps are lighter than they've ever been as she falls in the arms of Boy at the end of the song.

And then there are no more songs. I don't know how many there were. But when I look at Merile, I know there won't be more. Every single one of the discs is gone, shattered into black dust and rubble that has piled on the gramophone, the oval table, and at her feet. Yet, she cranks the gramophone as if she'd noticed none of that.

The darkness withdraws between two eyeblinks, and light returns to the room. Maybe it was never dark. Maybe I just imagined it. Maybe if I tell myself so many, many times, it will be as if I'd never seen what I saw. I can but try.

On the dance floor, my sisters curtsy to their last partners,

Celestia at Boots, Elise at Captain Janlav, and Sibilia at Boy. Celestia, Elise, and the guards stroll to the oval table, to catch their breaths and sip the punch and enjoy the sweet and salty treats. The ghosts trail after them, arms linked together. But Sibilia and Boy retreat to the other side of the room, to the sofa placed before the tall mirror.

I know I shouldn't look at them, it's not polite to spy, but I can't stop myself, because this at least is real. Besides, as I'm too far away to hear them, it can't really count.

Sibilia arranges her dress better over her knees. Boy tugs his trousers straight. He meets her gaze, asks her something. She giggles behind a raised palm. He places his hand on hers, and she nods. He leans toward her—I don't really know why. She whispers something short and turns her head aside. His lips brush against her cheek, and then both of them pull back and resume sitting on the sofa, blushing redder than the maple leaves.

"Here you are!" Captain Janlav's voice startles me. I jump a step aside. Did he catch me spying? That is, not really spying. "I was starting to wonder where you'd slipped off to."

I turn my gaze aside from Sibilia and Boy. I don't know what I saw, but now they've both already got up from the sofa. I'm not going to say a word about this to anyone, not even to the ghosts. But I must say something, and so I say, "I slipped nowhere. I was here all the time, watching you dancing."

Captain Janlav kneels before me so that his brown eyes are level with mine. He's always been nice to me. And tonight, he's the only one apart from Olesia who's come and talked with me. Merile shouting at me really doesn't count.

I toy with my hem as I sway from side to side. Knowing Elise and Sibilia, they might come and steal Captain Janlav away any moment, and then I'd be alone again. "I would have wanted to dance, too, but Elise and Merile wouldn't let me."

"I know." He pats my head, and his touch is solid and soothing. "You have to wait but a few more years."

This evening things have been happening too fast, and they continue to do so. Words come to me, and I let them out. "I always have to wait. I'm always too young."

"Oh, little Alina," he chuckles, "there's some good things about being young, too."

I glare at him. He's very wrong. There's nothing good about being the youngest. "Like what?"

He glances at my sisters and the guards, then winks at me. "You get to ride piggyback."

Ride piggyback! Elise and Sibilia always refuse to carry me piggyback. The last time I got to ride Captain Janlav was . . .

"Up you get." He turns his back to me. Without a second thought, I climb up. He prances his arms as if they were feet, and his red epaulets swoosh. Tonight no one is as they should be, and now he's a wild stallion. Like Bopol. "Ready?"

"Yes!"

Captain Janlav gallops around the room, though Celestia and Elise look at us, brows arched like angry gulls, Merile frowns in what I know is envy, and the guards laugh. I don't care. I giggle and flick his braids as if they were reins. "Gallop. Gallop."

He obeys me like a good steed should, but still he's not a real horse. I try and forget that, but can't. And too soon, he stops by the sofa and lowers me onto the floor. "How about that?"

I brush my hem down again, to hide my patched stockings. Piggybacking is fun, but so is . . . "I wish I could ride a real pony."

"Well, I can't help with that one," he says, as I knew he would. All the horses in the stables belong to Captain Ansalov. But then he lowers his voice in a way people do when they're about to tell a secret. "But soon you'll get to ride in a train again."

Elise really likes Captain Janlav, and I like him quite a lot. Maybe he really is my friend, too. I wink at him because that's what you do when you remind someone of a shared secret. "I don't think so."

"What do you mean?" His brows furrow, and he glances at Elise. Did my sister not tell him? Or did he simply forget the plan?

"Either we all go or no one goes, and I think it might be the latter."

He jolts like a spooked horse might, away from me. As he stares at me, eyes wide, I realize I've said a thing that should have been kept a secret, though I don't really know why.

Chapter 12

Merile

Sleep. I can't sleep. My companions snore between Alina and me, keeled over on their backs, with their tiny paws propped up, their tongues lolling out of their parted mouths, their bellies bursting full. The air smells of musk and wet fur, but it's not my stinky sillies that keep me awake. It's Alina.

My little sister was so very upset after the Ball. She cried for what must have been two hours, but wouldn't tell me why. She might have just been tired from all the excitement. Or she might have been afraid of the gagargi and the Great Thinking Machine, and who can really blame her when he as much as admitted to wanting to feed her soul to the machine! But I don't think it was a case of either. I've seen her cry enough times to be able to figure out what ails her.

Creak. There's a creak where before there was only silence, a long and sullen creak. It's the drawing room's door. Someone has pushed it open.

I stare over the blanket's edge at the door Captain Janlav locked behind him. I grip it with both hands, knuckles white, unable to move. Are Captain Ansalov's soldiers coming for us, in the middle of the night when Papa can't see what comes to pass? Is this what Alina somehow sensed? She knows more than she tells us.

The door creaks again. Now, it's being pushed closed. Ha! People don't close doors behind them when they're up to no good. I'm no longer at all afraid. Really, I'm not. I want to know who's in the drawing room.

"Rafa, Mufu." I keep my voice low because I don't want to wake up Alina. My sillies continue snoring. And smelling.

Groan. The long floorboards groan under the steady, cautious steps that don't belong to any of my sisters. Whoever walks in the drawing room doesn't know the silent path. I shall call them "mystery visitor."

"Mufu." I curl up and poke at my pretty companion. She flinches awake, but remains lying on her back. Her belly is so full it might just split open. "Watch over Alina, will you?"

Mufu's tongue disappears inside her mouth as she glances sideways at Alina. My sister is crying in her sleep. She hinted that she'd done something she shouldn't have done, but I've no idea what she meant because she refused to tell me more. "Just watch over her."

Mufu snuggles closer to Alina. It's safe for me to get up and investigate. And this time around, I'll be careful. I won't leave the room, not that that's an option, because Celestia has the key ring. Really, I won't be placing my sisters at risk even in the slightest.

Tiptoe. I tiptoe to the door and press my ear against the panel. The creaks are closer now, as if the mystery visitor were hesitant to go through with their plan, whatever that might turn out to be. And what could it be? I have no idea.

The steps stop, not behind this door, but before . . . At first I'm not sure, and then I am, because we've been locked in this house for so long that I've learnt to recognize every screech and sigh of every room we're allowed in. The mystery visitor stands before Elise's door. How curious! Who would have anything to say to Elise in the middle of the night? She's become friends with some of the guards, but surely whatever they have in mind can wait until morning!

There's a knock. Short and short. Long and short.

I hold my breath, excited, but nervous, too. Is Elise awake still? Sometimes she cries at night, even though she smiles through the days. Though lately, there's been less smiling and more arguing. Celestia and Elise think that Alina and I are too young to realize that they're fighting. Or not fighting. Disagreeing and avoiding each other. It started after the gagargi left. No, maybe even before that. Can it have something to do with him claiming that Elise had plotted against Mama and funded the revolution? But Sibilia said it was all lies. She did say that.

I hear Elise's door open, quiet words exchanged, the door closing. Plan. What if my sister has a better plan than Celestia? Irina and Olesia always caution us not to trust our older sisters. I've always told Alina not to believe everything the ghosts say. But what if they're right! What if it's not Celestia that's hiding things from us, but Elise!

There's no time to lose. I dash to the vanity desk's cracked mirror. "Irina, Olesia."

My heart pounds and my mouth turns dry. I need the ghosts now. They can go and eavesdrop on what happens in Elise's room. I can't.

"Quick." I tap my fingers against the mirror's surface. Rafa stirs from her sleep. She stares at me, her big eyes wide. I shake my head at her, lower my voice. "Quick."

But though I knock on the mirror's surface, the ghosts don't appear. Do they tire as we do? They did stay with us longer to-

246 • Leena Likitalo

day than they've done in weeks. Toward the end, they looked pale and weary, even more so than Alina.

"Come now."

And still nothing, not even a whiff of their perfume. It's agonizing. Do I spend more time trying to lure the ghosts in or . . . If I wait, I might miss something important. The ghosts might show up later or then not at all. Ah, this is such a difficult call!

I make up my mind and abandon the mirror. I take a spot next to the old armchair and press my cheek against the flaking wallpaper. The walls of this house aren't particularly thick.

"Please tell me, tell me now"—Captain Janlav's voice is unmistakable, especially since he's raised it—"what is this nonsense about none of you going?"

There's a lengthy pause. No doubt Elise considers what to say. She, too, must think how exactly did Captain Janlav learn of our plan? How did he? Surely no one has told him that it was Celestia who sent the gagargi away empty-handed, that she'll do so again and again until he lets us walk free.

"I don't know what you are talking about," Elise finally replies. I'd have said the same thing.

Two hasty steps. "Don't you take me for a fool! Oh, sweet woman, don't you dare to take me for a complete and utter fool!"

Silence. With my ear pressed against the wall, I can keep an eye out for Alina and my companions. She sleeps still, but Rafa and Mufu are wide awake. They've managed to roll over onto their swollen, round bellies. If I were to summon them, they'd obey at once, though they might not move terribly fast.

"Elise," said in a much softer voice. I shake my head at my companions. I'm not afraid. Elise is seventeen. She can take care of herself. "Do you think I have come to you now, in the middle of the night, to punish you? Do you really think so?

Answer me, woman. Do you really think so?"

"No."

Maybe I should feel guilty for eavesdropping on a conversation that might be meant to be private. But I don't. I know what I'm told and nothing more—I deserve to know the rest. I shall listen with great glee.

"Good." I imagine Captain Janlav as he must be, standing with his heels together, hands clasped behind his back, staring sternly at my sister. "I'm here to warn you as a friend. The game you and your sisters play is dangerous."

"Dangerous," Elise laughs. She's upset. I'd be upset, too, if someone barged into my room and started blaming me for things. "What a funny thing to say! Tell me, has there been a moment since my sisters and I boarded the train, since we arrived in this house, that we haven't been in danger?"

Silence. Thin and stretched, a very uncomfortable sort of silence.

"It's true that you have been in a certain degree of danger, but I have been always there to protect you."

"That you have," Elise admits, but she's not terribly pleased about it. Or she is, but she also sounds bitter.

Captain Janlav starts pacing the room, his steps taking him past the spot where I listen. He wouldn't be happy if he learnt that I'm listening to them talking. Too bad for him, but I, if anyone, know what it feels like not to get everything I want. And yet, I hardly ever rant about that.

"If Celestia refuses to go, you will no longer be my responsibility."

This is something I didn't know. Elise mustn't have known this either, because she asks, "Whose, then?"

Another annoying pause in their conversation. This one

being of the foreboding sort.

"Captain Ansalov's."

My knees buckle, and if I weren't leaning on the wall already, I'd do so now. Captain Ansalov is a cruel and ruthless man. He would have ordered me shot if Celestia hadn't intervened that night when I followed the magpie. But since the gagargi left, my sister has been very tired. Though she's the empress-to-be, I don't know if she could save me, us again.

"Do you know what his commands are?" My sister's voice is steady, though she, too, must be terrified.

"That's the very thing I wanted to warn you about."

"I see," Elise says. I want her to say so much more. Celestia promised us that either we all go or all stay. But Captain Janlav's words imply that neither option is really possible, that something really bad might happen to us if . . .

The realization rolls upon me like an imperial freight train, squeezing me under the clanking wheels and tons of iron. What if the ghosts were right all along? What if we really can't trust Celestia? What if she brokered a secret deal with the gagargi, one that she's too ashamed to admit aloud?

On the other side of the wall, Elise remains silent. Maybe she's realized the same thing, and now she's too frightened to do anything else. If I were in her shoes, I mightn't be able to speak either without my voice wavering.

"Elise . . ." Captain Janlav sighs so deep the floor squeaks under his boots. "This isn't only about you and your sisters."

Elise is the most graceful of us. I can't be sure if she really moves toward him, but I imagine her doing so. I also imagine her saying a very different thing than: "I know."

First Celestia and then . . . No, Elise is just upset. That must be it.

"You say so," Captain Janlav says, "but I'm not certain that you do. If Celestia doesn't return to him, there will be no end to the civil war."

I close my eyes because this is too much. Memories of the burning villages we passed on our way to Angefort return to haunt me. Ash. I can still smell the burning logs and ash, lost homes, lost lives, too. And then there is the news my seed brought to this house, the battles waged, people being shot or their souls ripped from their bodies. It feels to me Captain Janlav is blaming us for that, and it's more than a bit unfair.

Yet Elise replies, "I know that, too."

I stare at my companions, shocked. They look back at me, unshocked. It can't be true. The gagargi is to blame for everything. My sisters and I have done nothing wrong! How could we when we've been trapped in this house for half a year?

"If you were the empress, what would you do?"

I wait for Elise to say that she's not, that it's not for her to choose. But instead there's a silence longer than any before. And I do wonder then. Sibilia insisted that what the gagargi said on that rainy day in the dining room about Elise was simply twisted lies. But could it really be that what I heard with my very own ears was true all along, that my sister did indeed side with gagargi and betray our mother?

And us.

Truth. Now that I've guessed what my older sisters are hiding, or most of it in any case, I expected everything in this world to look different. But in the morning, the tables and chairs of the drawing room remain where we left them the night before.

There's no sign whatsoever of Captain Janlav's visit. Or there kind of is.

Leftovers. As I munch the leftovers from the Ball, soggy triangular cucumber sandwiches, hardened tiny sweet rolls, and softened meringues, none of my sisters speak. Even little Alina is uncustomarily silent as she toys with Rafa's tail. My older sisters sip the hot tea and swirl it in the chipped cups. Millie has taken away the punch, but there are red spill marks on the white tablecloth and the floorboards are sticky. The maple leaves have dried and crumbled into red fists. I don't like how they look.

When the swan clock strikes eleven, Celestia retreats to the divan before the fireplace. She says, "My sisters, today we shall not dance."

Elise and Sibilia nod in agreement, and even I'd guessed as much. Black dust stains our hems. There will be no more music in this house. Though it's not my fault the discs broke. Really, it's not. What was I supposed to do? Stop playing them midway through the Ball?

Celestia lies down on the divan, tired from dancing. Or from keeping track of her numerous lies. Elise resumes darning her stockings on the padded chair next to the gramophone. She glances at Sibilia, who cradles the book of scriptures on her lap, on the sofa before the tall mirror. Elise's lips are drawn into a spurious smile, and she's got thick blue circles around her eyes. I'm sure that even if I were to ask her why, she wouldn't tell me.

"But we shall resume the practices tomorrow," Elise states matter-of-factly. "Shall we not?"

Sibilia nods, maybe agreeing to more than dancing, but how would I know? Maybe all of our older sisters have been lying to Alina and me! Now that I think of it, ever since we left the Summer City, they have been exchanging meaningful glances and nods and shakes of heads when we're present. Not really telling us anything.

"Yes, of course we shall," Celestia replies.

I herd Alina to the carpet, to play with Rafa and Mufu. She's been wiping her cheeks too often this morning. But this time around, I can't tell her it's going to be all right. Not now that I know what she did. I figured it out last night. She's the one who accidentally revealed our plan to Captain Janlav! Even she, my sweet little sister, has been keeping secrets from me!

"Up," I whisper. I can't stand this anymore. I simply can't. "I need to get up for a moment."

Rafa and Mufu bounce to me. They wag their tails and stretch their backs, thinking we're about to go out. Though of course we're not going to do that. It's not yet the time for that. It's never time for anything in this house. Besides, my companions need to stay and keep Alina preoccupied. "You. You stay with Alina."

Ghosts. I need to talk with the ghosts about what I heard and realized last night. I don't yet know how I'm going to do that with my sisters present in the room. Maybe the ghosts can read my lips. Or my mind. But I do need to consult with them as soon as possible. It may be that they're the only ones who have been telling me how matters really stand, though I suspected otherwise for such a long time.

I slowly circle the room, holding the silver hand mirror before me. My sisters are too distracted to take note of me, Celestia napping, Elise busy with the needle, Sibilia immersed in her own secrets. Though she has the book of scriptures propped on her lap, she's not reading Papa's words. She's hiding a letter. I have no idea whom it's from or what it contains. I want to know the answer to both.

As there's no sign of the ghosts, I might as well.

"Sibilia. Sibilia, tell me . . ." I trail off as she glances at me from over the book's edge, chewing her lower lip. She's not sure what she's reading either. Wrong. Maybe she's only been wrong about everything and not intentionally misleading me.

Sibilia stares at me, at the hand mirror. She knows what I'm looking for. But this morning, she doesn't care about the ghosts. She returns to her letter, has no idea of the plots weaved right before our noses!

"Never mind."

I circle the room again. Ghosts. Where are the ghosts? I want to, need to talk with them. I don't have anyone else to turn to for advice. My older sisters never tell me anything. Or if they tell me something, it's not everything. And I can't bear this anymore, not after Captain Janlav as much as confirming what the gagargi said about Elise was true, not with knowing that Celestia, the very empress-to-be, has been conspiring with the gagargi behind our backs!

Darkest. I visit even the darkest corner of the drawing room and stay there for quite a while, despite the draft and the heavy shadows falling on me. I don't deserve to be kept in the dark like this, not when I have no, or almost no, secrets from my older sisters. I've had it with them lying to me! I've simply had enough! Whom am I supposed to trust when both Celestia and Elise have betrayed us?

But it's only on the fifth round around the room that the ghosts at last appear, in the tall mirror above Sibilia's sofa. They're barely more than mist. They must be exhausted from the dancing, too. Or from more than that.

I wave at the ghosts, invite them to join me, and retreat to the window closest to our rooms. Rafa and Mufu halt their play, one paw up, staring at me. I shake my head at them. Help. I don't need their help now. Or I do. They should stay with Alina. Even if this conversation kind of concerns her, too, my little sister is too young and frail to take part in it.

"How kind of you to join us," I greet the ghosts, turning around with the silver mirror held up so that I can spot where they decide to take shape. There, on my both sides.

Irina arches her brows at my tone. Angry. I didn't mean to sound angry at them. Or maybe I did. Does it even matter?

Olesia lowers her palm on my shoulder. She eyes me from head to toe. "My dear, you look positively vexed."

Point. Straight to the point, and that's what I need. Though I don't usually talk with the ghosts when my older sisters are present, today they're so deep in their own thoughts that if I keep my voice low, they won't notice a thing. Besides they've conducted their own secretive business unabashedly in my presence for months. "I am."

"Why?" Irina asks, curious.

"Right. You were right about Celestia and Elise." And I tell the ghosts briefly about the night before, Elise's mystery visitor, who turned out to be none other than Captain Janlav, and the following conversation, the accusations that my sister didn't deny, and the revelation that made me suspect that there's more to Celestia's plan than what she's shared with us. It wasn't Gagargi Prataslav who lied, but Elise! And Celestia has been conspiring with him toward her own ends!

"I knew it!" Irina clutches her fist against her heart. Olesia puffs her cheeks and seems to be holding her breath. "You cannot ever trust the older sisters!"

"What should I do?" The reflection shimmers. I realize my hand is shaking and the mirror shakes with it. Still. I force my hand to still. If neither Celestia nor Elise have our best interests in mind, then it's solely up to Rafa and Mufu and me to protect Alina.

"You must confront them," Irina says.

"When?" I whisper. I really can't call out my older sisters responsible to their actions when Alina is present in the room. Or can I?

"You are also an older sister." Olesia glances at Alina, who's playing with my sillies, so blissfully unaware of Celestia's and Elise's deceitfulness. "As a younger sister, what do you yearn for the most?"

"Truth." For there's still a chance, no matter how slight, that I may have drawn the wrong conclusion. I reply without hesitation, "I want to know the truth."

"Merile . . ." Elise's voice jitters, but she's not really concerned about me. I bet she's worried that I'm on the trail of her shady plans. "Is something the matter?"

Did she hear me talking? Would it make any difference anymore if she did? One look at the ghosts suffices to confirm the answer. I spin around. My ankle jolts. "Yes. Many things, in fact."

And then all my sisters are staring at me. Alina, with her deep-set eyes wide, has of course noticed the ghosts. Sibilia must have guessed as much, for she presses the book of scriptures shut. Elise and Celestia don't have a clue about the ghosts, and that serves them right.

"What is it, dear?" Elise wants to know.

Well, I've been told you shouldn't feel sorry for getting something you ask for. And she's definitely asking for it. "The gagargi really didn't lie. You schemed against our mother! And you're still thinking about siding with him!"

Elise stares back at me, her expression completely unreadable. My heart beats hollow notes. I wish her to raise her voice at me, be mad at me, tell me that I'm but a foolish child who's got everything mixed up.

But that she doesn't do. "Indeed, he didn't lie, and I don't regret deciding to make the world a better place for our people, for funding hospitals and orphanages, for supporting the troops that marched against their lords and ladies to put an end to their tyrannical rule. And yes, given even a half chance, I would do it again."

Her reply stuns everyone: Celestia, who must have known about this for a long time already, Sibilia, who obviously didn't suspect a thing, and Alina, who stares intently at our sister, or more exactly, her shadow.

"Huh." Irina drags her knuckles against her teeth. "That I didn't see coming."

"Me neither," Olesia agrees. "That girl is wicked."

And I guess that that is what Elise really is behind her faked smile and cheerfulness. I can see that clear at last. The question to ask is: is Celestia, too, someone else than she pretends to be?

There's only one way to find out.

"And you . . ." I stomp to Celestia, who sits with her back so very straight on the divan's edge. Captain Janlav's understanding about the deal she brokered with the gagargi differs significantly with the one she shared with us. "You lied to us about the plan, didn't you? You said either we all go or no one goes. But that's not the truth. You're going to save yourself and abandon us here, aren't you?"

"That is a very long list of questions," Celestia states. She slowly pushes herself up, blinks once, twice, as if chasing away dizziness. It takes her a considerable effort to get up on her feet. Regret. I regret charging upon her like this when I know she's still weak from facing the gagargi. But also, I don't. "I shall do my best to address your concerns."

I stagger back, for I expected fierce denial. And my oldest sister is so tall, so white, so much more than any of us, that at that moment I'm convinced that she never made a secret pact with the gagargi, that she indeed has a subterfuge to get us all away from here, away from his reach, a way of turning the world back to what it should be.

"My sisters, I will tell you the state of matters that I know to be true for certain."

And that's exactly what she does, and we listen to her, spellbound, Elise from the padded chair, Sibilia from the sofa, Alina from the carpet alongside with Rafa and Mufu. The ghosts hover to flank me, and I stand my ground as my sister finally reveals the truth.

The gagargi wants Celestia, the empress-to-be, to appear by his side at the autumn equinox. Hearts. He believes that if she were to stand by his side, he would win over the hearts of our people.

"If you were to do so," Elise interrupts our sister, not exactly hesitantly. Rather like she'd said the same words many times before without really being heard. "The civil war would end."

"Words of a traitor," Irina whispers in my ear, though war means bad, bodies scattered in mud and worse, and ending it sounds good to me. In principle, at least.

Celestia shakes her head slowly, as if she were disappointed in Elise making the suggestion in the first place. "I believe you are mistaken. For I don't think that he would stop hunting down those who sided with us even if I were to stand by his side. And if I were to do so, it would not be me. My sisters, you must understand that the gagargi also has it within his power to separate a person's soul partially from their body, to leave behind an automaton willing to obey his every command."

"I wonder how she learnt of that," Olesia mutters.

I wonder about the very same terrible thing. I snap my fingers, to summon Mufu. I swoop her up in my arms. Everything's better with my dearest companion close to me.

"I know for certain he would do this to me, and he would have the shell of a woman left behind do things I would never agree to do." Celestia strolls slowly to Alina. She leans toward our little sister, to lay a palm on her shoulder. "He would have her feed her sister's soul to the Great Thinking Machine."

Tears. I expect to see tears in Alina's eyes, for these words chill me so bad that I can't speak. But instead, having heard that her nightmares are what really awaits her, she grins at Celestia. "He can't have me. You won't let him have me."

I don't understand how she can sound so sure when Celestia has told us so many lies, when I'm more afraid now than I've been ever in my life!

Celestia cups our little sister's face and kisses her on the forehead. Rafa pecks her cheeks. "You are right. I will not let him. I fought him once . . ."

"Tell us about it," I plead with her. Powerful. I want my oldest sister to be powerful. Invincible. I don't want us to be this vulnerable!

Celestia draws away from Alina and turns to face Sibilia. "May I?"

"Why is she asking her opinion?" Irina's reflection shimmers. "She is the oldest."

But she's also my sister. And though I was right about Elise, I'm now pretty sure I was wrong about Celestia. She won't let harm befall us. She's far from defeated.

Sibilia nods, and I realize a curious thing. Some secrets are kept so because they belong to other people. How come I've never thought of that before?

"Thank you." And having received our sister's permission, Celestia tells of the furtive preparations and her confrontation with the gagargi in great detail. The ghosts and I behold Sibilia in wonder. Sure, I'd noticed her reading the scriptures, but I hadn't realized she'd grown to such power! And at the same time, I'm in awe of Celestia. How brave she was to face the gagargi alone! Though she was strengthened by Papa, there was no way of knowing if the plan would work.

"My sisters, I have kept the true result of our confrontation as a secret from you, and it was not my intention to give you false hope, rather to protect you from the desolateness of utter despair. I mentioned before that either we all go or no one goes. But my spell broke before I could imprint this on his mind. I managed to only convince him to leave and later send for me and one of my sisters."

"She failed," Irina states so coldly that my stomach cramps.

Mufu shifts on my lap, sensing my distress. I brush her fur from head to tail, several times in quick succession. The silver of the mirror shines softly under the light of the two chandeliers.

"What did she say before?" Olesia muses at last.

What exactly did Celestia say before? I close my eyes to recall her words. Did she lie about her meeting with the gagargi? No, she didn't exactly lie, but spoke of another possibility, of sending the gagargi's men away empty-handed as many times as need be.

"Why didn't you tell us before?" I ask, because, to be honest, she didn't gain us that much, regardless of her spell. Just a little more time together, a vague possibility of another chance to fight. "What will you do when he sends for you?"

"Will you gather around me, my sisters?" Celestia asks, sitting down cross-legged next to Alina. Rafa pokes my little sister with her nose, no doubt as baffled as I am to see her still so unconcerned.

Genuine. Celestia's request sounds genuine enough, and Sibilia does join her on the carpet without hesitation. I decide to do likewise and settle between her and Alina. Elise takes ages to make up her mind. Eventually, she rises up from her chair and glides to take her place between Celestia and me.

"Merile, you asked me what I shall do when he sends for me." Celestia takes hold of Alina's hand, Elise's hand. It's more than a gesture; a reminder, not a command. I lower the mirror on the floor and reach out for Alina's and Sibilia's hands. I can't recall the last time we were together like this. Was it on the train, after Celestia's previous plan crumbled?

"I shall do everything that is within my power."

But what Celestia doesn't say means more. The ghosts must have realized this too, because they draw away from us, so far away that I can no longer see them in the mirror. They understand that this moment is private.

"Everything," I whisper. Sibilia closes her fingers firmer around mine. "Everything may not be enough."

And that's a terrible thought. We're the Daughters of the Moon, and Celestia is the oldest. I always thought that that was enough. But now it seems that . . .

"I do promise you one thing, my sisters"—Celestia meets in turn Alina's eyes, mine, Sibilia's, even Elise's—"I will not let him take you from me. I will not ever leave you behind. Even if it will cost everything I hold dear in my life, nothing in this world, under the gaze of our celestial father, is as important to me as you are."

My eyes moisten. I sniff, because I'm twelve, and I don't cry. But Sibilia tears up openly and gasps for ragged breaths. Alina squeezes my hand. I echo the movement to Sibilia, and that's where the comforting ends, because Elise has remained unmoved all along.

Celestia has failed us. Fair. It's not fair to say so, because she tried, has tried as hard as anyone. And the reason she hasn't told us any of this before is that . . .

"She was protecting them."

I flinch so hard both Alina and Sibilia turn to stare at me. The hand mirror on the carpet shows nothing but my reflection. I shouldn't hear the ghosts. I study my sisters to see if they, too, heard Olesia's statement. Yes. Sibilia definitely did.

"I know," Irina replies. From the corner of my eye, I catch a glimpse of the ghost rubbing her chin. I quickly turn to behold Mufu. Wrong. It feels wrong to look at the ghosts when they think themselves invisible. "And don't I know it well."

"I . . . I'm not sure if I should say anything," Sibilia mumbles. I'm happy it's her speaking, that if someone will betray the ghosts, it's not me. She and me and Alina share a secret that doesn't really belong to us, that isn't ours to lay bare.

"Do speak," Celestia urges our sister. "This is the council of sisters. I will not shun anyone for challenging me." And with the last words, she turns to Elise. The traitor.

"You said . . ." Sibilia's hand turns clammy in mine. Let go.

Even so, I won't let go of her. "You said that you mightn't be able to defeat the gagargi as a Daughter of the Moon, but how about . . . That is, I'm no gagargi, but I think . . . Do you think you could defeat him as the Crescent Empress?"

What. What is she talking about? I stare at Sibilia, with my mouth hanging open. The ghosts stare at Sibilia, too. Celestia mentioned Sibilia learning a spell on her own, but could she really perform the most sacred of ceremonies?

"I've found a spell in the scriptures." Sibilia blushes furiously. Sweat buds on her forehead. Somehow, her red hair blazes more than it did last night. "If I had a swan soul bead, I might . . . But it's silly. Forget I spoke at all. We don't have one. Really, just forget my speculations."

"Irina . . ." Olesia nudges her sister. They're hovering right behind Sibilia now.

"Yes," Irina snaps. "Yes, I know."

"Look at them, Irina, the poor daughters. Do you really want their deaths on your conscience? What use do we have for it in any case anymore? We are as good as dead! Worse than that!"

Impossible. The ghosts are arguing so loud that it's impossible to ignore them anymore. Alina winces, shakes her hands free, and presses her palms over Rafa's ears. I hold on to Mufu with my thus freed arm. The ghosts' secret is not mine . . . "Anyone. Anyone who wants to speak can speak?"

"Anyone," Celestia replies, but her attention lingers on Sibilia. She's thinking our sister's words, as if she still knew more. "Anyone present in this room."

"Please, Irina." Olesia tugs her sister's arm. I don't know why they're so very present. Or I do. They've been fading for weeks, but now they're losing control of both their souls and shadows. "She is not like our sister. She would never abandon the girls. I know it in my heart as surely as I have ever known anything."

"Merile?" Celestia beholds me. She really wants to hear what I have to say. She's treating me like an adult. Which means I should act like one.

"Anyone present in the room, did you hear that?" I say loudly, hoping Irina and Olesia realize I'm talking to them. Nervous. I've never been this nervous. The ghosts have always been able to hear us, even when we can't see them. But it's a different thing to listen than to hear.

"Fine then." Irina sniffs, straightening her back. "Show yourself to them if you so wish. But if you turn out to be wrong, I shall never let you forget it."

Olesia beams. She shuffles hurriedly to the tall mirror, and upon seeing herself in the reflection, pats her bun and fixes an escaped gray lock. "You shall not regret this."

"Mirror," I whisper. "Celestia, Elise, look at the tall mirror."

Elise rises up first. Yet it's not her who offers Celestia a hand, but Sibilia. When all of them stand before the mirror, Olesia greets them with a warm smile. It's only after that that Irina glides to her sister.

Celestia nods as if she'd already known about the ghosts, but how could she? Elise is properly taken aback. That's what it feels like to be revealed a secret! Alina waves at the ghosts, cheerfully greeting them now that they really want to be seen. I take hold of her hand, and we dash to join our sisters with Rafa and Mufu.

"Greetings." Celestia bows her head at the ghosts. "Honored Irina, honored Olesia, it is a long time since we last met."

The way she speaks . . . She knows the ghosts from the time

before they became ghosts. How curious! And how many secrets has she got hoarded under that untouchable façade of hers?

"You were such a sweet little girl." Olesia pinches my sister's cheeks. Yes, they're familiar with each other. But even so, Irina remains still, a displeased frown on her steep forehead. "Look at you, all grown up! The oldest Daughter of the Moon! The empress-to-be!"

"Dear Olesia," Celestia replies, cheeks red, though the ghosts can't really touch us. "That is unfortunately all I shall ever be. I assume you heard us talking."

"Oh, we did," Olesia reassures her. She has no idea that Alina, me, and Sibilia saw and heard her and her sister, too, and it's better that way.

"You." Irina turns sharply to Sibilia. "Can you really perform the ceremony?"

Sibilia shifts her weight, wipes her palms on her hem. "I . . ."

"Speak up," Irina commands. "This is important."

"Perhaps," Sibilia replies. Irina glares up at the ceiling as if begging mercy from Papa. My sister draws her shoulders back and seems to grow in height. "Yes. Yes, I believe I can."

"Good for you then," Irina replies.

For a moment, I think this is it then. Everything. But then Celestia addresses the ghosts. "Irina, Olesia, you had a swan soul bead once. Will you tell us where you hid it?"

Indeed my sister knows many secrets. But even I realize that this one is dangerous. Swan soul beads are valuable, and stealing one . . . I'm happy to be distracted by the ghosts conferring.

"Shall we?" Olesia wraps her fingers around her sister's thin arm. "I would very much like her to become the empress. I don't like the looks of this gagargi at all. They should not need to consider siding with him to survive."

Irina casts a pointed look at Elise. I know what she's thinking. Elise can't be trusted anymore. But Celestia can. "Fine."

My sisters and I wait for her to continue, to give us hope. Anything.

"Look up," Irina simply says. "Look up at the shimmering lights to find the sacred swan."

Chapter 13

Sibilia

Dear Scribs,

This will be the last time I confide in you. Please don't feel sad, not for yourself and not for me either. Remember me with the same fondness I feel toward you, and guard my memories well. After all, we've both known since the beginning that this day would eventually come. The fountain pen is about to go dry. There's not that many pages left. The holy scriptures say that everything in this world will run its course regardless of what we do—but believe me, Scribs, when I say this, I've cherished and valued our friendship more than anything else in this house.

There's one more tale I want to share with you. I'm writing this in the drawing room—yes, I know, how shocking, dangerous even—but it seems only fitting to scrawl my final account under my father's gaze. And I couldn't anyway write in the room I share with Celestia. We have no light there, as we replaced the beads we unscrewed from the chandeliers with those from our and Elise's room. More about those beads later.

It's a full Moon tonight, and you know what this means. Oh, Scribs, my skin gets goose bumps even when I only think about it! I, Sibilia, wed Celestia to the Moon.

I know, Scribs, I can't believe it true either. But true it is! My sister is now the Crescent Empress, bless our celestial father!

Can't waste the last pages in something as trivial as gloating. I'll tell you about the ceremony, but not in too great detail. You understand, if I were to disclose everything, anyone who read my account might be able to figure out how to perform the rites, and that of course would be a really bad thing.

In any case, here goes.

After Captain Janlav had locked us into our rooms for the night, we waited till the house grew silent and then some more. While I reread the important bits of the scriptures, Celestia retrieved the key ring and the two swan soul beads from the secret locker at the back of the wardrobe. Dressed only in her nightgown, she looked strikingly bare. She has no more secrets from me, of which I'm glad. And I understand at last why she kept so many from me earlier—she was protecting me in the only way she knows.

I, on the other hand . . . Celestia doesn't know about me being up. I left her sleeping, a content smile on her face, and I'm pretty sure she won't stir before the morning. I've not yet decided if I'll tell her of my outing or not.

When the clock in the drawing room struck twelve, I pressed the book of scriptures shut (not that I could make out more than the shapes of the words in the dark), clutched you under my arm, and claimed the key ring from the nightstand. Celestia already waited by the door, holding a soul bead on each palm, close against her chest. I must admit, my heart beat quite wild as I turned the key in the lock. There was no sign of the ghosts, which was annoying, since they could have helped us secure the room. Scribs, I dreaded that Captain Janlav or one of the guards would enter the drawing room all of a sudden or midway through the ceremony so much that I hurried to place a chair against the door leading out. The floor squeaked under me, and I was acutely embarrassed about that as I returned to Celestia. She merely studied me from under her raised brows. I resolved not to take a step more than absolute need be before the ceremony was over.

"I'll let them out," I whispered. That, at least, was part of the plan.

Celestia nodded.

I unlocked Elise's door first. She waited behind it, the strangest expression on her face. Scribs, you know when a horse decides not to move and you can't coax it to take a step forward, not with a whip, not with a lump of sugar? As you surely recall, since my sister confessed funding the insurgence, she's been in turns very vocal and then withdrawn. Tonight, it felt to me as if she were set to stay in her room and not play her part in the ceremony, even though that would have ruined any chance we have for leaving this house together.

But before I could say a word, she glided past me directly to the curtains, there to immediately start unraveling the thread holding them together. Scribs, tell me that I just imagined it.

Thanks. I feel much better now. Onward with what happened.

I proceeded to let out Merile and Alina. I had it in my mind to caution them to stay silent and not move around the room, lest their steps wake up the guards. But as I pushed the door in, they were ready, the rats sitting beside them. And something about them made me hold my tongue. My sisters looked more mature than their years warrant, Merile thoughtful, Alina completely fearless. And the rats . . . they were beyond vigilant, blessed by Papa himself, not mine to command.

Once we were all in the drawing room, I sat down on the

sofa and closed my eyes to focus on the sacred ceremony that I was about to perform so very soon. Since the ghosts revealed the location of the swan soul and we decided to go forth with this plan, I'd spent my every waking hour practicing the spell and the rites to the degree that it was possible to do so. Yet, my thoughts strayed, just as they're straying now.

I don't know what to think about Elise anymore. Celestia sided with the gagargi because she was under his spell. Though Elise claims she was initially unaware of the gagargi being behind the insurgence, she doesn't regret supporting it. It's as if she's not at all sorry to see everything our family has worked toward for millennia crumbling before our eyes.

The ghosts call her a traitor. I really . . . Can we return to this topic a bit later?

Ghosts and the soul beads. I shall write about those first.

Who'd have guessed! Though Celestia had searched the house through for the swan soul bead she knew Irina and Olesia had brought with them, it had never occurred to her, or any of us, that they might have split it into two separate beads, that we'd basked in our heraldic charge's sacred light all along! No wonder our mother grew so afraid of her sisters' cunningness that she decided to send them here. And I do feel sorry for what they had to go through, live here so very alone for over a decade, and then meet their end at Captain Ansalov's hands! The thing is, even if they did plot against our mother once upon a time, they feel like family now. I know they'll do everything in their power to help us escape their fate.

I don't know how much time I spent with my eyes closed, wondering whether the ghosts would show up or not. I wished that at least Olesia would, because the ghosts were present when Mama wed the Moon and hence know how the ceremony should proceed in practice. That is, at that point, both Celestia and I knew how it should go in principle. But principle and practice are always two different things. Anyway, I had to remind myself several times that it mightn't be up to them to decide whether they appear or not. They're not in control of themselves anymore. They're fading. Soon, they mightn't be anything else but waning hauntings of a forgotten house.

I stirred to the sound of the curtains being drawn apart. Though the gap between the planks is narrow and the crack in the glass is small, barely the size of a copper penny, a thick, silvery beam of Moon's light flowed into the room. My sisters and I, we drifted to bask under our father's gaze.

This is when the ghosts finally appeared. Irina formed next to Alina, Olesia beside Celestia. In the Moon's light, they looked more real, solid.

Scribs, I'd grown so used to seeing them but in a reflection, that to see them—not in flesh, but in the ghostly version of that word—greeting our father, his daughters just like us, my heart swelled with a bruising feeling, a sort of foreboding melancholy. But at that moment, I knew that our father would always care for us all, that he'd forgive us, no matter what path we wound up following.

Celestia stepped forth, toward the window, and turned to face us. Dressed in her negligee, holding the two soul beads on her palms, she seemed to gleam silvery luster—no, to reflect the Moon's light. "Welcome, my sisters. Welcome, our honored aunts."

Olesia curtsied, but Irina didn't. She chose to remain still, taller, thinner, her outline sharper than that of her sister, with the gap between her and Elise sore like a ruined grin. She simply said, "The guards are asleep."

I glanced at the chair with which I'd barred the door, still happy that I'd chosen to do so. Even if the ghosts had checked up on the guards, there was no guarantee that one of them mightn't wake up.

Scribs, you're right, I'll be running out of ink and paper before I get to the ceremony. Hence, I'll be skipping the greetings and some other bits. I'll try not to leave out anything that might be of interest to you.

"Shall we begin?" Celestia asked, and not only to check if I was ready for my part, but to also verify from the ghosts that everything was in order.

I held my breath. Celestia and I had done our best to combine what I'd figured out from the scriptures and what the ghosts had told us about the ceremony. But how could we really know if we'd still got something terribly wrong?

"I see no reason for delay," Irina replied, and she was right. The late-summer nights are short still and the gagargi will be sending for Celestia well before the next full Moon. This might be very soon indeed.

This thought in mind, we hastened to our assigned places: Celestia at the exact center of the Moon's light, Elise to the right of her. My place should have been there, next to her, but of course tonight it wasn't, as I had the sacred rites to perform. Merile, Alina, and the rats gathered to the left of Celestia, uncharacteristically attentive. Irina and Olesia remained where they'd appeared. They were to be the rest of our family summoned to witness the most sacred of ceremonies.

Once everyone was in the right spots, I untied the knot securing Celestia's negligee. With my fumbling fingers, it took me two separate attempts to manage this, but once I did succeed, the garment slipped off her shoulders, off her. She stepped out of it, to reveal her unclothed body for her husband-to-be. In his light, she was slender and pale like a young birch, the shadows of her ribs the stripes. Rooted to this moment.

My sister said, "I am ready."

Scribs, speak of a pressure! I can't even begin to describe how nervous I felt as everyone turned to stare at me. For a moment, I couldn't breathe, let alone move. My sisters' fate, the very future of the Crescent Empire, rested in my clumsy hands! We had but one chance for the ceremony, only one swan soul. If I were to say the wrong words, mispronounce the glyph, if the beads were to slip from my fingers at the wrong moment . . .

"Sibilia." Celestia's voice was laced with confidence.

I drew a deep breath. She believed in me, and if she did so, it had to mean that I could really perform the ceremony. I pushed any opposing thoughts aside and strode to my place, before her.

"The sacred marriage that binds the Moon to the eldest Daughter of the Moon is the most blessed of unions," I said, and my voice didn't waver at all. More confident now, I opened you, Scribs, and turned over the right page. I cursed myself for having written sideways over the passages. But then . . .

Our father's light lit the paper white, and the black letters grew bolder under my gaze. Each word was so easy to make out, so easy to say. And so I recited our father's wisdom in a clear, loud voice, coaxing forth the glyphs that would bind my sister to the Moon. And they came to me, in orderly groups, though I'm no gagargi.

When the time came, Celestia extended her bare hands toward me, the soul beads resting on the cups of her palms. With each passage I read, the light inside the beads changed form. White threads surged under the glass, radiant but impatient. We'd speculated on the complications of one soul being split apart and being reunited later. The ghosts had reassured us that this should pose no risk. Or that was what the young gagargi had told them all those years ago.

And now that the final glyph emerged from amongst the words, I had to believe in the ghosts and the young gagargi I'd never met, that they'd been right, that they'd known what they were doing. Because as the master of all glyphs expanded in the Moon's light, winding more complex with each heartbeat, I for sure had no idea whether I was going to succeed or not. Scribs, there really was but one way to find out.

"Celestia, the oldest Daughter of the Moon," I addressed my sister, so very keen to pronounce the master glyph, but terrified as well. For the glyph was so impossibly elaborate, a hundred times more so than any I'd ever coaxed forth from the pages before. Being so for a purpose. "Will you marry His Celestial Highness, the Moon?"

"I will." Celestia smiled at me, and it was as if her whole being, her body was radiating the answer, her eagerness in the form of lustrous white light. I could feel my sisters', the ghosts' expectant gazes on us.

I willed myself to remember the glyph in its whole glorious intricacy, and then, Scribs, I closed you, and having no other place to put you, I clasped you between my knees. My hands shook violently as I extended them toward Celestia's.

She met me with the most trusting of gazes, as blue as the innocent summer days of our childhood. "Sibilia, the one our father has favored with the deeper understanding of his words, will you perform the rite?"

I forced myself to take a slow breath, and in our father's presence, I at last found calmness. My hands ceased to tremble, and Celestia placed a bead on each of my upturned palms. "I will."

And then, I pronounced the glyph that was the key to the Crescent Empire's future.

Scribs, I'm sorry, but I can't tell you of the things that unfolded next. It's not for selfish reasons, but a matter of necessity. My father's secrets are not for me to share. But I can tell you that the moment he took my sister as his wife was both beautiful and terrible, deafeningly loud and silent, short and long, and all the things in between.

This much I can say: the ceremony changed Celestia. Where she had been serene before, now her blue gaze is wide and deep like an ocean that knows no boundaries. Where her posture had been tall and proud, now it's even more so. And where she'd been fair before, now she gleams our father's blessed light even when he's not present.

"It worked," I whispered under my breath, but I didn't dare to move, as my knees had suddenly turned very wobbly and unreliable.

Celestia glided to me and took hold of both my hands. When she spoke, her voice was different, too. Imperial. "That it did, my dear sister. And we have you to thank for that."

I blushed despite myself as my sisters and the ghosts gathered around us. And it wasn't only to pay homage to the Crescent Empress, who stood before them still bare of any jewels and clothes, but also to acknowledge me for the part I'd played in the ceremony. It was a curious feeling, to be the center of attention because of something I'd done, rather than because of how I look, but I think I quite liked it.

This time around, the dizziness that always follows a spell came with a delay. When we broke off the embrace of sisters at last, Celestia guided me to the sofa before the windows, though I assured her I was fine. But when I did lie down on the sofa, I instantly dozed off. I came around only when my sisters had already swept the floor clean of the soul bead shards and sewn the curtains shut.

Alina dashed to check on me. "Are you all right? Please, tell me you're all right!"

I held a finger up, against my lips, to remind her to keep her voice down, but I did smile at her. I felt great, not only physically, but also because of what I'd achieved.

While I got my bearings—I might have been a bit dizzy still—Celestia saw Alina and Merile to their room and Elise into hers. Of the ghosts, there was no sight. They must have left us while I rested.

"How do you feel?" Celestia asked me when we were alone in our room. With our lamp no longer working, it should have been dark. But it wasn't, as my sister still radiated our father's light.

"Tired," I lied. In truth, now that I'd napped for a moment, I felt invincible and ready to face any challenge posed to me. Yes, Scribs, I recognize the ridiculousness of that thought all by myself. Hence the lying, though I'm not proud of that.

I undressed, and we went to bed, and there was no need to

talk more. We both knew what had come to pass and how it may yet alter the course of events.

Scribs, I've seen my sister tired and happy and worried. But never have I seen her in such an utter state of contentedness as when she closed her eyes. She's become what she was meant to become.

The Crescent Empress.

Sorry for the long pause, Scribs, I had to stop and really think about it. Here goes.

I wonder if in some convoluted way my sisters and I have become what we were supposed to become in this house, if we have done so due to the circumstances or because this was our father's plan all along.

Alina is no longer afraid of the things she sees or even the Great Thinking Machine. She believes in the promise Celestia made to her during the council of sisters, that we'll keep her forever out of the gagargi's reach. As a result, though her mind-rotting disease may have gotten worse, she seems healthier now than back at the palace, and in the end, I suppose, that's the thing that matters the most.

Since the magpie incident, Merile has grown up. Even though she still acts childish at times (like when she continues to insist that she and Alina really saw the witch in the garden once), I know in my heart that she would do anything to protect Alina. And there can't be a greater quality to cherish than utter selflessness. She's brave, too, and now that I further think about it, we should thank her for Celestia becoming the Crescent Empress. If she hadn't demanded answers, Celestia would have never conceded how dire our situation was, and the ghosts wouldn't have revealed the location of the soul beads.

Elise . . . I don't want to write these words, but Scribs, I need to get this off my chest. So, here goes, regardless of how terrible this might sound to you.

Elise isn't the sister I knew back at the Summer City, the buoyant girl I so envied. I don't think I can trust her anymore. I don't even want to talk with her. It feels to me as if nothing we ever shared was true.

And I really don't like the person my sister has turned into. These days, her opinions are so wild and outlandish that sometimes I think she'd still be ready to side with the gagargi regardless of what that might mean to us. The worst thing is that she seems to genuinely believe that that would be the right thing to do.

I don't know how she can do this to us, her family! The ghosts call her a traitor. Perhaps that's what she is.

Scribs, would it be such a very bad thing if I never said another word to her?

Can we continue with what happened tonight? Thanks.

When I was sure that Celestia was truly and deeply in the land of dreams, I got up as quietly as I could. I know, what a silly thing to do, but Scribs, tonight I felt as if I needed to get up, out into the drawing room, and meet once more with my father.

Hence, I retrieved the key to our room from the wardrobe's

secret compartment. I don't know how Celestia always opens it so easily, but I was sure I'd wake her up with all the prodding and pushing. Luckily enough, my sister remained fast asleep. I prayed thanks to Papa, snatched you with me, Scribs, and sneaked out.

In the drawing room, Moon's light trickled in through the holes of the sewn-shut curtains. My father's shine drew me to him, and I felt as if I were drifting, barely more than a ghost of myself. I hesitated to unravel the thread—Celestia never lets me touch it. I think she fears that I might accidentally snap it, and I'm tempted to agree with her. But tonight, there was no other option. I lowered you on the floor and set to work.

I thought I knew what to expect when I drew the curtains apart. But I was wrong. So very wrong.

The crack in the glass is at the same level with my eyes, and as the light seeped in, it felt as if I were directly meeting my father's gaze. I was blinded and granted sight. The world ceased to be and went on without me. I was no more, and yet I was more than before.

As I stood there, frozen, my father spoke to me, words of light that I didn't understand then, and have still not been able to figure out. There were images, too, or perhaps they were visions, but they went past so fast that I can only recall one. Merile's rats running through a dense birch forest, a bird black and white framed by the Moon's light. An echo of the future, perhaps?

To be honest, I have no idea.

I don't know how long I stood there. I don't really care. Eventually a cloud slipped to cover the Moon, and when it passed, my father had shared with me everything he wanted me to know. Yet I didn't feel like sleeping, rather like writing, and so I settled on the sofa chair closest to the window.

Tonight, my account has been full of important events that will no doubt bear historical significance in a century or two. But I think I've written enough of that now, wouldn't you agree with me, Scribs? Yes?

Good. For I only have two or so pages left, and I want to fill them with something lighter, but very personal still.

THE LETTER!

I've been dying to write about the letter since the Ball, but haven't. I needed to first make up my mind about a few things, including the kiss that could have been. Needless to say, I really haven't yet, but I'm ever so slowly running out of time to do so.

Here's what you need to know.

Celestia and Elise gave the letter to me to read while they fussed with my impossible hair. They reassured me it's from K, that it was smuggled here by the Poet, under the false bottom of the box of chocolates that left a bitter taste in my mouth. The letter might eventually do likewise.

Lately, I've been thinking about it and what came to pass after the last dance a lot, but funnily enough, not K. I know, unbelievable, considering how many of your pages I wasted drooling after him. I'm sure he's still handsome and all that. No doubt about that. But . . .

The letter says that he'll love me forever and was planning to gallop to my rescue. But then his family, who'd sided with us of course, had to flee the gagargi's persecution, and his parents forced him to leave the country with them. He's safe now, at the Southern Colonies, where the sun doesn't warm him like my smile once did, where the night is cold but not as cold as his heart is without a reassurance of my eternal love.

Once upon a time, the words would have sent me tearfully

brooding for weeks, if not for months. Or years. To be finally confirmed that he loves me! To know he's safe!

But I've had a lot of time to mull over both the first and only time we met and every word written on that precious piece of paper. I've come to realize that what I felt for him was never more than a passing infatuation, nothing upon which to build my whole life and existence. Nothing for which he should risk his life either—that I should have had the audacity to dream of this!

Scribs, I bet you noticed, I have my doubts about the letter's origins. I, too, have changed during our confinement in this house, but it might be that my older sisters haven't yet realized this. I know they have pitied me in the past—and possibly still do so—and I can't blame them. For months and months, I only prattled about my debut and wanting to be just like Elise used to be (the Moon bless that I never actually turned into someone like her). I do appreciate them arranging the Ball. It was fun while it lasted. And enough.

I can see beyond the surface now. The handwriting on the letter isn't that of my sisters. But who says they didn't ask one of the guards, Captain Janlav perhaps, to write it, in a well-meant attempt to console me? If that's what they did, I can say with a clear conscience that I won't hold it against them. And if the letter is really from K, I wish him all the best and that he won't cry after me for too long.

For even if we were to return to the Summer City, I don't think I'd like the life there. And though my sisters mightn't believe me—and hence I won't share this with them—even if we'll never leave this house, I don't feel like I'm missing out on anything. In the end, it's not the balls and dresses and music and refreshments that are important. But being content.

I'm not lying here, Scribs, it's the same thing as it was with the kiss. I thought I wanted it, but at the last moment, I changed my mind. Though Boy really likes me, and he's turned into quite a handsome lad (I don't know how I didn't see it earlier), I don't feel the same way about him (and it's not because I'd still dream of Captain Janlav. That, too, was just a passing fancy). There mightn't come another chance to kiss and be kissed, but for now it's enough for me to know that if I'd so wanted, I could have done both.

And with that said, I'm perfectly happy with my life as it is.

Scribs, I don't know if you can make out any of these words. The ink is running very low. And in any case, we've come to the last page. I want to thank you for your friendship and your company most loyal. You've helped me discover who I really am, and for that I'm eternally grateful.

Fare you well, my dear friend, I shall hide you in the secret compartment, for someone to find you.

For them to remember me.

Sibilia

Chapter 14

Elise

I'm not welcome. I'm akin to a weary traveler arriving at an inn, one who is turned away already at the gates. I'm akin to a tramp with an incurable disease that no one wants close to his loved ones in fear of contagion. I'm akin to a criminal who has broken the holiest of laws, one who has been judged before weighing the evidence. I'm akin to a woman who has knowingly betrayed the Crescent Empire.

My sisters and I no longer dance. Instead, after breakfast, my sisters play singing games. I don't attempt to join their company anymore, but remain by the oval table and patch whatever garment has once more fallen into disrepair. If I were to try and partake in their activities, they would politely shuffle to make room for me. But none of them would pass me the clap. Or they would pretend not to hear·my rhymes. Or then they would skip my turn altogether. These days, I'm more invisible to them than the fading ghosts.

The ghosts aren't with us today. If they were, there would be a gap between Alina and Celestia. They would whisper ill words about me. They would call me a traitor.

In a sense, that is what I am. I have thought of our options long and hard, and now my mind is made up. I must find the courage to persist, to make sure we do the right thing, even if it goes against what Celestia, the Crescent Empress, believes.

The clapping stops, the game ends. Alina and Merile giggle as they cuddle the two dogs. But when Alina notices me looking at them, she turns her gaze down as if my shadow were of more interest to her than what I might have to say. Merile wraps an arm around our little sister and bares her teeth. It's a warning. She doesn't want me talking to them.

"That was such great fun," Sibilia exclaims as she moves on to tend the dying fire. Though her enthusiasm is as far away from genuine as possible. We all know what awaits us. Some of us hide it better than the others.

"Yes," Celestia replies as she settles in her customary place on the sofa by the windows. She crosses her elegant hands on her lap, straightens her back. "That it was. Please, while you are at it, do toss a few more logs in. It is feeling a bit damp here."

With each passing day, Celestia and Sibilia look wearier. Though I haven't been privy to their schemes since I played my part in the wedding ceremony, I know what they are up to. Sibilia is strengthening Celestia.

It is foolish of my sisters to think that they could defy the gagargi's will. I have tried to reason with them, to no avail. As a result, I have been shunned out of the family as if I were no longer their sister. But regardless of what they might prefer, I'm still a Daughter of the Moon. I do miss Celestia, Sibilia, Merile, and Alina, I do long for their company, and I don't want our ways to part in anger.

For only a day or two can remain before the gagargi sends for us.

The sheet of paper and the pen burn in my dress pocket. Captain Janlav was suspicious, rightfully so, when I asked for them. He thought I intended to write a letter, smuggle it out of the house, plead with someone, anyone to come to our aid. I swore under my father's name that I wasn't planning any such thing. I went as far as to tell him the truth. Upon hearing from my lips that he and the guards are now closer to me than my own family, he took pity on me.

Of course I would love nothing more than all of us leaving this house together and living our lives happily ever after. But if worst comes to worst and the gagargi holds Celestia accountable for the deal she made with him, my sisters and I really need to decide which one of us goes with her.

And so, I abandon the chair, the oval table, the needle and the thread.

"Sibilia," I say in a gentle voice as I approach the fireplace, for my steps are silent and sure.

My sister flinches away from me, teeters on the divan's edge. She bends to pick up a poker, prods the pathetically burning logs. The fire spits sparks as if to despise my very attempt to talk with my sister. As if it knew that I chose her because she has the softest heart, because once we were best friends.

"You don't need a poker to protect yourself from me." And I laugh girlishly, as if her defensive mannerism hadn't hurt me deep inside.

Sibilia turns minutely toward me. Her gray eyes are watery, but not because of the smoke.

"I have something for you." I offer her the sheet of paper, the pen clipped against it. I pray the Moon she doesn't toss it in the flames, at least not before she has read my question.

Sibilia bites her lower lip. She has always kept a diary, but five days ago, she simply stopped writing. Either she ran out of paper or ink. Or both. Not of things to say.

"I shall just leave them here," I say, smiling benevolently. My sister, she's not stupid. She knows there's more to my kindness than a simple act of consideration.

And that there indeed is. If I can turn her to my side, then I have a chance of reassuring also my younger sisters, and then potentially even Celestia about the benefits of my plan.

Sibilia comes to me, as I had hoped she would do, after we're done with lunch. She takes a seat at the end of the oval table, farther away from me than I would prefer, but even this is better than nothing. My sister's excuse is a button that has come loose on the coat I sewed for her during the winter.

Celestia eyes us from over her teacup's chipped brim. It may be that Sibilia told our sister about the question and received her permission to proceed. It may be that neither came to pass. We aren't exactly forthcoming with information in this house.

If I were to wager a guess, I would say that Sibilia didn't tell her. For she fidgets with the needle for quite a while, until Celestia decides to stretch her legs and stroll around the room, before she slips the sheet of paper and the pen back to me.

My question stands bold and prominent on the very top.

Are you still upset with me?

Her answer is one simple word and yet a triumph in its own right.

Yes.

For this isn't the end, but the beginning. I quickly ink another question. I must not let the momentum slip.

Why?

She glances at me, her gray eyes bulging, as if she's wondering why I even need to ask. But she accepts the pen, scrawls.

I don't know you anymore.

I feel like laughing out of relief. For I was wrong about her! My sister is still so silly! But such a burst of emotion would only drive her farther away from me. And so I write in my elaborate, clear hand.

But you do know me. I'm the same Elise as always.

She reads my words, forehead wrinkling. Her hair gleams red-gold as she shakes her head. She disagrees with my statement, a reaction I didn't expect.

Perhaps in order to bridge the gap between us I have to push her just a little bit harder. I write at the beginning of the next line an offer she really can't refuse.

Can we still be friends?

She doesn't reply.

"Tabard . . ." Sibilia muses even as she stumbles on her hem. She manages to recover her balance at the last moment by taking support from the railing that our trailing fingers have worn smooth. "May I ask you something?"

It annoys me that Sibilia speaks with the guard, but wouldn't earlier reply to my simple question. My gaze meets briefly with Celestia's as she glances over her shoulder to check that our sister didn't hurt herself. She shakes her head at me, as if she did indeed know what I tried earlier, even as she ushers Alina and Merile down the stairs.

"Sure," Tabard replies, cheerful, though every day the stairway feels narrower, darker, like a tunnel diving deep underground, to gloom that no one should call their home.

"When you take the dogs out, where exactly do you take

them?" Sibilia asks when she reaches the second-floor landing. Alina and Merile run through the hallway, towing Celestia with them. They're eager to get out, to breathe the air there, even if it tastes of rotting leaves.

Tabard stares after them, unconcerned, for Beard is waiting by the next stairway. "We let them out in the garden and that's it."

Nothing more sinister, then. Celestia would have us think Gagargi Prataslav and all loyal to him are evil, though the beneficial reforms he has initiated for the good of our people are right here, before our eyes, depicted in the posters that she doesn't want us to even glance at. Plentiful harvests divided equally, to feed every man, woman, and child. No more soldiers sent to pointless wars. No more families torn apart. It's because of him and the Great Thinking Machine, but she refuses to hear of that, can't look past what he once did to her, an unjust deed perhaps, but a necessary sacrifice, no doubt.

"Never in the forest?" Sibilia keeps her gaze riveted on her clacking sabots. She didn't reply to my question. Even she might not side with me, but do as Celestia dictates.

"To be snatched by the wolves?" Tabard chuckles as we reach the last flight of stairs. He's oblivious to what's to come so soon. Unlike me.

I half expect to find the door leading to the cellar ajar. It's closed still, thank the Moon, though it may not stay that way for long.

"Last one in the garden is silly," Alina decides.

And she and Merile race toward the open back door with the dogs at their heels. It's gray outside, and yet the light paints a beam against the bare floorboards. Sibilia and Celestia follow this path.

"Missus," Tabard addresses me, hesitant. He tugs at the front of his faded blue shirt. "Everyone must go out."

"Oh?" I hadn't realized that I had halted, but that I had. I force myself to glide toward the gray light. I'm not afraid to die, the opposite. But if Celestia's plan, whatever it may be, doesn't work, I refuse to stay behind in this house, to follow Captain Ansalov's soldiers to the cellar, there to stand against the wall, to be shot dead.

For I'm of more use to our people alive than any of my sisters.

———

I let Tabard escort me to the porch. Captain Janlav is there already, smoking. I bum the last drag of his cigarette. Tabard and Beard are smart enough to realize that their company isn't required. They amble after my sisters, rifles strapped against their backs.

It strikes me how carelessly, in such accustomed manner, they carry death with them. It is as if they have forgotten what a single bullet can do, what it means for it to pierce flesh and bone, and then sink into stone that shall not bear anyone's name.

"Did it work?" Captain Janlav asks. He takes in my sour expression, sighs. "At least you tried."

Wisps of smoke drift from between my parted lips. In the garden, the purple bloom of thistles has been replaced by thorny spheres. The pale flowers of widow's lace have shriveled to ugly brown. I see the world such as it is, not as the idealistic version Celestia prefers. "Can we talk?"

Captain Janlav glances at my sisters, at Tabard and Beard.

My sisters are playing Catch the Goose, though the grass under their feet has waned.

"In private," I add, though during this hour, we're supposed to be out. No, that isn't how it is. My sisters and I aren't allowed to go out at other times, but the agreement with Captain Ansalov doesn't dictate that we couldn't stay in if we so decided. Celestia herself did so on a few occasions after her private audience with the gagargi. It really doesn't matter anymore if we deviate from the routines built to comfort my younger sisters.

Captain Janlav must have reached the same conclusion, for he turns on his heels and says, "Follow me."

And I think, he shouldn't have told me. For what feels like ages ago, I decided that I would follow him wherever he would lead me. Now, this decision overcomes everything else, anything else, I might feel.

It's dim in the library despite the duck soul lamps hanging from the high ceiling. I halt at the doorstep, for though I have visited many a great house before, countless libraries each more splendorous than the previous, the sight of this one takes me by surprise. With everything that has happened in this house, I expected the library to be unkempt or even demolished, but instead it's orderly and clean. The guards have made do with what they have, just like us. The shelves no longer line the paneled walls, but are placed adjacent to them, to form . . . the closest thing that comes to my mind is novice gagargi's cells. And the shelves don't bear books anymore, rather starched sheets have been hung against them to provide privacy. To our right, at the end of the room, a round table has been placed before the unlit fireplace, with an unfinished game of cards waiting, mismatched sofa chairs set in a circle around it. There are no mirrors on the walls—the ghosts can't enter the room. They will be blind and deaf to whatever happens here, and that serves them right.

A lanky shape springs up from one of the sofa chairs. A low, trembling voice—Boy—asks, "What's she doing here?"

Captain Janlav strolls to the youngest of the guards. He places a reassuring palm on his shoulder. But it's not this that has Boy gulping. He was brooding already before we arrived, no doubt crying after Sibilia's kindest rejection of his affections.

"She's with me," Captain Janlav says, nodding toward the open doorway where I chose to linger. "Now, lad, get out, will you?"

As Boy scampers up the aisle formed by the shelves, it occurs to me that I never learned whom it was exactly that Sibilia fancied. I decide it doesn't matter anymore, she wouldn't let me help her. I step further into the library, allow Boy past me. He halts only to push the door closed behind him.

And just like that, Captain Janlav and I are alone, and I feel better and worse.

For a part of me hopes that everything, even our time together, would come to an end sooner. I cling to the hope that somehow my sisters and I might yet avoid the inevitable fate that awaits us, and I'm certain I'm not alone in this thought. But I am alone.

"What is it that you wanted to talk about with me?"

The distance between us has grown too long. Summoned by his voice, I skim toward him. But I speak only when a mere two steps separate us. "I will go with Celestia."

His brown gaze lights up. "She's agreed to go to him? At last!"

"No . . . Not yet." It hurts me to see disappointment drawing his expression taut.

Sometimes I wonder how everything became so very convoluted, when eventually it's in my and my sisters' power to make the world right again. But it's as if Celestia were beyond reason now. She has no intention of cooperating with the gagargi, and yet she insisted on going through with the wedding ceremony. Though Sibilia is not a trained gagargi. Who knows if the bond she forged between my sister and our father will really last?

"But I will make her change her mind," I say, and mean it. Since Celestia is now the empress, to a degree at least, she must think of what's best for her empire, not her family. She must go to the gagargi, stand by his side at the equinox ceremony, and bring an end to the war she started. And if she refuses to bear the gagargi's seed, if the future of the empire becomes thus threatened . . .

Echoes of gunshots slash through the library, sharp and vicious, and then he's there, the man I once loved, his arms so firmly around me, his voice so soft in my ears. "Do not fear, Elise. They're merely practicing shooting."

As they have done every single day since Merile's folly.

"I'm not afraid," I reply, though that isn't the entire truth. I dread so many things, one more than the others.

If Celestia won't fulfill her duty, it becomes mine, and I won't shy away from doing what I must do to protect our people. And that's why I need her to go to the gagargi, why I need to go with her, to be there, to take her place. Unlike her, I will be willing. I will force myself to be. But even so, the gagargi may choose to put me under his spell, and I may become but an empty shell of myself.

Captain Janlav meets my gaze. "I'm in awe of your courage."

For a moment I can't speak, for I'm bewildered at his statement. My courage? What courage? I have waited for too long to make up my mind. And then I laugh, and I don't even know why I'm doing so. But it feels so good to laugh, to be the carefree Elise once more, though that I never was.

"What are you laughing at?" he asks.

"I have no idea!" I clasp his hand. And it's so warm and familiar, his skin against mine so stirring. An idea comes to me, a yearning, to be more precise. I have felt so alone for so long . . .

It's a blessing to know what I must do at last. But I'm not ready. Not yet. Though I'm prepared to sacrifice myself for the better of the empire, I don't want the gagargi to be my first man when there may never be more than necessity, no tender feelings between us.

"Come!" I gently pull Captain Janlav's hand. He, at least, I once loved. "Come with me."

"Where?" he asks, before realization dawns upon him. Why not be young and foolish this once, when there's no guarantee of tomorrow? Why not!

He takes the lead, and together we run to the very end of the aisle, to his cell. We shed our clothes, autumn trees shivering leaves, even before he parts the curtain. When we fall onto his bed it's just his skin against mine.

Afterward, we lie side by side, sweaty and out of breath. I enjoy his closeness, the warmth of a man caring. For a long, long while only my heart feels empty. I will soon be leaving my sisters behind, and though they might think otherwise, I take no pleasure in this.

Even though I dread ruining the precious moment that I long to last forever, I must speak, ask him, "When I go with Celestia, is there really nothing you could do for my sisters?"

It's well past the time for me to hope that someone would come to their rescue. I know they won't be able to escape, and even if they somehow could, they couldn't possibly find their way through the wilderness. They would starve or die of exposure. But if they remain in this house, their fate will be equally grim.

Thus, his reply takes me by surprise. "Tabard and Boy have volunteered to stay behind."

It's something, I guess, but not enough. "And what power will they hold over Captain Ansalov's commands?"

He turns to his side, to face me, his chest wide and muscular. He has a red scar on his left side, a slash from a skirmish fought not so long ago, no doubt in my mother's name. "Nothing but foolish dedication."

He's so close to me that his breath tickles my throat. No matter what awaits me, my father has granted me more than I deserve, and I feel guilty when I know my younger sisters will never receive such blessing. "As wonderful as that is, it might not be enough. Is there really nothing more?"

He brushes a lock behind my ear. He thinks of lying; I can tell that from the tenseness spreading across his shoulders. I lock gazes with him. Don't. Don't lie to my face.

"If they were younger, if they were smaller, if they could pass for peasant girls . . ." His voice breaks.

"I see." There's no hope for my younger sisters. There's nothing more I can do for them, and I can but accept it.

"I'm sorry." Captain Janlav's pine brown eyes fill with water. He must wonder if I'm angry at him, disappointed in his lack of a better plan.

"It's all right," I say, planting a kiss on his worry-wrinkled forehead. Our mother broke the empire. It's up to my sisters and I to fix it, regardless of what that might require from us. But until then . . .

"Kiss me again," I whisper, allowing myself one more fleeting moment of this terrifying, selfish pleasure. "Just kiss me again while there's still time."

Chapter 15

Celestia

It is a quarter to nine, and only forty-two days remain before the autumn equinox. Though I keep track of the hours, for a long time, I couldn't be sure of when our time in this house would come to an end. Yesterday, during our daily outing, the swans at the gate sang to me, and though my swan-self has left me, I haven't forgotten their language.

They sang it loud and clear. The gagargi's men are coming.

Many are the moments when I have felt alone and beyond exhaustion, trapped in this house. But I haven't shared this with my sisters. As I sit on the drawing room's sofa, my back straight, my hands folded on my lap, I maintain the façade of calm as I always do.

Alina, Merile, and Sibilia play on the carpet with the two dogs. Lately, Sibilia has been increasingly interested in the dogs. I don't know if it is merely because she ran out of pages and ink and can no longer keep a diary or because she knows every sacred passage of the scriptures by heart already.

Perhaps it is because she detests Elise's attempts to reconcile with her. The one, who betrayed our mother out of her own will, mends the sleeve of her dress on the padded chair next to me. The dull needle parts again and again the fabric so worn that no amount of thread will ever suffice to make it whole.

I am tempted to pace the room, worried of what may come to pass so soon. But it isn't my right to despair, not now when we are so close to the end, not even after the end. My duty as the Crescent Empress is to persist, and that I shall do. My beloved, the Moon, is on our side. I am stronger now than I have been ever in my life. But at the same time I am weaker, too. I have stayed up through every cloudless night, to bask in my beloved's light. My eyes ache constantly as if they had sunk too deep in my skull. An iron circle encloses my head, another, heavier one presses against my chest. One day they shall lift. One day my sisters and I shall walk free, even if it costs me my soul.

Though I don't know if that will come to pass tonight. My beloved, he hasn't shown me what he sees yet, and I do wonder at times if something went wrong during the ceremony. Questions crowd my mind, but there are never answers. Only light brighter or waning.

"What." Merile's voice is unmistakable, childishly confident. "What did you hear, silly?"

The black dog has trotted to the curtained window closest to our chambers, there to tense with one paw up, head cocked left. Of course it would be one of the dogs that heard the arrival of the gagargi's men first.

Sibilia's knees click as she gets up from the carpet, slowly towering to the full height she isn't yet accustomed to. She meets my gaze, but chooses not to say a word. We have talked of this moment before. As the older sisters, it is up to us to remain undaunted.

And then, though walls separate us from the autumn evening, we hear the howls of Captain Ansalov's hounds, the shrill wails not that far away from those of their kin, the wolves. Barks, too, cascading into cacophony. Someone is approaching the house. There are orders shouted, words replied, both too faint to reach us. But I know their meaning.

I rise up from the sofa then, with exaggerated slowness as if I were in control of the situation, though that I am not. Elise snaps the thread, quickly knots it to secure her handiwork, and places the needle and thread on the table, disturbingly excited. Sibilia stays with Merile and Alina, but her hand slips into the pocket of her dress, there to fidget with her pearl bracelet.

"They are coming," I say, for sometimes people are reassured by the simple act of the one they look up to stating the obvious. Mother once said that it makes them feel as if they could affect their fates. "Now we must wait."

The ghosts appear before the captains, guards, or soldiers do. Alina and Merile greet them, still unaware of how dire the situation may soon become. The ghosts' outlines are blurry, hems limp and heavy, hair untied, slowly swaying as if they were submerged in a river. The news they bear is important, but I can't rush these poor creatures any more than I can maintain the illusion of security.

It becomes apparent that the ghosts have lost control of their bodies. I shouldn't pray—for that rarely helps—but I do pray that they still have enough control left of their minds. I need to know what awaits us, though I have done my best to prepare for every eventuality.

"Troika," Irina wails. "Troika. Troika."

"Away," Olesia adds, and I can tell that they are trying their best, though each word costs them more than any have ever cost me. Soon there will be nothing left of them but a fading memory of younger Daughters of the Moon.

"Thank you." I nod at the ghosts. This is what I agreed with the gagargi. Though it is late already, whichever of the two captains enters the room, he will demand I leave this house immediately. Any more delays might mean that I mightn't arrive in the Summer City in time for the ceremony.

"Which one of us will you choose?" Elise asks, her voice bright as if she really expected me to follow through with the deal I manipulated the gagargi into accepting. She has changed more than I have, but out of her own will or under someone's influence, that I don't know. But I shall not forget she betrayed me once already, that she is young and idealistic, dangerous to a degree.

"Either we all go or no one goes." I repeat what I have said so many times before. I won't leave this house with one of my sisters and abandon the others in the hands of Captain Ansalov, regardless of what Elise may insist.

Sibilia nods at me, glares at Elise. Merile takes hold of Alina's hand. But little Alina, she seems completely unafraid, the last thing I expected. As I meet her gaze, I realize she is sure I will keep her safe, that I will live up to my promise to protect her from the gagargi and his horrid machine.

"Coming." Irina drifts to the door, fists clenched against her chin. As she quivers her shape disintegrates, her voice hoarsens. "Coming. Coming."

And then the heavy, determined steps already rattle on the stairs. Those familiar. Those these hallways haven't known for weeks.

"Let us be ready then," I say to my sisters, and step forth, to stand at the exact center of the room. My sisters hurry into an arc behind me, in the order of age, though Elise does so reluctantly. No matter what she claims, a part of her believes that I will triumph tonight. Indeed, the time has come for me to use the strength bestowed on me, that of my very own soul, to alter the mind of the person who steps through the door.

The door opens with a slow creak. The ghosts flee, out of their own mind or out of fright I don't know, and presently I must focus on the task at hand, the one that surpasses all others in its direness.

I pronounce the glyph.

"Evening." Captain Ansalov marches in, a letter with a broken red seal creased in one outstretched hand. His curly brown hair springs with his steps, but his beady green eyes are without emotion other than fierce devotion. From this I know the gagargi addressed the orders to him. He is in charge tonight.

Captain Janlav follows two steps behind Captain Ansalov, quick and sure with his movements, but undecided yet in his mind. I can tell this from the way he stares at Captain Ansalov, how his gaze darts from us to the door and the guards and soldiers that crowd the hallway beyond. His gaze meets Belly's, and the guard wide and tall closes the door before anyone else can enter the room. Though my sisters and I may have appeared meek in the captain's eyes for many months, he is no fool. He knows that I will not simply give up.

And this is exactly what I have counted on him doing, sealing us in with no unnecessary personages left to witness what may come to pass. I part my lips and let the glyph out. "Good evening to you, too, Captain Ansalov. Captain Janlav."

As the glyph transforms into a spell, it feels as if I were standing in the Moon's light. The silver threads of the spell bear my beloved's touch, and they are visible only to Sibilia and me. I feel inhumanly strong, almost invincible, but this is just an illusion. I didn't triumph over the gagargi, merely delayed this moment. I must proceed with the greatest care and caution.

As Captain Ansalov strides toward me, I wrap the threads into a cap around his head. He halts abruptly, a step away from me. Now that I am married to the Moon, his magic comes to me in a more structured, more understandable way. This spell is intricately woven, one for me to control, not one as wild as the one with which I so crudely attacked the gagargi.

"Daughters . . ." My sisters and Captain Janlav wait for Captain Ansalov to announce his grim news. Captain Ansalov clenches his jaw as I press the silver net through his hair, against his skull. He scratches the back of his head, fingers sinking deep into his thick curls.

Captain Janlav clicks his heels together. Though the silence has lasted for mere seconds, he is suspicious, aware that I may be trying something he might not even comprehend. He glances past me at Elise, searches for a confirmation. The walls of this house are thin—I have heard if not seen the bonds forged between them. I can discern all of this in his voice. "Good evening, daughters."

My sisters remain in the arc behind me, as I have earlier instructed them to do. Apart from Sibilia, they don't know about the glyph or the spell. Yet they have placed their lives in my hands. Alina, Merile, Sibilia, even Elise, they believe in our father's powers, if not yet in mine.

"Daughters. Celestia." Captain Ansalov brandishes the once-sealed orders. I ram the cap against his head, push it through the skin. I don't plan on altering his mind, rather the orders he thinks he has read. For the closer I stay to the truth, the easier Sibilia says it will be to make him believe what I say. "Gagargi Prataslav has sent for you."

I meet his gaze, boldly, as is the right of the oldest Daughter of the Moon and that of the Crescent Empress. His skull, though made of bone, yields under the spell. Captain Ansalov's body tenses, and his winter-bitten fingers curl tighter around the letter. Some might consider it terrifying to have this much power, to be able to change the course of events, history even, with mere words said. But this is how it has always been for the Crescent Empress. "My sisters and I are ready."

And from this moment on I am alone, as the empresses of the past have always been. I dare not to divide my attention to how my sisters fare, to more than one mind. I have chosen to tackle the more dangerous man first.

For mine is the touch of my father and my husband, and under it, Captain Ansalov's mind is red and raw, a tangle of orders received and followed. I sense this, though I don't know the details, I don't possess the skill to see them. But I can imagine their content. The orders are from those higher in rank than him, a few are from my mother, and then, some are from the gagargi himself. I can also sense that this isn't the first time his mind has been tampered with.

I had expected that with my beloved's help I would be able to separate these commands from each other with ease. But there is no way to further tell them apart. Quickly I realize the only available approach is to alter as many as I can. And that is what I do.

Three decades of service translates to hundreds, if not thousands, of deeds done in the name of those more powerful. I imprint my will against each order, perfectly aware that I am thus fast draining the strength my beloved blessed me with. But soon I realize, not Captain Ansalov's. His will has been eradicated so many times that the only thing that has persisted is a blind sense to obey without reason or thought for consequences; the only way for him to bear this is to enjoy doing so.

"Shall we, then?" Captain Janlav's question brings me back to the moment.

A headache buds behind my eyes, and the silver threads connecting me to Captain Ansalov's mind flicker. What I have done may suffice or then turn out to be nowhere near enough. At this point, perhaps the best course of action is to wait, simply maintain the spell with what little is left of my beloved's strength.

As I hold Captain Ansalov under the spell, he remains dazed, Captain Janlav suspicious. I rub my forehead, to clear my thoughts, before I can stop myself. The question to ask is: if Captain Janlav came upon a chance to protect my sisters and me, would he grasp it? Yes, I think so, he is a decent man, once loyal to my mother, now dedicated to our people. Having grown close to Elise, he will not willingly hurt us if provided with an alternative that doesn't put his men at risk.

"The order." Captain Ansalov glances at the wrinkled paper. Flakes of red wax shiver onto the carpet. I refuse to think of this as an omen, though a hundred white dots bloom before my eyes from the mere effort of prolonging the spell. "The order . . ."

Now Captain Janlav knows that I have indeed pursued the path of resistance. His lips part, but not to form a protest. It is more as if he were in awe of me. Intriguing. Though he knows me as the oldest Daughter of the Moon, doesn't know me as the empress, my powers shouldn't have come as a surprise to him.

"My sisters and I are ready to come with you," I repeat, meeting Captain Ansalov's eyes. His mind, it pulses under the spell, violent and violated. More orders surface, from this year or from decades past, that I can't tell even as I feel the last flecks of my beloved's blessing waning.

"The orders are to . . ."

I will myself behind the spell with my full mind, with my whole body. I will see my sisters to safety, regardless of what that might do to me. And so I alter the orders as they spring up in Captain Ansalov's mind.

A guttural grunt of refusal slips out from between Captain Ansalov's lips. But it is too late for him to repel me and of that I am glad. For every action I commit consumes a part of my soul. But I have no time to regret my choice, no regrets. And so I press the spell against his mind and everything it contains.

Captain Ansalov recoils. His eyes widen, then narrow. Captain Janlav stares at me, indecision marring his forehead. I arch my brows at him. What did he expect? A Daughter of the Moon simply giving up? And at the same time, I am equally surprised by my own power.

Captain Janlav's mouth pulls taut, and he strides to Captain Ansalov's side. He clears his throat as he claps his heels together. A part of me wants him to speak up, another part to forever remain silent. One of my wishes is granted. "We shall take the daughters with us."

Elise glides beside me, nods passionately. A peculiar, soothing feeling—relief, I realize—washes over me. She does care for our sisters. Given the opportunity, she is willing to protect them.

I share a quick look with her. Now that Captain Janlav has decided to side with us, we must leave this house, reach the troika, preferably the train, and be on our way toward the Summer City before Captain Ansalov can regain his composure. "We are ready."

For a moment that is so short, but so long still that I believe the fallacy, I think the situation is under my control. There is the slightest easing of tension. A flicker of hope in my younger sisters' personages.

Then Captain Ansalov blocks my way bodily, ending up so close to me that only a paper's width separates us. He smells of wet horses and gunpowder, not like my seed did, but terrifyingly familiar still. Under the spell, his mind shifts, like a rogue wave rolling against a rocky shore. "No."

I force myself to complete stillness. This is it then. When I thought of this encounter before, I knew it might come down to this. I must sacrifice myself to save my sisters. I draw more of my soul and enforce the spell.

"The orders are . . ." Captain Ansalov glances at the paper, at me. He crosses his hands behind his back. "The orders are . . ."

I fill in the missing words even as my knees buckle from their sheer intensity. "To take us to the gagargi."

"There are many orders . . ." Captain Ansalov trails off, shakes his head. He is a soldier at heart. It is in his nature to fight against the insurmountable odds, even if doing so may hurt him. And this is exactly what he does. "That. That is not. That is not—"

I push myself as far as I can. Farther.

As I am connected to his mind, I feel the exact moment of its shattering.

In the stillness that follows, that beyond the night's last hour, that of the morning's first, I realize to my horror that there is nothing more I can do. Captain Ansalov's mind is broken by the commands said decades ago, by my attempts to change them. Even if I were to drain my soul dry, I don't possess the skill to mend his mind. It becomes a meaningless endeavor to hold on to the spell, and so the best course of action is to simply let it fade.

"Captain Janlav..." Captain Ansalov's gaze steadies. He motions sharply toward us, a gesture of terrible inclusion. "Bring them with us to the cellar."

A chorus of gasps comes from behind me. I refuse to make a sound, though this command can't be the one he received from the gagargi. It can't be, for the gagargi needs me alive! But I can't allow terror to even touch me. I must understand where this command stems from to decide the best course of action.

"No, not that one." Captain Janlav places a friendly palm on Captain Ansalov's shoulder, but he looks past the captain at me. Having seen my powers, he wants to know if there is more I could do.

I dare not meet his eyes, answer him. I don't yet have a plan.

"The orders are to clean this house," Captain Ansalov insists. I realize it then, this order comes from the past. He doesn't know anymore which of the many orders crowding his mind he has already obeyed and which are yet to be fulfilled. In his confused state, he will not listen to my words. He is beyond my influence, that of my father.

Captain Janlav pats Captain Ansalov's shoulder, a jovial attempt to save what he can. "No, no, no, the orders are written and sealed. Shall we have one more look at them together?"

And it is only because Captain Ansalov is still befuddled that Captain Janlav manages to distract him and direct him out, his last favor to us out of loyalty for the ruler he once served.

———

I am not alone with my failure, but in the company of my sisters. I had thought through many scenarios, but none wound up like this. I was prepared to sacrifice my soul, my very life, but in the end, even that wasn't enough to keep my sisters safe. Defeated, I stare at the flaking paint of the pale blue door, closed and locked once more. For us, another one will not open. Or if it does, it will be that of the cellar, the one we shouldn't walk through.

My sisters wait patiently behind me. I can hear their nervousness in their shallow breaths and the floor creaking under weights shifted. Turning around, facing them, feels more challenging than confronting Captain Ansalov. "My sisters—"

"He would have helped us!" Elise claps her delicate hands against her chest, awed by the man she once loved, whom she can now admit she never stopped loving, impervious for a moment more to our impeding fate. "All this time, and I didn't know!"

"Well, now you know," Sibilia remarks, as disappointed as I am that our sister cares more for her heart's chosen one than our own well-being. She slips the pearl bracelet around her wrist. She fidgets through each pearl before she finds the courage to ask what I should have willingly provided. "What are we going to do?"

What pains me the most is to see the absolute trust in Alina's deep-set gaze, hope in Merile's dark brown one. Sibilia already knows, though she pretends otherwise. We have talked of this often enough. The grimness of our situation is only starting to dawn on Elise. She really thought she would be leaving the house tonight.

"We must decide together how we wish to proceed." And I lay down the facts and only the facts, no feeble promises of better prospects. I couldn't change the orders Captain Ansalov received. Captain Janlav's offer, born from a moment of opportunity, is something we can but forget. Now that the gagargi's orders are in the air for both his guards and Captain Ansalov's men to hear, defying them and engaging in a fight that is likely to end in gunshots and blood spilled is not something he is willing to risk.

"One." Merile picks the black dog up in her arms. It climbs to rest against her shoulder, prods my sister's neck with its nose. "So you must choose one of us to go with you?"

Alina intently studies my shadow, that of Elise. She nods to herself and kneels to summon the brown dog to her. "I know who you should pick."

Out of all of us, Alina is the one least afraid. She alone still believes that I will live up to my promise. A thought bordering on delirious comes to me. Could it be that my frail little sister can glimpse our future in the shadows? If I had thought to ask this earlier, could I have saved us? Could any knowledge have made the difference?

"Either we all go or no one goes," Sibilia repeats. She must have realized, too, that with his mind tampered with, Captain Ansalov will order anyone staying behind in this house executed.

"I don't agree with you." Elise has her chin angled up, gray eyes afire with defiance. "Celestia, you are the Crescent Empress. What will become of our people if we meet our end in this house? With us gone, there will be no one left to champion for them. Don't say no to the gagargi's generous offer for purely selfish reasons."

For a moment, there is but silence, for what else could there be? And in this silence, the room feels smaller, the shadows in the corners darker, the light of the chandeliers feebler, the carpet akin to sinking ground. Where once the whole empire was mine, now I am hesitant to confront my own sister. For I don't know if there is anything I can say to make her see that I am not defying the gagargi because I loathe him for what he did to me, what he did to us and our mother and her sisters. I am saying no to his plan to save her and our younger sisters and the whole empire from oblivion.

In the end, I don't have to say a thing. A thin, white shape forms beside Elise.

"Drinking," Olesia wails. Her shape is translucent. "Men drinking downstairs."

"Oh no," Sibilia gasps, a hand flinging to cover her mouth. "Celestia..."

I lift my forefinger minutely, a sign she shouldn't say more. Men drink to gather courage when faced with commands they aren't willing to obey sober. This is no longer my choice. The two captains will force me to go to the gagargi, to abandon my sisters. Or then, the order they think they must obey is the grimmer one, the one from the past that has already been once carried out, that led Irina and Olesia to their graves. But Captain Ansalov may not remember that, and it is my fault and no one else's.

"My sisters..." I have always known that as the Crescent Empress I might need to choose from two equally appalling options. But never did it even occur to me to speculate which of my sisters deserves to live the most. For that is a decision I can't make, one that I can't ask them to make for me either. "I..."

"Celestia, wait," Sibilia says, so quietly, so shyly, uncertain and yet so sure of herself. "There is one more thing that we could try."

"Tell us." Merile speaks in my place.

Without saying another word, Sibilia strides to the window closest to our rooms and yanks at the curtains. It takes her three attempts to fully part them. The thread tears loose just as we gather around her.

My beloved, he hasn't yet risen to the sky. Yet, where there should be but dark, a faintest silvery glow emerges. It finds its way into the room through the crack in the glass, the gap between the planks, past the open curtains. "Our father showed me something that for a long while only confused me. But I just realized what he might have meant. That is, I'm pretty sure I know what he was after."

The silvery light draws me toward it. My sisters and Olesia hear the call, too. It can be but a message from our father, for we are all his daughters.

"When I read the scriptures, I came across a spell that might enable me to change the souls between two willing bodies." Sibilia glances at Alina and Merile, and then . . . at the two dogs. No wonder that my sister is hesitant. Her idea is straight out of a children's story. "He has shown me the dogs running through the forest, following the magpie. I think that . . ."

She doesn't need to say more. She is suggesting switching Alina's and Merile's souls with those of the two dogs, to be guided to safety by the witch who demanded too much from me in her greed. And then she wants me to leave the house with . . .

"Could you bind the spell?" I ask, though this is a ludicrous conversation to have in the first place. But I must know the answer to make a decision of any sort. It is very challenging to maintain a spell while moving, and if the spell were to snap, the souls would no doubt return back to their original bodies.

"I'll stay here," Sibilia replies, her voice steadier than mine. "Captain Ansalov will have no reason to go after the dogs."

The rest of her plan dawns on me. She wants me to leave the house with Elise. Elise, of all people!

"No." I cup Sibilia's cheeks, kiss her forehead. My dear sister, the one I once chose to stay behind with me, the one I promised to never abandon, is ready to sacrifice herself to save her younger and older sisters—a duty that was mine, but which I couldn't carry through. "No, no, and no."

But my sisters care little of me rejecting the dreadful idea. They don't yet understand the price it bears, the sheer number of unknowns. What would happen to our youngest sisters once their bodies cease to breathe? Would they remain captive in those of the two dogs forever? Or would the witch know a way to bring them back?

"Yes, that's it!" Elise claps her hands. She isn't cheerful as much as relieved. "Celestia, can you not see it? This is our father's will."

Alina squeals with delight. "I'd be a dog!"

"But what of my dear sillies?" Merile asks in a quiet voice, though she must know the answer already. There is nothing left in this house for us, for them, but despair.

"Please, be quiet," I plead with them, pacing away from the pale light. Sibilia's plan is far-fetched, its implications more terrible still. If her spell were to fail, the lives of our youngest sisters would be forfeit. If it were to work, beyond all logic, beyond all sanity, four of us would have a chance to live. But one of us would fall.

"Rifles." Olesia's shrill whisper interrupts my train of thought. "Irina says . . . Men loading rifles."

"Father Moon, forgive me," Sibilia mumbles even as she

marches to me. She grabs my wrists and pulls me with her into the beam of light. "Will you show your wife your will and let us get on with it?"

Before I can tell her that it is outrageous of her to ask this of our father, demand my husband show me what he sees when he hasn't chosen to do so before, impossibly, the light turns luminous. I can't move, wouldn't even want to move, as it swallows me whole. My beloved reveals his blessed face to me, the drawing room fills with his silvery presence, and I can at last see that which has come to pass under his celestial gaze.

The Great Thinking Machine has grown in size. It is blacker than the night, an oiled creature with a thousand spindly, insect legs. It hisses in hunger, though dozens of men feed it small amber beads in a constant supply. Another group of men piles holed paper sheets in its gaping maw, questions that the gagargi demands answered. The cogs and wheels spin as the machine crunches through numbers without thought or care. All this is possible only because . . .

A peasant woman with more white in her hair than one of her age should have presents her newborn to a country gagargi. The man in black robes extracts the child's soul from the writhing body with practiced ease, a glyph pronounced, fingers flicked. The small glass bead fills with amber light. The baby ceases to move, to breathe, to be. The gagargi nods, satisfied with a job well done. He offers the limp body back to the woman. She attempts to hide her tears without success. This is the fate of every other child.

There are more visions of my empire, but they change too fast for me to catch more than a glimpse of each. But in many of them there are weapons fired without thought or reason, snow and frozen ground stained with blood, houses and fields left behind for someone else to claim. I don't know why my beloved hasn't shown this to me before, but now isn't the right time to ask. Not now when the vision changes once more, and I see with my own eyes the one that first confused, then inspired Sibilia.

A black dog, a brown dog dash through the midnight forest, thin tails extended straight behind them, ears pressed against their heads. Theirs is speed, theirs is devotion, as my beloved lights their way through the unnamed, winding paths. A bird black and white flies before them, wings beating fast, but whether it is fast enough . . .

"Celestia." Elise's whisper is soft, wavering. "Please come back to us."

I blink and find my sisters huddling around me, my beloved's light receding. I understand now what I should have realized on my own a long time ago already. When one is taking, one isn't looking. That is why I didn't see these visions before.

"What did he show you?" Sibilia asks, and my younger sisters stare expectantly at me. They know that I now know my beloved's will.

"I must return to the Summer City, there to put an end to Gagargi Prataslav's rule."

Men arguing. Glass shattering. Furniture being pushed aside. These harsh sounds carry through the house, and we hear them clear now. The impatience and anger unleashed.

"Hurry." Olesia flickers out of sight, back. "Irina says to hurry."

I have always prided myself on being able to think rationally even in the direst of circumstances, and this occasion is no exception. Sibilia's plan is our best and only option. It pains me to accept this, but there is no other choice.

I stoop down and pat my knees twice in quick succession. The dogs bounce to me, brown coat, gray coat gleaming under my beloved's light. I meet their big, round eyes. "Let me have a look at you."

My sister's dogs are more than themselves tonight. There is a deeper understanding present in their glistening gazes. They are ready to sacrifice themselves to save their mistress, her little sister. And for that I love them as if they were truly my sisters.

"Alina, Merile." I address our youngest sisters even as I rise up. Elise herds them before me, not quite able to conceal her own haste. Sibilia peeks out through the crack in the glass, the gap between the planks, thoughtful. Olesia falters out of sight, returns fainter, but there is nothing I can do for her. "I have seen what Sibilia has seen. Will you let Rafa and Mufu help you?"

"Yes!" Alina agrees as if she had been waiting for this moment for months and then again months. And perhaps she has.

"Other way." Merile pouts her lips. Tears glitter at the corners of her eyes. "There is no other way. Is there? One where . . ."

Elise wraps her arms around Alina and Merile. Regardless of what she insisted earlier, it isn't easy for her to part from them. It isn't easy for me either. I should have been the one to sacrifice myself, not Sibilia. "I am afraid there is none."

Merile blinks, frustrated and furious. Finally, she nods. "What do we need to do?"

Sibilia stirs by the window. Her gaze is full of wisdom and my beloved's secrets. For a long while after her debut, I wondered if my swan-self kept her word, if she flew to the highest skies, if she conveyed the news of my sister's coming of age to our father. Now I know she did. As I have been blessed by our father, so has my sister. "Not much. Elise, where did you put that needle?"

Elise quickly fetches the needle from the table while Sibilia instructs us to settle into a crescent so far away from the window that the beam of light barely touches our sabots. She nudges the gray dog before Merile, the brown one before Alina. I have no role in this ceremony. It is up to my sister to perform the rite.

The sounds from downstairs intensify. Men searching for courage have perhaps found it from the bottle, and have no other option but to cope with their commands. Olesia's shape shivers worse than before. She doesn't need to tell us to hurry.

"Father Moon," Sibilia addressed my beloved, her tongue clicking with the glyph, I recognize this now. "Four willing souls, four bodies, will you save your daughters?"

The silvery beam of light flowing into the room gleams in reply. My beloved has at last risen to the sky. The two dogs trot to the purest of lights. Alina and Merile follow them, as does Sibilia. Elise shifts to do likewise, but I seize her arm. This rite doesn't concern us.

My hand clenches blue bruising tight around her slender arm.

"Finger." Sibilia beckons Alina, the needle already poised.

Alina sticks her forefinger up. She winces as Sibilia stabs it. A drop of blood swells on her fingertip, scarlet in color.

"You, too," Sibilia says to Merile.

Merile hesitates. She glances at her dogs, at us. I meet her gaze. Does she not hear the sounds from downstairs? Does she not realize this is our only chance? I will my eyes to convey all this.

Merile sighs and extends her hand toward Sibilia. Our sister sinks the needle in her flesh.

Next, Sibilia squats down. The dogs offer their paws at her, one after the other. She draws their blood, her movements growing clumsier. "Now, what was the thing I was supposed to do next?"

There are footsteps pounding up the stairs. More than two pairs. Many more. The captains are coming for us with their men. But telling Sibilia to hasten the spell would only confuse her more. And if even this were to fail, more than one of us would fall.

"Ah, that bit." Sibilia swiftly rises up. She waves wide circles with her hands. She lets another glyph out . . .

If I had thought my beloved's light bright before, I had no idea of how bright it could be. The Moon's light floods the drawing room so bright that for a moment I can't see. When my vision returns, Merile and Alina are already changing. They writhe and whine. They shiver and shine. Then their gazes dull, their souls leave their bodies.

And the dogs before the girls change, too. They curl down, twitch, go limp. Did the spell not work? Or did it go wrong like so many things have done of late?

But no, the dogs stir, bounce up to their feet. Now their big eyes glint with confusion, not with fear. They open their mouths as if to speak, but only a curious growl comes out. They glance up at me.

"It worked," I say. The impossible, the improbable worked. I bless my beloved's name.

Sibilia purses her fists against her hips, satisfied. Elise's lips part as she wonders at the girls that are not our sisters, the dogs that are.

The footsteps reach the hallway beyond the locked door.

"My dear sisters . . ." I must persist, hold on to my composure just a little while longer. As much as I would like to, there is nothing I can do for Sibilia. I can't switch places with her, for she must stay behind for the spell to remain intact. And intact it must stay for the two captains to believe Alina and Merile dead. That is the only way for them to flee. However, it is up to me to save Elise and myself, even if she has acted treacherously in the past. I don't yet know what consensus the captains have reached, but I pray to the Moon that they are still willing to obey the gagargi's original commands. "Let us be brave."

A mere heartbeat later, the door swings open. Olesia shimmers, disappears out of fright. Or altogether. I wish we could do likewise, but we are not yet ghosts.

"Daughters." Captain Janlav enters first, his eyes hard as beaten copper. The offer born from opportunity is gone, as I knew it would be. I can but accept this.

Captain Ansalov strides in after him, the bayonet attached to the end of his rifle gleaming in my beloved's light. Beyond the open door, in the hallway, wait both the guards and the soldiers, every single one of them armed. The tension between them is so dense that one could march on it.

"We meet again." I spread my arms in a greeting fit for an empress. Let them see me as I am, not as a woman afraid of her life, that of her sisters. Beside me, Elise smiles more luminously than ever, disquietingly ecstatic. Sibilia whispers what may be a prayer. The dog-girls stare at their feet. The girl-dogs sit against their feet.

Captain Ansalov staggers to a halt. He isn't intoxicated, but broken inside. I look past him at Captain Janlav, Beard, Belly, Tabard, Boots, and Boy. The hardness, determination of the youngest of them is merely a shell for a boy not ready for the deeds that men bearing rifles must do. Whether the guards are ready to admit it or not, for these past seven months, three weeks, and twenty-one hours, they were our family as much as we were theirs. And though they knew that this is how it would eventually end, they must have hoped that something, anything would change along the way, that it wouldn't come down to this.

But now it has.

"Well?" Captain Ansalov snaps at Captain Janlav, and I can read the consensus they reached from his impatience. He is beyond certain that I will not bend to the gagargi's will, that my life and that of my sisters will soon be in his hands.

I say the words that pain me more than anything the gagargi ever did to me. "Elise and I are ready."

Sibilia and the dog-girls are allowed to follow us to the hall where Captain Ansalov and his soldiers wait, rifles ready. Of the two ghosts, there is no sign. I don't think anyone of us will see them ever again.

My heart sinks as I notice the door leading to the cellar is ajar, for my sisters and I know what this means. But there is no taking back my words, the decision that in the end wasn't even mine to make.

"Sibilia . . ." I embrace my sister, the one who is to stay behind, to walk down the stairs into the darkness, never to see light again until she rises to the sky, there to forever bask by our father's side. Tears throb at the back of my mouth, and though I haven't wounded my flesh, I taste blood. I wish there was some greater wisdom for me to share as my final words to her, but there is none.

"Oh, Celestia, it's all right! It's all right to feel!" My sister places her palms on my shoulders, her gray eyes completely tearless. "I'm not afraid. Truly, I'm not."

I have never heard such sincerity and honesty in anyone's voice, and it is only because of that that I can bring myself to part from her. She is so brave, much more so than I am. My little sister, the dreamer who taught herself what I couldn't learn even when guided by the best of tutors!

As Elise says her good-byes, or perhaps she begs forgiveness from Sibilia, I bend and kiss each of the dog-girls on their foreheads. They peck small kisses on my cheeks. They stamp their feet. If they still had tails, they would wag them. "Farewell, my dears. Farewell!"

Captain Janlav clears his throat. He is anxious to leave this house behind, to gain distance between himself and what will soon happen here. "Celestia, Elise, let us be on our way."

Despite his words, I kneel to pat the girl-dogs, my sisters Alina and Merile. There isn't much time left, but I don't know when—if ever—I will see them again, if someone will eventually find a way to summon their souls back to human bodies.

"Run," I whisper in Alina's ear, to Merile, "run as fast as you can and never look back. Run as soon as you see our father's light."

Captain Janlav pushes the door open. "Now."

The girl-dogs dart forth, past his worn boots, into the true night that awaits only some of us. One brown dog, one black one, two Daughters of the Moon, soon become but shadows. Elise and I follow Captain Janlav to the yard.

———————

As the troika speeds through the night, I hearken my ears to the sounds I know to expect. Elise leans against my shoulder, eyes closed, unable to hold back tears. Despite what she may have done in the past, I am not cruel enough to deny her comfort at this terrible moment. I cradle her slender palms between mine. Her fingers are colder than mine, her heart, too.

I know now what lies beyond exhaustion, at the end of everything. Numbing vulnerability, but also the frailest flicker of hope, the belief that our father, my beloved, will protect us.

And then, gunshots, followed by faraway barks.

About the Author

Photograph by Writers of the Future

LEENA LIKITALO hails from Finland, the land of endless summer days and long, dark winter nights. She lives with her husband on an island at the outskirts of Helsinki, the capital. But regardless of her remote location, stories find their way to her and demand to be told.

While growing up, Leena struggled to learn foreign languages. At sixteen, she started reading science fiction and fantasy in English. The stories were simply too exciting not to finish, and thus she rather accidentally learned the language.

These days, Leena breaks computer games for a living. When she's not working, she writes obsessively. And when she's not writing, she can be found at the stables riding horses.

TOR·COM

Science fiction. Fantasy. The universe.

And related subjects.

*

More than just a publisher's website, *Tor.com*
is a venue for **original fiction, comics,** and

discussion of the entire field of SF and fantasy,

in all media and from all sources. Visit our site

today—and join the conversation yourself.